ONLY UNI

BOOK 2

Camy Tang

ZONDERVAN®

ZONDERVAN.com/
AUTHORTRACKER
follow your favorite authors

Only Uni
Copyright © 2008 by Camy Tang

Requests for information should be addressed to:
Zondervan, *Grand Rapids, Michigan 49530*

Library of Congress Cataloging-in-Publication Data

Tang, Camy, 1972 –
    Only uni / Camy Tang.
      p. cm. — (Sushi series; bk. 2)
    ISBN-10: 0-310-27399-4
    ISBN-13: 978-0-310-27399-8
   1. Dating (Social customs) — Fiction. I. Title.
PS3620.A6845S87 2007
813'.6 — dc22

                                   2007029336

Published in association with the Books & Such Literary Agency, 52 Circle, Suite 122, PMB 170, Santa Rosa, California 95407-5370, www.booksandsuch.biz

Interior design by Michelle Espinoza

Printed in the United States of America

08 09 10 11 12 • 24 23 22 21 20 19 18 17 16 15 14 13 12 11 10 9 8 7 6 5 4 3 2 1

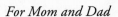

For Mom and Dad

ONE

Trish Sakai walked through the door and the entire room hushed.

Well, not exactly pin-drop hushed. More like a handful of the several dozen people in her aunty's enormous living room paused their conversations to glance her way. Maybe Trish had simply expected them to laugh and point.

She shouldn't have worn white. She'd chosen the Bebe dress from her closet in a rebellious mood, which abandoned her at her aunt's doorstep. Maybe because the explosion of red, orange, or gold outfits made her head swim.

At least the expert cut of her dress made her rather average figure curvier and more slender at the same time. She loved how well-tailored clothes ensured she didn't have to work as hard to look good.

Trish kicked off her sandals, and they promptly disappeared in the sea of shoes filling the foyer. She swatted away a flimsy paper dragon drooping from the doorframe and smoothed down her skirt. She snatched her hand back and wrung her fingers behind her.

No, that'll make your hips look huge.

She clenched her hands in front.

Sure, show all the relatives that you're nervous.

She clasped them loosely at her waist and tried to adopt a regal expression.

"Trish, you okay? You look constipated."

Her cousin Bobby snickered while she sneered at him. "Oh, you're so funny I could puke."

"May as well do it now before Grandma gets here."

"She's not here yet?" Oops, that came out sounding a little too relieved. She cleared her throat and modulated her voice to less-than-ecstatic levels. "When's she coming?"

"Uncle picked her up, but he called Aunty and said Grandma forgot something, so he had to go back."

Thank goodness for little favors. "Is Lex here?"

"By the food."

Where else would she be? Last week, her cousin Lex had mentioned that her knee surgeon let her go back to playing volleyball three nights a week and coaching the other two nights, so her metabolism had revved up again. She would be eating like a horse.

Sometimes Trish could just kill her.

She tugged at her skirt—a little tight tonight. She should've had more self-control than to eat that birthday cake at work. She'd have to run an extra day this week . . . maybe.

She bounced like a pinball between relatives. The sharp scent of ginger grew more pungent as she headed toward the large airy kitchen. Aunty Sue must have made cold ginger chicken again. Mmmm. The smell mixed with the tang of black bean sauce (Aunty Rachel's shrimp?), stir-fried garlic (any dish Uncle Barry made contained at least two bulbs), and fishy scallions (probably her cousin Linda's Chinese-style sea bass).

A three-foot-tall red streak slammed into her and squashed her big toe.

"Ow!" Good thing the kid hadn't been wearing shoes or she might have broken her foot. Trish hopped backward and her hand fumbled with a low side table. Waxed paper and cornstarch slid under her fingers before the little table fell, dropping the *kagami mochi* decoration. The sheet of printed paper, the tangerine, and rubbery-hard mochi dumplings dropped to the cream-colored carpet. Well, at least the cornstarch covering the mochi blended in.

The other relatives continued milling around her, oblivious to the minor desecration to the New Year's decoration. Thank goodness for small—

A childish gasp made her turn. The human bullet who caused the whole mess, her little cousin Allison, stood with a hand up to her round lips that were stained cherry-red, probably from the sherbet punch. Allison lifted wide brown eyes up to Trish—*hanaokolele-you're-in-trouble*—while the other hand pointed to the mochi on the floor.

Trish didn't buy it for a second. "Want to help?" She tried to infuse some leftover Christmas cheer into her voice.

Allison's disdainful look could have come from a teenager rather than a seven-year-old. "You made the mess."

Trish sighed as she bent to pick up the mochi rice dumplings—one large like a hockey puck, the other slightly smaller—and the *shihobeni* paper they'd been sitting on. She wondered if the *shihobeni* wouldn't protect the house from fires this next year since she'd dropped it.

"Aunty spent so long putting those together."

Yeah, right. "Is that so?" She laid the paper on the table so it draped off the edge, then stuck the waxed paper on top. She anchored them with the larger mochi.

"Since you busted it, does it mean that Aunty won't have any good luck this year?"

"It's just a tradition. The mochi doesn't really bring prosperity, and the tangerine only symbolizes the family generations." Trish tried to artfully stack the smaller mochi on top of the bottom one, but it wouldn't balance and kept dropping back onto the table.

"That's not what Aunty said."

"She's trying to pass on a New Year's tradition." The smaller mochi dropped to the floor again. "One day you'll have one of these in your own house." Trish picked up the mochi. Stupid Japanese New Year tradition. Last year, she'd glued hers together until Mom found out and brought a new set to her apartment, sans-glue. Trish wasn't even Shinto. Neither was anyone else in her family—most of them were Buddhists—but it was something they did because their family had always done it.

"No, I'm going to live at home and take care of Mommy."

Thank goodness, the kid finally switched topics. "That's wonderful." Trish tried to smash the tangerine on top of the teetering stack of mochi. Nope, not going to fly. "You're such a good daughter."

Allison sighed happily. "I am."

Your ego's going to be too big for this living room, toots. "Um . . . let's go to the kitchen." She crammed the tangerine on the mochi stack, then turned to hustle Allison away before she saw them fall back down onto the floor.

"Uh, Triiiish?"

She almost ran over the kid, who had whirled around and halted in her path like a guardian lion. Preventing Trish's entry into the kitchen. And blocking the way to the *food*. She tried to sidestep, but the other relatives in their conversational clusters, oblivious to her, hemmed her in on each side.

Allison sidled closer. "Happy New Year!"

"Uh . . . Happy New Year." What was she up to? Trish wouldn't put anything past her devious little brain.

"We get red envelopes at New Year's." Her smile took on a predatory gleam.

"Yes, we do." One tradition she totally didn't mind. Even the older cousins like Trish and Lex got some money from the older relatives, because they weren't married yet.

Allison beamed. "So did you bring me a red envelope?"

What? Wait a minute. Was she supposed to bring red envelopes for the younger kids? No, that couldn't be. "No, only the married people do that." And only for the great-cousins, not their first cousins, right? Or was that great-cousins, too? She couldn't remember.

Allison's face darkened to purple. "That's not true. Aunty gives me a red envelope and she's not married."

"She used to be married. Uncle died."

"She's not married now. So you're supposed to give me a red envelope, too."

Yeah, right. "If I gave out a red envelope to every cousin and great-cousin, I'd go bankrupt."

"You're lying. I'm going to tell Mommy." Allison pouted, but her sly eyes gave her away.

A slow, steady burn crept through her body. This little extortionist wasn't going to threaten her, not tonight of all nights.

She crouched down to meet Allison at eye level and forced a smile. "That's not very nice. That's spreading lies."

Allison bared her teeth in something faintly like a grin.

"It's not good to be a liar." Trish smoothed the girl's red velvet dress, trimmed in white lace.

"You're the liar. You said you're not supposed to give me a red envelope, and that's a lie."

The brat had a one-track mind. "It's not a lie."

"Then I'll ask Mommy." The grin turned sickeningly sweet.

"I wouldn't do that if I were you." Trish tweaked one of Allison's curling-iron-manufactured corkscrews, standing out amongst the rest of her straight hair.

"I can do whatever I want." An ugly streak marred the angelic mask.

"Of course you can."

Allison blinked.

"But if you do, I'll tell *Grandma* that I found her missing jade bracelet in your bedroom." *Gotcha.*

"What were you doing in my bedroom?" Allison's face matched her dress.

Trish widened her eyes. "Well, you left it open when your mom hosted the family Christmas party ..."

Allison's lips disappeared in her face, and her nostrils flared. "You're lying—"

"And you know Grandma will ask your mommy to search your room."

Her face whitened.

"So why don't we forget about this little red envelope thing, hmm?" Trish straightened the gold heart pendant on Allison's necklace and gave her a bland smile.

A long, loud inhale filled Allison's lungs. For a second, Trish pan-icked, worried that she'd scream or something, but the air left her noiselessly.

Trish stood. "See ya." She muscled her way past the human traffic cone.

She zeroed in on the kitchen counters like a heat-seeking missile. "Hey, guys."

Her cousins Venus, Lex, and Jenn turned to greet her.

"You're even later than Lex." Venus leaned her sexy-enough-to-make-Trish-sick curves against a countertop as she crunched on a cel-ery stick.

"Hey!" Lex nudged her with a bony elbow, then spoke to Trish. "Grandma's not here yet, but your mom—"

"Trish, there you are." Mom flittered up. "Did you eat yet? Let me fill you a plate. Make sure you eat the *kuromame* for good luck. I know you don't like chestnuts and black beans, but just eat one. Did you want any *konbu*? Seaweed is very good for you."

"No, Mom—"

"How about Aunty Eileen's soup? I'm not sure what's in it this year, but it doesn't look like tripe this time—"

"Mom, I can get my own food."

"Of course you can, dear." Mom handed her a mondo-sized plate.

Trish grabbed it, then eyed Venus's miniscule plate filled sparingly with meat, fish, and veggies. Aw, phooey. Why did Venus have to always be watching her hourglass figure—with inhuman self-control over her calorie intake—making Trish feel dumpy just for eating a potsticker? She replaced her plate with a smaller one.

Lex had a platter loaded with chicken and lo mein, which she shoveled into her mouth. "The noodles are good."

"Why are you eating so much today?"

"Aiden's got me in intensive training for the volleyball tournament coming up."

Trish turned toward the groaning sideboard to hide the pang in her gut at mention of Lex's boyfriend. Who had been Trish's physical therapist. Aiden hadn't met Lex yet when Trish had hit on him, but he'd rebuffed her—rather harshly, she thought—then became Christian and now was living a happily-ever-after with Lex.

Trish wasn't jealous at all.

Why did she always seem to chase away the good ones and keep the bad ones? Story of her life. Her taste in men matched Lex's horrendous taste in clothes—Lex wore nothing but ugly, loose workout clothes, while Trish dated nothing but ugly (well, in character, at least) losers.

Next to her, Jennifer inhaled as if she were in pain. "Grandma's here."

"No, not now. This is so not fair. I haven't eaten yet."

"It'll still be here." Venus's caustic tone cut through the air at the same time her hand grabbed Trish's plate. "Besides, you're eating too much fat."

Trish glared. "I am not fat—"

Venus gave a long-suffering sigh. "I didn't say you were fat. I said you're eating unhealthily."

"You wouldn't say that to Lex." She stabbed a finger at her athletic cousin, who was shoveling chicken long rice into her mouth.

Lex paused. "She already did." She slurped up a rice noodle.

Venus rolled her eyes toward the ceiling. "All of you eat terribly. You need to stop putting so much junk into your bodies."

"I will when Jenn stops giving us to-die-for homemade chocolate truffles." Trish traded a high-five with Jenn, their resident culinary genius.

"Besides, chocolate's good for you." Lex spoke through a mouthful of black bean shrimp.

Venus, who seemed to know she was losing the battle, brandished a celery stick. "You all should eat more fiber—"

Trish snatched at a deep-fried chicken wing and made a face at her. "It's low carb." Although she'd love to indulge in just a little of those Chinese noodles later when Venus wasn't looking . . .

She only had time to take a couple bites before she had to drop the chicken in a napkin and wipe her fingers. She skirted the edge of the crowd of relatives who collected around Grandma, wishing her Happy New Year.

Grandma picked up one of Trish's cousin's babies and somehow managed to keep the sticky red film coating his hands from her expensive Chanel suit. How did Grandma do that? It must be a gift. The same way her elegant salt-and-pepper 'do never had a hair out of place.

Then Grandma grabbed someone who had been hovering at her shoulder and thrust him forward.

No. Way.

What was Kazuo doing here?

With Grandma?

Her breath caught as the familiar fluttering started in her ribcage. No, no, no, no, no. She couldn't react this way to him again. That's what got her in trouble the last time.

Trish grabbed Jenn's arm and pulled her back toward the kitchen. "I have to hide."

Jenn's brow wrinkled. "Why?"

"That's Kazuo."

Jenn's eyes popped bigger than the moon cakes on the sideboard. "Really? I never met him." She twisted her head.

"Don't look. Hide me."

Jenn sighed. "Isn't that a little silly? He's here for the New Year's party."

Trish darted her gaze around the kitchen, through the doorway to the smaller TV room. "There are over a hundred people here. There's a good chance I can avoid him."

"He probably came to see you." A dreamy smile lit Jenn's lips. "How romantic . . ."

A mochi-pounding mallet thumped in the pit of Trish's stomach. Romantic this was not.

"What's wrong?" Venus and Lex separated from the crowd to circle around her.

"That's Kazuo."

"Really?" Lex whirled around and started to peer through the doorway into the front room. "We never met him — "

"Don't look now! Hide me!"

Venus lifted a sculpted eyebrow. "Oh, come on."

"How does Grandma know him?" Jennifer's soothing voice fizzled Venus's sarcasm.

"She met him when we were dating."

"Grandma loves Kazuo." Lex tossed the comment over her shoulder as she stood at the doorway and strained to see Kazuo past the milling relatives.

Venus's brow wrinkled. "Loves him? Why?"

Trish threw her hands up in the air. "He's a Japanese national. He spoke Japanese to her. Of course she'd love him."

Jennifer chewed her lip. "Grandma's not racist — "

Venus snorted. "Of course she's not racist, but she's certainly biased."

"That's not a good enough reason. Don't you think there's something fishy about why she wants Trish to get back together with him?"

Venus opened her mouth, but nothing came out. After a moment, she closed it. "Maybe you're right."

Trish flung her arms out. "But I have no idea what that reason is."

"So is she matchmaking? Now?"

"What better place?" Trish pointed to the piles of food. "Fatten me up and serve me back to him on a platter."

Venus rolled her eyes. "Trish — "

"I'm serious. No way am I going to let her do that. Not with *him*." The last man on earth she wanted to see. Well, that wasn't exactly true. Her carnal body certainly wanted to see him, even though her brain and spirit screamed, *Run away! Run away!*

"Was it that bad a breakup?" Lex looked over her shoulder at them.

Trish squirmed. "I, uh ... I don't think he thinks we're broken up."

"What do you mean? It happened six months ago." Venus's gaze seemed to slice right through her.

"Well ... I saw him a couple days ago."

Venus's eyes flattened. "And ...?"

Trish blinked rapidly. "We ... got along really well."

Venus crossed her arms and glared.

How did Venus do that? Trish barely had to open her mouth and Venus knew when she was lying. "We, um ... got along *really* well."

Jennifer figured it out first. She gasped so hard, Trish worried she'd pass out from lack of oxygen.

Venus cast a sharp look at her, then back at Trish. Her mouth sprang open. "You didn't."

"Didn't what?" Lex rejoined the circle and the drama unfolding. She peered at Jenn and Venus—one frozen in shock, the other white with anger.

Trish's heart shrank in her chest. She bit her lip and tasted blood. She couldn't look at her cousins. She couldn't even say it.

Venus said it for her. "You slept with him again."

Lex's jaw dropped. "Tell me you didn't." The hurt in her eyes stabbed at Trish's heart like Norman Bates in *Psycho*.

Well, it was true that Trish's obsessive relationship with Kazuo had made her sort of completely and utterly *abandon* Lex last year when she tore her ACL. Lex probably felt like Trish was priming to betray her again. "It was only once. I couldn't help myself—"

"After everything you told me last year about how you never asked God about your relationship with Kazuo and now you were *free*." Lex's eyes grew dark and heavy, and Trish remembered the night Lex had first torn her ACL. Trish had been too selfish, wanting to spend time with Kazuo instead of helping Lex home from one of the most devastating things that had ever happened to her.

"I just couldn't help myself—" Trish couldn't seem to say anything else.

"So is Kazuo more important to you than me, after all?" Lex's face had turned into cold, pale marble, making her eyes stand out in their intensity.

A sickening ache gnawed in Trish's stomach. She hunched her shoulders, feeling the muscles tighten and knot.

Her cousins had always been compassionate whenever she hurt them, betrayed them, or caused them hassle and stress by the things she did. She knew she had a tendency to be thoughtless, but she had always counted on their instant hugs and "That's okay, Trish, we'll fix it for you." But now she realized—although they forgave her, they were still hurt each and every time. Maybe this was the straw that broke the camel's back.

"Where's Trish?" Grandma's refined voice managed to carry above the conversations. "I'm sure she wants to see you." She was coming closer to the kitchen.

"I can't face him." Trish barely recognized her own voice, as thready as old cobwebs. "I can't face Grandma, either." A tremor rippled through her body.

Venus's eyes softened in understanding. "I'll stall them for you."

Trish bolted.

Out the other doorway into the living room. She dodged around a few relatives who were watching sports highlights on the big-screen TV. She spied the short hallway to Aunty's bedroom. She could hide. Recoup. Or panic.

She slipped down the hallway and saw the closed door at the end. A narrow beam of faint light from under it cast a glow over the carpet. Her heart started to slow.

Maybe she could lie down, pretend she was sick? No, Grandma might suggest Kazuo take her home.

She could pretend she got a phone call, an emergency at work. Would Grandma know there weren't many emergencies with cell biology research on New Year's Eve?

The worst part was, Trish hadn't even gotten to eat yet.

She turned the doorknob, but it stuck. Must be the damp weather. She applied her shoulder and nudged. The door clicked open. She slipped into the bedroom.

A couple stood in the dim lamplight, locked in a passionate embrace straight out of *Star* magazine. Trish's heart lodged in her throat. *Doh! Leave now!* She whirled.

Wait a minute.

She turned.

The man had dark wavy hair, full and thick. His back was turned to her, but something about his stance . . .

The couple sprang apart. Looked at her.

Dad.

Kissing a woman who wasn't her mother.

TWO

Trish stared at them.

They stared back.

Nobody moved.

She waited for him to say something. He was the one caught, shouldn't he say something? She wasn't going to say anything. What could she say? "Well, hey, Dad. Introduce me to your adultery partner"?

Maybe something melodramatic like, "How *could* you?"

Or maybe voicing the rumbling, burning in her chest with, "You selfish, detestable worm."

The woman regarded her with expressionless eyes. She was beautiful. Trish hated her.

Maybe Trish should say something to her like, "Why'd you have to go after a married one?" or "Are you married, too?"

The room began to tilt and dip. Trish sucked in a dry breath and realized she had stopped breathing. The murmuring from the cracked door behind her eased into the quiet room like waves at the shore, lapping toward the beach.

"Where's Trish?" Grandma's cultured voice carried over the din from the family room.

Suddenly, Grandma didn't seem so bad anymore.

Trish turned and flung open the door. Leaving it wide open, she walked out into the hallway. She slapped the wall switch to turn on the hallway light and flood her path.

She focused on the cream carpet. She hated it. It was pure and clean and soft.

Jenn rounded the corner into the hallway and nearly collided with her. "You better come rescue Venus—" Her face flipped from cool to concerned. "What's wrong?"

Trish opened her mouth, but the only thing that came out was something between "erk" and "ugh."

Jenn got the "really concerned" face. "Trish?" She peeked over Trish's shoulder.

"No!" It came out sounding like a croak, but she got her point across. With shaking hands, she prodded Jenn back down the hallway. After initial resistance, Jenn complied. Like she usually did.

They erupted into the living room filled with relatives, most of them eating. The noise was too loud, the lights too bright. Trish had a fleeting fantasy of shrieking, "Shut up!" and then racing out of the house.

This was too much. She needed to go somewhere with her three cousins and best friends, where she could rage and cry and doubt and scream and cry some more.

She needed to leave, but in order to do that, she had to find her other two cousins to inform them they were leaving with her, and she had to find Grandma. Oh, and avoid Kazuo. "Where's Grandma?"

"In the kitchen."

Trish pushed her way through people. "I have to say hello and then tell her we're leaving."

"We're leaving?"

"And Lex and Venus, too."

"They are?"

"It's an emergency."

Jenn's eyes got round. "Oh. Okay."

"But I have to avoid Kazuo."

"Why?"

"Because I don't want to see him." Actually, she wanted to see him too much. "Can you divert him or something if he comes near me?"

"He's already diverted. He's talking with Venus. In the kitchen."

Rats. "Okay. Um ... I'll pop in and say hi to Grandma—"

"She brought him to see you. She'll call him over."

Jenn was too logical for Trish's overworked brain right now. "Well, do something so he can't. And I'll tell her we're leaving."

"She's not going to like that." Jenn bit her lip.

No, she wasn't. And although Lex and Venus seemed to enjoy antagonizing Grandma, Trish and Jenn liked to keep her happy. Life was easier that way. Trish swallowed a sob. "I don't want to talk to him."

Jenn's brow furrowed. "Why don't you wait here instead of seeing Grandma just yet? I'll get Lex and see if she has any ideas." Jenn switched directions and dove into the crowd of people.

Good thinking. Trish backed into a vacant corner in the living room and tried not to eye the food on people's plates. Her stomach rumbled. She smoothed the creases on her skirt—did she have cornstarch from the mochi on there this entire time? Plus some sticky patch that was probably a gift from Allison, the brat.

"Trish, there you are."

Nononononononono. "Grandma, I was going to find you." She gripped her hands in front of her chest to try to keep her heart from flying out. She sucked in her gut and tried to shrink a little.

Grandma always made Trish feel hulking and fat. She never seemed to eat—even at lavish family gatherings like this—and she always wore the most fab business suits that must take off at least ten pounds from her already-slender figure. She fingered the gold filigree pin on her cream lapel as she waltzed up to Trish's corner.

"You're looking good. New haircut?" Flattery might work. Trish was *so* in the doghouse for not coming up to say hello to Grandma as soon as she arrived.

Grandma patted her permed gray-bronze curls, but her perfectly stenciled lips never broke their straight red line. "I've been searching for you."

"Oh?" She widened her eyes and hoped she looked innocent rather than like a deer in the headlights about to be completely slaughtered. She clenched her hands at her stomach to stop it from gurgling.

"I met Kazuo yesterday when I was in Japantown."

"You did? But Kazuo doesn't work at the sushi restaurant anymore." His "artistic loner" personality hadn't won him any friends with his coworkers, so when they had to lay off someone, he was the first man booted. His parents in Japan had responded with larger monthly checks so he didn't have to find another job.

"I saw him outside the Shiseido shop. He seemed rather sad, so I talked to him."

That, or she had wanted to pick his brain about why they broke up. "He seemed happy the last time I saw him." Well, as happy as brooding Kazuo ever got.

"He told me he hasn't seen you for a few weeks." Grandma's stern expression melted. Her bright brown eyes pleaded with Trish. "I hoped you two would get back together. He's such a good boy."

"We weren't right for each other." *He just made me feel beautiful and loved.* No, she had to remember the bad times. Trish had a flashback of Kazuo in one of his frustrated artistic rages, flinging paint on his masterpiece and raining spit on her shocked face as he ranted.

Grandma's gaze dropped.

Trish's heart fell a notch with it. "I'm sorry. I know you liked him."

Grandma sighed.

Trish wrung her hands. "We really tried hard to make it work." Well, *she* tried. He just agreed with her when she wanted to talk things out, and then tried to make love to her with his words and gaze.

Grandma's face suddenly came to life, sparkling like the diamond choker at her throat. "Well, Kazuo is here tonight."

"Uh . . ."

"And he says he's a different person now, and he wants to try again with you."

Kazuo had said he'd try harder or turn himself around after every fight they had. "But . . . Grandma . . ."

"Isn't that romantic? Girls love when men chase them."

Trish couldn't picture Grandpa ever chasing Grandma. More like the other way around. "But I don't like Kazuo anymore."

Grandma's immaculate Shiseido makeup cracked as she frowned. "Trish, I can always tell when you're lying to me."

She bit the inside of her lip. *Everyone* could tell when she was lying. "It's kind of like french fries."

"What?"

"You know how we all love french fries?" Well, with her slender figure, Grandma might not know. "But they're bad for you. Very, very bad. Lots of calories and bad carbs."

"I don't know what that—"

"Kazuo is like french fries."

Now Grandma was looking at her like she'd given a speech on DNA cloning vectors.

"I do still like him. But long-term, he's very, very bad for me. So I'm going on a diet."

Grandma patted her arm. "Well, you could stand to lose a few pounds, dear."

What? "That's not what I meant."

"And I'm certain Kazuo would appreciate a more youthful figure on you."

Youthful? She was only thirty. "I'm not fat."

"No, you're not fat, but you're not as slender as Lex."

Lex was an athlete and she exercised 24/7. But Trish consoled herself with the fact she actually had a bosom. "I'm not like Lex—"

"Kazuo loves you just the way you are."

"But I don't want him to love me."

Grandma's eyes took on a sharper cast, and her voice had a ring of steel like a samurai drawing his sword. "It would make me very happy if you two would get back together."

Trish blinked. Was that a threat? Grandma never threatened her. Sure, she threatened Lex and Venus because they went out of their way to annoy her, but Trish? Grandma loved Trish. Trish always had boyfriends to bring to family parties. Trish listened when Grandma said she wanted her to get married. Trish wanted to give Grandma great-grandchildren.

Grandma's hard look made her squirm. Well, maybe she'd at least talk to Kazuo. It was the middle of a big party. Nothing would happen, right?

"Where is Kazuo?" She fiddled with her earring and half-heartedly flickered her gaze around. Maybe if she didn't look too closely, he wouldn't show up.

Better yet, maybe he'd be so captivated by Venus's drop-dead-gorgeous face and figure that he wouldn't want to see Trish. Although the thought of him and Venus twanged in her breastbone like a snapping guitar string.

"I'll go get him." Grandma disappeared faster than a ninja.

Trish considered — for a brief moment of insanity — simply walking out the door. But imagining Grandma's wrath kept her chained to the floor. Even an army of rushing Japanese warriors — like in that Kadokawa movie *Heaven and Earth*, which she saw in the original Japanese, thank you very much — was preferable.

How sad. She was less afraid of death by dismemberment than displeasing Grandma.

He appeared through the crowd of people like a ship parting the waves. His emotional pull on her sucked at every square inch of her skin like a vortex trying to drag her into a black hole.

She wasn't going back to him again. No matter how absolutely muscular and protective he looked in that black turtleneck sweater —

No, stop thinking about his muscles.

A woman nearby gasped. Yeah, Kazuo had that kind of effect on women. Something about his silky long hair pulled into a ponytail and his dark, fathomless eyes —

Stop thinking about his eyes.

"There you are, Trish." His deep voice had that sexy lisp of an accent that marked him as a Japanese national. Trish wondered if anyone had thought to record his voice on MP3 to fall asleep to —

Stop thinking about this man and sleep, you idiot.
She was doomed.

"Hi, Kazuo. Did you eat yet? Good party, huh? My relatives always have great food. Did you know that some of my aunts and uncles married Chinese spouses? So they bring a lot of really great Chinese food to these family parties. My cousins Venus and Jenn are half-Chinese. They both speak Chinese. Jenn speaks Mandarin and Venus speaks Cantonese because their dads are . . . well, Chinese. And—"

"I've missed you, Trish."

He said it with a kind of strong, passionate look, the kind that preceded some heart-pounding grabbing and kissing.

No, no, no. No kissing in the middle of the New Year's party. Trish swallowed and eased backwards.

Kazuo leaned toward her.

Besides, what was she doing thinking about kissing when she'd just caught her father kissing another woman? She had to get away from her parents, from the party, from Kazuo. "Kazuo, you know we're like oil and water—"

"You are my muse. I am an empty shell without you." He reached out one long-fingered hand, pale and graceful, barely smoothing over her cheek. It made her tingle. "I need you to breathe life back into me."

She had life. Lots of life. And she liked his touch way too much. She drew a shaky breath, filling her lungs with his sandalwood scent, sharp and musky. He'd make her the center of his world, and he'd hold her with those strong arms—

No. Remember? That was how she'd got herself in trouble in the first place.

Maybe God is punishing you.

The thought splashed like ice water down her back. All her problems . . . Dad and that woman . . . No, it couldn't be God punishing her for sleeping with Kazuo. That was silly. Besides, she'd . . . well, Kazuo wasn't exactly her first.

She jerked a step back and almost sent an aunty behind her slamming into the wall. "Oops, sorry." But she broke Kazuo's mesmerizing spell.

"Trish." Jenn suddenly appeared. Thank goodness. But hadn't she said she'd get Lex?

Trish straightened her back and stared up at him. "I was leaving, Kazuo."

His full lips curved up in a half-smile, and his eyes gleamed like black lacquer. "I'll drive you home."

Stupid! He took her words as an invitation. She gave herself a few mental smacks. "No, Jenn and I are leaving together. Girls' thing."

Jenn bit her lip.

Oh no. "What?"

"I drove Venus."

"She's coming too."

Kazuo's brow dented. "I was talking to Venus. She didn't say anything about leaving."

"She probably forgot." Kazuo didn't know that Venus never forgot anything.

"Trish, there you are."

Oh no. How could she face her mom after seeing what she just saw? She turned with an automatic smile plastered on her face and hoped she didn't look like she was in pain.

Mom's hands fluttered in the air as she made her way past an uncle and closer to Trish and company. Her straight hair was looking a little like a bird's nest as she swung her head back and forth, smiling at someone who followed her. "I want you to meet someone special." Her bright eyes twinkled up at Trish like an excited sparrow. "She happened to be invited by one of the aunties."

Mom pulled forward a tall, slender woman with jet-black hair falling like an ebony cascade.

The woman Dad had been kissing.

To her credit, her eyes wavered under Trish's shocked scrutiny. Her smile was small and tight.

Mom didn't notice. She clasped the woman's hand and beamed up at her. "This is my only daughter, Patricia. Trish, meet my old college roommate, Alice Ogawa."

THREE

They don't have Chunky Monkey."

"Cherries Garcia, either."

Trish wanted to shake the freezer case. "Whose idea was it to stop at the Swifty-Mart?"

Jenn pointed to the far corner where Lex was loading a family-sized nachos platter with cheese. "She complained about not getting anything to eat at the party before we left."

Trish pouted. "She's got eighteen percent body fat. She can eat all that stuff and never gain an ounce. Unlike normal people like me." She glared at the tiny freezer. "I need ice cream!"

Venus sashayed up. "I have nonfat frozen yogurt at my place."

"Blech." Both Trish and Jenn made faces at her.

Venus stabbed a manicured finger at Trish. "Then I don't want to hear any more whining about your weight."

Jenn bit back a smile and twirled a lock of her long hair.

Trish whimpered and leaned her forehead against the cool glass door.

Venus crossed her arms and sniffed. "And I hope you have a good reason why we had to leave early."

Trish couldn't remember what she had said to Alice. Hopefully nothing like "Why were you kissing my father?"

With brilliant timing, Lex had chosen that moment to find them in the midst of the crowd, Venus in tow. They'd made their excuses and left the party. Venus's apartment was closest, so they headed there—first stopping off for Ben and Jerry's.

Lex approached with a tray of tortilla chips globbed with fake cheese. "You ready to go? Why did we have to leave early?"

Venus's cold eyes glittered. "It better not be just so you could avoid Kazuo."

Trish's gut burbled. "No, it's not that." Well, it was partly that.

Why was she always drawn to the bad boys? Like Joss, the handsome poet whose verses made her insides melt, who could only write when he was high on cocaine. Or Franc, whose ballroom dancing skills—especially the salsa—made her feel as sexy and talented as J-Lo, although he'd also had several concurrent affairs with ballet dancers on the side. Or Rob, who had been a little too close to his young and pretty cousin; or Andrew, who boosted cars; or Karl, who had multiple body piercings, some in rather unusual places.

She was like a dieter pulled against her will toward In-N-Out Burger. No, even In-N-Out was too healthy. Okay, Fat Burger. A dieter pulled toward Fat Murd—er, Burger.

"I can see why Trish fell for him." Jenn's behind wiggled in the air as she rummaged in the freezer. She straightened with a carton of generic neapolitan. "Kazuo's really good looking."

Venus stabbed her with a look. "Kazuo's totally creepy."

Jenn ducked her head and went to go pay for the ice cream.

Venus shifted her attack to Trish. "You owe me big-time for distracting him in the kitchen. I thought it would be easy, but boy, was I wrong."

Trish cringed. She did owe her. Venus hated talking to men if she could possibly help it, and Kazuo probably drove her nuts. "He's not creepy. He's intense."

Venus's plucked eyebrow arched. "Intensely weird."

A woman looking at cold drinks a few freezer doors down turned to give them a strange look.

"Will you keep your voice down?" Trish hissed, then turned and gave the woman a weak smile.

Jenn returned from paying for her ice cream. She nabbed a plastic spoon from the holder on the industrial freezer door. "He seemed kind of like Viggo Mortensen in *Lord of the Rings*. Muscular, brooding, but poetic."

Hmm, good analogy. Hot but artistic. She could picture Kazuo in a cape with a sword—

Stop thinking about him, you dork.

Venus snorted. "That's fine in Middle Earth, not in Silicon Valley."

"Aw, come on." Lex jabbed her in the ribs with a bony elbow. "You didn't think he was at least a little cute?"

Venus's glare could have melted the cheese on Lex's nachos without the microwave. "You try talking with him about his painting. He makes absolutely no sense."

Trish couldn't argue about that very much. "He's very ... spiritual." He practically worshipped his art. She remembered cringing in the corner as he raged in front of his painting, begging his muse to inspire him, which didn't really make sense because supposedly she was his muse. Then again, being incomprehensible was pretty normal for him.

"Well? Why did we have to leave early?" Lex crunched a corn chip.

The words resonated in Trish's head, but she couldn't make herself say them out loud. As if they couldn't possibly be true unless she spoke them. "I can't tell you in the middle of Swifty-Mart. Can we go—"

Jenn stuck her spoon in her mouth so she could pry open her ice cream pint. "Mmfffn shoo?"

"What?"

Jenn took out the spoon. "Was it that Alice lady? Want some, Venus?" She offered her ice cream, a teasing glint in her eye.

"Are you trying to make me smack you? I'm on a diet. Alice? The one with your mom?" Venus turned to Trish. "She introduced her to Grandma in the kitchen. While I was fending off your creepy ex-boyfriend."

Trish stared at the goopy ice cream. "Maybe it would have been better if you hadn't distracted Kazuo."

Venus gave a disgusted noise. "Now you tell me—"

"What are you talking about?" Pieces of chips flew out of Lex's mouth. "You ran like you were on fire."

"I should have let Grandma find me. Or Kazuo. It would have been better." The rage boiled inside her, like ramen noodle soup about to overflow the pot. "How did my life get so complicated?"

Venus rolled her eyes. "How is facing Kazuo complicated? Just tell him off."

Trish gave an exasperated huff. "Grandma would have been so upset."

"So?" She shrugged.

Trish wanted to scream. "Why do you and Lex love to make her mad?"

"Because despite what she thinks, Grandma does not run our lives for us." Venus's mouth settled into an uncompromising line.

"Plus it's fun." Lex ate another chip.

Jenn squeezed her temples. "She takes it out on us, you know."

"Yeah!" *You tell 'em, Jenn.*

"That's why she brought Kazuo for Trish."

"Yeah! And if I hadn't run from him I wouldn't have seen Dad kissing Alice—" She choked. What did she just say? No . . . not in the middle of Swifty-Mart. This was a bad dream.

Everyone froze. Including the lady a few freezer doors down. The tinny music from the store speakers bounced along as if nothing was wrong.

"No way." Lex stared at her.

Venus grabbed Jenn's spoon and scooped a hunk of ice cream.

Jenn shoved the ice cream carton at her. "Are you sure?" She furiously twirled a lock of her long hair, her breath coming in gasps. "Where were they? Maybe you didn't see—"

"He turned and looked at me."

Jenn held Trish's anguished look for a long moment before dropping her gaze toward the cracked linoleum floor.

The woman next to them tsked. Venus glared at her until she scampered away.

Trish buried her head in her hands. She saw Dad's face, and Alice's. Her heart thudded in her ears with a dull sound, like one of those big *taiko* drums.

"What are you going to do?"

Trish couldn't tell who had whispered it. It was like curling smoke on the edge of the darkness in front of her eyes. There was going to be a huge fire. An explosion, more like.

Venus cleared her throat. "Well, you won't decide in Swifty-Mart. Let's go."

After leaving Venus's apartment, Trish was so nervous driving to her parents' home that she almost had a couple of accidents. Well, not involving other cars, at least — but slamming into the highway median probably wouldn't be good for her health, regardless.

Her mom's Avalon sat in the driveway, but not her dad's Highlander. She couldn't quite decide if she was happy or upset her dad wasn't home. Where was he? She tried not to feel resentment that he wasn't around or wonder who he was with. *Don't go there.* At least she could talk privately to Mom.

Trish geared up as if she were preparing to go into a cleanroom at work. Tissues? Check. Glass of water? Check. Pillow for protection from flying objects? Check.

She knocked on the bedroom door. "Mom?"

This was so wrong. A daughter should not have to tell her mother something like this. But Trish knew World War III would erupt if Mom found out on her own and then discovered Trish hadn't told her.

Not that this would have fewer casualties in figurines and other breakables, but at least Mom wouldn't be peeved at *Trish.*

She was sitting up in bed, reading a book. She blinked at Trish over the tops of her glasses. "Hi, sweetie. Why are you here? I'd have thought you'd have gone back to your apartment." Mom perked up. "Did you want to spend the night?"

"No." On the bedside table—glass of water, nearly full. Ooh, that was a lot of liquid that could wet the carpet. Trish swooped in and snatched it up. "Can I drink this? Thanks." She downed it in a few seconds.

Ew. Good thing she tossed it back so fast. "What is that?"

"Barley water."

"Yech."

Mom raised her eyebrows. "I didn't ask you to drink it."

What else was in grabbing and throwing range? Bedside clock and lamp. She grabbed them and laid them on the floor a good three feet away. "Mom, I have something to tell you."

"What are you doing? I need the light to read." She flapped her hand at the lamp as if that would bring it back to her.

Trish turned to the dresser and started scooping jewelry and a few Precious Moments figurines into the lingerie drawer. "Mom, you're not going to like this."

"Don't put away my figurines. Now I'll have to set them all up again." Mom sat straight up in bed and pulled back the covers to get out.

"I saw Dad kissing another woman."

Mom's naturally pale face whitened a shade, and she swallowed hard. She settled back into her pillows, breathing hard, her hand at her throat. "Was it tonight?" Her voice had become wispy.

What? This was unnatural for Mom. She was usually throwing curveballs at the walls at this point. Trish nodded, then realized her mouth was still open. She snapped it shut.

Mom's shoulders slumped. She curled in on herself and turned her head away.

"Mom?" She almost asked, "Are you okay?" but that would be pretty stupid.

"I ... your ... father ..." Trish could barely make out the words.

"Oh, Mom." Trish gripped one of the costume rings on her fingers. The cheap metal bent. "I'm sorry—Mom!"

Mom slumped over, unconscious.

FOUR

Trish hated how the hospital smelled. Bitterness had become a scent in the air, as hard to remove as cigarette smoke or cheap perfume. It clogged her lungs and made her gag.

Her cousins were on their way, twenty minutes tops. It wasn't soon enough. She wanted one person to hold her hand, another to talk with the nurses and doctors, and someone else to fill out the forms and try to get a hold of her father.

Oh, and she probably needed to re-park her RAV4. Although she didn't think she was *exactly* in the middle of the entrance way. She certainly tried parking closer to the side.

She kept rubbing her arms, partly to warm them, partly to massage the aching muscles. Man, for someone so small, her mother weighed a ton, even carrying her the short distance from the bedroom to her car. Or maybe Trish was a wimp. Miss 18-Percent-Body-Fat-Lex would probably say she lacked muscle tone or something like that. At least she'd been able to flag a few brawny paramedics to carry Mom into the emergency room. Where were they, anyway? They were cute . . .

Stop it! You have men on the brain. God might hear you.

After all, isn't that what this was about? Why else would this come crashing down on her two days after fornicating (yet again) with her ex-boyfriend?

She liked that word. It made her feel dirty and nasty and miserable, which is exactly how she wanted to feel right now. She deserved to be flagellated. Another good word.

The sliding doors whooshed open and Dad breezed in, curly hair disheveled. He looked so calm, Trish wanted to scratch the unconcern off his face.

"Where have you been? I've been trying to reach you!" Her voice had risen to a glass-shattering pitch. Her mind tried to tell herself to calm down, but her mouth kept going. "Every time I call your cell, it goes straight to voice mail."

"I hadn't turned it back on until a little while ago. I'm here now, pumpkin." He gave a grim smile and drew near.

"Don't pumpkin me!" She took a step away. "Where were you? Who were you with?"

He had the gall to open his eyes wide in innocence. "I was picking up your grandma." He gestured behind him.

She sailed into the room with the command of a steel battleship, her red and white scarf floating behind her like a Japanese flag. Trish cringed, wondering how much her screeching had carried and if she was in for another lecture about politeness. But no, Grandma swept past her to the nurses' desk where she started barking questions at the bewildered women.

She hadn't thought to call Grandma. Was she supposed to? Was Grandma peeved and ignoring her as unobtrusively as she could?

Her father knew her too well. "No, you didn't need to call her, pumpkin. She happened to call me right after I got your message."

Trish pressed her lips together and breathed harshly through her nose. "You should have been home, Dad." Although if he had, she wouldn't have gone in to talk with Mom and maybe she wouldn't have collapsed. But he might have been there afterward to help her take Mom to the hospital. Instead of out doing all kinds of things she didn't want to think about her dad doing.

"You took care of it so well, though." He gave her that encouraging smile that used to make her feel as tall, skinny, and gorgeous as a supermodel.

"Stop trying to make excuses. I had to take care of everything myself." Now she sounded peevish. Did she want to see him grovel?

To make him cry? To force a confession here in the middle of the waiting room?

He leaned forward to speak low in her ear. "What do you want from me? I'm here now. What happened is between me and your mom. It doesn't involve you."

"Yes it does. Well, no it doesn't, but it sort of does. Why did you do it, Dad?"

He looked off over her shoulder. And shrugged.

Shrugged!

She grabbed his lapels. "That is not acceptable!"

She smelled the sandalwood a split second before two arms came around from behind her and plucked her hands from her dad's rain jacket. Her shoulder muscles relaxed in automatic reaction as she breathed in. The warmth from his arms seeped through his own jacket and her sweater to wrap her like a shawl. His long-fingered hands clasped hers with tenderness, his thumbs smoothing over her skin.

Kazuo pulled her away from her father by wrapping his arms around her—well, wrapping her arms around herself, too. She didn't think he had intended to make her feel like she was in a straitjacket, but it was a nice straitjacket, anyway.

His breath made the wisps of hair near her ear flutter and tickle her. "It's all right, babe. I'm here. I'll take care of you."

It was so nice to hear that. After all the stress and confusion of trying to figure out what to do with Mom, with the nurses and doctors, it made her heart crack. Heat flooded her nose, and she squeezed shut her eyes as tears gushed. She dropped her chin down to rest against his sinewy forearm, feeling the rasp of his Northface jacket against her cheek.

A part of her mind—a very small part—warned her that she shouldn't be doing this, that she was walking down that dangerous path again. But the majority of her head and all of her hormones were thinking it was so nice to be held by male arms again, and Kazuo could be so kind when he tried.

"Trish!"

Venus's sharp voice made her jump, cracking the top of her head back against Kazuo's chin. She pushed against him, but his arms wouldn't let go easily. It was like trying to peel off cobwebs. She finally jabbed him in the ribs.

Venus had struck a pose in the middle of the room, hands on hips, leaning on one leg. "Didn't we just pray for you a couple hours ago at my apartment?" Even her unwelcoming posture didn't deter some of the other men in the room from taking a second look.

Maybe Trish should rethink Kazuo, because he was one of the few guys who didn't seem attracted to Venus at all. Well, it probably helped that he'd spent time in conversation with her and knew her extreme views on the general uselessness of the male species.

Lex's look was hardly more welcoming. "Guess you didn't need us."

Trish chewed frantically on the inside of her lip and tasted blood. "Well, it's been pretty rough, and Kazuo just got here . . . Wait a minute, how did you know?" She turned to look up at him.

"I was with your grandmother when she found out."

Of course. She thought she heard Lex mutter, "Grandma's dating service never closes."

"Hey, where's Jenn?"

Venus waved her hand, which held her cell phone. "She called and said her mom is having problems tonight. She can't make it."

Oh. Aunty Yuki hadn't been looking too good after her last chemo. Now Trish knew how Jenn felt, seeing her mother so sick.

An Asian female doctor burst through the swinging doors. "Mr. Sakai?"

Dad zipped in front of the woman in a flash. Faster than Trish had expected him to, at least. She had to practically push Grandma out of the way as she got there.

" . . . heart attack. She's resting now. Immediate family can see her for a few minutes. Mr. Sakai, you and your daughter can follow the nurse over there."

Grandma's eyes darkened. "I'm her mother."

The doctor stared her down. "You told the nurses you're her mother-in-law, Mrs. Sakai."

Grandma sniffed and lengthened her neck, which didn't do her any good since she still stood a good five inches shorter than the doctor, who looked like she relished dealing with recalcitrant people.

Trish scurried after her father and the nurse through the swinging doors.

She almost burst into tears when she saw Mom on the bed. She'd aged ten years. Trish had rarely seen her mother at rest. Her eyes weren't darting around — instead, they stayed fixed on the TV set above her, and then lazily swung to Trish and Dad. Her hands weren't moving like they did even when she wasn't talking — they lay relaxed and open against the white sheets.

Man, they must have drugged her up good.

Her mom's gaze softened at the sight of Dad, which made Trish's fists clench at her sides. Dad could exert his charm with a look, and all was forgiven. Well, not for her.

Mom's eyes shifted to Trish, and pain flooded them.

What? She forgave the philanderer but blamed the bringer of bad news? So not fair. Trish rubbed her breastbone. It had only pricked a little. Just a little. It wasn't like a red-hot poker jabbed into her chest by her own mother.

They sat on either side of the bed. Dad picked up her hand — an unusual instance of PDA, probably trying to impress the nurse and ingratiate himself with his wife — so Trish took the other hand.

"Everyone's in the waiting room, Marian." Dad smiled at her, not too brightly, but not too sadly, either. The right amount of hopeful concern. He was such a faker. "I brought my mom, too."

Mom turned to Trish. "Did Grandma tell you about the rumors?"

Huh? "What rumors?"

Mom sighed, a deep heaving groan that seemed to deflate her. "I heard about it today. This morning. How you were sleeping around, so Kazuo dumped you."

"What? Dumped me? I dumped him! And I wasn't sleeping around." Trish's fingers twitched. She tried to relax her grip so she wouldn't squeeze and break Mom's fragile bones. "Those are all lies."

With a rasping breath, Mom sighed again. "Sweetheart . . ."

Dad leaned toward her. "You know how they are, pumpkin. Plus you and your cousins are so adamantly against going to temple. It makes people think you're judging them."

Trish chewed on her cheek even as her other hand rubbed at the pulsing behind her eyes. "You know that's not true." A pack of lies. Who'd say such nasty things? Kazuo's friends? Except he didn't have many friends. He was a typical artist — lonely and moody.

"They're only rumors . . ." Mom closed her eyes. She hated things like this, because she couldn't fix them. Especially not now.

Dad's sad gaze took in his wife's tired face. "Trish, why don't you go out to the waiting room? This is upsetting your mother."

And leave her alone with the lying weasel?

Mom's eyes opened a crack. "Go, Trish. I'll see you tomorrow."

Trish swallowed around the ball of fire in her throat. Prickling numbness raced down her limbs. She dropped Mom's hand before she could feel Trish trembling. She stood. "I'll see you tomorrow." She walked to the waiting room.

Grandma grabbed her arm. "Is she all right?"

"She's tired, but she's okay." Her cousins gathered near. Trish should have felt warm with so many people crowding around her, but she shivered and shifted from side to side on stiff legs.

Kazuo appeared next to her, and she felt a little spark of warmth in her heart. Not a good kind of heat, but at least she could feel something. His arm snaked around her in a concerned but rather intimate gesture.

Trish stepped away from him. They weren't dating anymore. She had to remember that, even though she'd like to just lean on him and let him take care of her like he used to.

Wait, what was she thinking? Her behavior with Kazuo might be the very reason all this was happening. She didn't know if God's wrath came down on people like this — did it?

Grandma sighed. "She's so young. Why did this have to happen to her?"

Why Mom? Why not Trish? Mom hadn't done anything bad. Well, apart from being a staunch Buddhist and only smiling politely when Trish talked about Christ.

Maybe because God knew this would hurt Trish more, to see her mom suffer. More painful *flagellation* for her *fornication*.

Or maybe because God wanted to give her a second chance. He let the Israelites repent tons of times, right? Maybe this was his way of saying, *Now is the time for you to turn your life around, babe.*

Trish sank into a chair. Kazuo tried to sit next to her, but Venus and Lex muscled in and flanked her instead. They knew her better than anyone — knew her nature, knew she needed protection from both Kazuo and herself.

Trish didn't care who sat with her. She no longer needed someone to hold her hand.

After tonight ended, she needed some time alone with God.

FIVE

A biologist's work was never done.

Not when cancer cells grew exponentially regardless of whether it was a regular workweek or the holidays. Trish spent most of New Year's Day—just a few hours after leaving the hospital—in her cell culture room at Valley Pharmaceuticals, doing damage control.

It wouldn't have been so bad if two incubators hadn't decided to give up the ghost over the New Year's weekend.

As it was, three of her studies had to be trashed, and she had been at work all day trying to salvage what cells were still alive. Her boss Diana was *not* going to be happy about this, because her boss's boss had been waiting on the results of the studies that were now in the biohazard trash bin. Emergencies piled on top of stress, piled on top of lack of sleep.

But nothing that one of Jenn's homemade dark chocolate truffles couldn't solve.

Finally done with work and relaxing at home, Trish sat in the dip in her living room couch, licked chocolate off her fingers, and stared at the closed Bible in her lap. She was procrastinating, but she couldn't seem to get going. A wound-up nervousness vibrated in her hands, in her legs, in the pit of her stomach. Or maybe it was exhausted energy from her sleepless night and busy day.

She stared at her goldfish, who piddled around in his bowl on the counter top. Gonzo the umpteenth—she named all her goldfish after her favorite Muppet character.

The train chugged by outside her apartment, leaving Mountain View for Sunnyvale. What time was it? Would her roommate Marnie come home soon? She'd been gone when Trish had dashed in for a change of clothes before heading into work. Good thing she only had a short commute to Palo Alto.

What would she do about dinner? She was too tired to cook. She could go out—there were lots of good restaurants on nearby Castro Street—but she hated eating alone. And even if Marnie were home, she wouldn't ask her along—she had given up trying to be better friends with her. When they'd first started rooming together a few months ago, she'd coaxed Marnie into going out to dinner with her a few times, but Marnie was always so quiet and closed that Trish ended up babbling like an idiot and feeling like one, too.

She really couldn't complain, because Marnie was a good room-mate—quiet, hardly any visitors except for her boyfriend, and about as neat and tidy as Trish, which was somewhere between "slob" and "a household with toddlers." Which reminded her, it was her turn to vacuum this week . . .

Stop it. Get going. She yanked open her Bible. She stared at the page a moment without reading anything.

Get a grip. Wait, maybe I should pray before I dive into this. She sighed.

Dear God.

The blank walls answered her, waving dusty cobwebs in the breeze flowing from the window. She really should clean up the apartment . . .

No, she needed to focus. *Dear God—*

A key rattled in the lock, then Marnie Delacruz ambled in. Her favored loose knit clothes in predominantly blues and greens made her seem even shorter and rounder than she already was. She looked like she always did—as if her pet had just died.

"Hi Marnie!" Trish infused excitement in her voice in hopes that Marnie would respond with something other than a grunt.

"Hi." Just that one word. Her full, un-lipsticked mouth set in its normal half-frown. She dropped her keys onto the kitchen counter and smoothed back her crowning glory, her waterfall of dark hair that fell to the back of her thighs. She pulled her computer briefcase off her sagging shoulder.

"You went into work today too?"

She ran a hand over her chipmunk cheeks—which should have made her look cheerful but didn't—and sighed. "Server crashed."

Trish winced. "Ooh, bummer."

Marnie shrugged.

Conversation over.

Well, Marnie did have a slight flush under her olive skin tone, and she looked a little sadder than usual, which Trish took to mean she was tired. Marnie tended to get even less talkative when tired—she often collapsed in front of the TV in a heap after a long day at work.

But today, Marnie surprised her. "Is your mom okay?"

Trish blinked at her for a few seconds before she swallowed her surprise. "Yeah. I talked with Dad." A stilted conversation. "She's doing okay."

"Heart attack?" Marnie opened the fridge.

"Yeah. They're holding her for observation." And probably to keep her heart-attack-inducing daughter away from her. "She's going to need quiet for the next few months. Someone with her to care for her."

"Your dad?"

Trish looked away. "Dad refused to hire a nurse, said he'd take care of her himself. I was surprised." She didn't understand. It would seriously cramp his tomcatting around. Maybe he hadn't wanted a nurse observing both Mom's health and his behavior.

Marnie popped open a can of soda. For some reason, she had a rather misty, faraway look in her large dark eyes that made Trish wonder if Marnie was coming down with something. "He must love her a lot."

Trish's stomach clenched, and she pressed her lips together so she wouldn't gag. She felt trapped—she couldn't talk to her mom about his affair while she was recovering, but she didn't want to talk to her father, either. For now there was nothing she could do. "I guess."

Slurping her soda, Marnie wandered into the TV area and peered at Trish's lap. "Doing your church stuff?"

She closed her glaringly blank notebook. What a great witness to her atheist roommate. "I just started. I'll go to my room if you want to watch TV."

Marnie dropped into the couch almost before Trish vacated it and reached for the remote control on the coffee table. "Yeah, I don't want to keep you from your Bible reading."

Trish gritted her teeth at Marnie's pointed tone. Sure, she wasn't the best Christian on the planet, but Marnie didn't have to mock her. She padded into her bedroom and shut the door.

Flopping onto her futon bed, she arranged her Bible and notebook in front of her. She bowed her head. *Dear Lord. Um ... well, I guess I haven't been reading my Bible like I should. I'm sorry about that. But I could use some answers now.* She felt a whining attack surge up, but she shoved it down. *I feel kind of weird coming to you now. I know my behavior lately hasn't been very Christian-like, and I'm sorry. I mean, I'm really sorry this time. A lot of bad things happened yesterday ... Well, duh, you already knew that. So I guess I'm hoping this means you're giving me a second chance to turn things around. Please help me. I don't deserve it, but please give me some grace.*

Trish filled her lungs until her ribs felt tight and stretched. As she exhaled, peace like a slow, gentle wave washed over her heart, sweeping the jittery tension away. She flipped the Bible open, and it landed at the beginning of 1 Corinthians. She started reading.

Her heart skipped a beat as she read chapter one: "He will keep you strong to the end, so that you will be blameless ..."

Blameless. She'd like to be blameless and pure, instead of a mess. And did that verse mean Christ would keep her strong so she could stay blameless?

Could she be blameless again? Could she regain what she'd lost? Well, not literally—she knew she couldn't regain her virginity, which she'd carelessly lost several boyfriends ago, unknown to her cousins. But could she regain everything else? Her chastity, her cousins' love and support, her ruined reputation?

She'd always treated God kind of like a genie to save her when she needed Him. But now she wanted to be a better person. She wanted to make better choices. She wanted to be in a better place than the miserable dilemma she was in now, tempted by Kazuo's presence and by Grandma's approval of him.

She wanted her chastity back. If she could do that, then everything would be the same as it was before.

The Word spoke to her again in chapter seven: "I would like you to be free from concern ... I am saying this for your own good, not to restrict you, but that you may live in a right way in undivided devotion to the Lord."

Trish almost popped off her bed. Undivided devotion to the Lord. That's the spiritual place she needed to be. God wanted her to be devoted to *Him*. Undividedly.

Undistractedly.

Wait a minute. Undistracted? Guys distracted her everywhere. Her eye always roved around. She always yearned and wondered, *Is he available? He's cute. Oh, and his friend is darling. Aw, he's being nice to that old lady—he must be a great guy ...*

But if she was undistracted, she'd only be thinking about the Lord's affairs, like it said in the seventh chapter of 1 Corinthians. Although to be completely honest, that sounded kind of boring.

Undistracted devotion. Hmm. She'd have to think about that later.

All week Trish continued through First and Second Corinthians, taking notes and jotting down verses that leaped off the page. On Thursday night, she sat in her bedroom reading 2 Corinthians, when a verse struck like a lightning bolt. She gasped and straightened her spine with a jerk.

Unfortunately, at the time she was perched on the seat-back of her chair with her toes dug into the seat cushion. Her sudden movement tipped her balance and propelled the chair backwards.

Trish's arms flailed in a blur before her eyes, and she toppled with a sound like a cat hacking up a furball. She landed hard on her tail-bone and collected two rug burns on her elbows. In a flurry of pages, her Bible flopped onto her chest.

Trish scrambled to her feet. Her bedroom shared a wall with the living room, where Marnie watched TV. She hoped the Spanish-language soap opera had muted her bumping across the carpet. She dropped her Bible onto the desk and pulled her chair upright, resisting the urge to give it a solid kick—her toes would lose, anyway.

Where had she been reading? Trish sat in the chair—properly, this time—and flipped through the creased pages. There, chapter five: "Therefore, if anyone is in Christ, he is a new creation; the old has gone, the new has come!"

She had always assumed it talked about the process of becoming a new Christian, but maybe it applied to old backslidden ones, too. Not that she was old, just ... well, old enough to know better.

She could completely shed her old self, her old problems, her old temptations (namely, Kazuo) and jump whole-heartedly into a new self. A new adventure for life. How cool!

"All this is from God, who reconciled us to himself through Christ and gave us the ministry of reconciliation: that God was reconciling the world to himself in Christ, not counting men's sins against them. And he has committed to us the message of reconciliation. We are therefore Christ's ambassadors, as though God were making his appeal through us. We implore you on Christ's behalf: Be reconciled to God."

Get back with God and tell others. Sure! She could do that. She had no problems talking.

Chapter six was more difficult for her to read: "Do not be yoked together with unbelievers."

She had read the passage a million times before, and it never registered. Maybe she'd been willfully blind about it, especially because she didn't see the harm in dating non-Christian guys. But if she devoted herself to God, she wouldn't even consider sharing her life with someone who didn't feel the same way.

Trish also realized the dire truth. Dating only Christian guys cut down her dating pool. Drastically.

She admitted that Christianity wasn't at the forefront of her thoughts whenever a cute guy passed by. Especially not if he gave her a second look. But only Christian guys? That was so hard. But if Kazuo had been Christian, he wouldn't have pushed her into sleeping with him, right?

Well, she hadn't exactly run away from him. And she'd really enjoyed the magical intimacy they shared. Why was it that all the guys who were bad for her made her feel so *good*? She didn't know any interesting or attractive Christian men. But then again, if she focused on God, she probably wouldn't even *care* about the lack of dating prospects.

There it was, printed in black and white. It was what God wanted for His children. And He gave promises if she obeyed: "I will receive you." Ooh, she wanted to be received in loving arms. "I will be a Father to you, and you will be my sons and daughters . . ."

Trish wanted the intimacy of being a beloved daughter. She'd lost favor with her cousins after they saw Kazuo embracing her in the middle of the hospital waiting room, and Grandma was withholding favor until Trish got back together with him. Her mom was really sick, and Dad . . . things were strained, to put it mildly. There was no one there for her.

And maybe once she was successful in becoming a better person — if she did enough things so God could love her more — then He might lead Mr. Perfect Christian Man directly to her. Didn't they always say you found what you were looking for when you stopped looking? It had worked for her cousin Lex and her great relationship with Aiden.

Trish definitely had that whole "burning" thing Paul talked about in 1 Corinthians 7 somewhere. She needed a good Christian boyfriend to depend on, someone to be strong so she wouldn't have to be.

She continued on. She had already filled pages and pages of her notebook with verses and thoughts.

On Friday night, Trish stayed home like an utter social failure to finish the last few chapters of 2 Corinthians. In chapter twelve of 2 Corinthians, she reached Christ's words to Paul: "My grace is sufficient for you, for my power is made perfect in weakness."

She burst into tears.

She was so weak, such a loser, such a *tramp*. But Christ promised to give her His power despite her weak-loser-tramp status. Paul himself said, "For when I am weak, then I am strong." If Paul could be flogged and jailed and still be faithful, then she could at least face morning traffic with fewer temper tantrums.

Sniveling and honking into tissues, Trish finished 2 Corinthians and jotted down her last note. She sagged back in her chair and took a deep breath, feeling the air rasp in her throat. A vague nervousness simmered somewhere south of her stomach, making her a bit queasy. This was something big.

Reconciled with Christ. Blameless. Undivided — undistracted — devotion.

Her nervousness rose to a rapid boil, and she started to hyperventilate. Could she do that? Turn her back on non-Christian boys — on *all* boys, because if she was looking at guys, even Christian guys, God certainly wouldn't give her one. Could she turn her mind and desires around so that she could achieve that undivided devotion? Jenn seemed to have that — she was such a good Christian girl. Could Trish learn to rely on God more than she did? Most of the time, she simply didn't remember to think about God.

She needed to pull a Nike and just do it. Commit to becoming a different person, a better person. Regaining her chastity, making everything like it was before.

The realization hit like a dash of cold water, calming her boiling tension, invigorating her senses with new purpose. She would change her innermost desires and make Christ her top priority. First and Second Corinthians could show her how to do it.

She sifted through her notes and saw many things falling into a pattern. Energy rushed through her hands and feet. She felt like she was back in school, and she finally understood a calculus concept that baffled everybody else.

I think I get it . . .

"Hallo?" Jenn's voice sounded scratchy with sleep.

"Jenn, I just exited the freeway. I'm on my way to your house."

"Trish? What time is it?"

"Let me in, okay? I called your cell phone so I wouldn't wake up your mom."

"What? What time did you leave Mountain View?" Trish heard Jenn fumbling for something.

"Well, I stopped off for coffee. I had to talk to you—"

"Trish, it's seven a.m. on a Saturday!"

Uh oh. "Um . . . Do you want me to come back later? I could drive around . . ."

Jenn sighed. "No, I'm already up. I'll unlock the door for you."

Twenty minutes later, Trish bustled into Jenn's kitchen. Jenn dozed while standing over the coffee maker and turned a bleary eye when she walked in.

Trish dropped her Bible on the counter. "Good morning. Did you make enough for me?"

"You said you had coffee already." Jenn gestured to the mucho-grande-popcorn-tub-size paper coffee cup in Trish's hand.

"Oh, I finished it."

"I'll make another pot for you. Will you let me have my one cup so I feel a bit more civilized?"

Wow, Jenn sure was crabby in the morning. Trish retreated to the breakfast table. "I'm sorry. I'm excited about what I read last night."

"What?"

"I figured out my problem is men."

Jenn didn't applaud. She circled her hand in the air, asking for more. "Isn't that every girl's problem?"

"Well, specifically, my behavior around men. I need to stop desiring Kazuo or any other guy. I need to regain my chastity."

"I guess that's a significant revelation." Jenn yawned. "What were you reading?"

"First and Second Corinthians." Trish bounced up and down in her chair. "I even memorized a verse: 'Since we have these promises, dear friends, let us purify ourselves from everything that contaminates body and spirit, perfecting holiness out of reverence for God.' Second Corinthians 7:1."

Jenn stared at her.

Could someone fall asleep with their eyes open? "Jenn?"

Jenn sniffed. "What."

"Oh, you are awake. Okay, so I decided I need a complete transformation to become completely devoted to God. So I came up with three rules —"

"Wait, where did you get those rules from?"

"Don't worry, they're from First and Second Corinthians. It was like God showed me all these verses, and three key themes kept coming up." She dug out a small note card from her Bible.

"Um, not to harp on this, but do you have biblical references?"

"Yes, and they're not taken out of context, either. Now be quiet and listen. Okay, rule number one —"

"Rule number one." Jenn sank into the chair across from Trish and propped her head in her hand.

"Don't look."

Jenn stared in confusion for a few seconds. "Huh?"

"I have to stop looking at guys."

"Are you going to blind yourself or something?"

"No, it's just that ... well, everywhere I go, I'm looking around, hoping to meet guys. I'm striking up conversations, checking him out, wondering if he's single, encouraging him ... I have to stop."

"Like I said, are you going to blind yourself?"

"Jenn!" Who knew quiet Jenn could be such a smart aleck at seven a.m.?

"Sorry, sorry. I'll be more supportive. But ... even Christian guys?"

"Well, if a guy is interested in me even though I don't encourage him, I'm not exactly going to blow him off. But this rule will ensure I don't forget God's will if I get tempted by some yummy but non-Christian guy."

"Is this rule really going to be able to do that for you?"

Trish gnawed her lip and glanced at her notes. "Uh ... I hope so. At least I know what my problem is now. It'll be a hard habit to break, but I need to stop doing it."

Jenn looked skeptical. "Okay, next?"

"Rule number two: Tell others about Christ."

"Like all the time?"

"Well, more than I'm doing now." Which was closer to never.

"You're not going to be preaching on street corners, are you?"

"No, but I work with nonbelievers. I can start telling them more about God." She envisioned striking up conversations while seeding cell lines, leading a coworker to salvation while bowed over a bio-chemical assay.

Jenn bit her lip. "You don't need to evangelize to everyone around you, you know. You can show God's love with your actions. Like forgiving whoever keeps stealing your ice cream from the company fridge."

"But those are Häagen-Dazs pints."

Jenn lifted an eloquent brow.

"Okay, okay. But won't people just think I'm being nice? They won't know it's because God has changed me into a fabulous new Trish." She flung her arms out in a "ta-da!" gesture.

Jenn didn't even crack a smile. "You're making it sound too easy."

"But I'll be motivated to do it, and God will help me. Which brings me to rule number three: Persevere and rely on God. Paul told the Corinthians to persevere, and that God would give strength, help, and grace in hardship."

"Following these rules won't automatically make you devoted to God."

"But if I follow these rules, eventually God will change my heart so that I will be devoted to Him."

"Where does it say that?"

"Right here in 2 Corinthians, after the 'do not be yoked' thing." Trish flipped pages. " 'I will be a Father to you, and you will be my sons and daughters, says the Lord Almighty.' See? I will become His daughter. I'll be a good girl instead of an embarrassment."

"I guess . . . you're right." Jenn stared hard at the verse.

"You have that *concerned* sound."

"Well, they seem kind of legalistic."

"No, they'll remind me of what I need to do. My new rules for living!" Trish flung her arms out again and almost knocked over her coffee cup.

"Keep it down, you'll wake Mom."

"Oh. Sorry." Trish leaned against the table. "So what do you think?"

"Don't get me wrong—realizing that you need undivided devotion to God is a good thing. It's a huge spiritual step. And they're good rules. I don't see anything wrong with them, and they're biblically-based."

Trish perked up like she'd found a five-dollar bill outside of a Starbucks café. "Then will you keep me accountable?" She was so proud of herself for remembering that she needed a prayer partner, let alone actually asking someone to help her.

Jenn's brow wrinkled. "Me?"

"Why not you?"

"Well ..." She twirled the ends of her hair. "Not that I don't love you, but you've always been closer to Lex."

Trish gnawed a little on the inside of her cheek and scratched the back of her neck. "Uh ... Lex hasn't been returning my emails lately."

Jenn's eyes cracked a fraction wider. "Is she okay?"

"Oh yeah. I think she's ... well, she might be mad at me." Her neck started warming up like she had a heating pad wrapped around it.

"Mad at you? For what?"

"At the hospital that night, Kazuo and I were ... sort of embracing."

"Embracing? At the *hospital*?"

Trish realized she'd embraced guys in worse places, but this time, she wasn't totally to blame. "He was holding me back from smacking my adulterous father. I think that's a good reason."

Jenn's gaze fell to the scarred wooden kitchen table. "Oh. Yeah."

"And Venus is always so busy at work."

"She works at a startup. Of course she's busy."

"Oh. So anyway, I really need you. I kind of feel like ..." Trish bit the inside of her lip. " ... like they've abandoned me." The way Trish had abandoned Lex.

She touched Trish's hand. "I'm sure they haven't."

"Well, it sure feels like it, since Venus is so busy and Lex isn't talking to me."

"Trish, she's not perfect. You hurt her, and she's going to need time. But she'll call you eventually. Besides — " But she swallowed whatever she was going to say. She started braiding a lock of her hair.

Trish stared hard at her. "What?"

"Well ..."

"Spit it out, Jenn."

She looked up at her. "We pick you up, dust you off, take care of your problems for you, and then you always seem to go and do the same things again."

"No, I d — " Well, last year there had been that whole "I'm not going to date" phase (à la Joshua Harris), which didn't last very long.

And then there had been that thing about going back to church, and she'd only gone a few weeks before slipping back into the habit of sleeping in on Sundays. There was the mess about getting intimate with Kazuo again after she'd sworn she was finally over him, which caused that minor thing about making Lex feel like she wasn't as important as Kazuo's loving attentions. And . . .

Jenn sat there blinking.

"This time I'm really serious."

"But how would anybody know that?" Jenn's question was sincere.

Trish sat back in her chair. How would anyone realize this was different from other impulsive decisions she'd made over the years? Because this really was different. She knew it without knowing how she knew. Deep down inside her, deeper than emotions. "How do I prove to them I'm sincere?"

Jenn continued to blink at her.

What could she do that would undeniably prove she had become a good, Christian girl, devoted to God, earnestly longing to serve Him and—

Wait a minute. Good Christian girl. Devoted. Serving. Who else served the church like no one else? The pastor.

"I'll get my MDiv!"

Jenn blinked faster. "What?"

"A Master of Divinity degree. Then no one can refute that I've really changed."

"You're going to go to seminary just to prove that you're changed? That's awful."

"It's not just to prove I've changed. Before this wakeup call, I wouldn't even have considered doing this. I feel inspired because God is going to make something new and terrific inside me." Trish nodded firmly.

"What are you going to do with an MDiv?" Jenn asked.

Trish waved a hand. "Anything. Women's ministry. Children's ministry. Evangelism deacon. I'm sure God will tell me."

"You're going to quit your job to go into full-time ministry?"

"What? No. A couple people from my church got their MDiv, but they haven't quit their jobs or anything."

Jenn had started twirling the ends of her hair. "I don't know, Trish ..."

"Why not? This is perfect. I'm always taking classes at the community college just for fun — I love taking classes."

"It's a lot of work."

"I'm not afraid of schoolwork, and I'm great with languages. I'm fluent in Japanese, and I learned some Chinese and Spanish — I'll bet Hebrew and Greek would be a breeze."

"I don't know about that. It'll take years."

"I'm willing to work for it, no matter how long it takes."

Jenn closed her eyes and rested her forehead in her hand. "It's too early in the morning for this."

"For now, can you be my accountability partner?"

"Sure, sure." Jenn sighed.

"Good. Kazuo goes back to Japan for good sometime this summer — his uncle is opening a new art gallery and promised to display Kazuo's paintings at the grand opening — but until then, maybe my three rules will help me transform myself so I won't be tempted by him."

"You won't run into temptation sooner?"

Trish snorted. "Where? At church? Everyone knows you never meet eligible men at church."

"How about your apartment complex?"

"Ewww. No way. They're all either married or packing massive emotional baggage. And I think the guy upstairs is doing something illegal."

"How about at work? They're all smart and have steady incomes?"

"They're not Christian, and most of them aren't cute. No temptation there." Trish got up to get coffee. "You'll see. I'll transform myself, and that MDiv will prove it's not temporary."

SIX

If Trish's supervisor went by "Asian time," Trish would be on time for the meeting even though the wall clock in the cell culture room showed ten past the hour. However, she didn't think Diana would find that Asian American joke very funny.

Trish yanked off her nitrile gloves and threw them at the biohazard container. The first official day back from New Year's holiday was always busy—Diana would understand that, right? She raced to the door of the cell culture room and happened to glance at the container. Rats, the cancer-cell-infested gloves had missed. She screeched to a halt, flung her body back, picked them up by a clean corner between thumb and forefinger, and dropped them into the red plastic bag.

Trish slammed out the door of the room. Tearing off her lab coat, she sprinted to the lab sink. She cranked the sink handle and a spray shot down from the narrow spout and ricocheted up into her face.

Spitting and shaking her head, she turned the water down so she could wash her hands. She pinched off tiny pieces of the paper towel before grabbing a mammoth handful to dry her hands and wipe her streaming face. Stupid towel dispenser. Oh, and the stupid water got on her new blouse. She scrubbed at the water stains as she raced out the lab doors and down the hallway.

Trish hurtled into her office room so fast, she bounced off the cubicle wall to an empty desk. She skidded around the edge of her desk in the corner. Paper towels flew everywhere when she dropped them to snatch a pen and her calendar.

She crashed through the door to the stairwell, then leaped up the stairs. By the time she reached the third floor, her chest heaved, and she expected to see her lungs fly out of her mouth with her next breath. She raced down the carpeted hallway to the conference room.

Outside the door, Trish glanced at her watch. With a grimace, she eased open the heavy oak door to peek inside.

Four pairs of eyes zoomed in on her.

Oops. "Sorry. I had a problem thawing cells this morning."

Her supervisor Diana waved her to a seat, then turned to speak to Trish's redheaded coworker. "Is the study ready to start on Friday?"

"Yup." She glanced at their other coworker. "Are you doing the assays on the samples?"

He stretched and nodded. "Got it covered."

Trish plopped into a padded chair and felt her bladder jiggle. She should have stopped off at the restroom. She downed so much coffee that she drank a lot of water to avoid dehydration — she hadn't slept through *all* her human physiology classes — which also meant she had to go a billion times a day. She squirmed in her seat but decided it wasn't too bad yet. Only then did she glance up.

Spenser Wong from the tumor research group sat across the table. *What's he doing at our group meeting?*

At the last interdepartmental meeting, Trish hadn't heard a word of his presentation. Instead, she drank in the sight of his lithe body and listened to his deep, dreamy voice and sighed over his chiseled, handsome face.

Pull yourself together.

Her coworker flourished a printed email. "Newark said they had a laboratory accident. Compound shipment is delayed."

Diana frowned. "When will they have it ready?"

Spenser shifted in his seat and stretched his arm as if it felt stiff. How could she listen to late shipments when tempted by those broad shoulders straining the knit fabric of an indecently snug shirt?

Stop looking. Remember your three rules. Trish whipped her head around to focus on Diana, as if compound insolubility fascinated her.

Movement at the corner of her peripheral vision screamed at her to look.

No looking. He's not even Christian. She gritted her teeth and forced herself to remember when she'd seen Spenser last week Monday, his eyes bloodshot and a headache creasing a frown in his forehead. They'd arrived at work at the same time, and she let them in with her card-key. He stumbled through the doors with a groaning "Thanks," then hauled himself up the stairs to his second-floor office.

He must be a party animal. Trish no longer drank, so she was now a good girl. *The old has gone, the new has come.*

The party animal twirled his pen as her coworkers brainstormed ideas to speed up the study.

"Couldn't we cover our bases and add another three groups?" There, that proved Trish wasn't distracted. She was paying attention.

Diana paused, then shook her head. "We don't have enough compound to do that. How about ..."

Trish admired Spenser's long fingers as he flipped the pen around and scribbled a few notes. The other hand reached up to massage his square jaw. "You could change the dosing schedule ..."

Trish drowned in the mellow sound of his voice, a sea of swirling, rich dark chocolate ... She jerked her head up and straightened her spine in her chair. None of that. He was a player, and no way would she ever be interested in someone like her dad. Why, last week she saw him flirting with that long-haired, leggy intern from Hong Kong.

"Okay, that's settled." Diana's voice pulled Trish back from a daydream about magically transferring all her own fat to the hips of the rail-thin Hong Kong girl. "Now for the big news. Our manager handed a new project to me yesterday. We've discovered a novel pathway to prevent bone disease. Trish, you're in charge of developing a cellular model to screen compounds."

Trish jolted in surprise so violently that she started sliding off her seat. She slammed her hands against the table so she wouldn't end up on the floor. Wow, she got to be in charge of a new pathway study! She eased her rear end back onto the cushion. "Really? That's great."

"Here are some scientific papers about similar cell models for unrelated indications." Diana pushed a pile of photocopied papers at her. "The problem is that the model has to be tested with biochemical assays—the scientific council wants concrete data, rather than anything ambiguous. This won't be like the other projects—histological stains don't give numerical results."

"What kind of assays? Will I need to order ELISA kits, or RIAs ...?"

"No, the other investigators in those papers developed special in-house assays."

Trish flipped through the papers and started gnawing on her inner lip. She had assay experience but not enough to develop one from scratch.

Diana wasn't finished. "Since Spenser has so much experience developing biochemical assays, he's been assigned to help you develop the model."

He met her surprised look with a cool one that dampened her excitement. He probably wished he could work with that prettier Hong Kong girl. He would have at least given *her* a friendly smile.

Diana had a calculating look. "Trish—there are three empty desks in your office, right? You're the only one in that room?"

Trish fingered the edges of the papers while something gurgled in her stomach. Funny, she had eaten that apple hours ago. "Yes."

"This is a high-profile project—everyone in the scientific council will follow this. You two need to work fast and efficiently to get this model ready to screen compounds by the end of the quarter."

Trish peeked at Spenser, but her gaze flitted away from his grim expression.

"So Spenser," Diana continued, "I want you to move your desk down to that room. You'll be Trish's new office-mate."

God, I want you to know that you have a very strange sense of humor. I can't believe I thought this would be easy. How can I keep rule number one with him in my office?

As soon as the meeting ended, Trish bolted for the door. She needed someplace quiet to recover from the shock. She headed for her office ... um, no. Bathroom break first.

The quiet in the echoing restroom didn't calm her. She washed her hands and wondered what to do. If only Spenser weren't so *yummy*. She would be aware of him every time he walked into the room. Whenever she opened her mouth, she would drool and babble like an idiot.

She needed to calm down. She entered her office, took a deep breath, and collapsed in her chair. Okay, reality check: Spenser was unhappy about the whole thing. Trish would be unhappy too, if she had to move to a different office. But she didn't know why he objected to working with her — he didn't really know her.

His disgruntled attitude cooled her ardor. Eye candy wasn't as sweet when it scowled at you, like Spenser did after the announcement at the meeting.

Trish should be overjoyed at his lack of interest. She was getting worked up for nothing. Smooth, sophisticated Spenser in his Structure khakis and Armani Exchange shirts wouldn't be tempted by the new Trish, proper and devoted to God. Besides, she wasn't supposed to encourage even a hint of interest. She'd be breaking rule number one.

She could be calm and professional.

Trish hid behind her computer monitor, which blocked her view of the doorway. She wondered when Spenser would move in.

He walked in a second later with a cardboard moving box. He dropped it to the floor with a *plunk* that betrayed his still-simmering temper.

Trish eyed his box. That was fast. "How long have you known?"

"My supervisor told me this morning so I would join Diana's group meeting."

Trish bristled at his clipped tone. *Grumpy.* She stared at his back, which wasn't *that* broad.

He tossed pens and his calendar onto one of the two desks at the other end of the room, ignoring the one right next to hers. Refusing to let him get away with his snot-nosed attitude, she leaned back in her chair. "Good idea. I'm sure it will be much easier to collaborate if I have to throw the data sheets across the room at you."

Spenser swung his head around to frown at her.

Trish's sense of humor took over, and she flashed him a cheeky smile.

He turned back to the cubicle he'd chosen, then looked at the one next to hers. His glower melted into a rueful expression. Then he had the audacity to wink at her. "You want me close so you can play footsies with me."

Trish's mouth opened in shock before she exploded into peals of laughter. "Yeah, right. Your ego's not going to fit into this office."

Spenser grinned. "My ego wouldn't fit into this building."

She hadn't thought he was able to laugh at himself.

He scanned the floor. "I need a power strip. Got one?"

Trish rummaged for the extra surge protector in her desk drawer and gave it to him. He glanced at the mess of papers surrounding the keyboard on her desk. "Are you finished with your last project?"

She caught where he was heading. "I'm writing the final report now. I'll be done by the time you get settled."

"Good. We can start on the model this afternoon." He gave her a satisfied nod. "I think we're going to work well together."

He transformed his brooding face with a blinding, charming smile — and dimples! He had dimples! — that made her mouth go dry and her stomach plummet to her knees.

Oh God, help me . . .

"Hey!"

Spenser heard Trish's complaint a split second before she smacked the back of his hand. "What? What's wrong?"

"Put on fresh gloves before you touch my pipettors." She continued aspirating supernatant from a 6-well cell culture plate.

Spenser pulled off his gloves, dropped them in the biohazard bag, and reached for new ones in the nearby box. "Want to check under my fingernails, too, Mom?"

She stuck out her tongue at him. "And remember to put that pipettor back in the right place this time, too."

He still didn't get how Trish's desk looked like a tsunami had hit, but her workbench had the neatness of Mr. Monk's house. "Bossy."

"Grouch. You've only been working with me a week and you're already complaining." But she smiled as she said it. "Here." She passed him the plate she'd been working on so he could do his DNA prep on the cells.

They worked smoothly in silence for a while. He tended to work quickly, but Trish kept up with him, passing him another plate just as he finished the old one.

"I'm done with the protocol for the mesenchymal osteoblasts." Trish pipetted supernatant into a microfuge tube.

"I'm almost done solidifying my assay for those. The cells—"

"I ordered them . . ." She stopped to think. "Yesterday. Did you double-check the micro-plate reader? That one tech from Virology always leaves a terrible mess—I mean, the last time there was reagent spilled all over the counter, and I never heard the end of it from the guys in Arthritis—anyway, he was the last one to use it."

Good to know, otherwise he might have lost an entire day in contaminated plates. "I'll check it today."

He had already figured out that Trish might act like a ditz sometimes, but she certainly wasn't one. It hadn't taken him long to realize a biologist wouldn't have gotten to her level of seniority without some brains behind the wide eyes and nonstop mouth.

"How's your mom's flu? Is she feeling any better?" Trish peered closely at the bottom of a well.

He pipetted cells into the Eppendorf tube. "Sort of."

"What do you mean, sort of?"

"You ever taken Chinese medicine?"

"No, but my cousins are half Chinese, and their parents do." Trish passed him another plate.

"Mom says, 'If bad taste means strong medicine, you're cured.'"

Trish snickered. "What's she taking?"

"Some new root that she boils on the stove. I walked into her kitchen and thought the cat had died."

Trish erupted into laughter.

He didn't expect the dazzling smile that made the laboratory lights seem dim. She turned the full force of that smile at him, making him blink in surprise. He felt like someone punched him in the stomach. He had never seen a smile that could make a guy grin back like an idiot.

"So does it work?"

It took him a moment to realize she'd asked a question. "She says it does, but when she drinks it, she looks like she's in pain."

Trish hooted. "That's what my cousin's mom looks like, too." She tucked her hair behind her ear and applied herself to her work, a smile still hovering on her mouth.

He'd never really noticed her features before, how pretty she was. And she was fun to be around.

She handed him the last plate. "I need more coffee."

"You had three cups this morning already."

She rolled her eyes. "Nag, nag, nag. I'm going to get something from the cafeteria." Her face lit up at the prospect of something nuclear-strength and venti-sized from the espresso bar.

He looked her in the eye. "Your coffee addiction is scary."

She laughed and left the lab.

The lab seemed darker without her in it.

She'd be a fun date.

In his office, Spenser studied Trish as she stared at her calendar, as if daring it to defy her careful planning. Her arched brows scrunched under a smooth forehead, already a bit shiny by mid-morning and framed by the straight dark hair that fell from her middle part, with wisps softening her face. She was always well dressed, but usually untidy by noon.

Spenser tended to prefer tiny, delicate girls. Trish was short, but not delicate. However, her jeans showed off nicely curved hips that weren't unattractive. She didn't walk—she bounced with confidence and energy. While she wasn't as trendy as his other girlfriends had been, she didn't dress like a slob, either. He wouldn't mind being seen with her on his arm.

So why not? He wasn't proposing marriage or anything. A date would be a casual way to get to know her better. If it didn't work out, he knew it wouldn't faze her efficient work ethic.

She didn't bother to look up at him. She frowned at her calendar. "Spenser, do you think we'll see any alkaline phosphatase on day three? Should we collect samples on day five instead?" Her head tilted, as if she still thought about her question even as she waited for him to answer.

Spenser heard a voice that sounded like his own. "Are you doing anything tonight? Let's go out to dinner."

SEVEN

N*o. Way.*

Did six-feet-of-gorgeous just ask her out? She must be hearing things. Was he asking out someone else?

No, he was looking right at her. Aside from the fact there were only the two of them in the room, guys generally didn't make direct eye contact with one girl while asking out another.

When the shock wave receded, her heart started to pound. Six-feet-of-gorgeous had asked her out! He hadn't even asked that Hong Kong intern to go out to dinner! (She knew because she'd rather slyly asked.)

Wait a minute, why had he asked her out? Miss Hong Kong was at least thirty pounds lighter and five years younger. Plus, Spenser was always talking with women in the hallways.

"Uh ... you mean on a date?"

Spenser's smile grew a little strained. "Sure. Why not?"

Oh no, had Trish been flirting with him? She'd been trying so hard the past few days to *not look*. It had taken a while for her to get used to the new Trish — the non-animated, proper, and rather boring good girl version. Maybe she'd unconsciously been spewing phero-mones, hence this surreal moment.

Rats! Six-feet-of-gorgeous had asked her out! She had been work-ing so hard to keep rule number one, but then he had to go ahead and drop this bomb in her lap. This was too much temptation for a girl to bear.

Because she had to say no.

"You're serious?" She chewed her inner lip. Was she crazy? What was she doing? She couldn't refuse the very man she'd been ga-ga over for the past two weeks!

"Yeah, I'm serious." His brow wrinkled and his tone buzzed with annoyance. "Why? What's wrong?"

"I'm flattered, but ..."

"But ...?" Spenser's mouth tightened.

Trish stood. She hated needing to look up at him so far. "Well, no offense but ... you're not Christian."

Okay, that hadn't come out sounding very good. Had she really said that?

He grew very still. Very, very still. He didn't even blink. Trish couldn't quite decipher his expression, and that scared her a bit.

"I, uh ... I want to date only Christian guys. You see, God is my top priority, and I want to date someone with the same priority." Trish gnawed the inside of her cheek, her eyes darting everywhere but at him, while she reached up to fiddle with all three of the earrings on her right side. "It's like a San Francisco 49ers fan dating an Oakland Raiders fan. Or a Giants fan dating an A's fan. Well actually, God's more of a priority for me than a football or baseball team, but you get the picture, right?" She lifted pleading eyes to him.

Was she crazy? The past two weeks had been horrible. A zillion times a day, she had to drag her eyes away from his dimpled smile and the adorable way his hair waved down over his forehead. It was soooo hard to ignore his muscular grace when he sat on the edge of her desk to discuss something.

"Ahem. Yeah, sure." His face seemed rather neutral. Was that good or bad? "So if a Christian guy asks you out?"

"Well, um ... I'm trying to commit myself whole-heartedly to God."

"And that means?"

"I want to become a better person and leave it to God to give me the right man, because on my own, boys make me do all kinds of crazy thi—Um, anyway, I came up with three rules."

"Three rules?" His eyebrows hit his waving hair.

"If I can follow them, eventually God can change my heart so I'll have undivided devotion to Him."

"So what are your three rules?" His mouth worked in and out. Almost as if he were trying not to laugh.

Trish crossed her arms and glared at him. "You're making fun of me."

He opened his eyes wide and held up his hands. "No, I promise I'm not."

She didn't trust that glint in his eye. "Okay, rule number one — no looking at guys or encouraging them. No drooling, no roving eye, no scoping them out as boyfriend material."

"Hmm." He looked like a clinical psychologist. Or rather, what she imagined a clinical psychologist would look like when confronted with, say, a patient who claimed that aliens had taken over her brain.

"What do you mean, 'Hmm'?"

He shrugged. "Nothing. What's rule number two?"

"Tell others about Christ. Be bold and on fire to spread the Word." Oops, maybe she shouldn't have said that with such relish in front of a non-believer, to whom she was supposed to be witnessing at some point.

"Ah." More head nodding. "Number three?"

"Persevere and rely on God in hardship. God will give me strength through trials, and I need to persist and trust Him no matter what happens."

"Oh."

Was she being a good witness for Christ in telling him her three rules, or did it make her seem like an idiot? "You think I'm just spouting off. I'm serious."

"I believe you."

She shot him a look that should have squished him like a grape under a car tire. "No, you don't. You're making fun of me."

"I wasn't making fun."

"You were trying to swallow your chortles of laughter."

"Chortles of laughter?" He waggled his eyebrows as he said it. "You're reading too many romance novels."

"Oh yeah? How would you know unless you read them too?"

"I read serious stuff. Like *Star* magazine." He gave his little-boy grin.

That stopped her mid-breath. She coughed. "You read *Star*?"

"I got a subscription free."

"Oooh, can I borrow it when you're done?" Goodie. She couldn't get herself to actually pay money for it, but she couldn't help reading it. It was more entertaining than reality TV.

"Is it in your rules?"

She wanted to smack that sarcastic smirk off his face. "My rules will work."

Spenser snorted. "You won't last a week."

"What are you talking about? They're good, biblical rules."

"They're legalistic. Rules don't change people."

"I told you, God will change my heart."

"You're being optimistic and idealistic. Think about it. No looking? Resisting basic animal attraction? Everybody's programmed with it."

Her words sliced out clear and slow. "Maybe *some people* think with their lower regions, but not everyone acts on their lust." *Like you did, chickie-babe?* She tried to slam a lid on the insidious voice, but it echoed through her empty places inside.

He snorted. "Not looking is like trying not to read. And the telling everyone about Christ? Most people are plain scared to even talk about God."

"I'm not." She really wasn't.

He loosed a superior smile. "Sure."

"I'm not—"

"And then, *persevere*? Everyone's inherently lazy."

"I told you, God will help me—"

"If rules could have made the Israelites faithful, they wouldn't have had to wander in the desert for forty years instead of entering the Promised Land."

"But my rules are good." She needed those rules to remind her, because otherwise she wouldn't think about God at all in the course of a day. "Wait a minute. How do you know about the Israelites?"

For a second he froze, as if thinking about his answer. "You assumed a lot, considering you don't know me very well."

"Assumed what?"

"That I'm not Christian."

"What do you—" It dawned on her like the undead-destroying morning sun in a vampire movie. "You're Christian?"

His face was neutral again, as it had been when she first turned him down. Now she knew why. She had totally blown it. "How can you be Christian?" It flew out of her mouth before her brain had a chance to censor it.

He looked like he'd swallowed a frog. "What do you mean?"

Was he trying to deny it? "You're always flirting with girls. Everywhere. In the hallway, in the parking lot, on the phone. Even on email, I'll bet."

A glowing red the same shade as New Year's firecrackers started sparking upward from his neck. "I do not flirt."

"Oh, sorry. You don't flirt—you smile excessively when you talk."

"How is my *friendliness* so bad?"

"Who are you trying to kid? You love women." Just like her father, who always got along with everyone—especially the women who came into Grandma's bank. She'd always thought he just liked working with new people, but look how faithful he was. "You're either dating *all* of them or you're leading them on."

Okay, that sounded completely irrational even to her heated brain, but she didn't care anymore. She was tired of men like her dad, like Spenser, who *got along* with lots of women. She wanted to date some socially inept geek who'd be too shy to even finish a sentence in another woman's presence. She didn't want to deal with someone she couldn't trust completely.

Spenser's face turned pinker than her aunty's neon-red *char siu* pork. "I am *not* leading them on."

"Faithful men don't flit from woman to woman. They stay with one wife their entire lives and don't have affairs with their wife's old college roommate and then pretend nothing happened and cause stress and headache for their children!" Oops, that sounded distinctly screech-like.

Spenser looked at her like she was certifiable. "What?"

"I would never trust a boy like you. I'd be the flavor of the week."

He froze except for a faint tremor that somehow seemed of earthquake magnitude. His color paled, and his jaw muscles started ticking.

Okay, that might not have been the smartest thing for Trish to say.

Spenser turned away from her slowly, as if every inch of movement took extreme effort. Uh, oh. Trish watched him, frozen to the floor, gnawing on the inside of her lip and tasting blood. She had to say something. But not just anything or he'd go nuclear. What could she say? There had to be something.

She didn't have the right to accuse him, considering her own male-laden past (although hers was *past*, while his was *present*, or at least as present as last week). She ought to say something, or she'd be just hypocritical and wrong. But what? Her brain wasn't working.

Halfway to the door, he threw back over his shoulder, "Well, let's hope you learn to trust me. We have to work together for the next several months."

As he opened the office door, she thought she heard him mutter, "Can't end soon enough for me." He exited with a firm tug on the door.

Her knees gave way, but she was too far from her chair and ended up bouncing off the edge of her desk. She dropped to the thinly carpeted floor with a sharp *whomp* on her behind.

What had happened? Had she really refused him? She couldn't even remember what she'd babbled about. Something stupid about sports teams. She whimpered and banged her head backward against her desk drawers.

Why did he ask her out? She'd been throwing herself into her work so she'd stop daydreaming about him. Of course, she hadn't really needed to daydream with him right next to her desk.

She banged her head again. Couldn't she have put it a little better? "No offense, but you're not Christian." Then, after all that, he had been Christian. But he flirted with anything in a skirt—she'd never be able to trust him, no matter what he said to her. She wouldn't have wanted to date him anyway. She wouldn't. She knocked her head against the desk drawers some more.

Still, good thing it was late Friday afternoon. She sighed, breathing in a rather nasty moldy odor from the ancient carpet.

Well, maybe it was for the best that they'd gotten the bad business out of the way. It would be infinitely more uncomfortable if they'd dated and it didn't work and then they had to continue working together, right?

She hadn't handled that well. Then again, she had done what she was supposed to do. When she'd thought he wasn't Christian, she'd held to the conviction that she wasn't supposed to date non-Christian guys. Plus, "Bad company corrupts good character." She had withstood temptation—and hoo-boy, what a temptation he was. He even made her forget about Kazuo.

Six-feet-of-gorgeous had asked her out. She sniffed, then moaned low in the throat.

She hadn't been doing so hot with rule number one in the past few weeks—she hadn't exactly been keeping her eyes to herself—but it would get easier, right? She was proud of herself for passing her first real test.

Wasn't she?

Trish was running late—so what else was new?—but since Lex was picking her up, she knew she had at least ten extra minutes.

The voice in her head screamed for her not to run with the toothbrush in her mouth as she dove under the bed for some sandals that weren't three-inches or higher. She had a more conservative pair somewhere, didn't she? Yeah, she wore them the last time she went to church — three weeks ago? Three months ago?

Yet a couple days ago, she'd dissed Spenser for not being Christian. The fact that he *was* Christian didn't really count because she hadn't known it at the time — anyway, she didn't miss the hypocrisy of her own actions and her lack of attendance the past few Sundays. She couldn't believe the horrid, judgmental things she'd said to him. Life ought to be like TiVo so she could rewind.

Well, she was going to church today, that's what mattered. If she could find a pair of shoes that didn't sparkle, stab, or glitter.

There, way under the bed. At least three years old, black and clunky. She swatted at the layer of dust and sneezed painfully through her nose because she didn't want to spew toothpaste all over the place.

She finished up in the bathroom, then slung open the accordion doors to her closet. Oops, that was a bit loud. Marnie hadn't come in until late last night and was probably still sleeping.

Rifling through her clothes, she looked for a Good Girl outfit. Not that any of her clothes were *indecent* — well, she had a few dresses that bordered on it — but her conservative church members would look askance at attire in the sanctuary that would be perfectly normal at Valley Fair Mall. She didn't really understand it, but there it was.

Too short. Too low. Too *pink*. Too clingy. Exposed too much back. Exposed too much leg. Exposed too much shoulder.

Didn't she have anything to wear to church?

Maybe something near the back of the closet. She hunkered down into a crouch. She picked up a fistful of dirty laundry from behind her hamper. How long had that been —

A piercing scream from Marnie's bedroom ripped through the air.

EIGHT

Trish started, then whipped her head around. She smacked her temple into the closet doors with a hollow-sounding *thud*. Stars exploded in front of her eyes.

Owowowow! She scrubbed at her throbbing temple as she tried to rise to her feet. "Marnie! Are you okay?" Her bedroom dipped and swayed, but she managed to stumble out to the living room and pounded on Marnie's bedroom door. "Marnie!"

The door didn't open, but Marnie started to howl and moan.

Trish hesitated a fraction of a second before trying the doorknob. She'd never walked into her room before, but Marnie's crying shot bullets of alarm through her. Bloodcurdling cries warranted invasion of privacy, right? The knob turned in her hand and she plunged inside.

Marnie sat on her bed, a small dark bump in the midst of her violent pink-blue-green-red-purple woven bedspread. She gripped her open cell phone with shaking hands. Even as Trish stood there, the phone broke with a plastic *snap!*

"Marnie ..."

A shallow cut on her roommate's hand shone red, and the sight of blood seemed to break her out of her anguished trance. She dropped the two pieces of her phone. Her wailing had softened to hyperventilating. "He ... broke up with me."

"Your boyfriend?"

"With a *text message*."

Ooooh. Trish's gut clenched as if she'd been punched. She couldn't imagine what Marnie felt. But here was her chance to win Marnie for God, right? "Um ... do you want to talk about it?"

"*No.*"

O-kay. Guess not.

Marnie leaped from the bed and started cramming clothes into a duffle bag.

"What are you doing?"

"I need someplace to think."

"Are you moving out?" Just like that? Trish still had several months left on the lease.

"No."

"Oh." Whew. "Do you need help?"

"No."

Well, no one could say she didn't try.

Marnie packed in less than four minutes. Trish knew because she stood helplessly in the doorway watching her and eyeing the wall clock at the same time.

As Marnie flung herself out the door, Trish hollered "Bye!" The only answer she got was a resounding slam.

She stood in the middle of the living room. Somehow the apartment seemed emptier than it had ever been before, even when she was here alone and Marnie was out. The walls started closing in — this wasn't some kind of creepy premonition, was it? She rubbed the goose egg on her temple. No, she must have knocked loose some brain cells.

Ding-dong.

Aack! That was Lex! She was late for church!

Even though Lex and Trish snuck into the sanctuary late, several heads turned to peer at them. Trish tugged on the hem of her shirt. It was one of her only ones that didn't expose her belly button.

They sank into chairs near the back as the worship leaders ended a song. Actually, it was the last song.

"You made us hecka late." Lex's huffy complaint tickled Trish's ear.

"You were already late."

"You made us even later."

An old lady in the row in front of them whirled to glare at them. "Can we discuss this later?"

Lex shifted her attention toward the front, the argument already forgotten. Lex might not care what people thought of them, but Trish didn't like the colony of earthworms niggling in her stomach when people gave them dirty looks.

At least Lex wasn't avoiding her anymore. She'd been lonely without Lex to confide in, laugh with, hang out and eat Ben and Jerry's with. Lex understood her like no one else, knew when to encourage and when to tell the stark truth. Trish vowed she'd never hurt her ever again. Never.

Trish slouched back in her pew. It was too warm in here ...

She awoke with a start. The pastor's gaze stopped on Trish. He lifted an eyebrow at her, then continued. "Let's pray."

She kept her eyes open, deathly afraid she'd fall asleep again if she closed them. Lex gave a soft chortle of laughter before she closed her eyes in prayer.

"Amen."

The worship leader smiled and pointed toward the back of the sanctuary. "Thank you for joining us at worship today. Please stay for refreshments in our fellowship hall upstairs. The stairway is across from the sanctuary."

"Who's the evangelism deacon?" She scanned her program. Pastor's info, worship leader's name, pianist, worship team, ushers, church administrative assistant ...

No deacons. She could ask the admin, Eleanor Falk, for the name of the deacon and to point him out if Trish didn't know him.

Her bladder made itself known. Again? She'd gone before they entered the sanctuary.

She had to hold it. For some reason, most people congregated in the hallway behind the sanctuary and not upstairs, so the hallway quickly became a sea of bodies. If Trish wanted to find the evangelism deacon, she had to do it pronto before the hallway filled up.

"Come on." Lex tugged at her arm. "I want to get upstairs for the food before the high schoolers eat everything."

The band of her slacks had cut into her stomach while she sat (and slept). "Uh—you go ahead."

Lex darted away.

Trish followed close behind and managed to shoot out into the hallway while it was still relatively empty. Then Monica Cathcart appeared from the kitchen and crossed toward the stairwell with a tray of *musubi* riceballs.

"Monica!" Mrs. Cathcart knew everybody. Good thing Trish had seen her.

Monica smiled. "Trish! Haven't seen you in a while. Good to see you today. Want a *musubi*?"

"Thanks." Ha! Lex should have stuck with Trish. She snagged a fresh rice ball. "Who's evangelism deacon?"

"Oh, Mrs. Oh."

"Huh?"

"Mrs. Oh. Short, Chinese, gray hair."

That only left a quarter of the congregation. "Can you point her out?"

Monica peered around the rapidly filling hallway. "I don't see her. Let me put this tray in the fellowship hall, and I'll come back and find her." She zipped away.

Oh, there was the administrative assistant, Eleanor. Trish pinballed around standing groups of chatting people, dodged the children's Sunday schools, which had let out, and accosted Eleanor as she finished talking with someone. "Hi, Eleanor."

"Welcome to our church." She beamed, deepening the wrinkles in her face, and grabbed Trish's hand in a loose clasp. "Is this your first time?"

Her smile froze. Had her attendance really been that bad lately? "I'm Trish Sakai."

"Oh, I didn't know Lex had a sister." Eleanor patted her hand, still holding on to it.

"I'm her cousin. I've been going to this church for ... a little while now." Years, in fact. Although considering Eleanor didn't even remember Trish's face from her 50th birthday party last year, or from her granddaughter's baptism the year before that, it probably wasn't worth mentioning.

"Well, I'm so glad you came up and introduced yourself. How friendly."

"Can you tell me who the evangelism deacon is?"

"Oh, would you like to volunteer?"

"Yes, it's rule number two — I mean, I'm feeling ... uh ... *convicted*, yeah, convicted to put more effort into telling others about Christ."

"Oh, well, that's wonderful. Our evangelism deacon is Mrs. Oh. Now where is she ..." Eleanor scanned the crowd around her, but considering her lack of inches, it wasn't much help.

"Trish, there you are." Monica appeared at her elbow. "I found Mrs. Oh."

"There she is." Eleanor pointed toward the left side of the hallway.

"She's the one in the blue dress." Monica also pointed in that direction.

The sea of bodies parted slightly and there stood a tiny old Chinese lady. She looked like she'd barely reach Trish's shoulder, and Trish certainly wasn't considered tall.

"Do you see her?" Monica stabbed her finger harder in Mrs. Oh's direction.

"Yes. Thanks." Trish shimmied between groups of chattering people before she lost sight of her quarry.

Mrs. Oh chatted amiably with the young woman next to her, then bent to pick up the woman's small daughter.

"Hi, Mrs. Oh."

At the sight of Trish, the woman's gentle and kind face lit up with a smile. "Hello."

"We haven't met before. I'm Trish Sakai."

"Oh, how *nice* to meet you!" Her welcome was rather enthusiastic, but it seemed she wasn't faking—that's how she really was.

"I'm interested in helping with evangelism—"

"You *are*!" Mrs. Oh's eyes opened wide enough to make the black mascara gooked on her short eyelashes unclump.

The young mother she'd been talking to eased backward in a subtle movement, but somehow it caught Trish's eye. A niggling started in Trish's stomach, but she firmly stood her ground. How silly to be uneasy. Mrs. Oh seemed perfectly nice.

"Mrs. Oh, I'm going to take Kaylie and go home." The young mother disentangled her daughter from the old woman, not a difficult feat since Mrs. Oh was so tiny. "I'll talk to you later. Bye!" Trish blinked and the woman was gone. Like Superman. Or Supermom. Trish tried not to feel worried at her speedy exit.

Mrs. Oh grasped Trish's hands in hers. "How *wonderful* that you want to serve on the evangelism committee!"

What? Committee? "Actually, I was hoping—"

"We could use *so* much help in organizing the Easter festival this year. It's our biggest outreach to the community—last year, over five hundred people attended!"

"Easter festival?"

"We need someone to be in charge. To get people to volunteer, to organize the schedule, to take care of publicity—not that much work."

"Five hundred people?"

Mrs. Oh clapped her hands and widened her pearl-pink smile, revealing pearl-pink smudged teeth. She had an awful lot of teeth, too. "And we could use someone to organize the Go-Go Group. We may be older but we're certainly energetic!" Mrs. Oh punctuated her proclamation with an excited fist in the air. *Rah, rah.* "We have wonderful outreach events like Craft Day and Japanese Luncheon. We really need someone to set up the kitchen schedule and make up fliers and get the seniors involved."

"Japanese Luncheon?"

Mrs. Oh's eyes started to blaze. "Oh, and the children's Sunday school needs someone to take charge. They don't have enough teachers and they always need someone to fill in each week. Why, last week the kindergarten class had almost fifty children and only one teacher!"

"Fifty children?"

"I've been trying to get someone to help, but now I have you!"

"To get people to help?"

"To do all these things!" Mrs. Oh's face had turned into a maniacal demon *noh* mask. "The first thing you need to do is set up the Easter Festival. Make a big sign-up sheet and put it up in the foyer. Then make an announcement at service. And you have to order the cotton candy machine and the popcorn machine and all the supplies for it, and you should ask around for the games they used last year, except I don't remember who owned which game. You'll also have to order that big inflatable jumping thing they used last year for the children, and then order all the prizes. Oh, but first see if people will donate prizes—you'll have to ask around ..."

The woman was completely *loco*.

Trish wanted to help, not run the committee for this insane old lady. If Trish accepted this, she'd walk straight into an organizational nightmare and black-hole-sized time suck. Besides which, people barely knew she even went to church, much less who she was. Why would they ever volunteer to help?

Back away from the crazy person ...

But Mrs. Oh grabbed Trish's hand again, probably sensing the quarry was about to flee. "We so need young people like yourself to take up leadership roles in the church. Do you have any friends who might want to volunteer, too?"

"Mrs. Oh, I don't think—"

"Hey, babe."

"Oh, hi Kazuo. Mrs. Oh, my friends are—Kazuo!" Trish did a double-take at his tall, dark presence right next to her. "What are you doing here?"

"I came to take you to lunch." He leaned closer to Trish and touched her back with his hand.

"Trish!" Lex stood frozen a few feet away, both hands full of paper plates loaded with rice balls, donuts, *inarizushi* cone sushi, and egg salad sandwich triangles. She rounded on Kazuo. "What are you doing here?"

"I came to help Trish."

Lex didn't have time to do more than widen her eyes a fraction before Trish jumped in. "I didn't invite him, honest! He showed up."

"Why, here are a few friends who might help!" Mrs. Oh tried to grab Kazuo's arm while keeping a firm grip on Trish.

Lex looked like she was going to lose her food as she moved to put her hands on her hips, but she remembered in time that she had those plates, so she tucked her elbows close to her ribcage instead. "Why are you here?" She glared pointedly at Kazuo.

"I'm taking Trish to lunch." Kazuo turned an impassive gaze on Lex.

Trish would have preferred he kept his big mouth shut, sexy accent notwithstanding. "He's not. I didn't ask him to."

"How wonderful that he did!" Mrs. Oh gave Kazuo a wide smile, which unfortunately looked a bit evil rather than encouraging. Kazuo leaped back a step.

Mrs. Oh advanced on Lex. "You've been coming to this church for a while now, haven't you? You really should think about volunteering—"

Lex's eyes became as big as the rice balls on her plate. "Uh . . ." Her gaze darted around before landing on Mrs. Cathcart in the far corner. "Mrs. Oh, Monica needs you." She whipped her arm in the direction of the other side of the hallway, dropping a chicken wing from the plate. "Right now."

Mrs. Oh's pencil-thin brows wrinkled. "She does?"

"Something about ..." Lex floundered.

"The Go-Go Group?" Trish supplied.

"Yes! The Go-Go Group." Lex gave a weak smile. "Something about ... uh ..."

"Cooking?" Monica could whip up a meal for an army—or at least her four teenagers—in thirty seconds flat. Trish tugged at her hand, trying to wrestle it from Mrs. Oh's grasp.

"Yes! Cooking."

"Oh!" Mrs. Oh released Trish and clapped her tiny hands together. "How wonderful! The Japanese Luncheon is next week!" She darted off.

Trish heaved a sigh even as she rubbed the raw marks on her wrist. That little Chinese woman had hard, sharp bones in her hands.

Lex turned to Kazuo. "This is considered stalking."

"Your grandmother told me to come," he said.

"What?" Trish and Lex snapped at him.

"You don't want to be around these strange people." He motioned his head toward Mrs. Oh's departed direction. "I treat you like the goddess you are." He reached out and ran a soft, comforting hand down her arm.

A delicious shiver followed his caressing fingers. Trish breathed deep and filled her senses with sandalwood and the musky smell of Japanese soap. He *had* treated her like the center of his universe ...

"Trish!"

Lex's screech sent a jolt through her floating body. Oh, right. Not hurting Lex anymore. Devoted to God. New person. No Kazuo.

She sighed.

"And your grandmother approves." Kazuo's eyes seemed so reasonable, so logical. Of course Trish wouldn't want to upset Grandma, right?

Lex snorted. "You're Japanese, and Trish is the next oldest single female cousin in our family. Of course she approves."

"We make a good couple." He smiled that secret smile, the one that always made him seem even more mysterious and otherworldly. The one he often smiled when he painted her.

Instead of taking her back to romantic memories, it unearthed the more unpleasant ones. "You didn't want me to be around anybody else. I'm only the model for your painting, just a possession." She'd felt like a caged bird, or a tethered cat.

"You are precious to me." His hand followed the curve of her face without touching her.

Precious? That made her feel kind of tingly inside . . .

Lex's mouth was doing the pinchy thing as she glared at Kazuo. "Oh, give me a break."

Trish dampened the tinglies. Where was her head? All her good intentions flying out the window as soon as he came within a few feet of her. "We don't belong together anymore. I'm becoming a different person. I'm following my three rules." Sort of. "I'm getting my MDiv. I'm devoting myself wholeheartedly to God."

Kazuo shrugged. "I can do that, too."

"What?" In unison again, Trish and Lex shared a bewildered glance this time, as well.

"I can learn more about God." He looked deep into her eyes. "For you, I will do it. I will come to church."

NINE

"D id you have to yank me away so hard?" Trish rubbed her bruised arm as she got into Lex's car.

Lex jammed her key into the ignition. "You are going to fall for him again."

"What do you mean?"

"I could totally tell he was being condescending."

"I could tell that too." Sort of. It was hard to think straight with him nearby. "I would never have believed him."

Lex snorted.

"I wouldn't. He's tried that before."

"He has?" Lex threw a curious glance at her before swinging the car out of the parking lot.

"When we first started dating, he'd go with me to church. At first he acted all interested, but then he would make us late. And he never wanted to meet anyone. Eventually we both stopped going."

Lex gave her a sidelong glance.

"I know, I know. I shouldn't have been so easily swayed. But now I'm free of him—"

"Not when he follows you to church." Lex signaled and switched lanes. "You know, you weren't exactly giving him the cold shoulder."

Well, that was true. "But I wasn't falling in his arms, either."

Lex rolled her eyes. "I guess that's an improvement."

"Of course that's an improvement. I told you this on the phone. I am the new, improved Trish!" She tried to fling her arms out but only smacked her hand against the closed window and narrowly missed poking out Lex's eye.

"Hey, watch it." Lex's expression, while kind, had that twist of disbelief. "Trish, I know you pretty well. You love people, you love meeting new people, especially guys. I've hardly ever seen you *not* flirt. No offense, but I have a hard time believing you this time."

Lex's blunt honesty annoyed her sometimes. She supposed it was a good thing that at least one of her cousins had the courage to tell her the bare truth about how she felt, but sometimes she wished Lex would just pretend to believe Trish and be all sweet and compassionate like Jenn. "I'm really serious. I'm going to wipe the slate clean." Too bad she didn't have one of those memory wipers she read about in that action romance novel she read recently . . .

Wipe the slate clean. That was it. "I'll go to a new church."

Lex paused to digest her words, then sighed. "There you go again."

Trish wanted to strangle her. "What? Why is that so bad?"

"You always go on to something new."

"That's not always a bad thing. In this case, it's a necessity. I can't work with Mrs. Oh. You heard her. I'd be doing everything except cleaning the church toilets. It'll be like selling myself into slavery."

Lex raised her eyebrows. "Good point. So which church?"

"How about Aiden's? He's still going to Valley Bible Church in Sunnyvale — by the way, when are you guys going to start going to the same church?"

Lex's mouth tightened. "We will eventually. Stop nagging me."

Oops, must be a sore spot. "Anyway, Aiden would introduce me around at his church, wouldn't he?"

Lex stiffened, but she made a visible effort to relax her ramrod straight shoulders. She still had that weird reaction, even after six months of dating him. Trish sighed. She should never have made a move on Aiden — never mind that Lex hadn't even known him then. Hopefully with rule number one, no looking, she'd keep herself from doing seemingly innocent things that would get her in trouble later. Like that whole deal with Aiden.

"He's okay with me, right?" Trish monitored Lex's face closely. "He seemed okay with me the last time I talked to him. Water under the bridge, and all that."

"Yeah, yeah. Sure." Lex blinked and kept her eyes forward.

Trish spun one of the earrings on her left side. "I'm sincerely glad you guys are dating now. I don't ... like him anymore, you know."

Lex's face relaxed completely. "I know." She turned a genuine smile at Trish. "I'm sure he'd be happy to introduce you around."

"Great."

A new church, a new adventure. Things were looking up.

She'd taken emergency precautions and gone to the bathroom before heading to her office. Was Spenser going to yell at her? Give her the cold shoulder? Pretend nothing happened?

"Um ... hi." Trish walked into their office on Monday morning.

"Hi." He didn't turn around from his computer.

She dropped her bag near her desk. "Had a good weekend?"

"Yeah."

She started up her computer. Sat and stared at the screen while it booted up and did all kinds of time-consuming things. Her chair was already pushed back from her desk, so she peered around the cubicle partition at Spenser, who sat engrossed in some spreadsheet on his monitor.

She jiggled her leg. Sighed. "Spenser, I'm sorry—"

"Look, can we—"

She swiveled her chair and held his gaze. His face wasn't mad or grumpy or disdainful, but he wasn't happy with her, either. Well, not that she expected him to be actually happy, but she had been hoping for—what? A little warmer neutrality? More willingness to meet her halfway?

This was weird. She felt like she was trying to make up with a boyfriend after a fight, not reconcile after dissing her coworker.

Well, she wasn't a coward. She straightened her shoulders and took a deep breath. "I'm sorry, Spenser, for assuming you weren't Christian and yelling at you and everything. And for any ugliness between us, because we have to work together, and I think we do that well, and I want this project to succeed."

He looked a little annoyed. Like she'd beaten him to the punch. She pushed down a quick blossoming of satisfaction in her heart — she was supposed to be nice.

"I'm sorry too. I should have told you instead of stringing you along."

Aw, that was a sweet apology, although she couldn't exactly tell him he was sweet — she'd had enough boyfriends to finally get that guys didn't like being described with the same term as a chocolate croissant. She gave a wide smile. "Thanks. That's nice of you to say that."

How weird. Spenser looked a little dazed. Almost dazzled. No, that couldn't be. Maybe he was confused. She didn't think she'd used any weird words from her British historical romance novels.

She kept smiling, trying to ignore the silence stretching tighter and tighter. Before the rubber band snapped, she tilted her head and blinked rapidly. "Spenser?"

He started slightly. Funny, she didn't think he was the type of guy to zone out. Of course, she zoned out a lot but she'd never met a guy who did that.

Her cell phone ring blasted through the small office. Saved by the bell. "Hello?"

"Hello, Trish."

"Oh, hi Grandma." She got that rolling-boil feeling in her stomach, the kind that usually came before a scolding. Why would she be calling?

"How are you doing?"

"Uh ... fine." Was there a polite way to ask Grandma to get to the point?

"How's your mother?"

"She sounded better the last time I talked to her on the phone." At least Trish hadn't had to talk to her father. She didn't think she could say anything civil to him just yet.

"I heard you needed an apartment."

At last, that's why Grandma had called. "No, my roommate's just been ... weird lately. What did you hear?"

"I was at Jennifer's house when you called her."

"My roommate is being really strange. I was just complaining to Jenn."

"That's why I'm calling. One of the apartments I'm renting vacated, and I had it completely remodeled. It's in Mountain View, although not as near Castro Street as you are now."

"I can't afford to rent an apartment by myself, Grandma."

She chuckled, which set off Twilight Zone music in Trish's head. Grandma rarely laughed, and not often with that condescending tone to it. "I'll give it to you rent free if you'd like."

"Oh ... That's really nice of you, Grandma. But don't you need the rent?"

"I'd do anything for one of my granddaughters."

This was way too creepy. Grandma was rarely stern or demanding of Trish — at least, not like she was with Lex and Venus, but then again, they'd walk off a bridge if Grandma commanded them *not* to. Grandma was a savvy businesswoman — look how she'd taken over Grandpa's bank after he passed away — and she never did something that would lose her money. Not without some kind of return.

How to phrase it so Grandma won't be offended? "That's so generous of you. But, uh ... I can't take it without doing something for you."

"Oh, no, dear. You don't need to do anything." Grandma was so good at the not-sincere-but-obligatory-first-refusal, she made it sound as if she really didn't want anything.

"No, I insist." She pressed her hand to her stomach. The rolling boil had started erupting and overflowing.

"You don't need to repay me, but there is something that would make me very happy."

"I always want to please you, Grandma." At least, that was true most of the time.

"You're not dating anyone right now, are you?"

"No."

"It would make me so happy to see you together again with Kazuo."

"What?!"

"He's such a nice boy. He told me he's so sorry for the argument that made you break up with him."

"I broke up with Kazuo because he wanted to imprison me in his art studio."

Spenser suddenly fumbled and dropped his calculator with a clatter. She turned to peer at him. "Is it okay? Do you need to use mine?"

"No, I'm good." He didn't look up at her.

Her cell phone crackled. "What? Trish, who are you talking to?"

"My coworker. Grandma, I don't want to get back together with him."

"You're so melodramatic. No one actually imprisons people. You've been reading too many of those scary books."

"No, that's Jenn. I read romances."

"Oh, the ones with all the sex in them."

"No! Grandmaaaaa—"

"Kazuo says he can't live without you. Isn't that romantic?"

It was. But without his powerful presence to cloud her brain, she could remember his impassioned rages, the way he wanted to control her, possess her. She couldn't put all the blame on him for wanting to sleep with her, because she'd gone more or less willingly into that, but his moodiness, the pagan way he worshipped his art, and his tendency to force her free spirit to adopt his loner qualities had made him seem like a stranger in her bed. "Grandma, he and I don't really suit each other." *Now that's an understatement.* But she wasn't about to admit the truth to Grandma because she wouldn't understand.

"I think you suit each other very well." Grandma's tone had hardened. "You know I only want what's best for you."

Why couldn't things go back to the way they were before? Grandma had always been pleased with Trish, primarily because of all Trish's boyfriends—well, except for the one with the belly button ring. Trish had never said no to Grandma for anything. Why was Grandma wanting something from her that she couldn't give? Why was she demanding this when Trish was earnestly trying to do the right thing for once?

"Grandma, you know I'd do anything for you—"

"Then why not this one thing for your Grandma?" The chiding voice made Trish seem like such an unreasonable child for refusing. "Do you know how much he loves you and wants you back?"

"Yes, I know he wants me back, but I can't."

"What do you mean, you can't?" There was a razor edge to her voice.

"I just can't." *I won't.* But she wasn't about to tell that to Grandma. Here was her chance for rule number three with Grandma. "I'm trying to be devoted to God—"

"God? What does God have to do with a boyfriend?"

"God will help me find a nice Christian boy." Even to her own ears, that sounded rather stupid. She thought she heard a snort from Spenser. He wasn't listening, was he?

"It always comes back to your religion. You put your God over your family. That's shameful." Her tone sliced into Trish with jagged edges. Grandma had never been so openly against Trish's beliefs before.

"I love my family. God is going to lead the right boy to me, and the whole family will like him." If all her crazy relatives didn't make him run away screaming.

"What if Kazuo is the right boy for you, and you're pushing him away?"

"Kazuo is not the right boy for me—"

"Are you sure you're listening to *your God* correctly?"

Trish had to unclench her jaw to answer her. "Yes, I'm listening to God—"

"You are disappointing your grandma."

Uh, oh. Grandma was talking about herself in the third person. Bad sign. "I don't want to disappoint you, but—"

"Grandma would be so much happier if you got back with Kazuo. Grandma will be terribly upset if you don't listen to her."

Trish's heartbeat did double-time with her breathing. She'd never had to defy Grandma. Never. But Grandma had also never asked her to do something so impossible.

"I can't." She barely heard her own voice. She wondered if Grandma heard her, if she'd have to repeat it. She tried to swallow but something big and sticky had lodged in her throat.

Grandma had good hearing. "Trish, Grandma is ... You've hurt Grandma a great deal." *Click.*

She actually hung up on her. Trish stared at the phone in her hand.

Her hands shook. She shoved them into her lap. Well, she'd done it. Defied her grandmother. Lightning didn't strike her dead, but then again, since she defied Grandma in order to please God, she didn't really think He'd do any more bad things to her. God was happy with her new determination, right? Even if she alienated the most powerful person in her large extended family.

"You okay?" Spenser's quiet voice soothed her raw emotions.

She glanced at him. His eyes were soft with concern.

"Yeah, I'm okay." She bit her lip and flickered her gaze to the phone. She attempted a smile. "Pushy grandmas."

He followed her lead. "Tell me about it. Chinese ones are just as bad."

"She's never attacked my faith before." It came out on a whispered breath. Why did she say that? Spenser wouldn't care. He wouldn't be mean, but she'd feel like a dork.

"Family's hardest."

"Huh?"

He turned to make eye contact with her. "Friends usually flow with it when you become Christian, but sometimes family members don't know how to handle it. Sometimes they feel betrayed."

"But I've been Christian a long time. Since college."

"Long enough for them to realize it's not just a phase. Could be they're afraid you're going to start preaching at them."

"Now? After almost ten years?"

Spenser shrugged and turned his attention back to his computer, but a bitterness had hardened his expression. "They're more afraid of what they'll feel if you do."

Why would Grandma feel afraid?

TEN

Introvert, she was not.

The thought of an entire new church was a little intimidating, but she may as well attack it with gusto, get the unpleasant part of being the new girl in the pew over with as soon as possible.

Aiden met her at the door to his church on Sunday. His half-smile wasn't cool—that was just Aiden. When he'd been her physical therapist, his expressionless face always drove her nuts and made her want to shake him up. She could admit now that pursuing him and asking him out—and getting soundly rejected—probably wasn't the smartest thing she could have done.

Things were okay now, though. She hoped. She hadn't actually spent any time with him since he'd started dating her cousin Lex.

"Hi." She gave him her brightest smile.

He remained unmoved. "Hi."

She bit the inside of her lip. "You're okay with this, right? Lex talked to you about my new devotion to God and all that?"

"Yeah. I'm happy for you, Trish." Still that neutral face. She wanted to grab his cheeks and rattle them back and forth.

"You don't look happy."

He raised an eyebrow at her.

"Okay, okay, never mind." Iceman.

"I really am glad for you."

His eyes were sincere, even if his face wasn't animated. Trish could live with that. "Thanks."

They sliced through the crowd of people chatting outside the doors — what was it with people always congregating to talk in the middle of major pedestrian thoroughfares? — and entered the massive foyer, dominated by a round table and a soaring flower arrangement. The heavy scent from the star asters made Trish sneeze.

"Let's get a seat before they're filled up. I'll introduce you to people later."

Trish smiled brightly at the scattered people they passed, but no one seemed to notice her. How big was this church anyw —

Oh my garlic, the sanctuary was as big as a concert hall. It was even set up like one, with a semi-circular stage and chairs fanning out in rows around it.

And lots and lots of people in those chairs. How strange to be practically anonymous in the middle of this huge crowd. She wasn't used to *not* being noticed.

They sat near the front with a good view of the stage. The worship team was in place, fine-tuning their instruments, doing last minute sound checks. The lead guitarist gave a thumbs-up to someone in the back of the sanctuary. Trish turned and saw an extensive sound system set up on a balcony. A long arm shot up from behind the equipment with a returning thumbs-up.

"Let's get seated, folks, and start our worship service this morning." The lead guitarist had a rather plain voice, but his twelve-string guitar rang like liquid music on her ears when he strummed a chord.

Worship music at her old church was fine. Simple, straight to the heart. But this worship resonated in her soul.

It wasn't the full band with acoustic and electric guitars, bass, keyboard, and drums. It wasn't the speakers, only a few feet from where they sat, blasting into her so that her bones vibrated with the music.

It was the songs, the atmosphere, the way the leader sang with so much transparency. No one stood to sing, but she felt the energy in her legs, the joy in her heart propelling her from her chair. She wouldn't block anyone's view since they were sitting near the edge. She shot up, raising her hands and worshipping with her entire body as well as her voice.

She felt like God had breathed into her.

She sat down after the music ended. The pastor was good. Down to earth. Told a few bad jokes. Used a lot of Bible verses and didn't raise his voice to get his points across like her other pastor did.

At the end of the service, she sighed deeply. "That was great."

"Glad you liked it." Aiden motioned toward the back of the church. "Want to meet the Singles Group?" They headed out the back of the sanctuary, through a door on the right side of the foyer and into a large social hall, with a smaller gathering of twenty- and thirty-somethings.

New friends. New guys. No, she needed to stop thinking like that. Rule number one. Rule number one.

"*Yowza.*" What a hunk! Tall and blonde, Matthew McConaughey in the flesh.

Aiden cleared his throat.

Oops. She winced. She wasn't doing a good job showing the new, utterly-devoted-to-God Trish. Aiden was going to think she hadn't changed at all from when she'd embarrassed herself over him.

"That's Ike."

Trish's appreciation factor plummeted. So that's the creep who came on to Lex — before she started going out with Aiden — and then two-timed her with some other girl. "Where's what's-her-name?" She couldn't quite keep the venom out of her tone.

"Lindsay?" Aiden's look was faintly amused. "Over there." He gestured.

Pretty, blonde, skinny. Way too many bangles on her wrists, didn't she realize she was a walking fashion faux pas? Hair horridly streaked by a very cheap salon. Trish could probably let her know of a better stylist ... but she wouldn't. Ha!

Okay, that wasn't the most Christian attitude, but she intended to stand up for her coz. Lex was worth a million Lindsays.

Lindsay glanced their way and caught sight of Trish. She abruptly left off chatting with her girlfriends and sashayed up to Ike, twining an arm through his as he stood with his hands in his jeans pockets. Gee, could ya be more possessive?

Trish nudged Aiden. "You don't have to introduce me to them, but I'd like to meet everybody else."

They approached a group of women—a spunky brunette, a cute redhead, a willowy blonde. "Hi, I'm Trish."

Their smiles didn't quite meet their eyes. Trish's smile faltered, but she reasserted it with determination. Most people were uncomfortable with strangers.

"Katy." "Kaitlyn." "Kassie."

"So, what—"

"Aiden." Ike came up. The three girls immediately perked up, but Ike focused on Aiden. "They need you up in the sound booth."

"Oh, okay." Aiden turned to Trish. "I'll be right back."

"Oh, sure. I'll introduce myself to people."

"I figured you would." His half-smile told her he didn't intend it in a mean way. She was glad he appreciated her ability to take care of herself in a crowd.

"So what do you guys do?" She glanced at the tricolored trio of friends and tried to look non-threatening but friendly.

Brunette flickered her gaze away, then back to Trish. "I'm an administrative assistant for a law firm in downtown San Jose."

"Oh, that's neat. My cousin Lex loves the admin at her company. She's a quarter Japanese and—"

"Oh, I'm sorry, I need to catch my friend before she goes. It was nice meeting you." Brunette nipped away.

"Nice meeting you," Trish told the empty space where she'd stood. She straightened her faltering smile and turned to Redhead and Blondie. "So what do you guys do?"

Redhead looked at Blondie before answering. "I'm an elementary school teacher."

"I'm a software engineer." Blondie inserted her answer as if she didn't want Trish to have to directly address her.

"That's neat." The uncomfortable silence grated on her like a rake down her back. "I have a cousin—"

"Do you always worship with so much ... uh ... energy?" Blondie's smile was friendly—marginally—but her cool gaze seemed faintly disapproving.

Trish's back slammed straight as a rod. She bared her teeth. "Oh, yes. It's very freeing." Music was the one part of her faith where she felt closest to God. Who was this chick to criticize how she worshipped?

"I'm sure." Blondie shared a secret, amused look with Redhead. "It's just very unusual."

"Well, I would never want to be a lemming." Trish blinked innocently at her.

Blondie's smile disappeared entirely. "It was nice meeting you. Come on, Kaitlyn." They disappeared faster than hot dog *musubi* at a church picnic.

Trish looked around. There was a group of guys nearby—one tall and skinny with a shock of red hair, one Stay Puft Marshmallow Man, and one small and dark like a mole. The latter two had glasses and pocket protectors, and the redhead kept his eyes glued to his feet.

Another group of guys nearby were at the very least weekend warriors—trim, carrying themselves well. Dressed in Dockers, Polo, Structure.

One of them—the one in a dark green Hilfiger shirt—happened to glance at her. He paused and made eye contact, then deliberately turned away.

The nerve! Was this entire Singles Group full of snobs? She marched over to the cluster of nerds. "Hi, I'm Trish."

"Jaspar." The redhead spoke to her Stuart Weitzman slides.

"Willie." Stay Puft had a wide, sweet smile like in *Ghostbusters*.

"Gerard." Mole Man peered at her through thick glasses.

Jaspar addressed her knees as he mumbled how he was a door-to-door salesman. Stay-Puft—oops, Willie was a manufacturing engineer, and Gerard was a programmer.

Their short answers didn't faze her. They'd loosen up if she gave them a little more time to get used to her. The shy ones usually did, anyway. "So what do you guys like to do?"

"Jaspar likes the movies." Willie motioned to his friend.

Jaspar's gaze suddenly popped up from her knees to her eyes. His vivid green gaze startled her more than the sudden action. "I love *Star Wars*. It changed my life. I liked the light sabers." He gyrated in a few wild moves. Trish leaned back to avoid getting brained by his fists, held together as if gripping a light saber. What a change from the shoe-talking guy from a minute ago. "I even had a Boba Fett costume, with replicas of all his weapons." Jaspar's eyes dropped and he seemed to deflate. "I used to be too into it, but I've been learning how to make Jesus my priority and still enjoy movies."

Trish blinked. Had he really said that? Sounded like something her third grade Sunday school teacher would have made her recite. Still, she wanted him to feel comfortable, not let on that she thought his choice of words was a little weird. "That sounds like me. I'm, uh . . . trying to make Jesus my priority, too." She loosed a wide smile.

How weird. The three of them had suddenly frozen when she smiled. Jaspar had been about to say something, but his mouth stuck open instead. Willie's smile was a little dazed. Gerard had erupted into a smile of his own which, although a little dreamy, made his entire face light up.

"Hey Trish." Aiden showed up. "Hi, guys."

The trio broke out of their reverie and greeted Aiden with comfortable familiarity. Gerard perked up. "Did you see *BattleBots: the Rematch* last night?"

While they chatted about some type of robot demolition show, Trish caught sight of Blondie as she strolled past with Green Hilfiger Shirt. Trish chewed her inner lip. She'd forgotten Aiden had been sitting next to her during worship.

After it seemed like they were done talking about the complete destruction of radio-controlled robot warriors, she leaned into Aiden. "You know, I'm sorry if I embarrassed you during singing. I always—"

"You didn't."

That was that. Aiden was so cut and dried, it always took her off guard, but the encouraging gleam in his eyes eased the tightness in her chest. He understood the unspoken question in her words.

Trish sighed. She wasn't attracted to Aiden anymore, but she envied Lex. Aiden was such a nice guy.

"Did you want to meet the worship team?" He motioned toward the open door of the social hall, where the worship team was strolling out with their instruments.

"I'd love to." She smiled at Jaspar, Willie, and Gerard. "Nice meeting you guys." She meant it — unlike the Tricolored Trio, they'd wanted to get to know her, and she'd felt free to be herself.

Aiden flagged down one of the guitarists, a dark-skinned woman. "Olivia, this is Trish. Today's her first time here."

Olivia's white teeth were like beacons in her oval face. "How great. Glad you could come today."

"Olivia's married to Ed, the worship leader."

"The guy with the twelve-string acoustic? It sounds so great."

"Thanks, honey. He loves that guitar." She adjusted her electric guitar bag on her shoulder, but didn't seem anxious to leave. "So what do you do?"

"I'm a biologist researcher."

"That's fascinating. Our sound guy is also a biologist. I'll introduce you later."

"I loved the worship." A glowy feeling radiated in her chest at the memory of the service. "It was so great."

"Now I remember you." Olivia's eyes crinkled at the edges. "You were the one standing near the front."

The glowy feeling dimmed a little and instead started squeezing her heart. "I hope I didn't disrupt — "

"Oh, no!" She reached out to touch Trish's arm. "It's always so encouraging to the team to see someone really getting into worship. I can't begin to tell you how much joy that gives me." She eyed Aiden with a mischievous glitter in her dark eyes. "Most people are a bit repressed."

Aiden gave a half-smile, but it lighted his eyes. "Everyone worships in their own way, Olivia."

She tapped him with a playful hand. "That may be so, but girls like Trish let me know without a shadow of a doubt that we're doing our job for God." She turned to her. "What made you visit our church today?" Friendly curiosity, not suspicion or gossip.

"I'm looking for a new church. I want to find somewhere I can serve." Suddenly Trish really wanted to serve here, with these people, despite the Tricolored Trio and the Weekend Warriors. Because of people like Olivia and Aiden, Jaspar and Willie and Gerard, who made her feel so comfortable being herself. Well, her new self. Not her old, flirty self.

"That's wonderful. What ministry have you done before?"

Trish opened her mouth, then had to shut it as the breath stuck in her throat. What had she done before? Helped occasionally to set up for coffee hour after service. Okay, like maybe twice. What else?

"That's okay." Olivia laughed. "You can ask our volunteer coordinator and he'll hook you up with something. Anything you want to do?"

"I'd like to do evangelism. I'm also going to get my MDiv." Wow, she was running off at the mouth. Olivia made her feel so welcomed, so comfortable—it seemed natural to overshare.

"That's great. Where are you going?"

"Actually, I'm looking for someplace. I searched on the Internet but I don't know which schools are good."

"I can recommend one—Western Seminary in Los Gatos. Several of my friends are in their program."

Trish felt like she received a free latte from Starbucks. She started rattling on as if she were on a caffeine high, too. "Thanks so much, that helps a lot. I'm really trying to turn my life around—well, Aiden knows because Lex told him but he also knew me before—but now I'm trying to become wholly devoted to God and not look at guys and share the gospel with people and rely on God more." She paused to take a breath.

Olivia stepped forward and enfolded her in a warm hug that smelled like cinnamon. "Oh honey, I'm so happy for you. I feel like God brought you directly to our church for a wonderful reason. And I'm not just saying that." She released her.

Trish was going to cry. "That's so nice of you to say that." She sniffed.

Aiden's hand appeared in front of her with a Kleenex.

"Thanks." She blew her nose. "Why do you have a Kleenex?" Not that Aiden wasn't sensitive or anything, but that seemed weird.

"Lex got emotional when she had knee surgery the first time, so I started carrying them when she had surgery the second time."

Olivia burst into laughter. "Smart man. Honey, you two need to start going to the same church."

"We're fighting about which one."

Trish wanted someone to fight with about which church to go to. God would surely give her Mr. Right once she got her life turned around, right?

Olivia was looking at Trish strangely — not in a bad way, but with a thoughtful cast to her face. "You said you were turning your life around. You've burned your bridges, right?"

"Huh?"

"Done what you can to completely turn your back on your old life? Addicts destroy their drug paraphernalia, alcoholics throw out all their bottles. I burned all my offensive language CDs when I became a Christian."

Trish hadn't thought of anything like that. She figured it was enough to go to a new church. But maybe she ought to do something more — something symbolic. "I'll think about what I can do."

A figure exited the sanctuary and headed toward them. Olivia spied him. "Oh, there he is. Trish, this is our volunteer coordinator. Spenser, this is Trish."

She couldn't make her mouth close. "You!"

Spenser — her co-worker, officemate, project-teammate. Spenser stopped in his tracks, his hands full of sound cords. "Trish."

She smiled weakly. "Hi."

"You know each other?" Olivia had an unreadable expression on her face. It was sort of amused, but also almost ... speculative.

"We're co-workers."

"Trish is thinking of joining our church." Olivia's smile at Spenser was a tad mischievous.

He paused. Stared at Trish. Back at Olivia. "God help us."

ELEVEN

Spenser huffed and ran to follow Trish as she marched out into the parking lot. Man, the woman could book it when she was peeved. He waited until she was closer to speak to her so he wouldn't have to yell. "I said I was sorry."

"Hmph." She kept going.

He knew her well enough now—he could tell she wasn't actually upset with him. She only liked to see him grovel a little. "I was sort of kidding."

"Oh, and that makes it all better?" Trish stabbed at the Unlock button on her car alarm remote. Taillights blinked halfway down the line of parked cars. "Oh, there's my car."

He rolled his eyes but then had to sprint to catch up with her. "Trish." He grabbed her arm to stop her in her tracks.

"What?" She turned a cool face to him.

He quirked an eyebrow at her.

She erupted into giggles.

Ha! She couldn't keep a straight face if her life depended on it. "Olivia said you wanted to volunteer for something?"

"Yeah."

"Oh, I get it. Your three rules?"

Annoyance flickered over her face. "You don't have to say it like that."

"Like what?"

"Like they're as real as Ravenous Bugblatter Beast Of Traal."

"Huh?" What in the world was that? Must be from those books she was always reading.

"You've never read *The Hitchhiker's Guide to the Galaxy*?" She looked at him as if he were a Neanderthal. "Never mind. You said I had a snowball's chance in you-know-where of keeping them."

He decided to keep his mouth shut before she got any more irritated.

She sighed. "Yes, I want to serve at the church. Whaddya got?"

"What, like a fast food order?"

She glared at him.

"Okay, okay. We need another vocalist on the worship team."

Her face lit up for a moment, like a child offered her first present on Christmas morning. Then the light snuffed out. "No, I don't sing very well."

"You don't have to — "

"Oh, I couldn't possibly. I'm not being falsely modest or anything Asian like that."

He shrugged. "Okay. Well, they need help in the kitchen for the Seniors' Potluck Dinner next weekend."

"Oh, I can do that."

"Can you cook?"

"Uh ... I need to cook?"

"It's called a potluck, but in reality, we cook stuff because the Seniors tend to all bring dessert."

"Uh ..." She bit the inside of her lip.

"You run twelve different types of assays at work — I'm sure you can follow a recipe."

"Okay." She opened her car door. "Can you email me all the details?"

"Sure. You're not going out to lunch with the Singles Group?" He'd been hoping she'd join them — not that the food was great at the diner they usually went to, but he wanted to snigger over the bad food with her like they did with the cafeteria at work. She'd get a kick out of the bright orange rice ...

"No, I told my mom I'd visit her this afternoon." Trish must have read the question in his face, because she continued. "She's recovering from a heart attack."

He winced. "Is she okay?"

"She's kind of weak. My dad's taking care of her." She turned her face away for a moment.

"Sorry about that. I'll pray for her." The words sounded awkward coming out of his mouth. He hadn't said them very often, even though he'd been a Christian since grade school.

Which was exactly why he took the volunteer coordinator position when the previous coordinator wanted to step down, and why he'd gone to Olivia and Ed about doing sound for them again. All because this one woman standing in front of him had assumed he wasn't Christian and made him realize that maybe he hadn't particularly been acting like one for the past few years.

"Aw, man! I lost a bow from my shoe. When did that happen?" She bent to inspect her turquoise-colored shoes.

Okay, well, she wasn't always the most serious person. But being mistaken for a non-Christian had blown him away, especially by someone who admitted she was backslidden and trying to pick herself back up again.

Trish straightened. "So, I'll see you tomorrow at work?" She flashed that amazing smile.

His breath caught for a second. He still couldn't get used to it. "Yeah. I'll send you info on the Senior's Potluck." His voice sounded a little strained as he tried to remember to breathe.

Something flickered across her face. She bit the inside of her cheek and fiddled with her earring. "It's okay that I'm not ..."

"What?"

"Well, I'm not ... I used to be ..." She gestured helplessly with her hand.

He had a feeling there was more that she wasn't saying. "You don't have to be perfect to serve God." After all, he only had to look at himself.

She seemed startled, but then she exhaled and her shoulders relaxed. "You're right."

"I'll see you tomorrow."

"Huh?" She lifted confused eyes over the SUV door.

"At work?"

"Oh!" Her cheeks started to turn pinkish. "Oh, yeah."

As she got into her car, he thought he heard her mutter something like, "As if I could forget . . ."

She needed references. Four of them.

Trish scrolled through the online application to Western Seminary and winced more and more as she saw yet another page to fill out.

She could at least get her boss Diana to give her one reference. But three others?

No one at the new church knew her. Maybe if she went back to her old one . . . ?

Thoughts of Mrs. Oh with a whip, standing over her as she washed dishes in the church kitchen, made her shudder.

She printed out the application, but it didn't look any shorter in hard copy.

Maybe her cousins could give character references. Lex went to her church — well, her old church — and Venus and Jenn . . . She'd never actually done any service with them, but that was okay, right?

Her phone chirped and she looked at the caller ID. Wow, great timing. "Hi, Lex."

"I got a call from Grandma." Lex's voice reminded Trish of a simmering pot of oxtail soup, frothing and bubbling.

"What about?"

"What else? When am I getting married? Aiden and I aren't getting any younger, yada yada yada."

"You didn't answer with your usual, 'We're going to live in sin and not have children,' did you? She ranted for days the last time."

Lex released a mirthless laugh. "No, this time was different."

"Why are you upset by this? Grandma usually doesn't bug you."

"This time she accused me of putting God before family."

Uh, oh. That sounded rather familiar. "Oh, really?"

"You wouldn't happen to know what put that in her head, do you, Trish?" She'd have to be deaf not to hear the steely threat in Lex's tone.

"I, uh ... might have talked with Grandma about not dating non-Christian boys."

"You did? *You?*"

Her cousin's incredulous reaction shoved a pole through Trish's normally-slouching spine. "Hey, I told you I'm becoming whole-heartedly devoted to God."

"I already told you I'm doing my best to believe you on the 'whole-heartedly' part."

"What? Traitor. Jutus."

"I think you're mixing Brutus and Judas."

"Whatever. It's not my fault Grandma's suddenly turned all Roman Colosseum on our faith."

There was a strange silence on the line. "Lex? You still there?"

"Have you talked with Mrs. Matsumoto recently?"

"How recent?"

"Jenn was telling me that she hasn't seen Mrs. Matsumoto hanging out with Grandma at all."

"They're both opinionated and strong-willed. Of course they're going to have tiffs. Give it a week. They'll be best friends again in no time."

"No, Jenn says this has been going on for months."

"Really?"

"And we all know Mrs. Matsumoto isn't exactly quiet about her faith in God."

"You think that has to do with Grandma being so against Christianity with you and me?"

"Could be."

Well, they were the only four Christians in their entire extended family. It was just that Grandma had always argued with Lex and Venus, never with Trish. What had Mrs. Matsumoto said to Grandma about God that got her girdle in such a wad?

Lex continued, "Anyway, the original reason I called was to ask how church went today."

"Oh, great! I met Olivia and we instantly connected."

"I love Olivia, she's wonderful."

"She gave me the name of a seminary I can go to."

"What? Seminary?"

"I forgot to tell you. I'm going to get my MDiv."

There was a long pause. "Why?"

Uh ... she couldn't exactly tell her the original reason was to prove to them that she was in earnest about her new resolve. Why did she want her MDiv apart from their approval? "I'm devoting myself wholeheartedly to God, and what better way than to get my MDiv so He can use me in other ways?"

"Um ... oh." Lex didn't try to hide her confusion.

"It's true. I'm filling out my application right now. Hey, can you write a reference for me?"

"A reference? From me?"

"I need one from Venus and Jenn, too."

Lex paused before answering. "I don't think Venus would do it."

"Sure she would—"

There was a muffling sound, then Venus's voice barked across the line. "You want me to do what?"

"Oh. Hi, Venus." Her abrasive personality always reduced Trish to Jell-O. "You're over at Lex's?"

"Yes. You want me to do what?"

"Uh ... write me a reference. For seminary."

"For *seminary*?" Venus's voice blasted through the phone, and Trish jerked it away from her ringing ear.

She switched her phone to the other ear. "I want to get my MDiv."

"This is just another phase. Like your 'I'm over Kazuo and getting back with God' phase, and your 'I'm going to become a Japanese translator' phase, and—"

"Hey, I did learn Japanese. I know more than you guys." Which had always earned Trish kudos with Grandma over her other cousins.

"Who cares? It's another phase. I'm not putting effort into a reference for something you'll drop in a few months because it's boring you."

"No, this is real this time. I can feel it, deep in my gut."

"It's indigestion."

How could she explain it to cynical Venus? Because she was right—Trish had lots of phases, but she somehow knew this time was the real McCoy. God had given her a massive wake-up call, and she wasn't going to risk something even worse happening if she didn't shape up this time.

"So, uh . . . no reference?"

"No. I'm going to tell Lex and Jenn not to do it, either, until you prove this isn't something temporary." *Click.* She hung up.

Hmm. Venus was more annoyed than her usual grouchy self. PMS?

So Trish needed some other people to write those references. Well, she had the Seniors' Potluck this weekend. She'd have to talk to Spenser tomorrow at work about other volunteer activities—getting to know people, figuring out who she could ask.

Olivia, maybe. She'd felt an instant connection with her, but maybe Olivia was like that with everybody.

Olivia's words about burning her bridges made sense. It probably wouldn't be enough to convince Venus, but it would be something symbolic for Trish. She just wasn't sure what she had to burn. How to commit herself completely to her new course? How to prove to Venus—well, and to God, too—that she wasn't going to turn back?

Her new church was the biggest step. Maybe she could formally have her church membership transferred. Was that enough?

No, she wanted something big, dramatic, bridge-burning.

Burning . . .

Her gaze strayed to her open closet door, to the psychedelic colors of her wardrobe. To all the too short, too low, too transparent, too skimpy clothes.

She got up and started pulling blouses from the hangers. Then skirts, then dresses. That blouse showed too much cleavage. The slit on that skirt was too high. That dress was slightly, well, backless.

This blouse exposed too much midriff, but oh, it was that delicious cherry bubblegum color she loved . . . Those pants had too low a waist, but they had the really cool embroidery on the sides . . . Her gold dress wasn't as backless as the other one, was it?

She ran her fingers over the rich fabrics. It was like throwing away her close friends. For some of them, she didn't even have the excuse that they didn't fit her anymore. She sighed and held the blouse up in front of her. She faced the mirror.

She looked like a prostitute. A *cheap* prostitute. The realization gave her a disgusted feeling like rotting flesh infested with beetles in the center of her stomach. Had she really looked like this?

She pitched the dress.

Okay, her closet was depressingly empty. She reached in and chucked a few granny dresses and some outdated slacks with waists up to her ribs.

Would her life be that empty, too? Being a good Christian girl hadn't been *uneventful* so far, that's for sure, but it hadn't been as fun as her old life. Then again, if the high road was easy, more people would take it.

Nothing. Her closet had nothing. Her life had nothing. She needed to fill both.

Good thing she loved shopping.

"Spenser, I need more work." Trish nudged the door open and strode to her desk.

He looked up from his computer. "Good morning to you, too. I had a lovely weekend. How was yours? Fine, thanks. I spent most of the day watching college basketball—"

"I would never watch college basketball."

"You're not following the conversation close enough. That was my response. Here's yours: I would never watch college basketball—"

Trish rolled her eyes. "Doofus. Pay attention. I need more stuff to do at church."

"Oh, you mean you weren't volunteering to do my assays today?"

She gave him a *How stupid do I look?* face. "Hmm. Let me think about it . . . *no*."

He sighed. "Can't blame me for hoping."

"You're lazy enough as it is." Which wasn't really true, but it was fun to rile him.

He gratified her with the expected defensive response. "I'm not lazy. What are you talking about? I'm busting my butt for you—er, this project."

"Well, bust your butt for me another way—I want more stuff to do at church."

"That's right, you mentioned that before the whole 'lazy' crack." He leaned back in his chair and raised his arms above his head, which unfortunately—or fortunately, if she was being brutally honest with herself—set off his nicely honed biceps and triceps and that lovely wide expanse of chest straining against the knit fabric of his Calvin Klein shirt—

Whoa! Slow down! Remember rule number one—no looking. No looking means no looking. Trish snapped her head forward and stared at her blank computer screen, which actually wasn't a great idea because then she saw that muscled torso in her mind's eye . . .

"Worship team."

"Huh?" She cast a quick glance at him, then away. The man was too handsome for his own good.

"You could serve on the worship team."

She snapped out of her dazed daydream about his dimpled smile. "Didn't we already have this conversation? I can't sing."

"Can't play anything?"

"Nope."

"Hmm." He looked away. He muttered something under his breath, but she didn't catch it.

"Anything else?"

"Sunday school."

"Children's Sunday school?" The thought made her pause. Could she really help children? With her past? God wouldn't strike her with lightning for corrupting kids, would He?

The old has gone, the new has come.

A cool wave washed over her soul, sifting the sand, leaving her heart feeling sparkly like water reflecting the sunlight. Maybe it wasn't an issue.

But kids? She'd held one of her cousins' babies once. Did that count?

"Preschoolers. There's only one teacher, and they could use another one."

That was okay. Kids that age liked games, right? Trish was terrific at games. "Will I be by myself?"

"No, it'll be you and the other teacher, at least until you feel comfortable."

"Okay. That sounds good."

"If you don't mind my asking, why the sudden rush to serve more? You haven't even done the Seniors' Potluck yet."

"Uh ..." Telling him she needed references for her MDiv seemed kind of selfish. "It's part of my new resolve. Rule number two—tell others about Christ." Yeah, that sounded reasonable, right?

"Okay. Speaking of the potluck, here's the information I got." He clicked his mouse and brought up a document. "I'll print out a copy."

"Good." She leaned over his shoulder to read while it printed. Something light—something very male and very nice—tickled her nose. Trendy cologne, but not doused in the stuff. A sharp, refined, James Bond type of smell.

It was ... quite heady. And not in a bad way.

She could see the curve of his cheekbones, the light sheen of oil from his skin, as well as a few pimple scars. She smiled to herself. The imperfections made him more appealing, somehow. Kazuo's face had been so perfect—

"Trish."

She and Spenser both jolted at the sound of the husky male voice behind them. The familiar way he said her name sent a shiver down her spine—a very excited shiver, which was bad because she didn't *want* to be attracted to him.

She straightened and turned. "Kazuo! What are you doing here?"

TWELVE

Spenser automatically turned his head to look when Trish stood to face Kazuo, but her body blocked most of his view. Good thing, too, because he didn't want to see that pale face again.

Because he'd pulverize it.

He turned back to his monitor.

"I told you not to come to work to see me." Trish's voice had become strident. It also sounded like she was walking toward the open doorway. "You never listen to me." The end of her sentence was muffled as she went into the hallway and the door clicked shut behind her.

Spenser hadn't heard Kazuo's name in years, until Trish had mentioned it last week in her phone conversation with her grandmother. He'd been startled, but thought she must be talking about a different Kazuo. After all, it wasn't an uncommon Japanese name.

But hearing his voice, seeing that glimpse of his face — it was the same man. He gripped the armrests of his chair, and the rubber groaned as he pressed his fingers into them.

Had he seen Spenser? Probably not, or else he might have said something. Both of them always bristled when they met. Old territorial responses.

It was stupid, Spenser knew. It was over and done with. So why did seeing Kazuo still bother him? There was a busted connection between his rational mind and the rage coursing through his veins.

So Trish had been involved with someone like Kazuo. It occurred to him that her moral about-face — including her three rules and her refusal of Spenser because he wasn't Christian—might be a knee-jerk reaction to breaking it off with her slick ex-boyfriend.

Then Spenser realized he could hear snatches of the conversation.

"I don't . . ." Trish sounded as if she'd run a five-minute mile. "I don't want to get back together with you."

"You are the beauty in every line from my brush." Kazuo's voice had a deep, smooth resonance. "I need you."

Kazuo wanted her back? She didn't want him, according to what she'd told her grandmother, but she had a mesmerized quality in her voice. Kazuo was weakening Trish's resolve.

The idea came into Spenser's head like a whisper. Soft, not fully formed, but there on the edges of his mind. Trish. Kazuo. Their push-pull.

What if a wrench came in between them?

Someone to distract Trish from Kazuo. He knew she didn't have any other guys calling her—at least in the past few weeks. Maybe if she had someone to compare Kazuo to, she wouldn't have to fight so hard to simply tell him to go away.

Spenser had wanted to go out with her once. Why not again?

The part about her assuming he wasn't Christian had cooled his interest. But she was still fun to talk to, fun to banter with, fun to annoy. She knew now he was Christian, so he was acceptable to her stupid rules. Was that in her rules, that she could only date Christians? He couldn't remember.

Regardless, Kazuo would be livid if Spenser could turn her away from him. He could do it.

He could go after Trish.

Trish whirled through the apartment, clearing, dusting, wiping, and vacuuming. Her head spun, but she got everything ready for Marnie, who was returning that afternoon. She even demolished the cobwebs in the corners of the ceiling.

She coached herself as she did a last-minute swipe of the counter. Marnie had sounded her normal quiet self on the phone, although a little fragile. *Don't alarm her. Don't say anything stupid or irrelevant. Be happy to see her, but not overwhelming. Be—*

A key turned in the lock.

She stuffed her dishcloth into the handle of the refrigerator and sprinted to the door. She swung it wide with a flourish—but not too exuberant. "Hi."

Marnie hesitated on the doorstep but didn't respond. Trish then realized she blocked the doorway. She stepped aside.

Still silent, Marnie shuffled into the living room and set down a covered basket along with her duffle bag. She shed her jacket while her eye lingered over the unusually clean living room.

She smoothed back her hair, shining gold-brown in the light from the picture window. Trish damped down a sigh of envy. Not quite as long as Trish's cousin Mimi's—the bane of her life, that little tramp—and not as smooth and kink-free. When Marnie turned to face Trish, the light silhouetted her plump form. Her eyes, large and velvety dark beneath angled brows, glinted with a strange hint of triumph.

"Welcome back."

Marnie's full lips curved into a mirthless smile. "I'm finally free."

Her husky voice flowed like molasses, but her odd sentence made Trish blink and straighten. "Huh?"

"From him."

Her ex-boyfriend, she guessed. "Oh. Good." She didn't know how else to respond to that. Her nose itched. Strange, she thought she had dusted.

Marnie hauled her basket and suitcase into her room.

Trish hesitated in the doorway and reached up to play with her earring, feeling pressure to fill the silence. "So where did you go? No, no, you don't have to tell me. You, uh ... look good." What was that silver thing Marnie pulled out of her pocket? "Did you see? I cleaned the living room. I didn't get a chance to clean the kitchen, yet, though — Wait, are those cigarettes?"

Marnie's sidelong look brimmed with disdain and a swirl of defiance. "So?" She drew the word out like a challenging drawl from a Wild West gunfighter.

Whoa. This was a different Marnie. "No smoking in the apartments — that's general policy. You know that." Marnie's expression made Trish feel like a stuffy Sunday school teacher. "You could smoke out on your balcony." She gave a weak smile, then a resounding sneeze. Hadn't she vacuumed the living room enough?

Marnie glared balefully at the tiny, rickety balcony. She inhaled deep, then snorted out a drawn-out sigh. "Oh, all right." She turned fierce eyes at Trish. "I would have thought you'd be more understanding."

Trish recoiled from her vehement complaint. "Uh . . ." That was the longest sentence she'd ever heard from Marnie.

Marnie turned away to unlatch the basket lid. As Trish started hacking and wheezing, she realized she was mistaken. She had dusted and vacuumed perfectly.

Marnie had brought home a cat.

"Marnie! *A-choo!* No roving — *a-choo!* — pets — *a-choo!* — in the building. *A-choo!*" Trish scrambled from the room to snatch a handful of tissues from the box on the coffee table. She gave a resounding honk as she blew her nose.

"No . . . pets?" Marnie lengthened and enunciated each word like a kindergarten teacher. Instead of putting the black and grey feline back in the basket, she stood like a statue while it squirmed in her vicelike grip, sending cat hairs flying in a cloud around her.

Tears streamed from Trish's eyes. "Put the cat away, Marnie — a-*choo!*"

Marnie's basilisk eyes speared Trish as she dumped the cat back in the basket amid yowls and mewls. Her full pink lips pulled together in a sulk. "What am I supposed to do with him? Drown him?" Her sarcasm bit like a length of barbed wire. She stood with arms crossed, glaring an insolent challenge.

"You know the rules. If they find out, we'll be evicted. You'll have to give him away or move out." She ruined the effect of her firm comment with a piffling sneeze.

Marnie's mouth narrowed. Then she turned around and addressed Trish over her shoulder. "Fine. I'll give him away."

Trish blinked. She felt as if her stomach had been stretched tight and then deflated. "Uh ... good." She marched out of Marnie's room and shut the door behind her.

Oh, she had been real smooth. She'd handled that brilliantly.

But she couldn't be blamed, could she? This was a completely different Marnie than the woman who'd run out the door last week. That Marnie had been quiet and considerate, if a little taciturn. This one talked back and smoked and brought a cat home.

Trish escaped to her bedroom and flopped backward onto her bed. She traced the faint stains on her ceiling while she heard the rustling sounds of Marnie unpacking and crooning to her cat. Would she really get rid of it?

Oh, well. She'd wait and see.

Spenser leaned back in his desk chair and tried to peek around the cubicle wall between them. "Trish—"

Her telephone rang. Again.

He glowered at his monitor while she answered. He had been trying to oh-so-casually start up a conversation all morning, but she kept getting phone calls. If it wasn't the representative for the cells she had ordered, it was Diana, who was writing an IND report and needed clarification on some study.

"Hello? Oh, hi Mrs. Navarre." Trish's desk chair squeaked as she swiveled back and forth. Then the chair screeched as she jerked to a halt. "Uh ... what smell? No, we haven't smelled anything in *our* apartment ..."

Spenser heard a faint gag, then silence. After a few seconds, it started to concern him. It didn't sound like she was breathing ... Oh wait, there was a gasp. Huh. That sounded like a croak.

"Cigarette smoke?" Her voice had jumped an octave and cracked at the end. "Your nephew smelled it in your bathroom? Oh, that's terrible. No! Don't tell the manager. I'm sure, um, that the smell will go away soon ... maybe the guys in the apartments upstairs ..."

Then her panicked tones calmed down. "Oh yes, I'm sure they're doing something illegal ... Yes, they do look like gangsters ... Well, thanks for calling ... Yes, I'll tell you if I start smelling it, too. Bye."

Spenser jumped in before her phone hit the cradle. "So, Trish, I was wondering—"

But she picked up the handset and dialed. "Marnie, it's Trish. Are you smoking inside the apartment?"

She had ignored him. Not to be conceited, but girls never ignored Spenser.

"Don't lie to me. Our neighbor called me complaining about a cigarette smell in her bathroom, which shares a wall with your bedroom and shares a vent hole ... How should I know? I didn't design the building ... You need to smoke outside ... We had this argument yesterday. It's the apartment rules ... Excuse me, but I didn't write those, either. You have to stop or else Mrs. Navarre will call the manager, and he'll come and smell the smoke and know it's from our apartment ... Because we could get evicted, that's why! ... Okay, fine. Bye."

"So Trish, I was wondering—"

The phone trilled again. "Hello? ... No, Marnie, we don't have any more spoons ... No, they didn't disappear. We only have eight and you used seven between yesterday and this morning. You'll have to wash one ... Well then, just stop using spoons. Bye."

"Spenser, you were saying?" Trish's head popped around the cubicle wall.

He glared at her.

"What?" Her brow furrowed.

Spenser, don't irritate her. You're supposed to be pursuing her, not letting her get to you. He impressed himself with his self-control as he forced his face to relax into a smile. "Um, so have you seen the trailers for that new movie *Beowulf*?"

"Oh. Yeah." The annoyed glitter in her eye dulled to blankness. "But I hate epics." She drew back into her cubicle.

He did a double-take and stared at the empty space where her head had been a second ago. *What happened? That was quick.*

Okay, bad move. He hadn't even started turning on the charm, and he alienated her with his movie choice. Huh. Trish wasn't like the other girls he knew. She wasn't about to give him the time of day if his conversation didn't interest her.

He'd have to figure out her preferences, then. He heard her yakking on the phone. *Well, I guess tomorrow ...*

The next day, Spenser found her early in the lab, perched on a chair at the workbench where she had tossed a stained nitrile glove next to a half-coated ELISA plate. One gloved hand held an Eppendorf pipettor, while the ungloved hand held her cell phone to her ear. Wasn't the woman ever off the phone?

"I know you spilled the sugar because the counter was fine last night, but I had to clean up the mess this morning." Trish swung her legs, which dangled a good twelve inches from the floor because of the tall lab chair, and kicked the cabinets under the lab bench. "No, it isn't just that one time. You also spilled grape juice on the carpet and didn't clean that up either ... The big deal? The big deal is that when I finally saw it and tried to clean it up, it had already set and stained the carpet. That'll get taken out of the deposit, you know ... Just clean it up when you spill it from now on. Bye."

The time was now. Spenser injected himself into the space right next to her, relaxing against the edge of the workbench and invading her personal space. Trish straightened her back to ease away from him, but her pupils dilated.

He was close enough to smell her perfume — something light, not flowery, more like a sophisticated fruit scent. Acqua di Gio? If he could catch her perfume, he was certain she caught his — Aramis, the new, expensive cologne he'd picked up this weekend.

He reached out to take the cell phone from her hand, letting his fingers brush an "inadvertent" caress over her fingers. Her breathing hitched, then continued at a faster pace. Her eyelids slowly closed and opened over dazed eyes.

Then her gaze flickered. She blinked. In the next second, she turned back to the workbench and reached for a fresh glove.

How had he lost her? "So what kinds of movies do you like?"

Trish quirked a suspicious eyebrow.

He met it with whiter-than-snow innocence.

"Romantic comedies." A hint of defiance colored her tone.

Blech. "What's your favorite?"

"I like them all." She wasn't making this any easier for him.

"What have you seen recently?"

"I watched *Pride and Prejudice* again."

Eeeewww. Wasn't that movie ten hours long or something like that? "So you like that actress ..." What was her name? "Gwyneth Paltrow?"

She nailed him with a glare like a spear thrown at his head. "She wasn't in *Pride and Prejudice.*"

"I was asking about Gwyneth Paltrow's movies in general." *Oooo, way to think fast on your feet.*

She jumped down off her seat, and the wheeled lab chair skewed sideways with her violent action. Spenser leaped back to avoid getting rolled over. She darted her thick-heeled boot out and hooked one of the metal legs to stop it from wandering away.

He'd lost his personal space advantage. Then again, she looked pretty dangerous, standing with her weight on one hip, menacing him with flattened eyes. Her mouth, however, had pursed into an annoyed pink rosebud.

The rosebud opened and snapped, "Are you patronizing me?"

Spenser's brain deserted him. "Uh ..."

"Go away."

Trish had her back to him as she stepped on the footrest to launch back onto the seat, so she didn't see his face, which probably reflected his thunderstruck reaction. He closed his mouth before drool slipped out, then exited the lab. Quickly.

THIRTEEN

Spenser attacked — er, approached Trish outside their building the next day. The wind tangled the wisps that escaped her ponytail, and she swatted at them with one hand while she snapped at someone on her cell phone, "Yes, it was serious! I sliced open my foot on that broken mug ... Well, I wouldn't have needed to be careful if you'd cleaned it up when you first broke it ... You're lucky it wasn't very deep ... No, you'll have to fix the garbage disposal by yourself ... Because if we call the manager, he'll smell the cigarette smoke and see the cat and we'll get kicked out ... Well, I told you to — hello?" She stared at her cell phone, mouth gaping. "I can't believe she hung up on me."

Trish twisted around to snatch at her purse straps and put her phone inside. Spenser walked up to lend a hand. She jumped away as if he carried the Ebola virus.

"Only trying to help." He put on an injured expression.

No effect on her. "I'm fine." Acid dripped from her tone.

She was just peeved because she was having problems with her roommate. Spenser plunged full-speed ahead. "I watched a romantic comedy last night."

He had the satisfaction of seeing her jaw drop and her eyes widen to the size of silver dollars. But she definitely wasn't as attractive as when she was flaming mad. She kind of looked like a goldfish.

"*Bridget Jones' Diary,*" he answered her unspoken question.

"Get outta here."

"No, I really did."

Her eyes narrowed in distrust. "Okay, how long did you last?"

"From beginning to end. I promise I'm telling the truth."

She crossed her arms, but reluctant amusement pulled at her mouth. "I'm impressed. What did you think of it?"

Here was the dilemma. With any other girl, he could get away with a white lie. But would Trish see through it?

Probably.

Other girls would get bent out of shape if he told the truth. Would Trish brain him with her purse?

Maybe not.

"It was okay." He shrugged. Maybe he could get away with a vague answer.

No such luck. "Define 'okay.'"

"Um . . ." Spenser paused, then abandoned caution. "To be honest, it was kind of stupid."

Her lips pouted in frustration. "No it wasn't."

"Well, it had all kinds of things that didn't make sense at all."

"Like what?" she barked.

"What the heck is a bloke?"

Then Trish's big, glorious smile opened on her face. The spotty gray clouds disappeared and the sun shone down. He found himself smiling back like a dolt — he couldn't seem to help it.

"You idiot, it's like British-speak for a guy. Man. Male."

Even though her words made him sound like a dummy, the low sound of her voice did strange things to him. There was a purring somewhere in his ribcage.

A footstep sounded behind him. He nodded at a coworker, Kevin Clark, who passed them to enter the building. When Spenser turned back to Trish, he found her eyes following Kevin as if he was filet mignon and she was starving.

Wait a minute. Kevin?

"Did you know that Kevin's Christian?" Trish's voice had lowered from normal to dreamy.

"What?" Why was she telling him this?

"I needed to ask him a question about the plate reader, and I forgot it was lunchtime —"

"Forgot? Isn't that bathroom break number thirty-five?" He needed to snap her out of this.

He earned a venomous look. "Anyway, I interrupted him doing his assignment for Bible study."

"So? Rule number one is—"

"I know, I know. No looking. I wasn't looking ... not really ..."

"What's there to look at?"

"Are you kidding?" She lifted her eyebrows. "Kevin looks like Keanu Reeves."

What? Spenser countered with a disbelieving snort. "Are we on the same planet?"

Her eyes squinched, and her mouth thinned into a toothpick line. "Well, he's not as cute as Keanu, and he doesn't have that sexy tousled look."

"He looks like he came straight out of prep school."

She ignored him. "But he's got shoulders out to *there*, and he cycles, and he fills his jeans in all the right places—"

"Hey, hey." He stabbed at her with his finger. "You've been looking."

Her face flushed. "Well ... and he has that strong jaw and those chocolate brown eyes. He's a little shy and quiet, but he qualifies as a hottie, I think."

Kevin? Dorky, skinny Kevin? Was she crazy? His frustration squeezed his throat shut, and he started to sputter. "You—He—I—"

Her brow creased, and she tilted her head. "You sound like a frog. What's wrong?"

A frog? Indignation clamped onto his tongue.

Trish's head tilted the other way. "I can't understand you if you won't finish a sentence."

He finally found his voice. "You prefer Kevin to me?"

Her confusion melted into a smug gleam in her eye. "First time a girl's preferred someone else to you?"

Spenser started sputtering again.

A wicked grin rolled across her mouth. "I'm honored to be your first."

His incoherent sounds deepened into a growl, and he stalked away.

I'm honored to be your first. Had she really said that? Trish surprised him. Last night, after reviewing that entire conversation in his head a couple hundred times, Spenser decided that it wasn't worth the repeated insults to pursue her.

This morning, he just wanted to annoy her.

He hunted Trish down outside the women's restroom — where else would she be? Talking on her cell phone — what else would she be doing?

"I've reminded you every day this week but you still leave your door open and the cat escapes . . . Because I got an emergency doctor's appointment and she gave me allergy medicine. Just because I'm not sneezing lately doesn't mean the cat dander isn't making my allergies go haywire . . . Well, the medicine isn't working . . . No, I don't want to go back for stronger stuff, this stuff is already giving me headaches . . . Because you promised to give the cat away. It's against the rules . . . I've told you before, I didn't write the rules." She snapped her phone shut.

Then her shoulders sagged, her eyes pooled with despair, and even her hair looked limp. Her mouth drooped in that interesting rosebud shape. "Her cat ate my goldfish. Gonzo."

His sarcastic remark died on his tongue. He wondered if she would deck him if he responded with a pun.

Then she looked past him. In an instant, she shed her distress like tossing off a coat. She bristled and rumbled low in her throat, and he could almost see porcupine spikes rise from her rigid shoulders.

One of the biologists from virology sauntered by with a loose-lipped smile for Trish. It looked like he intended to stop, but her eyes stabbed daggers at him and he scurried away.

Spenser raised a questioning eyebrow at her.

"When I got into work this morning, we passed through a doorway at the same time, and he was groping me."

That dog. Spenser clapped his jaw shut. The muscles in his cheeks tightened and spasmed. He inhaled a sharp breath. The next time he saw him—

"So I stamped on his foot, and he backed off. I was kind of disappointed I didn't get a chance to elbow him in the gut."

Spenser's righteous indignation deflated. Bloodthirsty girl. Trish obviously didn't need a knight in shining armor. He'd have to be careful about that personal space advantage next time.

"It's all your fault." She jabbed an accusatory finger at his face.

He jerked his head away before she impaled his eye. He grabbed the offensive digit and lowered it to a safer vantage point. "What are you talking about?"

"All these slimy guys are paying attention to me because they've seen *you* with me the past couple weeks."

"Hey, I didn't ask to get transferred to your group."

"Who cares? You've become the bane of my life!" She accompanied her melodramatic screech by flinging her hands up.

He should have been offended, but he saw the humor in the situation. Plus, it was fun to aggravate her.

Another guy approached them. Spenser leaned into Trish and propped his arm against the wall over her head. His proximity made her jump and back into the wall, and he eased closer. Her eyes flitted everywhere but at his face, and her breath quickened.

She didn't seem to mind Spenser the way she minded the guy from virology. When she looked up, she looked bemused and hypnotized.

After the guy walked past them, Spenser pushed away from the wall. Trish remained standing there, confused and dazed.

Then her eyes snapped into focus and started sparking at him. "Are you doing this to annoy me?"

"Partly." He gave her a cocky grin.

She growled. She sounded menacing even though he stood a good three feet away. Her hands tightened into white-knuckled fists, then she whirled and marched away.

He resisted the unwise urge to chuckle.

At eleven o'clock that same day, Spenser stalled Diana to cover Trish's tardiness to the group meeting. She awarded him during the meeting with one of those terrific smiles and a scrawled note on her notepad: "Thanks. I'll buy you lunch."

He was in her good books. Perfect timing.

Spenser and Trish returned to their building from the café with their lunch — him with the Friday burger special, her with fried chicken salad. As they entered the card-key doors, he set a gentle hand on the small of her back. She started, but didn't pull away.

Things were getting better and better.

"Trish, I was wondering ... There's a great new Italian restaurant that opened on Castro Street. Let's go tonight."

A piercing wail from the direction of her purse nearly shot his ear off. Her cell phone. Again.

"Why do you keep the ringer so loud?" He rattled a finger in his numb ear.

"I can't hear it otherwise. Hi, Marnie."

Her fingers suddenly lost hold of her plastic lunch container. Spenser congratulated himself on his Superman reflexes when he caught her salad.

Trish didn't even notice. "What? What was he doing there? ... How did he get a key? ... Grandma doesn't have a key, she couldn't have given Kazuo one ... He did *what?* ... I don't care if he did it to keep you company, neither of you are supposed to smoke in the apartment ... You did *what?* ... What do you mean, it's not very big? A burn spot is a burn spot. Our carpet is white, in case you didn't notice ... I don't know how to fix it ... Okay, bye." She snapped her phone shut and stared into space, immobile.

Spenser snapped his fingers in her face, balancing two lunch containers in the other hand. "Trish?"

She turned to him. Her eyes didn't quite focus, but at least he had her attention ... he thought.

"So, um ... dinner tonight?"

She blinked. "Huh?"

"Dinner. Tonight. With me." Spenser smiled his warmest, most charming smile. A light came on in her eyes ...

No, that was an inferno spitting flames.

"Dinner?"

Oops. She shifted moods faster than Dale Earnhardt Jr. shifted gears.

"How can you ask me out on a date when I'm going out of my mind?" She exploded into noisy sobs.

Spenser beat a hasty retreat. *Maybe next week ...*

When Trish had spent all her tears, she sniffled and made her way back to her thankfully empty office.

What was Spenser doing? He had made her very ... uncomfortable this week. A girl could almost believe those soulful looks ...

She had to stop that. He was up to something. He was annoying. Well, amusing, too. And at times he was quite, quite attractive. Trish let out a puff of air and started fanning herself with her hand. It had taken heaps of willpower to not respond to him this week. That strength must have come from God, because she knew she didn't have any when Spenser was around.

She wasn't really looking, not when he was the one being all weird with her. She did have to work with him. She could almost think he had forgiven her for dissing him.

She could almost think he was actually interested in her.

FOURTEEN

The church kitchen had twenty women and two children in it. One child was getting water from the faucet into a cup. The other child was stuffing Goldfish crackers into a drain pipe in the floor.

The twenty women bustled to and fro, oblivious to the potential havoc caused by Goldfish boy, so Trish nabbed him. He loosed a samurai war screech that brought the smoothly running kitchen to a halt.

Women stared. Trish could read their minds—the tow-headed boy she struggled with was obviously not her own.

She pointed to his hands full of crackers. "He was stuffing these down the drainpipe."

A blonde mother rushed into the kitchen. "Danny, there you are." She snatched him away from Trish as if she were a kidnapper.

Trish did the whole cracker and drain pointing thing. The woman laughed. "Oh, you must be mistaken. He was probably trying to get the crackers out of the drain. Now sweetie, how many times have I told you not to put your hand in small dark places? Let's wash you up." She exited the kitchen, cooing to her four-year-old.

Trish found herself the center of the entire kitchen's attention, from the teenagers washing pots in the sink to the grandmothers fighting with each other over the space in front of the stove.

"I'm here to help. Spenser said to show up—?"

"Yes, yes." A portly Asian woman stepped forward from where she'd been rooting in a massive set of cupboards. "Spenser told me. You're Trish?"

She nodded and smiled, but the pale-skinned bulldog face didn't smile back. "He said you can't cook."

Hoo-boy, it was going to be a long Saturday afternoon.

The woman—Kameko, so maybe her faint accent was Japanese?—shooed Trish to the triple sinks next to two perky teenagers, Molly and Mary. "Wash pots."

Well, she could do that. She attacked the burned bottom of a stock pot with vigor.

She turned to smile at—Molly? Mary? But the girl quickly averted her eyes and resumed chatting with her sink mate. "Did you see Ryan today?"

"Oh, he's so hot in his server's uniform."

"I wish we could have been assigned to serving tables." She pouted and swished her sponge over a glass bowl.

Her friend scowled at her. "We might have if you hadn't been flirting so much last year that you dropped the spaghetti on Mr. Romano's head."

"I wasn't flirting! Take that back."

"Will not." She thrust out her neck and dropped the frying pan she'd been scouring.

Maybe Trish needed to police them. "What grade are you guys in?"

Two sets of nostrils flared at Trish. "Tenth." Then the closer girl turned back to her friend. "I'm not going to take it back."

"What school?" Trish finished the stock pot and took up the girl's discarded frying pan.

"Belfrey. Who says I even want you to take it back?"

"Do you guys drive yet?"

"No. Are you saying you don't want to be friends anymore?"

"Got any boyfriends?" Trish started on the pile of cups and tableware in a dishpan.

One girl turned to her. "Like it's any of your business." Her head wagged back and forth like a bobblehead doll.

Immature little twit. Trish shrugged a shoulder. "I'm just curious."

"Well stay out of it." The girl tossed her long dark hair in a spoiled gesture.

"Guess you don't want to know about the girl I saw Ryan talking to." Trish finished the pan of utensils and tackled a stack of plates.

Two wide eyes fastened onto her. "What?" "Who?"

Trish assumed Ryan was the tall, lounging teen she'd spotted in the foyer in a waiter's black and white. The only one not working. "A cute blonde girl. Gorgeous curls." Never mind she was only about ten, with an obvious crush he was gently watering with his attention, while she tried to ditch the grandmother she'd walked in with.

"Who is that?"

"I don't know any girls with curly blonde hair."

"Unless maybe Shana got a perm and didn't tell anybody."

"I bet she would, she's so sly. She's always been in love with Ryan."

"Well, I'm done." Trish rinsed her last plate and stared at the two girls, still stroking their sponges over their dishes.

One of them scowled as she realized how bad they both looked with their unfinished dishes. "Here." She shoved her glass bowl in Trish's direction.

Trish reached out for it without thinking, but then the girl deliberately dropped the bowl onto the floor. The crash echoed off the large stainless steel air vents over the nearby stove.

Kameko bustled up and gave a long, drawn-out sigh. "So clumsy. Good thing the girls were almost done."

The two teenaged cats smirked.

Kameko didn't notice. She grabbed Trish's arm. "Come, I have something else for you to do."

The two girls facetiously waggled their fingers at Trish as Kameko turned away. Trish bared her teeth at them. They jumped.

Kameko tossed a command to the teens over her shoulder. "One of you clean up the glass."

Ha!

Kameko set Trish to chopping onions. This was going to ruin her manicure. She'd even splurged and gotten three little crystals on each thumbnail this time.

The onion skins were terribly slippery under the dull kitchen knife. She went slowly.

A woman came and swiped Trish's chopped onions into a bowl, then whisked back to the stove and threw them in a frying pan with a hiss. The peppery odor of fajitas filled the kitchen.

"Faster!" Kameko roared in her ear. She chopped faster. The knife slipped. Red blossomed onto the cutting board.

"Aaaiyeeeeee!" Trish dropped the knife with a clatter. She whirled as she jerked her hand toward her chest, splattering blood all around. A few drops melted into the chopped carrots on the cutting board of the woman next to her.

The woman turned to Trish. "Are you okay? It doesn't look too bad, but boy is that a gusher. I'll get the first-aid kit."

Trish dealt with reagents all day, but not blood. Certainly never *her* blood. The room started to spin around her. Her forefinger throbbed, and a headache slammed into her forehead, pulsing with the rapid beat of her heart. She was going to bleed to death ...

"Let me see." Kameko grabbed her hand, enveloping her finger in a huge dishcloth.

She squeezed so tight, Trish expected her finger to pop off her knuckle. "Owowowow!"

Kameko gave her a disgusted look from her dark eyes. "Hold still." She smoothed her other hand over her straight dark hair, pulled painfully back from her temples into a colorful be-ribboned clip.

"Um ... Kameko?" One of the other women called out while peering into one of the nearby stand mixers. "This cookie dough looks strange."

Kameko bustled over, unfortunately still holding onto Trish's finger so she had to stagger after her. "What's wrong?"

"Is it supposed to be this pink color?" The woman held up a glob of sugar cookie dough the color of a blush rose petal.

Kameko frowned. "No." Then she looked down at Trish's captured finger.

Trish peeked back at her onion chopping station and noted the blood splatter around the board. Including the stand mixer in its circumferential area.

Kameko's glare was fierce enough to bake the cookies without an oven. "Toss the batch." She spoke to the woman but kept eye contact with Trish.

The woman's eyebrows wrinkled. "Why? What's in it?"

"Biohazard." Trish piped up.

Kameko growled.

Trish shut up. She was only trying to help. "Biohazard" sounded much better than "blood."

"Oh, and the carrots probably got some, too." She pointed with her free hand.

Kameko rolled her eyes to the ceiling and said something in Japanese that Trish couldn't quite catch. Then she yanked on Trish's arm. "You are a menace to my kitchen." She propelled her across the busy space, bouncing her off a few women working, and shoved her toward the door. "I will get you a Band-Aid, and then you will go home."

"But I came to help." Trish almost swallowed her words as the woman pushed her toward the church office down the hall. "Are you sure this isn't too serious? I might need stitches—"

"I'll drive you to the ER myself if you will stop ruining the food." Kameko fumbled with a set of keys to the office door.

The background din from the social hall had always been a soft roar—probably due to all the elderly parishioners without hearing aids—but it suddenly rose to a football game-worthy ruckus. Kameko's unibrow wrinkled as she turned toward the open social hall double doors. "What's going on?"

A teen serving girl came running out. "Mr. Carter was complaining."

"What?"

"He's okay. He bit down on this." The girl held out her palm, where something tiny sparkled.

Oh, a crystal. Kind of like the ones on her manicure—

Correction—the ones *missing* from her manicure. From the scrape marks on her thumbnail polish, the onions and the knife probably had something to do with it.

How—? Oh. The onions the woman had dropped into the fajita pan.

She cleared her throat. "Kameko?"

"What?" Really, the woman didn't have to snap at her.

"You might want to check the fajitas ..."

FIFTEEN

On Friday evening, Trish drove home, preparing herself for battle. Somehow the "helmet of salvation" described in the Bible seemed inappropriate to deal with a chain-smoking slob and her flea-infested, highly-allergenic furball.

Aside from their tense phone conversations, face-to-face discussion with Marnie resulted in a limpid look and a dispassionate shrug, even when her cat had eaten Trish's goldfish. She couldn't understand where the cat kept all the hair it deposited; there was enough fur on the living room couch to clothe three cats and weave a rug.

As a last straw, the entire apartment reeked of cigarettes. The next time the landlord came for his rent check or to deliver a package or to fix the garbage disposal (which still didn't work), he would discover their secret and they'd be out on the street. Minus the move-in deposit.

Where had her quiet, only slightly messy roommate gone? Where had this stranger come from? She'd been hesitant to lay down any ultimatums because Marnie had been such a good roommate in months past, but lately . . .

Her stomach had been upset all week because of this. She couldn't take it anymore, although she had to be honest with herself that she appreciated the fact she was eating less because the stress had affected her appetite.

Trish rattled the doorknob as she unlocked it and flicked open the door. A round grey puff on the couch jerked in surprise, then dropped down onto a pizza box, hopped over a dirty plate, slithered through a stack of magazines, leaped over a pile of laundry, and whizzed into Marnie's open bedroom.

"Marnie, we need to talk!" Trish's voice cracked, spoiling her dramatic Xena: Warrior Princess pose.

Marnie sauntered out of the bedroom. A cigarette stuck to her bottom lip and rained ashes on the carpet. "About what?"

At the sight of her flaunting her ciggy, Trish shot a hand out to slap the door closed behind her. "Will you put that out?"

She responded to Trish's tirade with rolled eyes, pursed lips, and a snort of smoke from her nostrils. She turned back into her bedroom and returned sans cigarette.

Trish took a deep breath, but inhaled a combination of acrid smoke and cat hair, and started coughing. At the kitchen sink, she fired water into a glass. "Marnie, that's it."

After a fortifying gulp, Trish squared off in the living room. "Anyone who comes up here can smell the cigarette smoke. You have to stop it or find somewhere else to live."

She let loose a long-suffering sigh. "All right, I'll smoke outside."

"You said that last time."

She gave her a narrowed *What more do you want?* look. "I promise this time, okay?"

"And the cat has to go." She'd been intending to threaten to give it away herself, but Marnie's eyes shrank to little black beads, making Trish hesitate.

Even her rounded cheeks looked sulky. "I've been keeping him in my room."

"No you haven't. He's been shedding on the couch."

"It's not bothering your allergies anymore."

Trish clenched her teeth and counted to ten. *Don't get into it. Just lay down the law.* She enunciated each word as if she were crunching glass. "The—cat—has—to—go—tomorrow."

Then quiet, insolent Marnie exploded into a barrage of Spanish. The peppery words flew at Trish's face like a flock of birds, startling and flustering her. Thanks to Hispanic friends and her high school Spanish classes, Trish understood some of it. Something about stupid rules, and being chained by a — something she didn't catch — demanding to know why she couldn't do what she wanted since she was an adult and independent and — something else.

Then Marnie reverted back to English. "And you. Why can't you keep quiet about my cat? Why should I abandon my baby? You should be helping me keep him. That would be the *Christian* thing to do."

Marnie stalked to her room. She slammed the door so hard that the walls shuddered and a picture dropped to the carpet. Trish stood in the empty living room, staring at the closed door. It was almost as if the conversation had never happened. Her mouth opened and closed but she couldn't get anything to come out. She'd only be talking to herself again anyway.

Trish tottered into her bedroom and collapsed on the edge of her futon mattress. She'd been on edge and irate all week, what with a whining call from Marnie every day and then more problems to discover when she came home. Her feverish, heightened emotions sucked the energy out of her until she fell exhausted into bed each night. When she wasn't blazing mad, her anxiety swung into depression.

Her nose tingled and her eyes started to swell. She sniffed. The sound triggered a tightening in her chest, and she pressed her fist over her breastbone, as if she could keep her heart from pounding harder.

She couldn't take it anymore.

My power is made perfect in weakness.

The sobs and wails came heaving out of her. She had forgotten rule number three, to persevere and rely on God. She had forgotten her God. But He hadn't forgotten her.

Oh Lord, I totally failed on rule number three. I should have come to you first for wisdom and guidance. I should have prayed before ever agreeing to room with Marnie. But even after she moved in, I should have asked you for help.

Shoulda, woulda, coulda. It seemed her life was always like that.

I know this is a little late, but please give me wisdom about what to do now.

She still had to get her point across. She couldn't lie about the cat. She had to do the right thing, regardless of what Marnie thought Christians should do. It had *nothing* to do with the fact that out of all the cats in the world, this one was the feline version of Godzilla.

She would wait until Marnie had calmed down—tomorrow? Trish wasn't being a coward, she really wasn't—then give Marnie the ultimatum: She would have a week to get rid of the cat or move out. If she stayed, Trish would tackle the smoking after that.

She plucked a few tissues and blew her nose. Now that she had prayed, her head had cleared of cobwebs, and her stomach no longer quivered. She felt as if a hand rested over her heart, stilling her emotions.

Everything would turn out okay. She breathed a sigh of relief.

And then she sneezed.

The next morning, Marnie sat watching Saturday morning cartoons when Trish stumbled out of her bedroom toward the kitchen. She cast a groggy glance at the figure on the couch as she honed in on the coffeemaker.

She started the coffee, leaned her tummy against the counter, and closed her eyes, listening to the gurgle and burping of the appliance. She sucked in the aroma as it dripped into the carafe.

What was she supposed to do today? Something about Marnie. But Marnie was already awake. Trish sighed. She'd be coherent and halfway human in about thirty seconds.

She poured herself a cup and sipped. *Okay, brain, start moving.* Something about the cat ...

Oh. Trish inhaled and straightened for a moment before slumping back into a limp noodle posture that would have made her mother cluck. That's right, she needed to speak to Marnie. Well, no sense putting it off. "I need to talk to you—"

The telephone jingled. Trish had the handset at her ear before the second ring. "Hallo?"

"Marnie, *tienes que llamar a Mamá. Ella está preocupada por ti ...*"

Trish walked to the couch and held the cordless phone to her. "It's for you."

Marnie barked into the phone, "*Mamá, tienes que dejar de llamarme. Te estás poniendo pesada ...*

Trish had inhaled two more cups of coffee by the time Marnie hung up. Ah, she felt positively feisty now. "We need to talk—"

The razor-sharp buzz of the doorbell sliced through the room. Trish froze.

Marnie blinked at her for a moment. Then comprehension dawned, widening her liquid eyes and pulling her mouth into an *O* the size of a corn tortilla.

Marnie bolted for her open bedroom door, then slammed it shut. Behind her.

Trish gasped. The nerve! Abandoned by the very cause of the problem.

Bzzzz cut into her thoughts. She broke her head from the coffee fumes to sniff around the room. She dove for the bathroom, snatched up the can of air freshener, then raced around dousing the apartment, hopping over bowls and pizza boxes.

"Who is it?" Trish winced at her frenzied tone while she jerked open the tiny windows flanking the living room's picture window. *Oh, please, don't let it be the landlord ...*

"It's Mrs. Navarre, Trish. I signed for a package for your apartment yesterday."

She crumpled in sheer relief, smearing herself over the arm of the couch. *Oh, thank you, God ...*

"Trish? You still there?"

The click of a door preceded Marnie's cautious head peeking out. "You going to answer that?"

Trish's mouth dropped open. She couldn't find her voice, and "urk"-ing sounds came out of her throat. She gave Marnie a long, incredulous glare while she stalked to the door and yanked it open.

Mrs. Navarre jumped at her violent action but smiled as she offered the brown parcel addressed to Marnie.

"Thanks." Thank goodness for every single one of Mrs. Navarre's eighty years, and her failing sense of smell. The old woman nodded and walked away.

Trish kicked the door closed. She tossed the package on the counter, then advanced on Marnie, who stood by the couch. "We need—"

Yowl!

Trish catapulted down and almost cracked her head on the edge of the coffee table when she fell to her hands and knees. Marnie gave a muffled shriek and lunged for the floor behind her.

"You tried to kill my cat!" She picked up the mongrel, who spat a baleful *I will enact my revenge, you stupid human!* hiss at Trish before it affected a victim posture and screamed bloody murder.

Trish should have jumped up at the sight of the injured animal... but she didn't. She got to her feet slowly, then sighed. "Let me see."

Marnie squeezed the cat and twisted away, her breath coming in quick heaves. "You're trying to hurt him."

"I tripped. Over a cat who was supposed to be in your bedroom. Now let me see him."

Her acidic tone cured Marnie's hysterics. She held out the feline. Trish ran her hands over his fur in a body check. "Nothing's broken. I think he's okay."

"You stepped on his paw. Shouldn't you wrap it or something?"

"It's *your* cat—"

"*You* injured him."

She needed to pick her battles. After all, she still needed to talk to her.

Trish turned away so Marnie wouldn't see her roll her eyes. She dug an old T-shirt rag out of her closet, then returned to wrap the flailing limb. The cat recoiled at the sight of the large white swath and scrambled to get away.

Hmph. He wasn't *that* injured.

Trish grabbed the cat and wrestled it into submission so she could wrap the paw. Marnie crooned saccharine Spanish phrases and annoyed it by rubbing its tail.

Here was her chance. "Marnie—"

"Oh, by the way, I've decided to move out. I'll leave in two weeks." Marnie then launched into more Spanish to comfort her pet.

Trish's jaw fell and her chin bonked the cat on the head. After a moment, she realized how idiotic she must look—mouth open, squirming cat in her arms, a bulky T-shirt bandaged around its waving front leg. "Uh ... okay."

Marnie seized the cat, flounced into her bedroom, and banged the door shut.

Trish dropped onto the couch. Marnie's pronouncement had startled her, but relief flooded through her like water softening a stiff loofah. Her hands dangled from the arms of the couch, and she stretched her legs out, feeling her bunched muscles uncoil. *Thank you, God, everything worked out fine.* Except ... what was that brown, slimy, hairy stain under the coffee table?

Oh, great.

The cat had hacked up a furball.

SIXTEEN

Trish got a bad feeling about teaching when Mrs. Choi, the Sunday school coordinator, met her at the door and suctioned herself onto her arm, reminding her of the time when she had licked a frozen lamppost at the tender age of seven.

"I'm so glad you volunteered to help us, dear." Violet-and-fuscia colored eyelids blinked rapidly as Mrs. Choi led Trish into the foyer of the church. Another huge basket of flowers on the center table made Trish sneeze violently.

Mrs. Choi kept smiling and tried to surreptitiously wipe the spray from her pink jacket collar. Trish's *Danger, Will Robinson!* alarm triggered.

However, Mrs. Choi had a strong grip, so she couldn't pull away and run screaming from the building even if there was a seventy-five-percent-off sale at Bebe.

"Um ... what age?" Trish dragged her feet even as Mrs. Choi yanked her down a hallway leading from the foyer.

"The best ages for new teachers, fours and fives." Mrs. Choi's mocha-plum lips stretched wide to reveal coffee-stained teeth flecked with lipstick. She opened a bright yellow door to a cacophony of childish voices, undercut by an older woman's aggrieved staccato.

"Here's our other teacher, Griselle Oh."

"Oh?" It couldn't be.

It was. A younger version of Mrs. Oh stood in front of her, with a strange blue hat—no, that was a splotch of blue paint on her head. She turned to Trish with the sweetest smile this side of the Yangtze River, waving a blue-dyed hand.

The bottom dropped out of Trish's stomach.

Run away! Run away!

Mrs. Choi threw her to the wolves. "There you go, dear. Griselle will tell you what to do. Ta-ta!" She slammed the door shut as a few munchkins tried to make a run for freedom.

"Miss Oh, Susie spilled the glue." A miniature Poison Ivy from *Batman and Robin* tugged at Griselle's creased and stained slacks.

Griselle gave her a smile as if she were Miss Toddler America rather than the tattletale she was. "Now, what did we say about talking about things rather than helping with them?" Her dulcet tones belonged to Glinda the Good Witch, not a human being. "Why don't you help her clean it up?"

Trish blinked. She definitely wasn't up on Nurturing 101 like this chick. Griselle needed help? To do what, polish her halo?

Surrounded by children and standing next to Griselle, Trish had never felt so stained, and not by anything colorful like the hopefully water-based blue paint on the younger woman's hands and head.

Griselle turned to her, all sweetness and light, making her want to sink through the floor. "Welcome! I'm so glad you're here. I could really use the help and you're perfect." Her smile would have convinced Tony Soprano to give up the family business.

"I've never—"

"That's okay, that's fine." She straightened her tucked-in long-sleeved shirt—buttoned up to her chin, naturally—leaving a faint blue streak on the chambray. Her dark eyes widened in concern. "Oh no, Matthew is eating crayons again. Why don't you help Susie clean up the glue?" She shooed Trish toward the back of the large rainbow-colored room to a low, small-person table where a dark-haired girl smeared glue all over the surface in a massive white finger-painting project. Some of it had already begun to dry, and rivulets stood out against the cheap Formica.

"Susie, glue is for ... uh ... gluing." Trish nabbed the plastic tub before the girl could dip in for another reload.

She stared at Trish with wide brown eyes framed with thick, curling lashes. Then her eyes scrunched as she beamed at Trish, poofing out her dewy cheeks, made even more irresistible by the glue dabbing her nose. Trish could almost kiss her, except, well, the glue would probably stick her mouth permanently to Susie's face.

Susie went back to layering glue on the table. "Mommy says I can have a new pet."

"Um . . . that's nice. Let's play bulldozer, okay?" Trish brandished the glue container. "You're the bulldozer. You have to push all the glue into the container —"

"I think I want a kitty." Susie slapped her hand against the table. It splattered, and she laughed.

"A kitty's a good pet. Let's play bulldozer." Trish made bulldozer noises — which sounded more like a Porsche engine — and scooped the glue towards the edge and into the container.

"Or maybe a ee-gwana." Susie mimicked her scooping actions but shoved her glue over the edge and onto the floor.

Lovely.

Then she noticed a little boy on the other side of the table from her and Susie. A cute Asian kid with a crew cut. He'd dipped his hands into the glue and gotten it all over him. No, wait, was he —?

"Ewwww! No, don't eat that!"

He licked his fingers.

Trish reached across the table to grab his hand so he couldn't get more into his mouth. Or on his face, or in his hair, for that matter.

Griselle came up and heaved a sigh that somehow managed to have a smile in it. "Matthew, you shouldn't eat glue. Remember what I told you last time?"

He laughed up at her with the cheerful disposition of the ignorant.

"Last time?" Trish had a hard time keeping hold of his squirming hands, slimy with glue.

"He's going through a phase." Griselle rescued one of his hands as it sprang free from Trish's. "He's been putting everything in his mouth."

Yucko. His poor parents.

"Here, I'll take Matthew and Susie to clean them up. You take the kids out to the playground for playtime." She motioned to the door at the back of the room. A fenced-in blacktop playground was visible through the large picture windows.

Playtime. She could do that.

Opening the back door was like the trigger for Pavlov's dog. Children popped up from their seats and scrambled for the doorway, pushing and shoving to get out first. Oops, was she supposed to make them line up first or something like that? Well, too late now.

Two little girls set at each other as soon as they hit the plastic go-cars.

"Mine!"

"Mine!"

"Neither!" Trish picked them both up by the waist and a little boy nabbed the go-cart.

Both girls erupted into howls worthy of a catfight on *Jerry Springer*. One went limp and sobbed into her pink lacy dress. The other kicked and wound her arms, making her red shirt ride up past her belly button.

Trish got down to eye level and kept a hand latched onto each girl. Neither one met her eye — actually, Miss Red Shirt tried to bop her in the eye, but Trish chose to ignore that. "You two need to learn to share. Do you know what it means to share?"

All she got in response was despondent wailing from Pink Dress and enraged screeching from Red Shirt.

"Jesus shared everything, including His food."

"Iiiiiii shaaaaarre myyyyyy fooooood!" Pink Dress sniffled loudly.

"Well, you need to share the go-cart, too, sweetie."

"I got there first!"

"No, I got there first!"

The two started slapping at each other, so Trish scissored her arms apart to get as much distance between them without letting go of their chubby arms. "You need to share. Put others first."

"Then I'll never get on the car!" Red Shirt stopped kicking and started crying as well.

"Oh, you poor dears." Griselle magically appeared and picked up Red Shirt. "It'll be all right."

Trish followed suit with Pink Dress. "They were fighting—"

"Over the cars? Nothing new." Griselle kissed Red Shirt's tear-stained face. "There, there. Do you remember what we said about sharing?"

Red Shirt stopped crying and nodded.

"What did we talk about?"

"To let others go first."

"Did you do that?"

"N-no." The little girl sniffled and buried her face in Griselle's shoulder. What happened to the screaming, kicking little monster?

"So what do you say?"

Red Shirt looked over at Pink Dress, still sniveling in Trish's arms. "I'm sorry."

"I'm sorry." Pink Dress erupted into a radiant smile.

"There you go." Griselle set Red Shirt on her feet.

Trish did the same with Pink Dress. They skipped off together, hand in hand.

Trish stared after them. How had Griselle done that? Trish's shoulders sagged, and not from the strain of carrying the pink taffeta doll.

Griselle had cleaned the blue paint from her hair, and it gleamed in the fitful February sunlight like an ebony waterfall. Trish couldn't get her hair to look that fabulous—and straight, not a single wave!—no matter how much she spent on hair products.

"I set out the food for snack time, so it'll be ready when they come in." Griselle tucked a strand behind her shell-like ear, which had a single pearl stud that melted into the creamy whiteness of her skin.

Trish wanted to shoot herself. She sighed.

Griselle gave her an encouraging pat on the shoulder. "Don't worry. It gets easier the more you do it."

"Do we do Sunday school every week?" She had forgotten to ask about that.

"We go one month on, one month off, with another team of teachers. That way, we have a chance to enjoy the sermon and the worship."

Hmm. Trish would need to find something else to do, then, so she could stay busy and keep serving. Didn't she read somewhere, sometime (long, long ago in a galaxy far, far away) that the devil used idle hands or something like that? Plus, she needed more references for her MDiv application.

"Okay, everybody, snack time!" Griselle clapped her hands and everyone started running for the classroom doorway. Trish couldn't tell if it was the food or the fact Griselle was practically perfect that made the kids behave.

"Will I see you with the Singles Group for lunch after service?" Trish called over her shoulder at Griselle as she wrestled a ball from a screaming boy in green pants.

"No. Thank you, Natalie." Griselle took a Wiffle bat from a little girl and patted her on the head. "I don't really know any of the other singles because I go to visit my grandmother every Sunday after service, and on the Singles Group meeting night, I have another Bible study with women from my apartment complex. Not all of them are Christians, but a few are very close to coming to a decision for Christ." She dimpled at Trish.

Dimples, too! The woman didn't even have uneven teeth to mar her smile.

They corralled the final kids into the room, where the rest of them apparently already knew the drill and sat at their own places, not touching the cookies and milk in front of them. Waiting for Griselle to say grace.

Trish expected a heavenly choir to sing when she prayed. Then she mentally smacked herself for being so uncharitable. So the woman was a walking saint and Trish was not. No reason to get snippy.

Griselle's delicately arched brows wrinkled. "Where's Sara?"

"Who?"

Griselle pointed to an empty spot on the far table. "Where is she?" For the first time, panic tinged her calm tones.

They got on hands and knees to look under the tables. Griselle peeked in the cabinets in case Sara managed to get inside.

"Can she get outside the classroom?" Trish tried the room door but it stuck in her hand. "Hey, we're locked in—"

"No, there's a childproof latch." Griselle pointed to a metal switch higher up. "Twist that and turn the knob."

"Oh." Well, there was no way Sara could have gotten out of the classroom. She headed outside to the playground, Griselle trailing. They left the classroom door open in case chaos erupted while they were out of the room.

She looked behind the large storehouse while Griselle slid back the metal doors to look inside.

"Oh, there you are—urghk!" Griselle sounded a bit like she'd swallowed a live eel. Or a spider. Or something else equally nasty.

Stop it, be nice you meanie. "Are you okay?" She turned the corner of the storage shed to find Griselle a full ten feet away, her hand to her nose and a very unhealthy color to her face.

Trish peeked in through the open doorway at the teary-eyed little girl who squatted on the floor in the midst of broken toys and flat playground balls. "There you are, Sara—"

The smell assailed her like a dodgeball thrown smack in her face. "Hoo-boy! What died?"

Sara burst into a fresh round of tears.

Griselle's knees visibly shook, and she dropped into a chair by the playground fence. Her shoulders heaved as she tried to bring in more air.

"Careful, you'll hyperventilate." Trish eyed the rather scary color of her cheeks.

Griselle made an effort to slow her breathing.

Whew, the smell was strong enough to kill someone, but as a biologist, Trish had smelled far worse in the labs. She eased closer to the crying girl. "What happened, sweetie?"

"I couldn't make it to the bathroom." Actually, it was more like, "I coodt mek—" Sniff, snort, "—batchroom" but Trish got the gist of it.

"Oh, that's okay, honey." Well, not really, but what else was she going to say? *Oh, going to the bathroom in your underwear is completely acceptable adult behavior.* Poor kid.

"I'm too embarrssd." Sara's sobs were quieting.

"So you hid in the storage shed?" She kept her talking, waiting for the smell to air out.

"I'm all diiiiirty!" Sara erupted into new tears from her bottom-less fountain.

"I'll ..." Griselle audibly swallowed. "I'll take her in a minute." Her oval face reminded Trish of those powdery white mochi at New Year's. No, actually, she looked more like those green mochis with the bean paste filling—

No, don't think about food. She opened her mouth wider so she wouldn't accidentally breathe through her nose.

Griselle took several deep breaths—also through her mouth—while gripping the sides of the chair, then suddenly jammed her head between her knees.

This was not good. Should Trish—?

Ewwwww.

But poor Griselle. She really didn't look so good.

Something inside Trish uncoiled, like a rope knot loosening. She stared at the top of Griselle's head, still huddled between her knees.

"I'll take her."

Strange, that sounded like Trish's voice.

Griselle moaned but didn't move her head. "Thanks, Trish."

What? Oh. That *had* been her voice volunteering to take this smelly girl to the bathroom and clean up her ... er ... accident.

Oh God, help me.

And she realized that was one of the first times she'd remembered to pray to God for help. Hey, maybe she really was becoming more devoted to Him.

She took Sara's hand. It trembled in hers, so she gave it a comforting squeeze.

She was about to take her back in the classroom when she changed her mind and headed out the gate in the playground fence. Poor kid didn't need the others teasing her.

They circled the building and entered the church through a side door. In the women's restroom, she had to swallow the bile in her throat as she took off Sara's panties. She used up an entire toilet paper roll to scrub at it, then flushed the mess down.

Now what? The thought of putting the pair back on Sara was just wrong.

"Wait here." Trish darted out, reasonably sure Sara wouldn't wander around the church without her underwear.

She dove under the sink in the kitchen and came up with a jug of bleach. The biologist's best friend. Enemy of germs everywhere.

On the way to the restroom, Olivia entered the foyer. "Trish, there's someone who came looking for you."

A wriggling snake thrashed around in her gut, then was still. No, he wouldn't, would he? "I'm in an emergency right now—I'll talk to *her* later." Hopeful thinking, that it was Lex or Venus or Jenn. Even Grandma.

She soaked Sara's panties in the bathroom sink with a few splashes of bleach.

Sara rose on tiptoe to peer into the sink. "My panties will be wet."

"But they won't have any *E. coli*." Trish wrung the bleach out.

"Eee wha?"

"Bacteria. You know, germs." Trish squeezed the water out, then rolled the panties tight in a stack of paper towels. They came out only slightly damp. "There you go."

Sara, the ungrateful child, grimaced as she put them back on.

The smell of bleach, soaked into her hands, wafted around her as she followed Sara back to the classroom. Mission accomplished. Disaster averted.

She opened the door of the classroom to wailing and screaming.

Griselle's hair floated around her head in a tangled mass like that voodoo witch from *Pirates of the Caribbean*. Her color had gotten a little better, but she still looked like a mochi.

The kids, sensing weakness like sharks smelling blood in water, had decided to test their teacher's resolve with widespread chaos. Griselle took apart two boys with windmilling fists. In the corner, Susie had gotten hold of the glue tub again and was making table art. Matthew had half a toy car in his mouth.

Trish put her fingers in her mouth and loosed an ear-splitting whistle.

Silence, blessed silence.

Then one child started crying. A second joined her. Suddenly they all started wailing. Well, at least they weren't being disobedient anymore. But how to make them be quiet? The sight of Susie lavishing glue on the table made a light go off in her head.

"I have an idea!" Trish tried to infuse as much excitement as she could into her voice. A handful of children stopped crying. "How about next week, we all bring our pets to church?"

Griselle's eyes nearly popped out of her face. But the kids erupted into cheers and squeals of joy.

Horrified teacher ... happy kids ... horrified teacher ... happy kids ... Was there really a choice, here?

The classroom door opened and a few women squeezed in. Trish then became aware of the buzz outside. Service must be over. The cheerful kids made their parents smile warily as they filed in to collect their progeny.

"Good Sunday school?" One older Asian woman dressed in pale lavender came in to collect Matthew, probably her grandson.

"The kids were great." Griselle's tone gave no clue that she'd had anything but an uneventful hour. Only the slightly bluish tinge around her eyes hinted at anything wrong, and that might be attributed to the blue paint still flecked on her hands and her shirt.

The woman turned to face both of them, a soft smile on her pink lips. "It's so comforting to have pure young women like yourselves teaching these precious children about Jesus."

Trish's smile froze. She felt like a block of ice, immobile and heavy.

Pure? She wasn't pure. Not like Griselle. Should she continue teaching Sunday school, deceiving people like this who thought she was someone she wasn't? Her stomach churned more sluggishly as the woman beamed at her. Who was she kidding? Could she really become someone totally devoted to God like her past was erased? Life wasn't a whiteboard, or a credit card that could be demagnetized.

And then she saw him, a head above the other women coming and going. Kazuo's burning eyes found hers and wouldn't release her. He found that dark space inside her and made her feel set apart from the people around her, because she had tasted what they were too naïve to realize for themselves ...

No. She closed her eyes, shutting him out. That kind of thinking was an insidious spiral of poison in a glass of wine.

He made her feel special. Sparkling. Wanted. Real.

No. She was real. This person now was real. God had made her real.

But could He make her pure?

Did she really want to be pure?

"Trish." His quiet voice, adult and male and reasonable after an hour of childish babble, cooled her like a drink of water.

She opened her eyes and only then noticed the pungent odor overriding his sandalwood scent.

"You've been smoking pot." She pitched her hiss low enough that he had to lean closer to hear her.

He shrugged. "Just one hit."

"You're in church, you idiot."

He shrugged again. "No one noticed."

Trish tilted her head back and closed her eyes. Probably no one had noticed. Probably 98 percent of these people had never smelled pot in their entire, secluded lives.

He took her hand. Her eyes flew open, and she snatched it back, as much to avoid his insidious touch as to shake off the delicious shiver that climbed up her arm.

"You have to stop following me." She tried to frown at him, but it felt more like a pout. It was hard to stay mad when he seemed like such a pillar of sanity in the midst of the remaining children running wildly through the schoolroom.

"You belong with me." Somehow, the way he said it was romantic instead of stalker-creepy. "You don't belong here with these people." He never said the word *hypocrite*, but she could tell he meant it. "I love you for who you are, not who you're trying to be."

How did he know that? It was as if he could read her mind.

She had to find Aiden. Or Olivia. Or Spenser, even. She had to find help. She couldn't fight him herself. She turned and walked out the door, waving mechanically at Griselle as she went by.

Griselle gave her a pained smile. "Remember next week's Pet Day." If it weren't given in such a sweet tone, it would almost be like a threat, as in *Don't even think of leaving me alone with them next week because you designated Pet Day.*

As she expected, Kazuo followed her. A few church members gave him strange looks as he passed, and no wonder — in all black, hot as a blacktop court on a summer day, and smelling distinctly pot-like — no, he didn't stand out at all.

She only had to make it to the foyer before help arrived in the form of Lex. She must have decided to attend Aiden's church today. "Oh, thank you, God."

Lex's brow wrinkled. "Why?" Then she caught sight of Kazuo behind her. "What are you doing here?"

Yup, she could always count on Lex's non-existent tact-o-meter.

Kazuo's eyes gleamed dull and black like an anaconda. "Your grandmother told me to come here. I asked a woman who said Trish was in the 'fours and fives.'" However, when he turned to Trish, his countenance flipped from brooding to gentle and curious. "What are the 'fours and fives'? Those children?"

"Their ages." He hadn't spoken very nicely to Lex. The magnetic pull dimmed somewhat. Lex's rudeness to him was motivated by love for Trish, while Kazuo's rudeness to Lex was motivated by his possessiveness over Trish. While Trish was the first to admit it was nice to be wanted like that, no way did it come between blood.

Plus she was really glad Lex was here to keep her in her right mind. At some point she had to learn how to think straight when Kazuo was around.

"How did Grandma know I was here?" Trish addressed her question to Lex rather than Kazuo, so she clearly saw the guilty flash across Lex's eyes. "No way. You told her?"

"It was by accident, I swear. I was talking with Jenn at her house and forgot Grandma was in the next room with Aunty." Lex's glance flickered to Kazuo. "At least Grandma didn't show up with him."

True, but that didn't mean she couldn't show up later. Or sometime soon. "Can we go?" Trish looked around nervously and caught sight of the old woman in lavender who had commended her and Griselle in the schoolroom. The woman's gaze passed innocently over Kazuo, but suddenly Trish didn't want Kazuo there, with these people, with her. He was like a blemish on her skin. A mole or a scab or a big honkin' hump on her back. She didn't want to stay here, crowded by all these nice churchgoing people who had no clue of the cancer on her soul.

"Where's Aiden? Let's go." Trish latched onto Lex and "accidentally" stomped on Kazuo's foot when he tried to get close.

Unfortunately, he had on his steel-toed boots, which only caused a sharp pain to stab up her heel. "Yowyowyow."

He tried to close in on her with concern on his face, but she hopped away. "Good-bye, Kazuo."

She tried to make her voice firm, but her heart both fell and tightened because she knew it wasn't the last she'd see of him.

SEVENTEEN

Spenser knew he should let it go, but seeing Kazuo at church with Trish had been too much like déjà vu.

He banged on his keyboard harder than necessary as he wrote up his report. Trish had dated Kazuo—she should know what he was capable of, his persistence, his track record with women.

"Hey, Spenser." Trish rocketed into the office and dumped her workbag on the floor. Plastic crinkled as she unearthed her lunch. "Do you have any other things I can do at church?"

"You didn't like Sunday school?" He'd have thought she'd be great with kids.

She headed to the small fridge under one of the empty desks in the office. "Sunday school was fine, but it's only bimonthly, so I wanted something in addition."

"You're going to overcommit yourself."

"No I won't." She closed the fridge door and faced him with hands on her hips. "I am committed to becoming wholly devoted to God. I need to serve Him more. Rule number two is tell others about Christ."

Her rules again. "Was there anything you had in mind?"

She chewed on the inside of her cheek. "I don't really know many people at church."

Except for ex-boyfriends who visit.

You chump, let it go. Let Kazuo do whatever he wanted to do with Trish. She was a big girl.

No, he couldn't. Trish was no match for Kazuo — he mesmerized like a snake charmer. Kazuo would snuff out her cheerfulness and bully her into whatever he wanted.

It wasn't only for Trish that he wanted to do something. If giving her things to do at church kept her distracted from Kazuo, sure he'd help her out. Anything to keep Kazuo's hands off her.

Where was his file from the last meeting at church? Still on his laptop? He dug around in his bag. "There's always worship."

Trish flung her hands up with melodramatic force. "What about 'I can't sing' do you not get?"

"I know, it's just . . ." He hesitated rather than saying it. It had been a long time since he'd heard God's voice, and he felt rusty and stiff. "Every time I think of new stuff for you, the whole thing about worship comes into my head."

She opened her mouth, but he cut her off. "I know what you said. I'm telling you that the idea of you serving on the worship team isn't from me."

Her lips formed a little O. She studied her feet. "I don't know what to say."

"You don't have to believe me, but . . . I don't know, pray about it or something."

"Okay, but no promises."

He shrugged. "That's fine." He finally found the file on his PDA. "They need help at Katsu Towers."

"Old people?" Trish's face told him plainly what she thought about that.

"Assisted living. It's close to church, so they have a program for people to visit."

"And do what? Wheelchair races in the hallways?"

"What's your problem?" He wanted to reach out and shake her. "Don't you realize a lot of those people have family who never visit?"

She paled like she'd been dropped in sub-degree temperatures. "Oh, I'm sorry. Gosh, that's awful of me. I didn't know." She plopped down into her chair, then suddenly sat up, her spine straight as a serological pipette. "Of course I'll do it. When?"

"The team visits on Thursdays around four."

"I'll arrange to come into work early." She turned on her computer. "Email me the info."

"Bossy, aren't you?"

She gave him a look brimming with sass. "Are you going to not be such a weirdo this week?"

He hadn't been weird last week. The week *before* he'd been trying to get her attention, but last week he'd been ... well, friendly. Maybe that freaked her out—she'd turned red and tried to avoid him a couple times. "Yes, ma'am. I'll behave."

"Then I'll consider being less bossy." She turned to her computer. "Oops, I forgot."

"What?"

"I forgot to find out who the church admin was so I could put a want ad in the bulletin."

"They don't put want ads in the bulletin."

"Oh." Her shoulders sagged.

"But they have a bulletin board in the foyer."

"Oh, that big one? With all the fliers? I thought that was for church activities."

"They put want ads there too. What do you need?"

"A roommate."

"I thought you had one." Although from the overheard phone conversations, she sounded like a real pill.

"She's moving out. She can make someone else misera—um ... uh ..."

"Sounded like your ex wanted you to move in with him." He kept his eyes on his computer screen. Yeah, he was fishing, but ... okay, he was fishing.

Trish cleared her throat. "Just because he called begging me to move back in with him doesn't mean I'm going to fall down at his feet again and do it."

Judging from the sound of her voice when she had talked with him, it had been a temptation she'd had to fight. But her assertion made Spenser feel a little better, even if he wasn't about to admit it to anyone.

"How about the Singles Group? They have meetings on Wednesday nights."

That made her pause. "Really?"

"You could ask around there."

"Do you go?"

"To Singles Group?" Did she not—? Oh. She didn't know. "No, I don't go anymore." He couldn't quite keep the edge out of his voice.

"Why not? Hot dates on Wednesday night?"

She said it flippantly, but it knocked him like an uppercut. With brass knuckles. "Sure. That's all you think of me. Going out, partying every night." He stood.

She started at his harsh tone. "I'm sorry—"

"No, you're not. You always say what you mean."

"I was only teasing—"

"What do you think I do every night? Why do you think I always leave at five?"

She swallowed. "I didn't think—"

"You never think. You don't know a thing about me." She didn't have a clue what he did every single night, even on nights he came home exhausted, even on nights he could admit he wanted to be somewhere else and not be paralyzed with guilt for even thinking it.

"I have assays to run." He snatched his lab coat from the wall hook and gave the door a good slam on his way out.

He heard something crash on the floor. Sounded a bit like his PDA.

"Hi, Trish, it's Griselle."

The perky voice bounded through her cell phone. Trish switched the phone to her other side and rattled her finger in her partially deaf ear. "Hi. What's up?"

"My apartment Bible study had to cancel tonight, and I was thinking of going to the Singles Group meeting, and wanted to know if you're going?"

"Yes. It'll be good to see you there." She didn't mind meeting new people, but a guaranteed friendly face would make her more at ease. She hadn't seen the Tricolored Trio or the Weekend Warrior guys since she first met them a couple weeks ago, but the memory of their less than enthusiastic welcome still burned a little.

That's okay. She knew she didn't need everyone she met to like her. She knew it in her head, at least. It didn't mean she was woo-hoo happy when that didn't happen.

Griselle insisted on driving and picked her up in a comfortable sedan that was clean enough to eat off the floor mats. Trish said a sincere prayer of thanks that she hadn't exposed Griselle to the years-old french fries scattered over the floor of her little SUV, and the mound of tissues overflowing her car trash can—a plastic Safeway bag. Not to mention the food crumbs decorating the upholstery.

The church was ablaze with lights, and not only the social hall where the Singles Group met. "Is there another service going on?" Trish took perverse pleasure in the fact Griselle's car door stuck a little.

"No, but there are other Bible study groups that meet here." She activated the car alarm and led the way inside. "There's the men's group, the Working MOPS group, the youth group ..."

The Singles Group seemed larger tonight than it had been on Sunday, with people scattered around the brightly lit social hall in clusters as they caught up and schmoozed.

Griselle actually hesitated a little in the doorway. Trish blinked. She didn't think someone as perfect as Griselle would be shy. Well, here at least was somewhere Trish excelled.

She twined her arm in Griselle's and plunged into the room.

The first cluster of people near the door were the geeks—er, smart guys she'd met her first time in church. "Hi Jaspar, Willie, Gerard. Do you guys know Griselle?"

"I've seen you around, but you don't come to Singles Group very often, do you?" Willie gave a sweet smile. That was the most Trish had heard him speak.

"No, I usually have a Bible study at my apartment on Wednesday nights." Trish was suddenly glad Griselle was who she was — she didn't make these nice guys feel like geeks. *Stop it, stop thinking of them like that.* They were nice, smart, socially handicapped — er, no, that sounded kind of rude. Um ... socially inexperienced young men.

Certainly nicer than the Weekend Warriors, who'd gathered together again and seemed intent on ignoring her even though they were only a couple feet away.

Then she noticed that one of them — he wore an Yves Saint Laurent shirt — glanced over and did a double-take at them. No, more specifically at Griselle. At *all* of Griselle, from her shimmering hair (Trish had to get her hair care secret from her on the drive home) down to her sandals peeping from the hem of her flowered skirt.

What a slime! Which had nothing to do with the fact that his perusal completely bypassed Trish, who knew she ought to lose about ten pounds but certainly wasn't an eyesore.

At a break in the conversation, they said their goodbyes and went to mingle with other people. Yves Saint Laurent Shirt followed them with his eyes, which caught the attention of his buddies, but Griselle was clueless and Trish wasn't about to enlighten her.

Trish tugged Griselle to two women who looked friendly. They smiled at them at least, unlike the Tricolored Trio of girls — Blondie, Redhead, and Brunette — who stood nearby and looked away quickly. Trish knew some girls did that because they were shy, but she didn't think that was the case with the Trio. If Griselle weren't with her, she might have felt up to exerting herself and crashing their pink party just to annoy them.

Oh, she was so obnoxious. Lex must be rubbing off on her. Or maybe God needed more time for the "new creation in Christ" to kick in.

"I'm Marcy, this is Emmy. Have I seen you at church?" one girl asked Trish.

"I only started going a couple weekends ago."

"You haven't come out to lunch with the Singles Group?" Emmy, the tall girl, blew her silky brunette bangs out of her eyes.

"Not yet."

"You should come with us this Sunday." Marcy nodded, making her brown curls jiggle by her cheeks.

"You look familiar, but I don't remember seeing you in service." Emmy's eyes nearly crossed as she stared at Trish in concentration. "Where do you sit?"

"Don't you remember her?" The silky voice grated along Trish's shoulders like a rock against a serrated knife.

Except the question wasn't directed at them, it was overheard from the Tricolored Trio standing nearby. Blondie was leaning into her friends as if she were telling a secret, but her voice carried clearly. "She was the one two weeks ago who was trying to raise the roof during worship." Blondie tittered and her friends followed suit.

Marcy's cheeks bloomed a pretty English Rose red. Griselle looked confused.

Emmy turned around to glare at the Tricolored Trio, then stepped into the awkward silence staunchly. "I was so envious of someone who worshipped so ... uh ... fearlessly."

Fearlessly. Well, that was one way to put it.

"Hey, guys, let's get seated and start the meeting." At the front of the social hall, Ed and Olivia had set up their guitars.

Cool. Trish hoped for a chance to talk to Olivia later.

She and Griselle sat near the front, but to her dismay, Blondie and Co. sat behind them. "Hi there. Trish, right?" Blondie cooed. Like she hadn't been making jokes at her expense.

"Hi Blondie—I mean, Katy? Kaitlyn?"

"Kassie." She glared so hard, her thick curling lashes met and obstructed her blue eyes. Or possibly blue contact lenses, because they were way too jewel-colored in this sick fluorescent lighting.

Suddenly, the joy Trish usually had in worship dissipated, like an Airborne tablet in a glass of water.

She sat during worship, feeling miserable. She didn't want to sit there, but she couldn't feel the urge to stand like she usually did.

Ed gave the message, talking about submitting to God in hardship — yeah, yeah, rely on God, she already knew that — and then they were done. Refreshments had magically appeared in the back of the hall.

Olivia appeared in front of Trish just as magically. "What happened?" Her voice was short of a screech.

Trish blinked, then closed her mouth to end her goldfish impression. "Huh?"

"Oh, honey, did they get to you?" Olivia's dark eyes melted with concern.

"Uh . . . do you know Griselle?"

"Hi, Griselle, sweetie. My nephew's in your class."

Griselle nodded and beamed. "He's such a good boy."

"Now stop trying to change the subject." Olivia pinned Trish with a look sharper than a C-major-seventh.

She shrugged.

"Was it the worship music?"

"No, not at all."

"Then what?"

"What are you talking about?" Griselle flipped her gaze between the two of them.

"Unashamed worship. Which someone has forgotten how to do." Olivia's tone was dry.

"I just . . ." Trish sighed. " . . . want to be liked." Whoa, whoa, wait a minute, she hadn't intended to say that.

"By *those* girls?" Griselle stopped short of pointing at them, where they stood a few feet away.

"I know, I know, it's stupid. I don't know why, I just lost the desire." Trish hunched in her seat.

"Oh, honey." Olivia reached out to cover her hand with her golden-brown one. "You shouldn't be someone you're not."

"But the person I am isn't very nice." Trish stared at her feet. "Or rather, the person I was. When do people become made new?"

"In heaven," Olivia said.

"As soon as you accept Christ," Griselle said at the same time.

Trish blinked at them.

"Both." Olivia smiled.

Griselle cast a look around, then pulled down the neck of her navy turtleneck to expose a few inches of her collarbone.

Except Griselle's collarbone was covered in a riot of color. Tattoos. And a piece of a rather dirty word.

She pushed her neckline back in place. "I understand about the person you were. Are."

Trish couldn't talk. Sweet, perfect Griselle had a cuss word tattooed on her shoulder.

"I left my mom's church because I couldn't stand how people treated me. Not badly," Griselle hastened to add when Olivia opened her mouth. "Just so overly *concerned*."

I feel like a prostitute. Trish could think it in her head but not say it. *Not just because of Kazuo, but all the other guys I slept with, too.*

"Jesus set us free." Griselle grasped Trish's other hand. "Remember that even if you don't feel like it."

Prostitute. "I don't fit in—"

"Honey, be transparent, and the ones who matter will fold you in." Olivia squeezed her hand.

"That, or you recognize real quick who won't." Griselle pursed her mouth.

They meant to be reassuring, but Trish wasn't ready yet to give or receive love. It was easy to just be friendly, to get used to this new community of people.

At some point, she'd know what part of the old Trish was acceptable here.

EIGHTEEN

The smell assailed her as she walked in. A combination of urine, vomit, applesauce, and bleach. The bleach reassured her.

Old person smell. Nothing else quite like it.

No, that was mean. Was she getting cynical? Shouldn't she be turning into someone nicer? Someone God would actually like?

Christina, the director of the church outreach program at Katsu Towers, guided Trish through the sign-in at the front desk and upstairs to the third-floor rec room.

"Hi, Mr. Amberley." Christina had a perky smile for the man sitting in a wheelchair and staring into space. Or at least, down the length of the hallway.

Trish didn't speak until they'd gotten out of earshot. "Does he hear you?"

"Does it matter?"

Good point.

They entered a large room with huge picture windows. Several elderly residents did various activities, some reading, some playing board games or cards, and a large contingency of old women crowded around the TV set.

"Go around and say hi. If they don't want to talk to you or don't respond, don't take it personally. Hi, Mr. Lee." Christina turned to talk to a man near the window drawing on a pad of paper.

Trish wandered closer to the group near the TV. What were they watching? It wasn't English. It sounded sort of like Japanese but not quite. She had to tiptoe to peek between the gray heads clustered together.

On the tube, a gorgeous young Asian woman gave a resounding slap to an equally good-looking young Asian man.

The audience — the live one — erupted into cheers and cackles.

The young woman spat a line of the not-Japanese foreign language at the man, then stormed out of the room.

The audience clapped as she slammed the door.

"What is this?" Trish squinted at the TV.

"K-drama." One woman in a wheelchair looked at Trish as if she were mentally unstable.

"K-what?"

"Korean soap opera, dear." A woman with dark hair and very long white roots sat on Trish's other side and gestured to the TV set.

"You all speak Korean?" Most of the women were Asian, but some were Caucasian, and one was Hispanic.

An Asian woman with a red sweater tittered. "Of course not. We read the subtitles."

The TV had a commercial on. Trish hadn't even noticed the subtitles earlier. The show came back on, but it was the ending credits and a sneak peek at the next episode, which involved a lot of beautiful women and handsome men. Several ladies sighed, and the group started to break up.

"That's it?"

"There's another show we watch that airs tomorrow." The red sweater woman clapped her hands. "That one has the cutest doctor—"

"Do you think they'll arrest Hyun-Ki?" One woman brought her hand to her chest. "How awful that would be."

"He did it! What are you talking about?"

"He did not! It looks like he did, but I think he was set up."

"I think that mysterious woman in blue set him up."

"But why would she do that?"

Trish helped one woman to her feet so she could get into her walker. "You ladies are really into this."

"Oh, only some of us." The woman jerked her head toward the red sweater woman. "Last night, she wouldn't take a call from her son. Said he knew better than to phone her between eight and nine."

Trish giggled.

"You laugh at me, but you're jealous." Red Sweater gave an arch smile. "I'll think fondly of you all when I'm on my K-drama cruise next month."

"Oh, you." "Listen to her talk." "She'll probably get sick on the boat."

"K-drama cruise?" Trish wasn't sure she really wanted to know.

"It's rather interesting." The woman maneuvered her walker. "They take you to the island where they film several of the soap operas."

"Do you get to meet actors?"

"No, I don't think so. Although Millie went on a K-drama cruise last year and got an autographed picture of one of the actors. She treats it like it's an Academy Award."

"Come sit down, dear." Red Sweater gestured to a seat where several of them had re-gathered. "What's your name?"

"Trish." She was beginning to feel distinctly guilty for assuming the people in this place were just cheerful but quiet Alzheimer's and dementia patients. Plus, she'd enjoyed hearing about the K-dramas way too much. She was supposed to be following rule number two, tell others about Christ. Here was a perfect opportunity. "So ladies, did you know that just as there are physical laws that govern the physical universe, so are there spiritual laws—"

"Are you married?" Red Sweater leaned forward in her seat.

"What? No." What a question. "Um, there are spiritual laws which govern—"

"Boyfriend?"

"No. Spiritual laws—"

"Are you lesbian?"

"*No.*" Man, get old enough and people feel entitled to ask anything.

"Good." Red Sweater sat back in her seat.

Uh, oh. Not a good sign. "What do you mean?"

"Oh, nothing. I'm Clara."

"Martha." "Sumiyo." "Eliana."

"Nice to meet you." She would forget their names in the next second.

One shriveled Asian woman sat nearby, not quite in their conversational circle. She scowled, not saying a word. How rude.

Clara leaned close to Trish. "She's deaf as wood. We don't even know her name."

"Ah." Trish smiled at the deaf woman, and the woman frowned back. She almost expected her to hiss and bare fangs. *Woke up on the wrong side of the coffin this morning, did we?*

"Are you coming back next week to watch with us?" Sumiyo (at least, she thought that was Sumiyo) asked. "You should come half an hour earlier so you can watch the whole show."

Oooh, goody. "Okay. I'll come at three-thirty."

"It's going to be a good episode. The doctor's estranged father is coming back into town. I think he's going to kill him."

"You're so melodramatic." Clara didn't quite roll her eyes, but if she'd been a few decades younger, she probably would have. "I don't think it's anything that bad."

"How would you know?"

"I'm president of Young-Soo's online fan club. I would be the first to know if they're going to cut him from the show."

"The actor has a fan club?" And this old woman was savvy enough to go online?

"Where's your keychain?" "Show her your keychain!" Both Sumiyo and Eliana flapped their hands at Clara, who smiled like a cat in the cream (or a rat in the stinky tofu).

She brandished her keychain, which didn't actually hold keys—just dozens of fobs all picturing the same Korean actor. Oh, he *was* a hottie. Did rule number one count if Trish was looking at a picture of someone she'd never meet?

Eliana pointed to one of the fobs. "When he was in San Francisco, my niece went to his hotel and waited in the lobby until he came out."

Can we say, stalker?

"She got a picture of him." Eliana sighed dreamily. "I had it blown up into a poster in my room."

"*My* nephew tapes every episode for me on his TiVo and burns it onto a DVD." The fourth woman—Martha?—lorded it over the others for a brief moment as they all looked *wasabi* green with envy.

"My son's father-in-law watches these too." Sumiyo leaned in close. "He bought the entire season—had it shipped from Korea—and it cost a hundred dollars per DVD."

Trish felt her tonsils wave in the breeze through her wide open mouth. "Shut *up*!"

All four women—with the exception of the nameless deaf one, who hadn't heard her—drew themselves up straight in their chairs. "What did you say?" Clara had turned as red as her sweater.

Oops. "Sorry, it's a figure of speech. It means, uh … 'no way,' or 'I can't believe it.'" Internet fan club notwithstanding, she had to remember these ladies weren't her coworkers or her cousins.

They relaxed. "You shouldn't use that term, dear. It's very disrespectful."

"I won't." At least not around them.

"Trish, time to go." Christina came up to their group. "Hi ladies." They nodded hello.

She turned to the deaf-as-wood woman and raised her voice. "HI DEBORAH!"

Deborah glowered and turned her head away. Trish wasn't sure she actually heard Christina, but at least now she knew her name.

"Huh? Who's Deborah?" Clara looked around.

"Bye, ladies." Trish rose.

"No, wait!" Clara reached out and grabbed her hand. Man, the woman had a grip like a falcon. "I want you to meet my nephew. He's coming in a few minutes." Clara beamed at her.

Oh, brother. She was as bad as Grandma. "That's so sweet, Clara, but I'm sure he has a girlfriend already—"

"No, he doesn't."

The other ladies nodded to affirm that yes, he was a single male under the thumb of the family matriarch, who obviously wielded power even from her assisted living facility.

"Maybe next time, then." Christina managed to yank Trish's hand out of Clara's death grip. "Bye!" They escaped.

"Thanks, Christina." Trish rubbed her bruised wrist. Clara had a superhuman grip on her like Grandma—maybe old age gave them manacles of steel?

"I didn't do you any favors, unfortunately."

"What do you mean? I avoided her nephew." They exited the building.

"This week. Next week, you can be sure he'll be here."

Oh, no. Well, maybe he won't be cute. What if he was boring? She'd have to sit and listen. Or maybe she could make an excuse to watch the K-drama with them. It seemed kind of interesting . . .

"Not only that." Christina sighed. "The other ladies will make sure their nephews, grandsons, and any other single men remotely attached to them by blood will be there."

Oh, brother.

She gave Trish a twenty-four-karat grin. "See you next week!"

NINETEEN

Trish had that same premonition — *Today is going to be a really bad day* — when she went to church on Sunday. It didn't help that she'd overslept and was racing to get to Sunday school on time.

Once again, the Sunday school coordinator, Mrs. Choi, met her at the door.

"Such a wonderful idea about bringing their pets." Mrs. Choi didn't quite look Trish in the eye when she spoke. "I know you'll make sure no one gets hurt?"

"Oh, of course."

"Excellent." Mrs. Choi hightailed it out of there when Trish opened the yellow door to the classroom.

The sound alone should have penetrated the walls to reach the sanctuary, but maybe the architects had been intelligent and put extra insulation in between the drywall. Next came the crashing wave of putridity that made her gag.

Cages lined the rainbow-colored walls, and a few more were outside the back door in the playground area. Some kids hovered protectively over their pets, others flitted from cage to cage to annoy the residents within. It didn't look like there were as many cages as children, so apparently some had forgotten, and some probably hadn't been allowed to bring Precious or FiFi to Sunday school.

Griselle's hair had become a bush again, but she lighted up when Trish came through the door. Then alarm flashed in her eyes. "No, Bobby, it's not time to leave — Trish, the door!"

She slammed it shut before Bobby squirmed past her legs on his attempted prison break.

"Sorry I'm late, I oversl—"

"At least you're here now." Griselle tried to smile, but it looked a bit more like a tortured death mask.

"Okay, everyone, sit down and we'll start show and tell."

The class took some time to assemble. Good—the more time they wasted, the less time each child had to show off their pets. The less show time, the less time said pets would be out of their cages.

"Who wants to go first?"

Hands shot into the air.

"Bobby, you go first."

Whines rose like a symphony, then abruptly stopped when Griselle waved her finger.

Wow. How'd she get that to work? The magic finger.

Bobby got up, went to his glass cage, and emerged with—

"This is Sammy, my snake."

"Oooh." "Aaaah."

Ewwwww. Trish tried to stealthily back away.

"He eats mice."

One girl shrieked and dove for her cage, where she wrapped her body around it. Hmm, one guess what her pet was. Trish had a vision of Sammy eating Mousey to the sound of wails and cheers.

Nope. Not while Trish had breath in her body and legs that ran faster than a snake.

"Thanks, Bobby. Next?"

Susie got up with a terrified kitten. "This is Kitty, my kitten."

These kids weren't too good on the originality scale.

"She eats mice, too." Susie crossed her eyes at Mouse Girl, who started to sob.

"Ah, thank you, Susie." Griselle had a pretty firm arm—she managed to manhandle Susie from the front of the room before she could wreak more havoc.

"Sara, you're next."

She snatched something from her cage, then hustled to the front of the room with it cupped in her hands. "This is Hammy, my baby Russian Dwarf hamster."

Where?

Ooooh, it was super tiny, fitting with room to spare in Sara's hand. Aw, what a cute little ball of fur—

"Eeek!" Sara jerked and dropped him.

Oh no. Poor guy, was he okay? Trish dove for the little waddling fuzzball.

"I'm bleeding!" Sara extended her hand to Griselle, where a river of red streamed down onto the carpet.

"What happened?" Trish cradled Hammy, who was only a little longer than her thumb, glad she'd gotten it before a child had accidentally stepped on it or—

"Yow!" A battery of stabs into her hand made her jerk it open. Hammy dropped right into a child's lap.

The hamster had bit her. Several times. And Trish was bleeding like Sara.

Hammy went on the rampage, taking a chunk out of the leg of the unfortunate girl he'd landed in. She screamed and kicked, sending him flying into another child's lap.

The boy picked him up.

"No, don't—!"

Too late. Hammy sliced at the kid's finger tendons. "Aaaaaah!" The boy shook his hand, but Hammy hung on.

Tenacious little bugger. Ignoring the blood dropping down her hand, Trish reached for the flapping hamster, but Hammy let go and flew into the crowd of children.

They'd figured out Hammy wasn't as cute as he seemed, and they scattered. Which would have been good except that they prevented Trish from reaching the child whose lap the attack hamster had fallen into, Matthew.

He picked it up.

"No, Matthew—"

A kid flew into Trish's legs, and she toppled to the floor. She almost landed on another child except she shoved her arms out like a push-up to prevent herself from doing a WWF body slam on the unsuspecting victim.

She crawled forward, getting kicked in the head and torso by screaming children, half of whom didn't even know what they were running from. *Must . . . get . . . Hammy . . .*

She reached Matthew. Who sat there calmly, smiling up at her with his shining dark eyes. He had a tiny prick of blood on his lip.

Hammy was gone.

No way. He didn't. He couldn't. His mouth wasn't big enough, was it? Granted, Hammy was very small. Also, Matthew had been a python lately and swallowing everything, but . . .

Matthew burped.

Griselle dropped to the ground beside them, blood smeared on her cheek. She stared at Matthew, then at Trish. "Oh, no."

"Oh yes."

"Maybe Hammy is around here somewhere . . ." Her gaze darted at the carpet around them.

"I don't hear any more shrieks of pain, do you?"

Griselle bit her lip.

"What's going on?" The male voice cut through the childish murmurs. Silence reigned, just like Griselle's magic finger.

"Spenser!" And Trish with her wide load sticking straight up in the air. Lovely. She scrambled to her feet so he wouldn't have to view it for longer than necessary. "Oh, close the door — !"

He shut it before Bobby made bail.

Griselle rose to her feet also, but she'd turned rather pale. Did she like Spenser or something? Not that Trish was jealous or anything. It wasn't like he'd be good date material for Trish, but she could see how he'd be a fun . . . well, amusing date for some other girl. Funny, some sharp pains had started dicing up her stomach.

"What are you doing here?" Trish tried to discreetly wipe the blood from her hand onto her jeans.

"I heard the screaming and came to see if it was serious."

"No, no problem." Trish stretched her mouth in what she hoped looked like a real smile. "Just a few excited kids. A few pets."

"Uh ..." Griselle gave her a swift kick to the calf.

"What?" she hissed.

"Hey, buddy, how're you doing?" He strode into the room, straight for Matthew. Aw, he was pretty good with kids. He must've thought Matthew was scared, and that was why he was sitting in the middle of a cleared floor with frightened children lining the walls.

He picked Matthew up. "What's this cut on his lip?"

"It's nothing. We'll tell his parents later." Ow, Griselle kicked her again.

He gave her a rather strange look. Actually, it was the kind of look of someone who knew something and was trying to decide if they were going to tell her or not. Trish didn't trust Spenser further than she could throw him. "What is it?" she asked.

"What's what?"

"Too late to look innocent. What's going on?"

Griselle was gnawing on her lip again. Oh, great. She was in on it, too. Trish hated being the odd man out.

Griselle was easier to lean on. She directed a sharp look at her. "What's going on?"

"Uh ..." She glanced nervously at Spenser, who bounced Matthew gently.

"*Spill, Griselle.*"

Spenser saved her. "Matthew's my son."

"What? Shut *up*!" Trish felt the floor drop out beneath her. Or maybe that was wishful thinking. Or maybe that was actually the bottom of her stomach. "You're — married?"

"Was." His mouth tightened a fraction — so slight, she almost didn't notice it. It was more like a hardening of his jaw, even as he smiled and joked with Matthew. *His son.*

Trish would never in a million years have suspected Spenser of having a child. Then again, she was constantly realizing she didn't know him very well. The way he cradled Matthew made him seem older and somehow softer, showing his tender side. It made him even more handsome ...

"Now you spill." His eyes had become fierce — Simba protecting his lion cub. "Why's he bleeding?"

"Uh ..."

Trish looked at Griselle, but she'd backed off a couple steps. "It was your idea, Trish."

"Traitor." Except it was true.

Matthew had started to squirm, so Spenser let him down. He straightened and crossed his arms, drawing himself up to his full height. Trish didn't exactly have a pair of stilettos on that could help even out the height difference.

"Well, you see, we had them all bring their pets to Sunday school."

"Gee, I'd never notice."

She glared. "Don't be a smarty-pants."

"Don't change the subject."

"Right. Well, Sara brought her hamster, whose name is Hammy. Was Hammy."

"Was?"

"Well, first let me say, the hamster was evil."

Sara let out a wail. "No he wasn't! Hammy was a good boy."

Trish rolled her eyes. "Hammy had teeth like a Black and Decker chain saw."

Griselle nodded so hard, her hair bobbed. "That's why some of the children have bites. Trish, too."

"You do?" His brows knit.

"It's nothing." She shoved her hand behind her back. The "nothing" had started to throb like a *katana* sword wound, but she wasn't about to let him know that. "Anyway, we were trying to protect the children."

"You didn't protect Matthew very well." His eyes had become fierce again.

"Hey, I told him not to pick up Hammy." Trish shoved a hand to her hip. "It's not my fault he didn't listen. And he obviously didn't get bitten very hard if he swallowed—uh …"

Spenser closed his eyes and squeezed the bridge of his nose with forefinger and thumb. "Let me guess. He ate the hamster."

"I'm sorry. I couldn't get to him in time. I was tripping over kids—"

"He's got the fastest hand-to-mouth in the west." He shot a pained look at his child.

Matthew laughed at his dad. "Yum!"

Ewww.

Spenser scratched his head. "Hamsters aren't poisonous, are they?"

"I don't think so."

He sighed. "I'll take him to the ER."

Matthew perked up. "Nurse Betty!"

Trish raised her eyebrows at Spenser. "Matthew knows the ER nurses by name?"

"More importantly, they know *him* by name."

Poor dad.

Griselle had started calming the children down, and Matthew came up to his father. His brow had clouded. "Daddy, I don't feel so good."

Trish and Griselle's eyes met across the room, mirroring each other's panic. "No! Not here!"

Spenser grabbed Matthew and took off. Trish ran to shut the door behind him, but not before Bobby finally squeezed through.

"Freedom!"

Trish scowled at the taillights in front of her. Her neck felt stiff, and she hunched over the steering wheel. Traffic never ceased to amaze, even on a Sunday—accidents in both directions on 85. A band of ruby lights ahead stretched alongside a chain of diamonds to her left.

In all the rush of the disastrous show-and-tell, she'd forgotten to find out who the church admin was so she could get her roommate want-ad put up on the bulletin board. She considered calling Spenser — no, he was probably at the emergency room with his orally-fixated heir.

Aiden? He'd know. She didn't have his number on her cell — she didn't think she had his number, period. She plugged in her Bluetooth wireless headset and commanded up Lex's number.

"Hey. I need Aiden's number."

"Why?"

"Don't sound so suspicious. Remember, I'm a new person —"

"Okay, okay. You're becoming devoted to God —"

"*Wholly* devoted to God."

"Wholly devoted to God. So why?"

"I need the admin's number from church."

"Oh. Here's Aiden's number."

Trish dialed and got his voice mail. "Hi, it's Trish. I forgot to find out the admin's number. I need to post a want ad for a roommate. Can you call me back? I don't have a church directory or anything yet. Thanks."

The thought of another roommate like Marnie made something bubble in her stomach, but she couldn't pay the rent alone and the lease had four months before it ended. If only she could screen applicants. *Please submit résumé and references . . .*

Single career female needs female roommate for two-bedroom apartment in Mountain View, near Castro Street and CalTrain station . . .

Trish reached her exit and flew onto the off-ramp, but jammed on her brakes at the mass of red taillights. What was up? Another accident?

A fire truck roared past with no lights or siren. Great. More traffic, and it was over so she couldn't even rubberneck the dramatic wreck.

Trish's landlord surprised her by approaching as she turned into her parking stall. She hauled herself out of the RAV4.

He spoke without preamble in his heavy Taiwanese accent. "Your roommate, she smoke."

Trish's chest tightened as if someone pressed against it, trying to ram her breastbone into her spine.

He wasn't finished. "She smoke much. Fire alarm!" His face flushed bright red and his breath heaved in his distress.

Trish hoped he wouldn't have a heart attack right in front of her. "She's moving out—"

"Big fire! Living room all burnt!"

Oh no! Trish's legs slipped out from under her. She sagged against the truck. The fire truck she had seen . . .

The landlord grabbed her limp wrist and slapped a folded piece of paper in her hand.

"You leave! Tomorrow!"

TWENTY

I'm homeless. Mom is going to have a cow.
Then Grandma's going to have a heart attack.

Then maybe Dad will have one, too ... No, that's really mean. Plus he's been taking good care of Mom, and apparently not seeing any other women the past few weeks.

But regardless, Mom is going to have a massive cow.

A spasm twitched through the hand holding the pipettor, and Trish discharged cells all over the sterile surface of the cell culture hood. She grunted in frustration. She stopped herself from smacking her forehead with her other gloved (biohazard-contaminated) hand.

Trish reached for a paper towel and the bottle of ethanol, trying to focus on work, desperate to make yesterday go away. Marnie's hysterical screeching, the charred, stench-filled living room, the eviction notice in her hand.

She had to find another place to live. Marnie and her furball had unfairly been able to move into her uncle's home this morning (and even Walnut Creek wasn't far enough away for Trish's taste). Trish wasn't so lucky. Her parents' house in Morgan Hill lay an hour and a half away — a horrendous commute, and too small for her, besides. They didn't even have an extra bedroom, so Trish would have to sleep on the sofa. When they bought it, Mom had protested the size, but Trish suspected Dad wanted someplace small after she moved out to *prevent* her from ever moving back in.

When Mom found out, she would freak. Coming off a heart attack, even though she was doing better according to their last phone conversation—not a good idea. Even if she were healthy, Mom would lament and Trish would never hear the end of it: *How can I ever face my friends at the Buddhist temple when they find out you've been kicked out of your apartment? Oh, the shame ...*

It was useless to reason that no one would find out unless Mom told them, but that was beside the point. If one person found out, the entire tight-knit Japanese community would know within forty-eight hours.

At Mitsuwa, the Japanese market: *Did you hear about Marian Sakai's daughter? She got thrown out of her apartment.*

At Gombei, the Japanese restaurant: *Did you hear the news? Marian Sakai's daughter burned down her apartment.*

At Shuei-Do, the Japanese mochi shop: *Did you hear? Marian Sakai's daughter got arrested for arson.*

Uncle Charley would call and demand, "What's this I hear? Marian's daughter broke out of jail?"

Maybe Trish could put off telling her parents until she found a new place.

Focus. She had to stop thinking about Mom. She needed a roof over her head. Where could she go? Her company sat in the middle of an old, wealthy residential neighborhood of Palo Alto where she would have to search hard to find a cheap apartment. She could look further north or south, but she had to limit her search area or else face more than a one hour commute each way.

Wait, rule number three—she was not going to forget rule number three again.

Where can I call to reserve a moving van?

Rule number three—persevere. Rely on God.

Oh, reminder to self: go through the Receiving dock and find cardboard boxes.

Okay, let's persevere. Wasn't there more than that ...?

I wonder if I can borrow Jenn's new truck instead of hiring a moving van.

If she persevered, she would achieve undivided devotion to God. She would regain her chastity. She would be a better person. She would get her MDiv. God would send the perfect man to her.

Okay, granted, her love life seemed pretty trivial in comparison to her homeless status. Trish blew out a gusty sigh. Maybe she ought to read her Bible.

She finished seeding the cells. After sliding them into the incubator, she left the lab and headed for her office. She had stowed an extra Bible in her desk drawer somewhere.

She alighted on 2 Corinthians chapter four. "We have this treasure in jars of clay ..." Paul described strength and fortitude in trials, and how that power came from God, not from within himself. Perseverance meant relying on God's help through the hard times, whatever happened.

Reading the verses calmed her. The niggling worry of moving van rentals intruded as she flipped the page, but it disappeared as she read a few verses down.

Paul described his trials as "light and momentary troubles."

She needed to put things in perspective. She faced homelessness, not being fed to the lions in Rome.

"So we fix our eyes not on what is seen, but on what is unseen." Translation: *Stop having hysterics, babe, and trust in God.*

Okay, Lord, I'm going to actually rely on you this time — woo hoo! — unlike that whole miserable Marnie thing. Thanks for these verses. They make me feel better.

Please give me wisdom about what to do now. Please help me not go all crazy about stuff that isn't important. Oh, and help me to have the right attitude.

And please, please, please help me find housing.

Spenser was perfectly groomed to woo Trish. Or annoy her. Or both.

He parked his sports car in the shade, then did the confident Hong-Kong-film-star-swagger from the parking lot into the building. He entered the office and stopped dead in his tracks.

"What's with the boxes?"

Trish glanced up at him. Her face paled, and she gave a nervous smile. "Um ... temporary storage?"

Spenser hefted a box with something clinking in it and removed it from his desk. "This isn't a public storage facility."

"It's only until I find a new place."

"What's wrong with your old one?" He could barely squeeze into his chair.

"It's ... um ... unavailable at the moment."

He gave her a long, hard look.

She caved. "My ex-roommate burned it down yesterday."

"What?"

"The windows exploded out, and the living room is completely trashed. Luckily it didn't get to the bedrooms."

"Where are you going to stay? Here?"

"No!"

"Then where?"

"Uh ... someplace temporary." Her eyes drifted to a bag where an old sleeping bag peeped out.

"You can't stay here."

"It's only for a few days. I've stayed overnight plenty of times for timed dosing studies."

"Someone might need to move into one of those desks." Spenser flung his hand out toward the other end of the room, but it collided with a box that clanked and rocked on its precarious perch atop a table lamp.

"Oh, come on. Who's gonna need the space? Our department is at its max in head count, so we won't be hiring anytime soon."

Spenser, calm down. He'd had fun annoying her these past weeks, but after seeing her on Sunday, he realized that while he'd originally pursued her to stick it to Kazuo, he liked Trish for herself. She was fun to banter with, and she'd handled the Sunday school class well considering she'd been up against a psycho attacking hamster.

And Matthew was fine. More importantly, he'd babbled about Miss Sakai on the ride home from the ER.

So now, he wanted to see Trish smile.

Remember, you are Chow Yun-Fat.

With lazy, half-lidded eyes and a conciliatory smile, Spenser walked around the cubicle wall — more like waddled through the sea of boxes — to lean against her desk, close to Trish's chair. "You're right. Sorry for complaining."

Her eyes flew to his face in shock, then flitted away, darting to her monitor, keyboard, lap, calendar — anywhere but at him. He saw her chest lift as she inhaled, but she took her time exhaling.

These were all very good signs.

"Do you need help mov —"

Her cell phone blipped with a single, ear-piercing chime, and she twisted her chair away from him.

But as she turned, the edge of her seat clipped his knee. A spear of pain shafted him all the way to his hip. *Stabbing, throbbing, aching, flaming, sizzling . . .* With an inarticulate moan, he crumpled to the floor. He landed on his uninjured knee while his hands cupped the other. Another moan leaked from his mouth as he folded in half. His forehead touched the floor, like he was bowing toward Mecca.

"Oh, Spenser, oh, are you all right? What happened? How did —"

Trish's voice faded into a choking gurgle as Spenser heard a firm footfall behind him.

"Um . . . hello?" The higher pitched but masculine voice made Spenser freeze.

No.

With effort, Spenser uncoiled and flipped over to sit on the floor. His hand grasped the edge of Trish's desk, and he hauled his body up. The sudden rush of blood caused his knee to feel like it would burst.

Kevin Clark stood in the doorway. Yes, Keanu Reeves, "shoulders out to there" Kevin. Dorky, skinny Kevin, whom Trish had raved about only last week.

Great.

Kevin shifted the box in his hands. "I got notice today that I'm transferring to your department. They want me to work on your high-profile project."

Trish glanced around at her stacked boxes and winced. "I'll clear space for you right away."

"That would be much appreciated." The lightest hint of sarcasm tinged his voice. "I also need a workbench in your lab."

"Oh, I'll show you where you can set up." Trish pulled him out the door — almost before he could drop his box — and down the hallway.

Spenser glowered at their backs. So much for "not looking." All Keanu had to do was show up and she was climbing all over him.

He was a little disappointed in her. Despite the fact Trish had seemed attracted to him, she hadn't given in to any of his overtures. Granted, he'd had rotten timing in some cases.

Spenser shoved a box with his foot before remembering his knee. With a yelp, he collapsed into his chair.

As soon as her computer clock hit twelve noon, Trish whipped out her cell phone and dialed.

"Valley Bible Church, this is Kat. How can I help you?" The voice sounded young — not an older woman.

"Hi Kat. My name is Trish Sakai, and I'm a new member."

"Oh, cool. Welcome."

"Thanks. I want to put a want ad on the church bulletin board. I need housing."

"Oh, no problem. What do you want the ad to say?"

"'Single Christian female needs housing . . .'" Yadda, yadda, yadda. She rattled off her cell number and email address.

"Gotcha. You moving out of your parents' house?" Kat's tone was conversational.

"Actually, I, uh … well, my apartment sort of had a fire."

"What? Are you serious?"

"It was my roommate!" She had to make that clear. Otherwise, no one would want to live with a potential pyromaniac.

"Oooh. Bummer! Well, you might get housing quicker if I sent out an email to the church e-distribution list."

"The church has a distribution list?"

"Oh yeah. I'll put you on it, too."

"That would be great. Thanks." She hung up.

Trish dialed a number from her Internet search this morning. "Hello, I'm calling about the apartment for rent on California Avenue—"

"Oh, it's already been let."

"But the ad appeared online this morning—"

"I decided to let it to my brother-in-law."

She resisted the urge to growl at the apartment manager and hung up.

She dialed another number. "Hello, I'm calling about the apartment for rent on Blossom Avenue."

The man went on to describe a large apartment that sounded pretty good.

Trish tried to hide her excitement. "Can I come by to see it tonight?"

"Sure. Oh, I should mention, the rent price published in the ad is wrong."

Something heavy like wet snow settled on her chest. "So what is it?"

"It's missing a zero."

What? "That's out of my price range."

"Yeah, lots of people have said that." His woebegone tone didn't make her feel sorry for him.

She rang off and dialed another number. "Hi, I'm calling about the apartment. The ad wasn't very clear about where it is."

"Oh, it's off of Greenway and Hamilton."

That sounded familiar ... wait a minute. "Greenway? Where that kid got shot last week in a gang war?"

"Yeah. But the neighborhood is really very safe."

Riiiight. I'd love to live in your 'hood. "Ah ... maybe not—"

"At least come see the apartment. You'll see the area—"

"Lemme-think-about-it-thanks-bye." She hung up.

A whining groan puffed out of her mouth. Her last lead, in gang territory. What was she going to do now?

A rap sounded at the doorway and deep male tones rang, "Trish?"

She looked up into Keanu—er, Kevin Clark's wide smile and blue eyes. Woo-woo. Oh my, he was simply gorgeous. Although a little ... prissy in the way he stood there in the doorway. With his hand on his hip, as if he were striking a pose. No, that was ridiculous. "Hi, Kevin. Finished setting up your lab bench?"

"Yes. Let's go out for lunch today. You'll like this new California Mediterranean restaurant that opened on San Antonio Road. You'll want the salad—it's fabulous, with feta and three types of olives."

She blinked in surprise. Oh she would, would she? "I don't really like olives—"

"They also have wood-fired pizzas. I think my favorite is the goat cheese one, but the rosemary chicken comes a close second. You'll like the rosemary chicken. Girls always do."

She crossed her arms in front of her chest. "Oh really?" Why had she never noticed the way he seemed to make decisions for everyone around him?

Well, it might have to do with the fact that she'd had exactly two conversations with the man, each about a minute long, and both about assay reagents. She couldn't lie—both times she'd had a hard time keeping track of the conversation because she'd been daydreaming over his handsome face. She'd never known he was a metrosexual under all that eye-gazing goodness, now a little tarnished. It seemed rather paradoxical, Keanu on *Queer Eye.*

"They also serve some fabulous homemade soups."

Was that the second time he'd used the word *fabulous*? She didn't think she'd ever heard a guy use that word except on reruns of *Will and Grace*.

"I had the mushroom cream the other week and it was their best yet. But you won't care for it. It was more earthy-tasting, and girls don't like earthy."

"I love mushrooms—"

"But you'll like their Cherries Jubilee. I prefer their Grand Marnier soufflé myself, but you won't like that ..."

She sat mute as he babbled on, wondering how to make him leave. Or at least stop talking. How could she communicate with a guy who never listened to her? She slashed through his tirade about romaine versus iceberg lettuce. "Kevin, I'm very busy—"

"—and they use the outer leaves, too. Travesty."

"Please leave—"

"—but they wash the lettuce thoroughly, I'll give them that much—"

"I'm going to check email." And she did, while he rattled on about organic baby carrots. She contemplated what he'd do if she raised her Nine West boot, laid it on his immaculate khakis, and gave a good shove.

"So are you ready? Trish?"

"Huh?" She turned back to him. He was done with the dissertation on cold-pressed flaxseed oil?

"Shall we go?" He gestured toward the door.

"Go where?"

He cleared his throat and spoke with exaggerated care. "Lunch."

What conceit. She'd had quite enough of his conversation, thank you very much. Guiltily, she realized that if she'd been following rule number one, this wouldn't be happening. So what if he looked good in his biking outfit? He had the personality of Prince Humperdinck from *The Princess Bride*, and she wouldn't be subjected to it now if she hadn't been sending out flirty vibes. "Sorry, Kevin, not interested."

He stood frozen for a minute, as if he didn't believe she'd refused him. "Why not? What's wrong with you?"

With *her*? "Nothing!"

"Well then, why wouldn't you want to get to know me?"

She was going to do him bodily harm. Except that was sort of illegal and she liked these new slacks she had on and didn't want to get blood on them.

An email from "Church Administrative Assistant" appeared on her screen. One quick glance jerked her upright in her chair. She grabbed the phone and dialed. "Kat, you mistyped on the email."

Her blatant disregard of his monologue got through to Kevin. "Trish, it's extremely rude of you—"

"What did I mistype?" Kat asked.

He mimicked holding a phone handset—"to call someone while I'm standing here—"

She glanced at her computer. "You wrote, 'Single Christian female needs housing after burning her apartment down.'"

He pressed a hand to his chest—"since I was carrying on a conversation with you first—"

"Oops. I'll send a retraction," Kat promised.

He circled his hand in the air—"but I suppose I'll excuse you—"

"Thanks, Kat."

Kevin glanced at the ceiling—"because you may not realize it's a social *faux pas*—"

Kat giggled. "What a way to gain a reputation in your new church, huh?"

He gestured in her direction—"since you are a foreigner and all—"

"You can say that again. Bye." Trish rounded on Kevin. "What did you call me?"

Her fire-breathing roar startled him. He unwisely repeated, "A foreigner?"

Trish drew a sharp breath and swelled her chest like the dragon in Disney's *Sleeping Beauty*. "I am a third generation Japanese American, you ignoramus!"

Cultured, groomed Kevin had obviously never been called an ignoramus in his entire life. The blood drained from his face — which had probably had a mud facial in the past week — leaving him the same color as his spotless cream Oxford shirt. His lips opened and closed before he remembered to purse them shut, and his eyes bugged out, making him look distinctly chihuahua-like.

He sniffed, aiming his nose toward the ceiling, and peered down at her like a monarch upon a peasant. Then he flounced out of her office.

Maybe she shouldn't have alienated him. After all, she did have to work with him now. Although to be honest, it would actually be a relief if he gave her the silent treatment or something like that. The man could *not* shut up.

This added more stress to her already considerably stressful life. Well, she had broken rule number one with Kevin earlier. Blatantly, despite her protests.

Was this God punishing her some more?

Very early Tuesday morning, Trish walked to the park near work and shivered on a bench beneath a few redwood trees. Flowers dotted the cement walkways that cut through the grass, still silvered by dew except where the early sunlight made it evaporate in steamy wisps. Occasional finches and sparrows flitted by, but the only other people were a few volleyball players enjoying an outdoor doubles match. Two tall Caucasian men with gorilla arms against a tall Asian guy and a Caucasian woman at least as tall as her partner. The Asian had a narrow but dashing face while his body corded with muscles, but Trish didn't feel even a twinge of interest.

She heaved a long, slow sigh. Who cared about guys when she was homeless? The gang-territory apartment was looking better and better.

Maybe she should suck it up and pay for an expensive apartment to buy her time to find something better. She wasn't poor, but she hadn't been scrimping and saving for a house like Lex had, and she didn't have a generous cushion in the bank. How long would she be able to live with rent that ate up four-fifths of her monthly income?

She could try to squeeze her stuff into her parents' tiny home, but she didn't think she could survive the commute — three hours every day. Plus she didn't want to have to move in with her adulterous rat fink father, on whom she'd wasted thirty years of unctuous adulation.

(Oooh, unctuous adulation. Who said reading romances didn't make a girl smarter?)

She hadn't talked to anyone about her dad since the news had put her mother in the hospital. She needed to do *something* at some point, but how to pick a good time to confront her parents about something that might tear their marriage apart?

The housing in the Bay Area was supposed to be a renter's market right now, but yesterday had turned up nothing. Why the sudden drought? Wasn't God going to come through for her?

Her cell phone pierced through the quiet, making the Asian guy miss a spike. "Hello?"

"Is this Trish? This is Mrs. Choi, from church."

She was going to be fired from teaching. She'd sent Griselle into a nervous breakdown. One of the parents was suing the church. "Everything okay with Sunday school?"

"Oh, yes, dear. This isn't about that. Are you still looking for housing?"

Trish shot up from the bench. "Yes!"

"Well, my nephew George — I don't know if you know him, he doesn't go to our church anymore. He bought a house in San Jose, but he decided to go on a yearlong overseas mission. He left for training in Missouri and asked me to find someone to rent his home. To pay the mortgage, you understand."

She crossed her fingers. "Where in San Jose, and how much?"

"Near the border of Los Gatos, near Camden Avenue and 85. But the rent is a bit expensive . . ." She named a price.

Trish broke into a frenzied happy dance in the middle of the park. A wiggly terrier barked at her, and its owner tugged it away, casting her a nervous glance.

"Mrs. Choi, that's quite a reasonable price. Are you sure that's correct?" *You didn't forget a zero or anything like that, did you?*

"Oh no, it's correct. George sold some stock and paid a large down payment, I believe. That's the amount of his monthly mortgage payments."

Trish could have kissed George. Wonderful, financially responsible young man. Should she take it, sight unseen? Well, it was George's house or the 'hood. Trish didn't know San Jose very well, but Los Gatos reeked of affluence. It was also about thirty minutes from work. Even if she didn't like the house, she at least had a place to stay while she looked for other housing. "Mrs. Choi, I'd love to move in. As soon as possible."

"Oh. Why don't you move in tomorrow? Here's the address . . ." It was off of Highway 85. Better and better. "I'll meet you at the house tomorrow. Around noon?"

"Yes, thanks, Mrs. Choi."

Trish hung up with her heart still pounding with adrenaline. She had so much to do. She needed to call Jenn, who had promised to let her use her brand-spankin' new SUV—Trish had only had to bully her a *little*—and to help her move. She hadn't told her mother about anything—Marnie, the fire, the eviction—so she needed to break the news to her today. *Oh joy.*

But at least Trish had a place to stay. *Thank you, God. I'm sorry I ever doubted you.*

"Venus, I love you, but you're taking up valuable car space." Trish leaned against the open passenger side window of Jenn's SUV when they drove into her company's parking lot.

Venus motioned back with her head. "Lex brought her car, too."

Oh, good. She turned her head to see Lex drive up in the used Toyota Camry she'd bought last year. While it wasn't new, it was still ten years younger than her last klunker. Since Lex had driven, Trish supposed it was better that Venus take up car space than try to help move her stuff in her little sporty convertible.

Trish was very glad no one came to work that Saturday morning to witness the four cousins carrying boxes out the back door of Valley Pharmaceuticals. She'd stored her futon bed in Venus's living room, and she didn't have as many boxes as she thought. There was room to spare in Jenn's truck, Trish's little RAV4, and Lex's Toyota.

"Why don't we put everything into two cars and drive together?" Venus leaned a hip against Jenn's truck.

Jenn put a box into her trunk. "Let's leave Lex's car."

"No, can't." Trish stuck a box into the truck. "Security would tow it."

"Well, then, let's leave your car. They won't tow that." Venus moved to remove a box from Trish's backseat.

They crammed the SUV and Lex's car, with just enough room to spare for Trish to ride with Jenn and Venus.

"And we're off!" She trailed her arm out the backseat open window as they headed out of her company parking lot, Lex's car trailing behind them.

"Hey, you guys!"

"What's that?" Trish tried to lean forward, but the lamp on the middle console nearly took her eye out. "That sounds like Lex."

She managed to shove the lamp aside and saw Venus lifting a walkie-talkie to her mouth. "We're here, Lex." Venus turned her head toward her. "Aiden gave her his walkie-talkies when he heard we were caravanning to your new digs."

"Oh. That was smart." Trust a guy to think of something practical like that.

"Hey!" Lex's voice crackled over the walkie-talkie. "Ask Trish about her mom."

Venus reached back between the lamp and a box of kitchen appliances to hand the walkie-talkie to Trish.

"Uh . . . hello?"

"So how's your mom?" Lex asked.

Trish put the walkie-talkie close to her mouth. "She's okay. She almost looks like she's back to normal, except she looks a little tired sometimes."

"How's your dad?" Jenn asked from the front.

Trish didn't answer immediately. The thought of him still made her stomach gurgle. Or maybe that was the breakfast burrito she ate this morning.

"So how's your dad?" Lex asked through the walkie-talkie.

"He's fine, I guess." Then she realized she had forgotten to press the button, and she had to repeat it for Lex. This was just a weird conversation.

"Did you hear any more about him and Alice?" Lex asked.

"No."

"Did you talk to him about it?" Venus turned to look back at her.

"Are you kidding me? He's my father, and he's Asian. We've never had a deep, serious conversation in my life."

Jenn sighed. "Not all Asian men are uncommunicative, you know."

"Yeah, well, my father is. He made Mom give me the sex talk — which I totally didn't understand because Mom kept not finishing her sentences, she was so embarrassed — and when he didn't like my boyfriends, he always made Mom talk to me rather than telling me himself."

"He does love you, though." Jenn sighed again, and Trish's annoyance dimmed as she remembered Jenn's heartache at the sporadic visits from her father after her parents' divorce a few years ago. And Venus's dad was cold and aloof, giving his approval sparingly — at least Trish's father had always been warm and welcoming to her and her friends.

"I can't talk about it with Mom when she's still so fragile."

The walkie-talkie crackled. "Have you seen him since then?"

"No, just talked with him on the phone. We always talk about Mom and keep it short."

"Maybe he and your mom are working it out themselves." Jenn twisted around to check behind her as she switched lanes.

Venus snorted. "Do you honestly believe they're talking about it?"

"Well, he's been really attentive to Trish's mom. It's not just guilt. That does say something."

"That's true."

Trish wanted to believe it and yet she was afraid to hope.

Silence reigned in the car except for Trish giving directions every few minutes. Finally Jenn asked, "How's your MDiv thing going?"

"I've been doing a lot of volunteer work lately." Like helping young children swallow hamsters and watching Korean soap operas. "In a few weeks, I'm going to ask people for references. Then I can finish the application form and send it in."

"See, Venus? She's really serious about it." Jenn sounded satisfied.

"Well, she still hasn't done it, so you haven't won yet."

"Excuse me, I'm right here. You bet on me?" Trish shoved the lamp further aside. She could see the outline of Venus's cheek, which had reddened.

"We didn't exactly bet on you ..."

"I'm sure you'll do it." Jenn exited the freeway. "Your motives are different this time—you're not just looking for something new to do."

"Turn left, then go straight down Camden past two stoplights." Trish re-read her notes, scribbled down when Mrs. Choi had given her the directions. She sat back in her cramped seat. Were her motives different? She hadn't really thought about them very much when she first started doing the whole MDiv thing. Well, actually, she'd wanted to prove to her cousins she was serious. But hadn't she also wanted to prove it to herself?

"Okay, turn right here." Her heart pounded as she drove down the quiet, tree-lined street. Jenn let out an envious, "Ooo, what a neighborhood."

Beautiful houses paraded down the block. Although small in size and a bit old, all of them flaunted manicured lawns and preened with the sharpness of conscientious care.

"Okay, turn left here."

The side street bore houses not quite as well-kept, but still respectable. Oh, except for that hideous house at the end of the block ...

Ominous premonition tugged at her. Her gut quivered and her throat tightened. *Please don't tell me...*

They came to a halt in front of the dilapidated wreck. "Number 5271." Trish wanted to howl.

Paint peeled from the siding in long jagged strips. Waist-high weeds crowded the front yard, and crawlers spilled into the cracked sidewalk where an ancient tree drooped dead branches over the street. Weeds dripped from the rain gutters, and a flat basketball slumped on the roof. Oil stains lay like bombing practice targets on the driveway, while the garage door cracked open at the bottom. Trish doubted it would open at all.

They parked on the street and climbed out of the cars. To reach the front door, they swam through the weeds on stepping stones drowned in the sea of vegetation. Cobwebs clothed a small, dingy front window and the rusted screen door next to it.

Lex pulled a handful of weeds and swept the cobwebs from the window. They peeked through gaping holes in the curtain but couldn't see anything. A twist to the doorknob confirmed the lock worked.

Trish stumbled back to the truck and sagged against it. She felt like Cinderella, radiant in her new gown on the night of the ball, entering the palace ... to find everyone had gone home already.

They went back to the cars. She wanted to drip down the side of the truck, but Jenn rubbed her shoulder. "Cheer up, Trish. It's only temporary until you find something else."

"I don't think I'll even be able to live here."

An old, gigantic town car pulled up to the house and Mrs. Choi emerged, stunned and dismayed. "Oh my goodness. Trish, I'm sorry, I didn't realize the house was like this."

Trish let out a sobbing whine. What could she do? Where could she go? Things couldn't get any worse.

Then a white Toyota Avalon coasted into the driveway. *Oh, no.* Trish's mother had shown up.

TWENTY-ONE

Mom, what are you doing here? You drove from Morgan Hill?" *Why did you have to be here to witness this, the supreme example of your progeny's stupidity and plain bad luck?*

"Your dad drove me into San Jose for the planning meeting for the *Obon* dance."

Oh, yes. There was the slimebucket now, sitting in the driver's side. "Are you okay to be doing so much so soon after your ... you know?" Trish had been going by how Mom dealt with the whole thing, and since Mom had yet to say the words "heart attack," Trish followed suit.

"Of course. I wanted to see your new place, considering you waited until yesterday to tell me."

Ah, no disgruntlement in her tone, not at all.

Trish's petite mother studied the ramshackle building. Her mouth wrinkled in distaste, and she raised a trembling hand to smooth down her hairdo—permed, ultra-short, and a mahogany color too brilliant to be real, although she'd been too ill to get it touched up so the gray roots were showing. "Is the address correct?" Desperation tinged her voice.

"Yes, Mom." This was the frosting on the cake. Why did her mother have to put in an appearance? Trish already felt abominably stupid in front of her cousins and Mrs. Choi. She didn't want to have to deal with Mom's rolled eyes and *Oh my goodness, what kind of* baka *daughter did I raise?* looks.

Mom would needle her until she discovered that Trish had taken the place sight-unseen, and then she'd never hear the end of it. *You didn't look at the place before you agreed? Triiiiiish!*

But Mom didn't say anything like that. "Maybe it looks better inside?" She gave an over-bright smile, but was so much more reserved than Trish expected that she almost fainted with relief.

"That's a good idea."

After introducing a wary Mom to an apologetic Mrs. Choi, Trish appropriated the key, marched up to the front door and hauled the creaky screen door aside. She fumbled to undo the bolt lock.

Venus sniffed. "Do you smell something funny?"

Trish paused. She smelled mold from the eaves, moss from the cracked stone front step, and a hay-ish scent from the weeds on the front lawn. "No." She shoved the door open with a shuddering groan.

The smell assaulted them in a *whoosh*. Mom scrambled back a few paces while Trish gagged, paralyzed in the doorway.

Decomp.

Trish recognized it from work, but it didn't make it any more bearable. She ducked sideways and stared hard at the weeds peeping from the base of the exterior wall. She wondered if she would hurl her lunch. Venus, who had been the next closest to the door, had retreated a few feet away, face white and eyes closed. Jenn, Lex, Mom, and Mrs. Choi had backed up almost to the sidewalk.

After a few minutes, the smell lessened enough to allow them to peek inside. The light streaming from the doorway revealed a long hallway. On the left was a rather nice archway into the living room, where various dark stains dotted the carpet.

They inched down the hallway into the kitchen, dimmed by curtains on the window over the sink. She shook them open in a cloud of dust. Sunlight filtered through the grimy glass to reveal walls patterned in faded avocado-green and burnt-orange. To top it off, the light illuminated the puke-yellow color of the curtains.

There was the culprit. The smell of decomposition came from an unfinished hamburger on the counter—George's trash, probably. Maggots overran the paper plate, and a few flies buzzed.

"Eeeewwww! Eweweweww!" Venus ran shrieking from the kitchen back into the hallway. Her screams warned her other cousins to stay back, although Mrs. Choi peeked in with trepidation.

Sissies. Trish called to Jenn, "Give me that extra plastic bag you always keep in your purse. And a few paper towels." She went to the window and flung open the glass. She managed to knock out the screen frame and started gently fanning it to get the flies and the smell out of the house.

Jenn dug into her gigantic tote bag purse and handed the bag and towels to Trish with an extended arm, not getting any nearer to the kitchen than she had to.

Trish got the plate and maggots into the bag. "Outta my way!" Women scattered. She headed down the hallway out the door.

She started when Dad met her at the front step. His face had screwed up tight. "What's that smell?"

Intent on her mission, Trish didn't have time to feel awkward. "Old hamburger. Out of the way, Dad."

"Oh. Give it here, I'll take care of it." He reached for the plastic bag.

"What? No, this is gross, Dad." It startled her, although it shouldn't. Dad always took care of the dead squirrels and birds in the backyard, the dog poop in the front yard, even that possum roadkill on the street when she'd been twelve years old.

It was just weird, seeing him be so *normal* when things should be horribly *abnormal* between them.

He snatched the bag out of her hand and headed toward the old garbage can on the side of the driveway. "Might be bleach under the sink," he threw over his shoulder.

Trish stood there a moment, watching him. Then she turned back into the house.

Sure enough, a dusty bottle of Clorox under the kitchen sink, along with a stiff sponge. Trish turned the faucet handle over the stained porcelain sink. The water flowed brown at first but lightened to clear. She wet the sponge.

Dusty beige tiles ran in rows on the countertop, and missing grout left dark rough crevices between. She poured some bleach over them and scrubbed with the sponge.

By this time, her mother ventured into the kitchen and grimaced at the grease-coated cabinets. Lex glanced up. "Eew."

Trish followed her gaze to the ceiling, stained dark and dotted with rounded blobs of grease. While they took in the horror over their heads, the kitchen light flickered on, blinding them.

"Moooom!"

"I wanted to see if the electricity was turned on."

"Oh, it should be." A smile trembled on Mrs. Choi's mouth. "Until he flew to Missouri a couple days ago, George lived here."

"He did?" Trish tossed the sponge into the sink.

At that moment, the refrigerator rattled violently like an old asthmatic man clearing his throat, then hummed. Lex opened the door before Trish could shout a warning.

Luckily, there wasn't anything living inside. A couple soda cans and a Hostess fruit pie—*George refrigerates his fruit pies?*—but the rubber sealing around the edge of the door caught Lex's attention. "What's this?"

They both peered at an icky brown substance slathered into the folds of rubber, cracked with age. Then a distinctive smell teased Trish's nose. "Peanut butter." They slammed the door shut.

Trish scurried from the kitchen but tripped over a lump in the hallway where the carpet bunched up. She slammed into the wall, and her hand came away sticky. She glared at the carpet. "Great, it's loose."

Venus glanced down. "Humph." She bent to look closer. "Hardwood floors underneath."

Trish didn't care. She hesitated at the door to the bedroom before easing it open.

George had camped out here. Literally. A North Face tent sat in the middle of a rather clean shag carpet, but there was no other furniture. The sliding closet doors revealed wire hangers dangling from a dusty, sagging wooden beam.

Emboldened by the marginally habitable room, Trish pushed open the bathroom door — which opened a foot before stopping with a *clunk* against the toilet. "You're kidding, right?" She squeezed in, but had to step into the open shower to close the bathroom door.

An old-fashioned sink crowded the toilet, with a teeny mirror that sported a narrow shelf. Talk about no counter space. She tugged at the mirror, relieved to open a rusty but somewhat clean medicine cabinet, although it missed one of its shelves.

She glanced down to inspect the linoleum — old, browned, and curling at the edges. But something small and white lay near the door and the edge of the shower. Trish stared hard, then realized that where the linoleum curled away from the wall, a mushroom grew in the floor.

A faint drip reached her ear. She folded in half to squint in the dimness under the toilet. She heard the *clunk* of the bathroom door against the toilet bowl and Jenn's voice. "Trish?"

"Is there a light switch near the door?"

The sound of fumbling, then the buzz of the light and a coughing chug from the electric bathroom fan. She found herself staring at a puddle of grimy water under the toilet. The drip came from a loose valve. She reached to see if she could tighten it, then heard a bloodcurdling screech.

Trish jerked and smacked her head against the toilet bowl. Rubbing, she peeked up at Jenn, then the ceiling.

At first she thought someone had painted a mural on the flat ceiling, using designs of dark-colored oil paints in subtle shades of grey, brown and forest green.

Then she realized it was a huge layer of mold.

She shrieked and leaped over the toilet, but her action slammed the door shut. The giant mold seemed to snicker threateningly. She screamed again and jumped into the shower so she could yank open the door. She shimmied out of the bathroom.

She and Jenn cried and clung to each other for a moment. Still panting, Trish turned when her mom called her from the door to the garage.

The stale airless smell enveloped her at the same time as the cool dimness, but the crack at the bottom of the slightly open garage door shone a narrow strip of white. At a flick of the light switch, a bare bulb buzzed to life. A cockroach scuttled away, and she noticed dusty cobwebs, dead leaves and tiny black pellets along the walls.

Venus noticed them too. "Ew, rats."

"But the smell in here is stale." Mom snapped off the light. "They may be old, and the rats might be gone."

"Let's hope so."

"I'm so embarrassed." Mrs. Choi wrung her hands. "If you don't mind staying here while you look for a new place, I won't charge rent."

Trish ran her eye over the dingy walls, into the danger-zone kitchen, and glared at the closed bathroom door. But she could use George's tent in the bedroom. She could bathe at the showers at work. As for the toilet ... well, the green monster was only partially over the toilet, so if she had to, she could sneak in, do her business, and sneak out without disturbing it.

"Thanks, Mrs. Choi." She didn't really have much choice — she was friends with the security guys at work, but they couldn't turn a blind eye on boxes in her office any longer. They'd transported the boxes here, and she had no where else to put them. "The only thing is my futon bed." No way was she putting it inside this house.

"Why don't you run it over to our home?" Trish's mom raised her penciled eyebrows as if to say, *Isn't that the obvious solution?*

"My bed isn't going to fit in the house." Not that it fit all that well in the puny living room at Venus's condo. She'd used that menacing growl of hers as she made Trish promise to have the bed out in a week.

"You can put everything in the garage, and we'll park the cars in the driveway until you find a place."

Her mother's calm voice and sensible suggestion eased Trish's worries. "Thanks, Mom."

"Why don't you all come on over now and stay for dinner? I made chicken *hekka*."

"Yummmm." Lex and Trish both smacked their lips.

At Mrs. Choi's inquiring look, Trish translated, "Japanese country-style chicken stir-fry that's actually kind of soupy."

Jenn rolled her eyes and turned to head outside. "Trish, you could make *sashimi* sound complicated."

She followed her cousin down the hallway. "Well, *sashimi* must be complicated even though it's just raw fish, since the sushi chefs in Japan have to train for years before they can work—"

"Don't be lecturing me, of all people, about culinary arts."

"Oh. Yeah." She shut up. Jenn could cook circles around most of the aunties, although none of them would ever admit it.

They tromped down the hallway, sprinted past the living room archway and escaped out the door. Trish turned to Mrs. Choi. "Thanks for letting me stay here." Sleeping on her office floor in a sleeping bag was making her back hurt.

"It's the least I could do. I'm so sorry I didn't look at the place before offering it. George only told me that he had bought it, where it was, and how much rent to charge."

"That's okay. At least I have a temporary place to stay that's close to work."

"Do you think you'll be able to find something?"

"Now that I'm not under time pressure, I'm sure I will. This last week must be a fluke—normally there are plenty of apartments available."

Mrs. Choi smiled. "That's good, dear."

"I promise I won't be here long." Trish walked toward their cars. "One week, tops."

Trish was going to be totally abandoned in her worship tonight if it killed her.

Well, not that worship was really supposed to kill a person, but she wouldn't let Blondie — Katy? Kaitlyn? Kassie? — dissuade her from going all out. That little blonde chick could take herself to another Singles Group because Trish was a force to be reckoned with.

She marched into the social hall, ready to take on lions. Except Blondie wasn't there. Rats.

More people than normal filled the small number of folding chairs, so Trish settled near the front on the side. Up front, Olivia gave her an encouraging smile. Nice to know someone appreciated her no matter how she worshipped.

Off and on, she'd been thinking about what Spenser had said — how the worship team had kept coming up in his head when she talked to him about volunteering. She'd figured out that Spenser wasn't the total playboy he'd originally seemed like. In fact, she hadn't even seen him talking to that Hong Kong intern at work. The only girl he talked to was ... well, her.

Something warm and chocolatey stirred in her stomach.

Ed and Olivia started worship. Trish closed her eyes ...

... To be rudely jostled as two latecomers practically tackled her to get to the seats beside her, which were the last empty ones available.

Oh. It was Blondie. With a gorgeous male friend.

He smiled at Trish, who couldn't help but notice that he had the high cheekbones and deep cut jaw of Johnny Depp from *Pirates of the Caribbean*, but without the scruff on his face and with cleaner teeth. His smoothed-back hair gleamed a little more golden than Captain Jack's, and much less oily.

Blondie's smile showed an awful lot of teeth as she introduced him. "Trish, this is Jack."

In the flesh, indeed. "Hi."

Still with that feral smile, Blondie leaned in close enough for Trish to see the faint smear of Berry Bliss on her teeth. Her lips barely moved as she hissed. "Jack isn't Christian, so don't you be scaring him away with your weird hand flinging."

Not Christian? Scared away? Well, yeah, Trish could see how that might happen.

But she was supposed to be totally abandoned tonight! What happened to her resolve not to let Blondie ruin it for her?

But what about rule number two? Tell others about Christ. Or at least don't scare them away their first time at Singles Group.

The music started. Olivia's eyes softened, then drooped as Trish remained sitting, miserable. Olivia's disappointment ground at her like pepper in a spice mill. Or cheese in a hand grinder. Or nutmeg in a mortar.

Great, now her stomach started churning.

The melody passed over her head. Trish was drowning, letting the waves wash over her. But after a moment, she closed her eyes and sang, letting the words of the song stir her heart. She raised her hand to her chest to feel it beating.

Blondie jostled her arm.

Was that on purpose? How mean. Trish hadn't been intending to raise it all the way up or anything like that. She glanced across Blondie at Captain Jack. He smiled, enjoying the music even though he didn't know the words.

Trish huddled in her seat.

Ed segued into the next song, a powerful ballad that felt like it deserved banners of victory waving over the Singles Group. Her heart swelled, and she leaned forward.

Blondie pinched her leg.

Ow! Now that was uncalled for. Trish rubbed the spot as the stab subsided. That would leave a bruise. Blondie wasn't fighting fair, and they weren't even at war. But they would be if she didn't leave off. Trish sharply nudged her knee into Blondie's bony one.

Then Ed started her favorite song.

"Your mercy comes to me now ... I lose myself when I come before you ... You are everlasting ..."

What was more important, Blondie's friend or bringing God glory? She'd come tonight, determined to worship Him with reckless abandon, but she'd been distracted, jostled, and pinched. Was it wrong to put her worshipping before Captain Jack's first experience at church?

But it wasn't *her* worshipping. It was *God's* worship. She was stinting, like skimming the whipped cream off a white chocolate mocha.

"Consume me, Lord ... transform me from the inside out ..." She closed her eyes and felt the words imprinted on her heart. Her hands came up.

Another pinch from Blondie, but without opening her eyes, Trish slapped her hand away.

"Your light shines ... never ending ... I long to bring you praise ..."

She longed to bring God praise, as much praise as she could give him from her little (well, not *that* little) body. He deserved all of her, He wanted all of her.

"My soul cries out ... I long to bring you praise ..."

Trish shot to her feet, throwing her hands up in the air. Her fingers hit something—maybe the chair back—but she didn't care. She felt like a bird rushing out of a cage, a dog snapping a leash. She had wings, and she was flying right to God.

The worship set ended too soon. She stood there in the resonance of the last guitar strum, head bowed, taking a last sip of the divine Spirit that had filled her heart.

She opened her eyes and sat down. Where had Blondie and Captain Jack gone?

Oh, there was Blondie, walking back into the social hall. Sporting a huge black eye. She glared at Trish kind of like how the crazed serial killer looked in the movies before hacking off the victim's head.

Blondie flung herself into Captain Jack's empty seat, leaving a gaping hole between them. "You are a menace." Her voice had enough venom to poison a small reservoir. She gingerly laid an ice pack over her eye.

"What do you mean?"

Blondie turned purple. Well, at least her entire face matched her eye, now. "You idiot!" Her lips curled out to expose her teeth, which ground together. "You socked me in the eye when you stood up."

Oh. "I'm sorry."

Blondie rolled her eyes and flipped up a hand. *Talk to the hand.*

"Where did Captain Jack go?"

"Who?"

"Uh ... your friend."

"Well, you can be happy you condemned his mortal soul."

Wasn't that a little dramatic? "I don't understand."

"He left as soon as you jumped to your feet."

The fizzy, freeing feeling in her chest suddenly froze and slammed into her gut. "He did?"

"He'll never set foot in a church again, thanks to you."

TWENTY-TWO

There should have been a sign — *Bad Wednesday afternoon with the old ladies straight ahead!* — when Trish pulled into the parking lot. She knew because of the overwhelming number of rice rockets — souped-up Honda Accords, Acura Integras, Mitsubishi Eclipses — and newer-looking SUVs packed into all the parking spaces. The more expensive cars had parked sideways to take up two spaces, the cads.

After parking down the street, she headed inside. She'd arrived early as instructed — she'd gotten into work extra early so she could leave early. She'd arrived even before the other volunteer, Christina. She had to admit she was rather curious to see what the big deal was about those K-dramas.

Her pace slowed as she passed a cherry-red Mazda convertible in neglected condition, with a few small dents and bruises, tires that needed to be replaced soon, and filthy windows. And an ancient Lemon Tree air freshener hanging from the rearview mirror.

No. It couldn't be.

She whipped out her cell phone. "Lex, I need serious help."

"What?"

"I've been volunteering at Katsu Towers — "

"You? At an old folks' home?"

"It's *assisted living.*"

"Okay, whatever." Lex's voice was dry.

"I just arrived, and *Kazuo's car is here.*"

"How'd he know you'd be there?"

"Grandma probably heard from one of the ladies in there, and she told him. I need you here to help me fend him off."

There was a moment of silence from Lex. "Trish, it's not like he's jumping you every time he sees you."

"No, but I ... kind of want to jump him."

"Ooooh. You need help to fend *you* off."

Put like that, Trish sounded pathetic. "Yeah, I guess."

"You're lucky. Today's a slow day for me at work."

"You can leave early? You won't get in trouble?"

"I'll be there in twenty."

"Thanks."

Trish shut her cell phone. She almost regretted calling in the reserve, but she wasn't strong enough. Even the thought of Kazuo's dark eyes made her breath quicken, and that was not good.

One day she'd be strong enough. Wasn't this like that verse in Corinthians, about the "way out" of any temptation? Lex was Trish's way out.

She stomped through the front doors of Katsu Towers. Why were the bad boys so good-looking? God should have given all the bad apples ugly mugs and jiggling beer bellies.

He saw her as soon as she passed the front desk, a decidedly non-ugly, non-beer-belly specimen of the male species, and she hated herself for the blip of her heart when she saw him. She drew her lips down in a frown. "What are you doing here?"

"Your grandmother's friend—"

"Never mind." Why even bother to ask? Of course it was Grandma's nefarious scheming, who else would it be? She probably had spies all over Japantown, which included Katsu Towers. "I'm here to volunteer, not talk to you."

Of course, her treacherous body swayed toward him even as she said that. He smelled clean and exotic, sandalwood with the distinct tang of Japanese soap.

"I can help you." He smiled. He sounded so reasonable.

No, he wasn't reasonable. He was sneaky and sly even if he didn't seem like it right now. He was dangerous and good-smelling and —

Stop that. Focus. "Fine." She marched away from him and upstairs. As soon as she entered the general rec room, the ladies came at her like a slow-moving flock of chickens, clucking and giggling.

"Trish, I want you to meet my nephew ..."

"This is my grandson ..."

"Where's my son? Oh, there he is. Come here and meet Trish ..."

Kazuo stuck to her side like a sword to a samurai's belt, and he glowered at each and every male relative the old ladies threw at Trish. Some of the guys were as annoyed as Trish at their matchmaking matriarchs, and once they did their duty, they left.

Some were mere boys who gave Kazuo a *Down, Cujo!* look. Others were belligerent — back went the shoulders, up went their chins. Kazuo's stance never relaxed.

Some of the guys weren't bad looking, but most of them were either too young or they were older with baggage — the kind of "baggage" that left a pale strip of white on their tanned wedding ring finger. Plus she wasn't disposed to like any man who came at Grandma/Aunty/Mom's beck and call.

As she smiled politely at each of them, she started to wonder if she was supposed to evangelize to them. After all, rule number two and all that. She tried it on one of the more persistent ones, a guy in an American Eagle T-shirt that was way out of place on his forty-something person. "Do you believe in God?"

"Uh ..." He fiddled with his jacket buttons and glanced nervously at Kazuo, who hovered over her shoulder. "Sure." Not a rousing affirmation. Trish wondered if the guy had ever been inside a church.

"Do you have a personal relationship with Jesus Christ?" She had this down pat. She'd finally memorized all the points from her Four Laws tract last week. This would be great —

Except the guy straightened and backed slowly away from her as if she were a nuclear weapon. He wore a too-bright smile. "Nice meeting you, Trish." He ducked out.

Hmph. Well, at least it got rid of him. Eventually, they all said polite good-byes and left her alone.

Maybe Kazuo was good for something, after all.

She happened to glance up and catch Deborah — the deaf-as-a-doornail old woman — sitting on the opposite side of the room from last week. Her outraged eyes bit into Trish like a dozen rabid dogs. Or maybe a dozen rabid toy poodles, anyway. She could almost read Deborah's mind — *This isn't a brothel, you hussy!*

She wasn't a hussy. Trish swallowed and looked away. It wasn't her fault the old woman was deaf and couldn't understand what was going on, on top of being crabbier than apples.

"Hurry, the K-drama is starting!"

The magic words made the women flock to the television set. Kazuo watched with his arched eyebrows furrowed. "K-drama?"

Trish followed in the wake of wheelchairs, walkers, and canes. She glanced back at Deborah, who pinched her mouth and turned her head away from the cattle call of bodies. A desert island, sitting by herself at the far end of the room. She didn't even try to get up and walk to the TV set with everyone else. Surely she could read the subtitles?

A majorly cute Korean guy — maybe the actor on Clara's keychain fobs — vowed his undying love to an incredibly beautiful Korean woman. In the next scene, an unsavory man brandishing a knife carjacked the hero. The thief was robbing him when the man tried to take the knife away, and he got stabbed!

It cut to commercial.

Wow. This was addictive.

Apparently Kazuo thought so, too. He glared at the set as if willing the commercial to end with his radioactive brain waves so the rest would play. "This K-drama is very good." For him, "very good" meant absolutely riveting, surprising, and immensely wonderful.

Kazuo and Korean soap operas? Who'd a' thunk?

"Oh, there he is." Clara reached over from where she sat to grab Trish's arm. "Meet my nephew."

She motioned to an Asian man who stood in the doorway to the rec room. He strode across the room with power and arrogance in every step, and Trish hated him on sight. It reminded her of Kazuo's demanding attitude when they'd been dating and he'd been in the midst of painting yet another "masterpiece." They were all "masterpieces," and she had gotten tired of being the focal possession in his collection.

She glanced at Kazuo, still staring at the TV. She hadn't thought of him once while the K-drama had been on, whereas at any other time, she wouldn't be able to make her brain stop dwelling on undwellable things. Should be a clue to her when a soap opera could distract her from a man.

She stepped away from the TV crowd as Clara's nephew came closer. She crossed her arms over her chest as a shield when he had the nerve to peer down his long, straight nose at her. Or at least try to. Up close, he was only a couple inches taller than she was. She got a good view of his excessively oily forehead.

She put a hand up to her own face. Man, she was leaking oil like an old car. She needed to talk to her cousin who sold Mary Kay about what products she could use.

"I'm Lawrence." He didn't even attempt a smile.

"Trish."

"You volunteer here at my aunt's facility?" He cast his gaze, tinged with disdain, around the room.

"I just started."

He looked at his watch.

"Nice meeting you." She turned to walk back to the TV set. Oh, the commercials had ended. Good.

"Oh, wait, that's right." He pointed a bobbing finger at her. "Aunt Clara said you work for a pharmaceutical company?"

"Valley Pharmaceuticals." Over his shoulder, the TV distracted her. The soap opera's villainess, Eun-kee, looked upset. Oh, the man she secretly loved, but who suffered from unrequited love to another girl, had walked into the room. Uh-oh.

"Ah." Lawrence erupted into million-dollar smiles. "How's that going?"

She trusted him as much as that Korean guy trusted that chick. "Uh ... okay." What was Eun-kee saying? Trish was too far away to see the subtitles. Looked like she was cussing him out.

"What department are you in?"

"Osteoporosis." The hot Korean guy was backing away from Eun-kee now. "Cell culture research."

"So ..." Lawrence leaned in closer. "What are you working on?"

Trish's "potential skunk" meter fired, and she snapped back to attention. "I can't disclose that, it's proprietary information." Her voice came out hard and sharp. Hopefully she pricked him enough that he wouldn't keep going down this line of questions.

He had alligator skin. "Aw, come on. Just a hint. I won't tell anyone."

Suuuure. Just his stock broker. "Do you need a dictionary?"

"Huh?"

"You obviously don't know the meaning of the word *proprietary*."

His smile and his half-lidded eyes screamed condescension even before he unwisely opened his mouth. "Now, Tina—"

"Trish."

"—let me explain how companies *really* work ..."

She already knew he had absolutely nothing meaningful to add to the conversation—such as it was—so she turned her eyes back to the TV. Eun-kee and the man were struggling. When did that happen? The villainess seemed to be wanting to embrace him. Uh oh, what was he going to do?

" ... so you see, only that little date on the patent really means anything ..."

Eun-kee had something in her hand. Where did she pull that from? She had on the filmiest dress, it barely covered her—

Bang! The sound resonated through the rec room. The women in front of the TV jumped in their seats. What happened? Trish squinted at the screen, but she wasn't close enough to clearly see ... Wait a minute.

" … and really, when you think about it—"

"Oh my goodness, she shot him!"

It took a second for her to realize she'd shouted her thoughts out loud, and that she'd interrupted Lawrence, and that it was obvious she hadn't been listening to him, and that he was looking at her like a particularly nasty fungi under the microscope.

He sniffed through his long nose—and so straight! It made Trish want to break it for him, except that was rather violent and it was usually Lex who was violent, not Trish—and puffed out his chest so she could see the lack of muscles under his polo shirt.

She smiled. "Nice meeting you, Lawrence." She hustled back to the TV.

Rats, it was commercials. "What did I miss?"

The ladies were more than happy to enlighten her. "She shot him in the shoulder."

"I thought it was the heart."

"No, that might be fatal. It has to be the shoulder because they can't cut his character."

"Maybe they'll draw out his death over a few weeks."

Clara touched her hand. "How did you like my nephew?"

Trish shook her head and sighed melodramatically. "He doesn't appreciate K-dramas." She infused as much disappointment and disdain as she could into her tone.

The women gasped as if she'd said he was an ax-murderer.

Clara laid a hand over her heart. "I would never have insisted he meet you if I had known."

"Your friend certainly likes K-dramas." Sumiyo pointed toward Kazuo, talking animatedly with another lady about the show. A sly smile. "He'd make a good husband. No fighting over the remote control."

Oh brother. Hmm, wonder if Grandma had asked them all to plead Kazuo's case for him? It wasn't entirely unlikely. "We don't suit." She tried to look happy about it.

Kazuo appeared as if summoned. "I must ask you something."

It silenced all the chattering women in a heartbeat. They turned bright, expectant eyes on the two of them, who were conspicuously standing on the fringes of the TV-watching group.

Oh, no.

"I need you back in my life. You are my muse, my creativity. How can I show you that I am nothing without you?"

Coming off of Lawrence's arrogance, Trish had an easier time resisting Kazuo. "You'll find someone else —"

"I heard you are in need of housing again."

Well, she had told Mom. Of course Grandma would find out, and she apparently did a lot of talking to Kazuo. "I'm fine. I'm in temporary housing, and I'll find something —"

"Since you refuse to live with me, I will leave my apartment."

"But your parents pay for your apartment." And pretty steeply, too.

"I will leave so you can live there. I need you. Come back to me." He grabbed her and kissed her.

Kazuo kissed perfectly. His firm lips were urgent but not brutal, his hands clasped her waist with the force that said, "I need you," but not too hard, the heavenly scent surrounded her . . .

"*Trish!*"

The voice screeched through the stars she was seeing and sent her crashing to earth. She managed to yank herself away from him and turned.

Lex stood in the doorway, hands on hips, fire coming out of her nostrils. Well, not really, but she was certainly mad enough.

"I promise, it's not what it looks like —"

"It is what it looks like." Kazuo tried to embrace her again. She shoved him away.

"It looks like you're kissing him back pretty good there, Trish." Lex's gaze skewered her.

"No, *he* jumped *me*, I promise —"

"Oh, it was so romantic." Clara beamed at them.

"It was not romantic!" The blood rushed to her head and pulsed so hard, she felt like her hair stood on end. "It was awful!"

"Didn't look too awful from here." Lex leaned on one leg and crossed her arms.

"I don't need temptation like that. You saved me from temptation. I really needed you." She was grasping at straws, but Lex's shoulders relaxed, even though her look screamed, *You are an idiot.*

"Well, here I am. Let's go." Lex turned to leave.

"Uh ..."

"What?" She clinked her keys. "Are you seriously telling me you want to stay?"

"Stay with me." Kazuo reached out his arm, but Trish slapped his hands away.

"Can I, uh ... finish watching the K-drama?"

TWENTY-THREE

I thought I was going to die." Trish tossed the remnants of their Chinese dinner—homemade from Jenn's magic wok—into her dingy kitchen's temporary trash can, a paper bag from Albertson's. "Not just the kiss, but his declaration. The ladies acted like it was a marriage proposal."

"Well, that's pretty big coming from Kazuo, right?" Jenn's voice was muffled as she talked into her chest (as usual). She scrubbed at their chopsticks in the sink.

"That wasn't big. He was trying to break down your defenses." Venus scraped the last of the leftovers into a Tupperware container.

It was seriously raining on her venting session that Venus had happened to be at Jenn's house when she called to invite her here for dinner (well, actually she called to beg Jenn to cook for her because she couldn't stomach another night of fast food). Not that she didn't love Venus, but while Jenn would commiserate, Venus would tell it like it is. Trish was not in the mood for realism.

"When we left, it was pretty anticlimactic. Actually, all Kazuo talked about was the cliffhanger at the end of the K-drama."

Jenn started laughing.

"Jeeeeeennnn."

"I can't help it," she wheezed. "Maybe you can bribe him away with a K-drama cruise." She giggled.

Trish leaned against the counter. "Lex hated the K-drama. She kept whispering that she thought we should leave while he was preoccupied."

225

Jenn hooted. Even Venus gave a shout of laughter.

"Laugh it up. You're not the ones staying in a dump."

"How's apartment hunting?"

"I can't find a thing. I don't understand it. I can't stay here any longer."

"At least the smell is gone."

"I had to borrow an industrial-strength coverall from the clean-room at work, then I swept out the living room and left the windows open for a few days."

"How about the bathroom?" Venus peered at the closed door.

"Oh, uh . . ." Trish swallowed. "I try not to use the toilet, and I don't look at the ceiling. I've been showering at work."

"You poor thing. Sounds stressful." Jenn's voice oozed warm fuzzies that wrapped around Trish and gave a sympathetic hug.

"Oh, come on," Venus said. "It's like camping."

Trish lifted an eyebrow. "This from the woman who thinks staying at a 3-star hotel is 'roughing it'?"

"I can't go anywhere that doesn't have wireless Internet and a pool." Venus pouted.

"At least a forest smells better." Trish paused, then gave the news that weighed on her heart. "Grandma called tonight."

Both her cousins sobered.

"She offered that apartment again. Rent-free, if I'd get back with Kazuo." She chewed her lip. She hadn't exactly told Grandma no, but she hadn't said yes, either.

"Don't do it." Venus was firm.

"God will provide housing for you," Jenn declared. "Don't let Grandma tempt you to do something God wouldn't want from you."

"She said, 'Kazuo's a wonderful man, and you don't want to be the next oldest single female cousin when Lex marries.'"

Venus chortled. "You should tell Lex what she said."

"Are you kidding? If Lex had been here, she'd probably have started a fight with Grandma."

Venus snorted. "If Lex weren't Christian, she'd live with Aiden and never marry him just to give Grandma grief."

"You're so mean to Grandma." Jenn spoke with the firmness of an old argument. "She only wants a large family."

"She wants to *control* her large family." Venus's look was dry.

Trish couldn't really argue with that. She was one of the last people who'd want to upset Grandma, but even she knew Grandma had a thing about micromanaging. Lives, in particular. "I just feel so guilty. Grandma's never been mad at me like this before."

"She's your grandmother, not God," Venus said back.

Well, that put things in perspective. She'd call Grandma tomorrow and tell her no. Would she have decided the same course of action if Venus hadn't kept her accountable? She was so weak . . .

"Well, I'll keep looking for housing."

Jenn finished washing up the few dishes. "There are new listings on the Internet every day."

Trish nodded, her spirits rising. "There's got to be something near work and in my price range opening up soon." She stuck her hand on her hip and chirped, "I mean, it's not like God doesn't want me to find an apartment, right?"

Trish needed to go to the bathroom. She was at work—it shouldn't have been a problem. No scary bathrooms here.

Except that twenty minutes ago, with her arms coated in orange-brown cell culture disinfectant, she'd put it off because she didn't feel like going through a major wash cycle to get the super-detergent off her skin. Now, with her bladder ready to explode, she set the stainless steel sheet down, whether half-scrubbed or not, to make a run for the ladies' room.

Her gaze landed on her cell phone, resting on the dry countertop, out of reach of the detergent and water. With stomach gurgling painfully, she had called Grandma, but her nausea had only gotten worse when she got Grandma's voice mail. Trish had left a quavering message for Grandma to call her back. She wouldn't call right this moment, would she? Trish would only take a second to go to the bathroom.

She stripped off her gloves. They hadn't protected her forearms, but they allowed her to give her hands a quick rinse so she could touch doorknobs without fear of smearing orange Betadine all over them. She scrunched paper towels to dry her hands, then turned around.

Spenser stood directly behind her.

"Aaaaaaaaah!" Her scream made the glass windows to the biohazard hood resonate in counterpoint.

She tripped backwards, but her flailing arm knocked into the plastic pan filled with orange-tinted soapy water. *Whoosh!* The water cascaded onto the floor.

"The incubators!" Trish grabbed a stack of paper towels and raced to the edge of the puddle that lapped near the cell incubator units on the far wall. If water got to them, they might break or compromise the cell plates of studies inside.

The throbbing in her pelvis intensified in protest that she wasn't headed for the bathroom. Trish gritted her teeth and laid down more paper towels. "What were you doing there? Trying to give me heart failure?" She didn't look up at him as she spread smaller stacks of paper towels on the edges of the mini ocean to try to stem the flow toward the several-thousand-dollar incubators. "I didn't even hear the door to the room open."

No answer. She turned around to an empty cell culture room. Had she dreamed he was there?

Nope. He'd been smart. His head and a mop handle appeared in the glass window in the door. When he re-entered the room, he slammed the door with a deliberate flourish.

"Ha, ha. Very funny." Trish ran for more paper towels to border the edges of the spill. "Did you hear me just now?"

"No, but I knew what you were going to be saying. Something about how you never heard me come in." He reached out with the mop and caught an orangeish rivulet that made a run for the far incubator.

She scowled at him but couldn't deny it. How did he do that? He must be able to do that with all the girls. Well, except that they'd have to be invisible if he'd been talking to any lately, since she hadn't seen him playboy-ing around.

Don't go there, you dummy. She'd already blown her chances with him.

The Betadine water was also heading — although more slowly — toward the biohazard hoods on the opposite wall. She needed to stem that while Spenser saved the incubators, but the floors there were disgusting. She knew because she'd been intending to clean them.

She *really* wanted to go to the bathroom. She danced from foot to foot as she slapped on another pair of gloves, which stuck to her damp skin so she couldn't fit her fingers in all the way With glove fingers flapping, she grabbed a stack of paper towels and ripped off the paper wrapping, made slightly difficult by the half-on glove. She stopped the closest finger of water creeping toward the equipment.

They worked in silence. She happened to glance behind her and caught sight of Spenser's rather nicely muscled back. *Oh, my.*

And he had to see her now, like this.

She detested Betadine. It got rid of anything resembling a germ or mold, but it foamed up so much that she needed to do numerous wet swipes when she cleaned. Inevitably, Betadine, suds, and water ended up all over her.

She already had huge water splotches on her faded T-shirt — selected in anticipation of this thankless chore — and her jeans sported dollops of suds. Her hair had escaped her ponytail, so wisps stuck to her cheeks and probably stuck out of her head at wild angles. She usually had orange streaks across her face, and she saw an orange smudge on the bottom edge of her safety glasses.

Trish felt about as attractive as Shrek.

Plus her bladder screamed bloody murder at her.

She knew she really shouldn't be staring at the attractive sight of Spenser's backside moving while he mopped up the water . . .

He turned and caught her staring.

Heat rushed to her head and she knew she must be an interesting purple color, clashing with the orange goo on her skin.

Spenser gave her a wink before he turned back to mop more of the water.

Aargh!

She threw a stack of towels at another flank of invading water. "Since you're here, I might as well tell you. I decided to volunteer for worship. I already called Olivia, and I'll start next week."

He grunted. "I knew you would, eventually."

She had to stem a rapidly moving pool so she couldn't turn and give him a swift kick in that nicely shaped behind.

"What changed?"

"Singles Group on Wednesday night." Yuck, this floor was grimy with spilled cell culture reagent. "I couldn't help myself during worship." And might have condemned a poor boy's eternal soul, but that was between him and God, right? "I knew I was pleasing God doing it, because I was being myself."

"It's kinda cool when you get into worship, you know."

Trish jerked up but bonked her head on the underside of the cell culture hood table. "It is?" She rubbed her crown with her forearm so she wouldn't get detergent in her hair.

"It's . . . I don't know . . . inspiring."

She liked being inspiring. "Thanks."

Her cell phone suddenly blared. She took small satisfaction that Spenser jumped a few inches. He actually had a couple moments of hang time.

Then the realization that the call was from Grandma slammed into her chest and stopped her breathing. She tried to strip off her gloves, ripping the nitrile cuffs, as it rang again. *Breathe, come on, you have to breathe to answer it.*

She splashed water on her hands and blotted her orange-dyed fore-arms with paper towels. Her entire arms had started to shake like she had palsy. The room began to spin. She couldn't make her diaphragm work to suck in some air ...

"Are you breathing?" Spenser's concerned voice came up behind her. He whacked her between the shoulder blades.

She coughed, hacked, and wheezed in a painful gush of air. She flipped open the phone. "Hello?"

"Trish, it's Grandma. Was there something you needed?"

My life intact once you find out what I'm going to say. "Grandma. I, uh ..." She crossed her legs and jiggled her foot in mid-air. She so needed to *go.* "I'm not going to take your apartment." Something to be said for a teeny weeny bladder, it made that almost easy to say.

Silence on the line.

"Grandma?"

Click. Dial tone.

The sound screwed into her chest with wrenching twists. Grandma must be completely and utterly ticked off.

Trish rarely upset Grandma like that. Hardly ever. She'd always secretly sighed in relief when Grandma's wrath fell on Lex or Venus without touching her. And now ... She was going to throw up, because her stomach felt like she'd drunk sulfuric acid.

Spenser reached in and took her cell phone away. His hands were so warm, they burned her fingers. Then his arms, clothed in an orange-streaked lab coat, wrapped around her and pulled her close.

Expensive cologne, undercut by the fresh scent of Lever 2000 soap and a deeper thread of musk. He even blocked out the harsh tang of the Betadine. For a moment, she felt completely at peace.

She suddenly noticed her heart beating harder — funny, she thought it had stopped. The ache in her chest didn't go away, and she still wanted to hurl, but both feelings had dimmed as if Spenser had turned down a stove burner.

Then she had to pull out of that warm scented embrace. She grabbed her stomach even as she headed for the door.

"Are you okay?" Spenser's finger plucked at her sopping wet T-shirt sleeve before she moved around him.

She didn't even pause on her way out. "I need to go *bad*."

He'd enjoyed holding her. At the same time, he'd felt like a fraud.

He sprinkled paper towels to hold back the slower edges of water, then went to tackle the water inching toward the biohazard hoods until Trish came back. What a mess. Both this, and this thing — this strange, existent yet non-existent thing — with Trish.

Originally, he'd liked her a little — enough to ask her out. Then she assumed he wasn't Christian, which pretty much socked him in the gut and made him back off real fast.

He'd gotten to know her better. They'd become coworkers, comfortable with each other. Then he discovered she'd dated Kazuo, and his brain started messing around with him, like thinking the plan to pursue her just to mess with Kazuo was a good thing. She hadn't bit, at first, but once he toned down the flirting, she'd been more receptive, especially lately.

How weird. He'd never had to stop being charming to get a woman's attention.

Now that he was realizing that she was different — that this was different from what he'd felt for anyone else — he realized he'd shot himself in the foot. He had to tell her about his ex-wife and Kazuo. The fact he'd kept it from her was not only going to royally hack her off, it would ruin any chance of her believing that his interest in her was real.

She'd realize that his earlier, heavy-handed attention had been with ulterior motives. She'd never trust him. She'd never believe he was different now.

Lately his actions, originally motivated by his history with Kazuo, had brought him to a place where he could hear a still, small voice telling him to get back with God. He had to tell Trish about his ex-wife, Linda, and Kazuo. It wasn't right for Trish not to know, even if she never forgave him for his actions.

He needed to gain her trust first.

TWENTY-FOUR

The living room light in the empty apartment flickered wildly, creating an eerie effect with the dingy walls and stained carpet. The combination grease-animal-puke smell didn't make Trish gag like George's house had, but it wasn't something she wanted to breathe for longer than a minute.

She'd already looked at dozens of apartments the past few weeks, but this one took the cake. Every surface in the bathroom boasted a stain, crack, mold, or all three. The miniscule kitchen looked like it had lived through a couple small fires. Even worse, small pieces of dried dog poop stood out as black lumps amid the dark stains in the carpet, fused to the synthetic pile.

Trish turned to the wiry Vietnamese man who shadowed her. "You want *how much* for this apartment?"

"No' me. Owner want one-tao-san." His eyes, weighed down by wrinkles, cast a knowledgeable look at her, as if to say, *Yes, girlie, I know it's a dump.*

Trish twitched aside the musty curtain to peer at the pothole-dotted road, lit by a lone orange street lamp. A heavyset figure bundled in a trench coat strode down the sidewalk. He met a skinny Asian kid in baggy jeans—they paused, exchanged something, then swept around each other, like dancers in a ballroom, to continue on their way.

She wondered if her RAV4 parked at the curb would still be there when she went outside. "I don't think so."

"You call me you change yo' mind."

"Okay."

Locking herself in her car, she fumbled with the ignition key. This was the last stop for tonight, and the last on her list of apartments for the week.

A rap on her window made her heart leap into her throat, choking her scream. The large figure she'd seen from the window now stood outside the truck.

"Hey, lady? Want some—"

She jammed her foot on the pedal and squealed away.

In the sane light of morning, Trish darted into the bathroom to use the toilet. When she finished, instead of pulling the door shut behind her, she stood—safely—in the doorway and glared up at the amoeba growing on the ceiling. She could swear it snickered at her when she nipped in and out each morning and evening.

She padded into the kitchen. The groutless countertop depressed her, as did the avocado-orange-ochre color scheme. She hadn't used the refrigerator because of the germ-infested peanut butter still slathered into the rubber seal, and she'd be happy if she never saw another Baja Fresh burrito or In-N-Out hamburger or even Mr. Chau's Chinese fast food.

She stalked to the living room archway and sneered at the carpet. The morning light revealed each hideous stain. She'd love to rip that thing out and toss it away. Well, she'd like to watch somebody else do it.

Although, she could. She wasn't crippled or anything. There hadn't ever been a need for her to do anything like that for herself. She could—possibly, maybe—fix things up a little if she were going to stay here.

She wasn't, was she?

She hadn't found a single suitable place to live. She'd driven into every neighborhood in Palo Alto, Mountain View, Sunnyvale, Cupertino ...

To be honest, this house wasn't any worse than some of the nasty apartments she had seen. Why would she pay to live in those places when she already lived here rent-free?

She wouldn't hate the house so much if she cleaned up a bit more. She hadn't intended to stay for long, and she spent so little time inside the house that she hadn't bothered to do much. She'd done some heavy cleaning at her parent's house a few times—not that she'd enjoyed it, and she only did it for them because they'd bribed her with something—but she'd done it.

She eyed the dim living room. Venus had said there were hardwood floors underneath. Maybe she could go on the Internet and figure out how to pull up carpet. Maybe it wasn't so hard . . .

Well, she couldn't do anything without George's—or Mrs. Choi's—permission. She didn't want to pay for any major repairs out of her own pocket, but she could ask Mrs. Choi if she'd allow her to live here for reduced rent in exchange for some home improvement. Trish didn't think George would complain about returning to a cleaned and repaired house. She wasn't certain what sort of financial arrangement Mrs. Choi had with her nephew, but no harm in asking.

It was *only* until she found an apartment. She wasn't about to give up on that front.

Repairs couldn't be that hard, right? She could vanquish the beast on the bathroom ceiling with a misting of bleach, squirt grout in between the kitchen tiles, maybe swab the grease off the kitchen ceiling and cabinets with some alcohol or something. After pulling up the carpet, she'd just sweep a bit, right?

For cheap rent, Trish was willing to do light grunt work.

"Are you sure?" Mrs. Choi's stenciled brows wrinkled across her white powdered forehead.

Trish sat at Mrs. Choi's Formica kitchen table and pretended to sip the glass of barley water she'd been given. She shifted against the sharp crack in the vinyl seat that dug into her tush. "I'm sure." She ignored the fluttering in her chest. "But I'd need reimbursement for the cost of any repairs. I'd trade my labor for the lower rent."

She took another sip of the ghastly water. It smelled musty, like Mrs. Choi's house, and she could taste a hint of anise seed. Like most Asian mothers, Mrs. Choi believed that the nastier something tasted, the better it must be for the body. Trish considered "accidentally" knocking the plastic tumbler — a relic of the seventies — onto the yellowed linoleum floor, but she knew Mrs. Choi would get her another one filled to the brim. Besides, she'd feel horrible causing a mess in the ruthlessly scrubbed kitchen.

"No, I hate having you stay in that horrible place. It must be terribly unsanitary." Mrs. Choi patted a strand of jet-black hair into place. Trish didn't think her own hair had ever been that color.

"It's been a few weeks, and I haven't found any other housing yet. I'm getting tired of all the grime in the house, and I'd like to clean up a bit."

"No, I couldn't take advantage of your valuable time. Don't you have parties to go to, or young men to date?"

Ah ... no comment. "I don't mind. I feel terrible for using up utilities for two weeks without paying anything."

"Oh, that's nothing." Mrs. Choi smiled, her fuchsia lips like a neon pink crescent moon on her pasty white face. Although she looked a bit frightening, especially with her heavily kohled eyes, she had a heart of purest gold, transparent as glass.

"This would be a super deal for both of us. I'd get cheap housing and George would get cheap home improvement." *The reprehensible worm.*

"No, I'd feel awful making you do that for George."

She knew the older woman wanted to let her do the repairs, but her traditional upbringing had taught her to keep refusing. How many times would Trish have to insist before she caved in? This was like trying to wrestle a restaurant bill from her stubborn father.

But she was just as skilled in guilt trips. "I'll do the repairs and pay for it myself if you won't—"

"Oh, no. I couldn't let you do that. Let me at least reimburse you. Yes, that sounds good. And no rent."

"Mrs. Choi—"

"No, you can't pay rent if you're going to fix the house up." Her look dared Trish to defy her logic.

Well, no use quibbling over something minor like that. "All right, thanks. I appreciate that."

"If you need help, call me."

Trish smiled, imagining portly Mrs. Choi hauling carpet out of the house with her bowlegged rocking gait. Then again, she had four grown children and still lived on her own.

"Thanks. I'll call if I need you."

"What do you mean? If I spritz bleach onto the ceiling, won't it disappear?"

Spenser raised an eyebrow at her. "Are you kidding? Mold like that? It's probably already deep into the wallboard."

"Are you sure? How do you know?" Trish gnawed her lip. "How can I fix it?"

"Hire somebody."

"Can't. I'm exchanging my rent for labor."

He let out a hoot of laughter. Her gaze darted around the restaurant and she hissed, "Behave yourself. Everyone's looking."

She settled down to take another bite of her wood-fired pizza. When that pompous windbag Kevin described the new California-Mediterranean restaurant, Trish had been intrigued and Spenser accepted her lunch suggestion with alacrity.

She deliberately plucked a strand of gooey cheese from her pizza and licked her fingers. Spenser's neat side hated when she did that. "Kevin was right about the rosemary-chicken pizza." Despite his numerous faults.

"I think Kevin's afraid of you."

"What do you mean? He barely speaks to me. He sticks his nose in the air and looks at me like I'm lower than a piece of gum on the bottom of his Hermès shoes." Actually, she'd love to see him step in a piece of gum and mar those expensive things. On his salary? Or maybe they were fake.

"Of course he's scared of you. Why do you think he's coming in so early in the morning? It's to avoid you."

"Because he thinks I'm the black plague."

"He thinks you're mean enough to *give* him the black plague."

She chomped on her pizza. She hadn't exactly been diplomatic that one time she talked — er, yelled at Kevin, but she hadn't actually been an ogre, right?

Why ruin a yummy lunch with an irritating topic? "How do you know so much about home improvement?"

He relaxed into a smug smile. "I did all the repairs at my townhouse when I bought it."

Humph. Probably bought for him by his wealthy parents. After all, he was from Atherton.

He must have interpreted her facial expression, because his mouth hardened. "I worked during college and invested wisely — and, I'll admit, luckily — so that I could afford a 20-percent down payment. I didn't have any help." The words came out sharp and succinct.

That impressed her, but no way would she let him see that. "I didn't say anything."

"Humph." He chomped into his pizza, eyebrows drawn low over glittering eyes.

Maybe she should have gushed all over him, because she might need his help? Nah. He would quirk his eyebrow at her and say, "Whatever you want from me, the answer is no." She sighed, then shoved a forkful of spring salad greens into her mouth.

His glare melted into a disinterested mask. "I could help you go online and figure out how to do it."

She nearly spit her food out. "Waw-wa?"

"Clean the mold. You should at least do that, even if you can't replace the wallboard."

Trish wanted to ask him where this streak of helpfulness came from. She also didn't quite trust him, not after that Sunday school Pet Day. She still felt a twinge of guilt every time she looked at him and remembered his son swallowing the hamster.

Trish didn't want to be in his debt. She gulped her food down. "That's a good idea." At least she didn't have to surf the web by herself.

"What else is wrong with the place?"

"There's a mushroom growing in the bathroom—"

"Uh oh. On the floor? Near the shower?"

"Yeah."

"Something's leaking. The joists might be rotted. Huge remodel."

Her heart dropped to somewhere near her bellybutton. "Oh. I've been showering at work, so my biggest concern is the mold on the ceiling."

"What else?"

"Grease on the kitchen ceiling and cabinets, grout missing from the kitchen tiles, carpet is stained. I'll need to strip that off."

"That's a lot of work, but not impossible."

Trish just wanted to use the toilet without fear of being smothered by a falling blanket of slime. Was that so hard? She groaned.

"Go online. Bound to be information there."

I have lethally toxic mold in my bathroom! Trish leaped from her office chair as she read the online article.

The janitor, used to seeing her at work so late, glanced up as he walked past her office, but didn't stop.

There might be *Stachybotrys* mold on the ceiling. Causing all sorts of health problems and even death.

Well … she hadn't had any of the symptoms listed in the article, but then again, she hadn't been in the bathroom that often. And … it seemed to cause death mostly in infants and those sensitive to respiratory allergies, but *still*.

Okay, so maybe she didn't have toxic mold. She needed to get rid of it. She could get respiratory masks from work and borrow that coverall suit from the cleanroom again. She needed lots of bleach.

Even aside from the mold in the bathroom, home repairs would be massive in manpower and cost. The carpet removal would require major muscle and long hours of pure grunt work. She needed a ladder to remove the kitchen ceiling grease and the bathroom mold.

Did she want to do this?

Did she have a choice?

She wasn't the neatest person, but even she couldn't stand the disrepair and mess any more. The way her apartment hunting was going, she might be at George Choi's Home Repair Hovel for longer than she'd like.

The scarcity of decent apartments amazed and appalled her. How could there be nothing suitable in three weeks? It was almost as if God was plotting against her.

Maybe He is.

Now why in the world would He want her to live in that miserable hole? Trish was doing her best to follow rule number three and persevere, but she couldn't take much more. Hadn't she prayed hard enough for housing? She had been in tears some nights as she begged God to deliver her from that Abyss of Abhorrence.

Then again, she hadn't been praying for God's will, had she? For a rescue, but not for guidance.

If He wanted her to stay and do the home repairs — more than she had intended to do, anyway — that meant she'd stop looking for apartments. Not even peeking at the online listings. Could she really do that?

Even as she sank into her office chair to pray, she started to whimper. "Oh God, *please* don't make me stay there."

Okay, that wasn't very submissive.

"Oh God, do I have to stay there?"

The heavens were silent. Or it could be because it was close to ten at night.

"Lord, do you want me to stay there?"

Still silence — no rushing winds, no bolt of lightning, no voices in her head. But she did remember the unusual, inexplicable lack of apartments in an area famed for being rife with decent housing.

Only God could do that.

Trish blew her nose and heaved a sigh that blew air down the wrong pipe, causing a coughing spell. After recovering, she bowed her head and nodded to the empty room.

"Okay, Lord, if you want me to, I'll stay."

TWENTY-FIVE

Trish sat in church and wanted to cry.

Okay, Lord. You seemed to want me to stay in that wreck of a house, and I agreed to obey you. Don't you think I deserve a little bit of good fortune at some point? Like about now?

Apparently not.

Blondie made a dramatic point of getting up and moving farther away when Trish sat down in the row in front of her. Then the little snob whispered to the older woman on her right, who shifted her ample bum a seat over while casting a wary eye at Trish. As if she would jump up and start waving her arms and prophesying.

She couldn't lie — she felt like a leper in her lone seat with a small sea of empty chairs around her. She fiddled with her hands in her lap while her heart jackhammered in her chest. She supposed she was lucky no one could see her rapid pulse or the burning headache behind her brow bone, and hopefully her makeup hid the bags under her eyes.

Despite her non-magnetic personality at the moment, she wanted to cry for different reasons. Namely, the despair she felt this morning, seeing her dumpy house in the cold light of day and realizing the sheer amount of work ahead of her. She, who had about as much of a clue as Inspector Clouseau.

She watched the worship team setting up on the slightly elevated stage. They worked seamlessly, like a colony of ants or bees, each doing their own job. Even Spenser appeared every so often to check various cords and mics before returning to the soundboard on the balcony at the back of the sanctuary.

Where would she fit in here? Why had she given in to Spenser's insistent recommendation for the worship team? First rehearsal for her would be Friday night. Not that she actually had anywhere else to go on Friday, which was depressing in itself. She'd get up there on the stage and totally suck, and then she'd look even more stupid than she did now, with empty chairs on all sides of her. She might as well have those yellow *Danger!* signs plastered front and back.

"Hi." Griselle plopped into the seat next to her.

"Hi!" Her relief made that come out a tad exuberant. She toned it down. "How are you doing?"

"Oh, great." Griselle adjusted her cream turtleneck sweater.

"Isn't that stuff hot in the summertime?" Poor girl. But she honestly couldn't see her exposing her cuss-word-laden shoulders to the congregation without causing at least one coronary.

"I wear light cotton stuff. When I get enough money, I'll have them removed."

"All of it?"

"Actually, I'll keep some, partly because it's expensive to have them all removed." She leaned in closer. "I kind of have a lot of them."

Trish was liking this chick more and more. "Cool."

Griselle smiled. "I volunteer at a Pregnancy Crisis Center, and the tattoos make me more approachable to the girls who come in, if you can believe that."

"I can." Some of the girls probably had tattoos of their own.

"Oh, I found out today you volunteered for the worship team."

"Well ... I'll try it. I guess I'll have to give up Sunday school if I continue with it, huh?"

Griselle nodded. "But God really provided. One of the pastor's nieces moved back, and she used to work the fours and fives. She called me yesterday. Now you don't have to worry about Sunday school at all."

Instead of relief, Trish felt kind of deflated. Unneeded. Like the church was just giving her things to do to keep her occupied. She mustered up a smile for Griselle. "That's great." The music started, saving her from having to think up other nice things to say about her replacement teacher.

"I will worship with all of me ... I want to be a fool for you ... Can I be any less?"

And she did worship with all of her, swaying and dancing in place, hands raised, offering as much of herself as she could. Who cared if people stared? Who cared if no one else joined her? She reached for more of Christ as she belted out the lyrics, feeling the words etch themselves on her heart.

Maybe the congregation would be happier to have her up front making a fool of herself rather than in the seats?

Stop thinking that way. She didn't know why, but somehow she knew God wanted her to serve on the worship team, for some reason, in some way. Because really, if He hadn't wanted her up there, He shouldn't have told Spenser three times to suggest it.

"Let me be Your hands and feet ... Show me where ... Show me who ..."

Deborah.

The woman's face flashed in front of her closed eyes and wouldn't fade away. Scowling, alone, ignored. It didn't seem right.

Okay, that was weird. Did God want her to help Deborah somehow? She couldn't make her a nicer person or restore her hearing ...

Wait a minute. Maybe she could.

"I don't understand." Trish pounded on the counter of the Katsu Towers nurse's station, which had taken her almost twenty minutes to find. She would have thought it would be more accessible, considering the people who lived there.

The nurse's face blushed an unpleasant purply-orange. "It's policy—"

"But this is stupid."

The nurse frowned deeper, if that were possible. "I don't make the policy—"

"Deborah hasn't had a hearing test in years—you said so yourself. Why can't I take her? No one can talk to her because she's deafer than a stone."

"You're not family—"

She flung her arms out. "Well, I wouldn't want to belong to her family, if only her nephew ever visits, and that's only once every six months."

The nurse pressed her lips together, obviously regretting telling Trish that piece of information. "Fine. Why don't I have you talk to the director?"

"Uh ..." Nurses she could nag, but what would she say to the director of the facility? "Isn't that awful high up for this little teensy problem?"

The nurse smirked, then picked up her phone and dialed. After a brief exchange, she gave Trish a triumphant V-shaped smile. "You can head up to the seventh floor, room 702."

Oh, man. She wasn't equipped for dealing with these upper-management types.

But Venus was! She whipped out her cell phone and dialed as she headed into the elevator.

"What do you need?" Venus asked.

"Hello to you, too."

"I'm a little busy, Trish."

"Well then, why did you bother to answer?"

"Because it was you. Again, what do you need?"

Trish explained while waiting for the elevator doors to open.

"So what do you need me for?" A rapid *taptaptaptap* sounded in the phone—Venus rapping her pen against her desk.

"What do I say to convince him? I'm terrible with these official things." She entered the elevator and pushed the button for the seventh floor.

"Just be logical."

"Excuse me? You do realize you're talking to Trish, here?"

Venus sighed, but it held a hint of amusement, so that was a good sign. "Tell the director that Deborah's hearing can cause legal problems for the facility if she's endangered in any way because she couldn't hear something or someone. Like in a fire, or if there's an accident with the wheelchair races in the hallway."

"*Muah!* You're awesome. Anything else?"

"Since you're an official volunteer for the facility, it's perfectly acceptable for you to run the residents to doctors' appointments."

"Oh, okay. Great."

"But Trish, isn't Deborah the crabby one?"

"So?"

"Are you sure she wants to get her hearing tested?"

"Of course she would." Trish exited the elevator on the seventh floor. "Why wouldn't she?"

The meeting with the director went swimmingly.

The meeting with Deborah, not so much.

Maybe because her hearing was so far gone, the old woman refused to talk to Trish and kept glaring and frowning. Trish thought she even growled once, but she wasn't sure. Deborah snatched her hands away when Trish tried to get her up to walk her out.

"DOCTOR!" Her voice was starting to go hoarse from shouting. "I'M GOING TO TAKE YOU TO THE DOCTOR!"

Deborah finally raised her sparking eyes to Trish's mouth as she said that last sentence. Then comprehension dawned and her mouth formed an O. She nodded and stood.

Trish heaved a sigh and got Deborah to the SUV without incident. She'd made an appointment for today with the primary care doctor listed in Deborah's chart, which hung conveniently on the door to her room.

However, in the doctor's office, the nurse said she needed Deborah's actual insurance card.

"Why? Hasn't she been here before?"

"It was years ago, and we need a new card."

Trish called the nursing home and had to wait while the nurse — the irate one she had argued with earlier, unfortunately — looked for Deborah's insurance information and faxed it to the office. The nurse had to get the insurance company on the line to verify Deborah was still covered.

Then the nurse said she needed a credit card.

"What? Doesn't she have some kind of Medicare or Medicaid or whatever old people have that pays for everything?"

The nurse gave her a look that said, *Come back when you have a clue what you're talking about.*

"How were her past doctor's visits paid for?"

The nurse looked at the file. "Her nephew gave his credit card."

"Is it on file?"

"Yeeeess ..." The nurse tensed, not liking where this was going.

"Well, if I get him to approve the charges, then it's fine, right?"

She visibly relaxed in her seat behind the counter. "Oh. Yes, if he approves the charges."

"Fine, do you have his phone number?"

The nurse's eyes shifted away. "I don't know if I'm supposed to do that ..."

"If I cancel this appointment, I'm sure he won't be happy to be charged the cancellation fee." Trish stabbed a finger at the sign on the counter stating a forty-dollar charge if any appointments were cancelled less than twenty-four hours ahead of time.

The nurse bit her lip, then rattled off the phone number from Deborah's file.

"Hello?"

"Hi, my name is Trish Sakai. I'm a volunteer at Katsu Towers and I'm with your aunt Deborah."

"Is she okay?"

"She's fine. I'm here at the doctor's office for a hearing test, but I need you to approve charges to your credit card for the appointment."

"Why does she need a hearing test?"

"Uh ... because her hearing is completely *gone*?" What a moron. He'd have known that if he'd visited her more often.

"How much is it going to cost?"

"Does it matter?" Her voice was starting to climb an octave. She took a deep breath. "Your aunt couldn't hear a fire alarm. Or a plane about to crash on her head. Or a mugger following her on a deserted street." Not that Deborah would be out at night, but still.

"She's perfectly safe at that facility."

"The facility said she could be a legal liability because she couldn't hear a nurse's instructions. And did I mention she can't hear a fire alarm?"

Trish could almost hear him pouting. "Fine. But don't go buying the most expensive hearing aid—"

"I won't. Here's the nurse." She handed the phone to her.

After some nodding and murmurs, the nurse closed Trish's phone. "He said he wants to approve any hearing aid you get her."

"That's fine. He's paying the bill, after all."

They only had to wait a few minutes before a nurse took Deborah and Trish in back. But when the nurse led her to the room where she'd get her hearing tested, Deborah took one look at the equipment and started backpedaling.

"What's wrong?" Trish tried to pull her into the room, but Deborah snatched her arm away and dug her feet in. She shook her head angrily, then crossed her arms over her chest.

"Oh, great. This is wonderful. Do you know what I've had to go through to get this test for you? Don't you want to hear again? People would talk to you." Trish flung her arms around in frustration. "God told me to serve you—well, I can't say He actually spoke but it was pretty clear because it was in the middle of a great worship set and I felt really close to Him—and you're not making this easy for me to help you."

Deborah stuck her hands on her hips and her chin in the air.

The nurse tactfully interjected. "Why don't I leave you two in an examination room for a few minutes?"

Once ensconced in the room, Trish seated Deborah and herself. What good was this? It wasn't as if Deborah could hear her. Maybe she could write it down? She picked through her purse and unearthed a few old gas receipts. She wrote "hearing test" on one of them and held it in front of the old woman.

Deborah grabbed the paper and brought it to within three inches of her face.

Oh, man. She needed an eye test, too.

"No."

Trish started. That wasn't her. That was . . .

"No." Deborah's voice rasped with disuse and sounded a few hundred decibels louder than normal people—even normal old people. She held the gas receipt back to Trish. "No hearing test."

"Why not?" She grabbed another receipt and wrote the question down.

"I like not being able to hear."

"Huh?"

"I don't want to have to listen to them talk, talk, talk. I *see* them talk, talk, talk, all day." Deborah sighed. She looked tired just thinking about those women talking to her.

All that hassle, and Trish needn't have bothered. No hearing test, although the deaf old woman obviously needed it. Trish looked at the floor. She heaved herself to her feet and stuck a thumb toward the door. "Well, let's go, then."

But Deborah snapped out and grabbed her wrist. "No, I don't want to go yet."

"Why not?"

"I came with you because you were going to take me to the doctor."

Trish gestured to her ears. "You said you didn't want—"

"I don't want a hearing aid. I want glasses."

Oh, right.

Deborah smiled then, for the first time since Trish had met her. "I want to be able to read the subtitles to that show they're always watching."

TWENTY-SIX

Trish hoped she wouldn't pass out.

She'd never been behind a mic before. She also had never been in front of an audience before, if she didn't count those times she made a fool of herself at karaoke.

She fidgeted as Spenser adjusted her mic stand in relation to the monitors edging the stage. Thankfully the stage was only a foot or two off the ground, since her fear of heights probably would have reared up to make her day even worse. Of course, the first row of pews was within a few feet of the stage, so if she got dizzy and fell, it would only be into the arms of whoever sat there. Probably some grumpy old man. Or if she was lucky, it would be Blondie and her posse ...

"Relax." Olivia stood next to her, tuning her electric guitar. "You did fine at rehearsal on Friday night."

She'd done better than she'd ever expected. Since she couldn't play an instrument with much proficiency but enjoyed singing, they'd put her on second mic. She'd warned the rest of the team — probably fifty times — that she didn't sing well, but when they set up the sound and started rehearsal, it hadn't sounded bad at all. She could barely hear herself, actually.

She shuffled the papers on her music stand in front of her, but she knew all the songs already. The lyrics were only there for moral support.

"Okay, gang. Let's pray." Ed set his acoustic guitar in the stand and the team gathered around him in a circle on the side of the stage.

Ed started, and they each prayed in turn. Trish's heartbeat ramped up from a cool samba to pounding hip-hop. She *hated* praying out loud in front of people, and she was perfectly atrocious at it. The rest of the team offered up prayers for the pastor, for the congregation as they gathered for service, for the music and how God could use it for His glory. Eloquent prayers. Prayers God wouldn't cringe to hear.

Finally it was her turn. For a second, she couldn't breathe. But something in her nose saved her by making her sneeze — a loud, rousing *A-choo!* that hopefully didn't mist the others too much.

She took a deep breath, tried to ignore the shaking of her hands. "Dear Lord ... uh ... help me not mess up. Amen."

She thought she heard Olivia stifle a giggle. Well, at least Trish was entertaining. She was done, that's all she cared about.

They took their places and Ed greeted the congregation to give them a few minutes to get to their seats. Personally, Trish would have yelled, "Sit down, people!" but she supposed that wouldn't be very polite. Ed opened up the worship service with a prayer.

She stood there behind her mic, staring down at the floor because she couldn't look out at the congregation. She didn't even listen to the prayer, just kept herself aware of the cadence of his voice. Her hands had frozen. She could barely open her fingers. At the same time, ants crawled up and down her legs and she couldn't make her feet stop shuffling. Finally Olivia took a discreet step sideways and pressed her shoe over Trish's tapping toe. She only removed it when Ed was closing up the prayer.

" ... Amen." Ed opened with a full chord from his 12-string acoustic guitar.

Oh my gosh, they'd started! She had to look up, because obviously the mic couldn't pick her up if she didn't look up and put her mouth in front of it. But did she want to be heard? She didn't want to look up.

Then Ed started singing, and the words filtered through her racing thoughts. "I leave my baggage at the door ... I surrender it all ... This is a time to worship you alone."

Suddenly she opened her mouth and put her chin up, although she closed her eyes. She supposed people would think she was into the worship, which she was, versus scared to look out, which was also true. But then the words came to her and she forgot everything else.

"I surrender it all ... You alone deserve this part of me ... You alone deserve all praise ..."

Hey, this wasn't so bad. She hadn't messed up any words in that song. She had a hard time hearing herself, though—must be the combination of the other instruments and the congregation singing too. She wondered if next time she could ask Spenser to up her volume in the monitors.

The song flowed into the next, and again Trish gave herself into worship. She didn't feel brave enough to raise her hands, but the words flowed out of her as an offering to lay before His throne. She forgot—almost—where she was, and instead focused on praising Him.

"Help us to live in you ... Until the day you make all things new ..."

She found the courage to open her eyes.

Her heart crashed in her chest. People stared at the words projected on the large screen above and behind the worship team, but their faces were so *dead.* Some sang. Some didn't even bother to open their mouths to try. Several people had pinched looks on their faces as if they were simply tolerating this noise until the pastor would come up to speak.

Her eyes squeezed shut. She couldn't look at them—she could barely keep singing. Their expressions shoved concrete blocks into her heart, pulling it deeper into a cold ocean of despair. Why did the worship team play up here, when the congregation could care less? Why sing?

Wait, what was she saying, *Why sing?* Just because she stood up here in front didn't mean it was any different from other Sundays. She had no problems singing on any other Sunday (or Wednesday night

Singles Group, she added spitefully) no matter what anyone else was or wasn't doing around her.

She flung her arms up and belted out the chorus with all the earnestness she could wring from her lungs.

"Your mercy comes to me now ... I lose myself when I come before you ... You are everlasting ..."

Then she really did forget where she was. She finished the song and opened her eyes, startled to see the mic at her nose and the congregation behind that.

Except this time she saw a few people scattered here and there — some sitting with hands raised and eyes closed, others standing with their entire bodies worshipping. The sight made her smile so broadly, her cheeks stretched and ached. Her chest filled with air and she almost felt as if she'd float away.

Maybe God really had spoken to Spenser about her being on the worship team. Maybe she had a purpose here.

It was the last song before the pastor's sermon. Trish closed her eyes and gave it her all.

"You are the only place I'll ever go ... And one day I'll arrive where you are ... For now I'll fall before you ..."

Her hands reached for Him, and the words came from her gut. The darkness behind her eyes helped her to focus on Him, only on Him ...

Bonk!

Her nose crashed into the mic. Rather hard, too. She opened her eyes.

Huh? Where was her mic?

Crash!

Her blow — or rather, her nose's blow to the mic — had sent the mic and stand tipping backwards. It flipped over the monitor squatting low on the edge of the stage and plopped into Mr. Yamaguchi's lap.

Ed faltered for a moment. Olivia stopped playing for a second. The drummer missed a beat.

Then they kept going.

Should she break from formation and run to get the mic stand from Mr. Yamaguchi? He blinked at the stand for a second before setting it on the empty seat beside him and picking up on the chorus.

Trish stood up there, feeling rather naked without the mic stand. Her head was on fire—she could almost smell singed hair—while her hands, gripped at her waist, had frostbite. Why couldn't she be like Nightcrawler from the X-Men and *bam!* disappear in a cloud of sulfur?

And then—*thank you, God*—the song finally ended. Trish raced down the stage to rescue the mic stand, but Spenser beat her to it.

"Who's at the soundboard?" she whispered. She handled the stand while Spenser inspected the mic. The pastor had gotten to the podium and started his sermon, valiantly ignoring them as they righted the equipment.

"Ed's nephew is with me the next few weeks learning to do the sound, so I left him there." He frowned at the mic.

"Is it broken?" Would she have to pay for it? She'd heard they were thousands of dollars. *Well, dummy, you're the one who broke it.*

"I think it's okay. It would have been worse if it were on."

Oh, whew ... Wait a minute. "What?"

"They didn't tell you?" He turned innocent eyes to her. Trish tried to ignore the fact that they were a delicious Godiva dark chocolate brown.

"Tell me what?"

His gaze flitted away. "Well, you were so worried about how you sang, and I can understand, not that you sing badly, because you sing better than you think ... Usually people are nervous when they hear themselves in the speakers or the monitors ... You did great because you couldn't hear yourself. Did you notice? I noticed."

He was stalling. And babbling, too, which was even more freaky. "What are you talking about?"

"I, uh ... turned off your mic."

TWENTY-SEVEN

Griselle's voice stopped her on her storming march out to her SUV in the church parking lot. "Trish, wait up."

She stopped and whirled. "He turned off my mic!"

Griselle paused with a neutral expression on her face, as if unsure whether to press forward or back away from the crazy woman. "I'm sorry."

"I don't sing that badly, do I?" Her eyes started to sting.

"You were great." Griselle patted her shoulder.

"No I wasn't. No one could even hear me."

She snickered. "I hate to break it to you, but you sang loud enough for the first three rows to hear you quite well."

She didn't know why, but the news brightened her mood. "Really? Oh." Not that her purpose of singing on the worship team was to be heard. She was supposed to be helping lead the congregation in personal and collective worship. Of God. Still, it was nice to know she hadn't been totally useless.

"Are you doing anything on Tuesday night?"

"No." Her sad social life.

"Want to come with me and work at the Pregnancy Crisis Center?"

Trish's initial reaction was no. How could she possibly help girls when she herself was only now regaining her chastity? How could she counsel anyone when she needed counseling herself on how to live a life God would be pleased with? She'd been a Christian, yet she had deliberately disobeyed Him. "You don't feel ... I don't know, guilty for working with them? I mean, both of us have done things we're not proud of."

Griselle's eyes softened, and her smile became blindingly brilliant. "Our pasts are just that—past."

Funny, her past kept biting her in the butt every day. When would she finally be forgiven? When would she finally be free?

"Trish, anybody can work there. More than that, you need a heart to help them. They can sniff out a fraud pretty fast."

Did she have a heart for them? Could she be honest with them about her past mistakes when she could barely be honest with herself, with her cousins? Did she care enough about those nameless other girls to let it come across?

Did she want any of them to end up victims of men like Kazuo? Or to hop from boyfriend to boyfriend, seeking love and tossing men aside aimlessly and heartlessly? To disappoint their cousins, to garner an unsavory reputation in Japantown, to have their psychotic grandmothers come after them . . . ?

"I'd love to help." She didn't only want to help, she wanted to swoop in and save them, but without the red and white spandex and cape. She wasn't sure if she could, but she also remembered rule number two—tell others about Christ. God would help her keep rule number two.

"Awesome. I'll pick you up on Tuesday night and drive us to the Crisis Center. It's in downtown San Jose."

"Where are you going?" She heard his smooth, seductive voice and caught a whiff of sandalwood a split second before the tall shadow covered her.

"Nowhere." Trish rounded on Kazuo. "Stop following me everywhere. This is getting majorly creepy."

And actually, he did look kind of creepy with that melodramatic lock of hair over intense eyes, which hid a horrid artist's temper and a collector's possessiveness.

Funny that she remembered that about him right now, so different from even a few weeks ago. Maybe God was changing her. Or maybe it was the fact Griselle stood nearby with a look on her face like she'd swallowed a slug.

"By the way, Griselle, this is Kazuo. My *ex*-boyfriend."

Normally sweet, polite Griselle acknowledged him with barely a nod. She took a step back. "I'll see you——"

Trish grabbed her—maybe a little harder than she needed to. "No, stay. Please?" Griselle's physical presence gave her more strength to face Kazuo, who looked like he'd have cheerfully wanted her gone.

He reached out long, graceful fingers to Trish's cheek. "I want to be part of your life again."

She hesitated only a second this time before pulling back. It was easier to avoid his PDA with Griselle right there. "I'm trying to become a different person."

"But I love you the way you are."

Oh, man. He was good. She needed to get herself away from him before he said any more disgustingly self-esteem-boosting things like that. "I didn't like who I was." *That scared, easily-swayed girl who dated you.* "Why can't you accept what I want for myself rather than what you want for me? That isn't love."

He hesitated. Had she gotten through to him finally?

Nope. "I want what's best for you because I love you."

He'd missed the point. Why was she surprised? She was tired of talking in circles with him, so she turned to Griselle. "Let's go to lunch."

Kazuo perked up. "Where?"

She firmed her mouth and looked him in the eye. "Not you. We are over."

A flash of fire streaked across his dark eyes.

Trish didn't back down. *Go ahead, Kazuo. Unleash your temper here, in the middle of the church parking lot. Remind me why I shouldn't melt into your arms again so that my body will finally listen to my head.*

Instead, he banked that dark fire. It was almost as if it had never broken out at all. He turned to walk away. "Enjoy yourself on Tuesday."

She couldn't suppress the shudder that ran through her.

She'd be okay tonight if she could stop being a basketcase. Easier said than done.

Trish entered the glass doors of the Pregnancy Crisis Center behind Griselle's lithe figure. The girl walked with so much bounce in her step, like she hadn't a weight on her shoulders at all. Not even a couple cuss words.

Griselle greeted a couple other girls with friendly hugs. "Trish, these are the other counselors, Pamela and Cheryl."

Such sweet girls. Pamela, the brunette with long wavy hair, gave her a wide smile. Cheryl's blue eyes lit up when she said hello.

Trish felt covered in ectoplasm.

No, that was basketcase-ness. She didn't even have a physical daily reminder of her past like Griselle did. She was a new creation in Christ. She was going to make a difference for Him tonight. She'd finally get to fulfill rule number two, tell others about Christ, which she'd been slacking at lately.

"Tonight is support group." Griselle led the way through a side door into a largish room with a circle of chairs. "You'll get to meet some of the regular women who come for counseling, but mostly there are newcomers every week."

"So I won't be manning the hotline phones?" She was partly relieved. She'd probably freak out herself instead of calming down some hysterical or depressed girl on the telephone. Yet she was also disappointed she wouldn't have the chance to snatch some poor girl from the fires of guilt and depraved sin.

Get a grip. They're pregnant, not serial killers. Hopefully.

Several young women came a few minutes before seven, many of them obviously pregnant. Pamela and Cheryl started the support group promptly on time, although many women snuck in afterward.

"Rosa, how has your week been?" Cheryl's pearl-pink lips gave an encouraging smile to the short Hispanic woman.

"Not too bad." Rosa rubbed her burgeoning stomach. "Carlos only came by my sister's house once this week, and Luisa's kids were already inside so we could lock and bar the door when he started screaming and pounding."

Whoa, momma. Trish's sob story of her demented artist boyfriend was a picture of suburbia in comparison.

"You should buy a gun." One girl with black makeup gunked around her eyes (how could she see with all that on?) nodded. "You don't have to shoot him, just fire it, and he'll be scared and take off." Trish told herself to stop staring at the girl's black leather and studs, trying not to cringe every time she moved and the metal seemed to pierce her.

"How're you doing with your boyfriend, Felicity?" Pamela nodded encouragingly at the leather chick.

Felicity?

She shrugged. "He tried to stop me from going out with my girl-friends. Said he needed me at home. He even took away my car keys and dropped them in the toilet."

"My ex-boyfriend did that!" Trish shoved forward in her seat. "How did you get them out?"

"My neighbor's a plumber. I got him to get them out for me after I clocked my boyfriend." Felicity smiled in satisfaction.

"Clocked him?"

"With one of his free-weights. He never did that again."

"Oh." Trish sank back in her chair. Sure, if she had risked *killing* Kazuo, she'd probably have escaped him much sooner.

"Tell us about yourself, Trish." Cheryl did some bobble-head action.

Now? "I've, uh ... never been pregnant."

"That's okay." Griselle patted her knee. "We're here to offer support. We're all women here."

Hmm. Well, she didn't quite have problems on the same scale as Rosa and Felicity, but she also hesitated to lay them out in front of

Pamela and Cheryl. What would they think of her? They seemed like such nice girls. What would they think to find she wasn't a nice girl?

Griselle caught her gaze.

Ah. Got it.

She took a deep breath. *His compassions never fail, they are new every morning.* "I escaped from my ex-boyfriend. He was possessive." That was one way to put it. "But I see him all over the place, and he wants me back, and he makes me feel like I'm sexier than Angelina Jolie, and I can't stop myself from wanting to get back with him, too, until I remember — or at least try to remember — how he used to treat me and how miserable I was because he never let me see my friends and it was all about him, but when I'm right next to him, all I can think about is that I want to kiss him." She gasped in a breath.

"Me too." Another Asian girl spoke up in a thick accent — Thai? Vietnamese? "My ex keep coming around. I tell him go away, but then he smile, and I tell him come inside." Her mouth turned down and her shoulders sagged.

"But it's even worse." Trish was like a busted dam, and it was all coming out. "I broke up with him, then I slept with him again. It was so stupid. I feel like a slut."

"Only once?" Rosa patted her shoulder. "I kept going back again and again. You were smart to wise up sooner. They're so good at putting on an act, until they hit you again." Rosa sighed and rubbed the sleeve of her flower-print dress. Several other women nodded.

Pamela took her hand. "In cases like that, maybe you need to try to avoid them. Sometimes it's impossible." She shrugged. "But when you can, stay out of situations where you can be manipulated or tempted by them."

"Yeah, if I see my ex, I make sure I show him my brass knuckles so he knows not to come too close." Felicity tossed her rat's nest hairdo, which flopped back down on her leather-clad shoulders. "I don't really hate him, but I don't want to get close to him, either. In case he turns on the charm."

"They do that so well." Trish slapped the arm of her plastic chair. "It's not fair. It's not like I can turn off the switch."

The other women chimed in. "And you brain get all fuzzy." The Thai girl circled her finger near her temple.

"And they say they've changed."

"And they say they love you."

"And a part of you really wants to believe it."

"And — what's that?" Rosa pointed at the window covered by horizontal blinds.

"What?" Trish's heartbeat crescendoed like the finale of a Taiko drum performance.

"Somebody was watching us."

"Oh, Rosa, I hope it wasn't your ex."

"I hope it's mine." Felicity cracked her knuckles and stood.

Trish had one of those weird feelings that sizzled down her spine. On one hand, it dissipated her panic. On the other, dread weighted down her chest because she really didn't want to deal with this. "Wait, Felicity." She got up. "Let me go first."

"Oh, be careful, Trish."

"Take this." Cheryl handed her an aluminum bat that happened to be propped up in the corner. Well, this *was* downtown San Jose.

She exited the room and stepped into the hallway. No one except that really sinister flickering light. Okay, first on her list was to stop watching those scary movies with Jenn all the time. Her heart would pound straight through her breastbone any second now. At least Felicity was right behind her — she could hear her chains clinking.

She turned the corner —

"Aaaaiiiieeeee!"

She dropped the bat and started slapping at him. "I knew it was you! You're such a creep! Why do you keep following me?"

Kazuo turned his shoulder to take the brunt of her nails. "I was concerned for you."

"Concerned, my foot!" She stomped on his instep.

"*Ittai!*" He hopped on one leg.

"This your ex?" Felicity peered at him. "Looks like you don't need help."

Kazuo set his foot down gingerly. "I want to talk to you."

"Well, we were just talking about you." Trish folded her arms. She could honestly say she didn't even want to be in the same room with him. Maybe because they'd been talking about far more abusive men, maybe because she'd been reminding herself how abusive he'd been.

Those women were more important than he was, and she honestly enjoyed being here with them. For the first time since she'd known him, she wasn't torn at all about where she'd rather be. She stuck her nose in the air. "It is in my best interest not to converse with your sorry carcass."

"Car-kass? I am a car?" He frowned, his accent more pronounced in his pain. "I just detailed my car."

"This isn't the best neighborhood." Trish turned to head back into the room, Felicity ahead of her. "I'd go back to where you parked it to make sure it's still there."

Trish heard his feet pattering and the slam of the front door.

Well, she knew how high she was on his priority list.

TWENTY-EIGHT

A re you stealing that?" Spenser stopped and leaned against the office doorjamb.

Trish's eyes bugged out. "No. As if."

"Looks like stealing to me." She was so easy to rile.

She responded as expected, much to his entertainment. Her hand slammed on her hip and her eyes sparked. Her other fist shook the Tyvek suit at him. "I used this earlier today, and I'm taking it home to use one last time."

"Doing what? Experimenting with the bacteria at home as well as work?"

Her nose shot up. "For your information, tonight I'm going to bleach some mold to death."

"Oh, that's right. That going well?"

"I scrubbed the walls down earlier this week. This weekend, I'm going to pull up that nasty carpet. There's hardwood floors underneath, you know." She smiled, quite pleased with herself. She'd probably never even changed a lightbulb before moving into her current candidate for *Flip That House*.

"You've been busy."

"Tell me about it."

The truth about Kazuo and his ex-wife had been gnawing at Spenser's gut, and he knew he needed a good moment to come clean. He also held out a small hope she'd forgive him. So, he'd been thinking of sticking his neck out and asking her to dinner this weekend.

Guess that plan was out, but he could still spend time with her. "I'll help you."

"What?" Trish couldn't seem to make her jaw work and close her gaping mouth.

"I can pull up carpet." He wasn't an imbecile.

She frowned and her torso tilted sideways as she checked him out from head to toe. "You can?"

His mouth closed, and he glared at her before he caught the quirk in the side of her mouth. She'd got him. He sighed. "Tell me where you live and what time you want me to be there."

"You're serious?"

"I covered myself in orange goo for you the other week."

She smiled, a rather nasty one. "That *was* rather amusing."

He took a step backward. "I guess you don't need my help ..."

"No! No, I do." She flapped her hands at him as if that would keep him from walking away. "Thanks for the offer. Ten o'clock?"

"Great." He'd probably get lunch with her, and the work shouldn't be too hard.

Covered head-to-toe in a Tyvek suit, complete with hood, safety goggles and a mask, Trish clambered up the ladder and spritzed bleach solution onto the natural mural on her bathroom ceiling. She stumbled down the ladder and escaped to the doorway, breathing in the chilly night breeze from the wide-open front door and kitchen windows. The bathroom fan coughed and gagged as if it would die any moment, but it had run for a solid half-hour already. Maybe it was a hypochondriacal electric appliance.

So, Spenser had offered to help her pull carpet tomorrow. She'd been shocked and still couldn't figure out why he'd offered. Seemed kind of strange. He couldn't be interested in her, could he?

Her heart fluttered, and her gut simmered. No, she should ignore her excitement—*No looking!*—and treat him like a coworker and a friend. For the sake of her three rules and to protect her heart against his charm, and because of Kevin's unwanted attention that one time. Thankfully, Kevin had been ignoring her, although he'd deigned to say good morning last week.

Back to Spenser. She would be businesslike and efficient when he showed up tomorrow. She would toil and sweat and show her most unattractive side. She wouldn't flirt or laugh, or even smile at him.

Hmm, I wonder what I should wear . . .

Spenser couldn't imagine anything more revolting.

He stood in the archway to Trish's living room. This close to the carpet, he could smell the faint musty odor. A mosaic of browns and grays colored the surface in ancient stains.

She glanced up at him with apology on her face. "You don't have to stay."

The temptation to cut and run tugged at his feet. That or bolt for the open door so he could hurl his breakfast into the weeds.

He could tell her about his past another day, another time. He wasn't even sure if he'd find a good moment to spill his guts about Kazuo and Linda.

Trish opened and closed her hands, as if wavering between shoving him out the door or grabbing him by the shirt to keep him from escaping.

But then she turned toward the carpet, and her shoulders sagged. She seemed to shrink under the weight of the work ahead of her. If he didn't know her already, he would have suspected her of playing his emotions to get him to stay, but this was Trish. "Don't worry, I wouldn't desert you like that."

She smiled, magnificent and beaming, brighter than the sunlight outside, so infectious that it made him grin in return. He couldn't understand how she always did that, and why it always surprised him.

She set him up with a mask, safety glasses, heavy gloves and a utility knife, and they started at opposite ends of the room. They cut the carpet into four-foot widths, making it easier to tug the pieces from the tackless strips, although she still had a hard time. But she persisted, as if she had a personal stake in the removal of that nasty carpet.

She yanked up a stubborn piece. "If only my dad could see me now." Her voice had a bitter, metallic tang to it.

"Why?"

"He told Mom he didn't think I could do the repairs. Ha! I showed him." She rolled up the carpet she'd unhooked. "I took your advice and did Internet searches to figure out how to pull up old carpet. Oh, and I secretly raided my dad's Time Life books."

"My dad had those. He actually used them, too. He would work on the house while Mom took my brothers and me to church on Sunday."

"He didn't go, too?"

"Not at first, but he did later. I miss him. He passed away when I was in college."

"Oh, I'm sorry." The droop in Trish's mouth fascinated Spenser, even though dust and grime coated her hair, even though she wore no makeup, even though her baggy clothes did nothing for her figure.

He could segue the moment into Kazuo. No, too abrupt, too much like a confession spilling out. He didn't want to sound *guilty* for not telling her about his past history with Kazuo. Maybe he'd mention his own struggles with faith. Then she'd understand how he hadn't handled that situation in a very Christ-like manner . . .

She turned to a new section of carpet farther away from him. Too late. The moment was gone.

They removed all the carpet—from the front room, the hallway, and Trish's bedroom. He noticed the folded camping tent and lack of furniture. "Where will you sleep?"

"I'll set the tent back up after we clear off the carpet pad. I have an old sheet to lay down on the floor."

He frowned at her.

She shrugged. "What else can I do?"

He had no answer.

They hefted the last of the carpet outside to the dumpster she had rented. They started pulling up the tackless strips with crowbars, but one mighty heave sent a piece of wood flying up to graze the back of his wrist. Spenser bit his tongue hard before he could let loose with a vehement cuss word.

"Are you okay?"

Spenser grimaced at the beads of blood from the scratch. It burned, but it wasn't deep. "I'll be fine."

"I have a first aid kit. Let's clean it so it doesn't get infected."

"No, it's not that bad."

Instead of insisting and dithering over him, she shrugged and went back to work. Spenser stood there in shock. Weren't Asians supposed to offer multiple times because people always refused the first time? He felt gypped. Well, he couldn't renege like a wuss. He tackled the wooden strips.

The rest of the tackless strips came off smoothly. The carpet pad, however, had reached its last legs years ago. Exposed to the light, it fell apart in their hands, leaving pieces stuck under the staples. They picked at the crumbling bits, trapped by so many staples that Spenser wondered if the person who laid the carpet pad had been obsessive-compulsive.

Trish laughed at the staples. "Looks like whoever did this had fun."

He grunted and yanked at another staple. His jaw ached from being clenched, and sweat trickled down his gritty face in sticky rivers. She didn't look much better, but her staunch persistence forced him to keep up his pace. His fingers felt worn to the nub, and he'd never get the little foam crumbs out of his nails, blackened like he'd been digging coal.

He'd lost any desire to bring up anything personal.

They took a late lunch where they laughed and bantered together. He couldn't ruin the atmosphere between them. He'd wait until after they were done.

They went back to work and pulled off the carpet pad and most of the staples by late afternoon. They were almost done when his pliers slipped, and he ended up pinching a chunk of his skin. With a strong grunt, he grabbed his hand and sat up on his heels.

She peered at his hand. "Did it break the skin?"

"No, doesn't look like it."

"We should bandage it. It's all red."

This time he didn't refuse. They washed their hands and she took care of his injury. He watched her bent head, her serious face.

She was beautiful.

There was a brief silence. Here was his chance. "I wanted to get back at Kazuo." Stupid! He couldn't have put it a better way?

"What?"

He paused to relax his jaw. "Kazuo's the reason my wife left me and Matthew."

She turned so pale, he grabbed her in case she passed out. She shook his hand away. "You've known Kazuo from before?"

"We're not exactly friends."

He could almost see her brain wheels running, the pieces clicking into place. "That weird week you kept asking me out ... that was right after Kazuo showed up at work that one time."

Busted. "Yeah." This wasn't going well. Every deepening line between her brows and around her mouth made him feel smaller and smaller.

"You said you wanted to get back at him?"

He didn't say anything.

"You mean you used me like a Kleenex? Is that what it was? This whole time? Even this?" She flung her hand out toward the living room as her voice rose in pitch.

"I stopped asking you out because I liked being around you and being your friend." He grabbed her arms and held on even though she tensed under his fingers. "It's not about Kazuo anymore."

Her face had closed up. He'd never seen her so cold, without any kind of movement or emotion.

"I know what I did earlier was wrong, but God's been working in me. That's true even if you never believe me."

She turned her head away from him and pulled out of his grip. "Leave." She wasn't being hysterical. He knew she would be later.

He exited the front door, heard it slam behind him, and got into his car. Now she'd probably avoid him like the plague.

Wait a minute.

No.

He couldn't believe he hadn't thought of it sooner.

He fumbled with the handle and thrust the car door open. He raced up the cracked driveway, waded through the weeds, pounded on the closed front door.

She didn't open it.

"Trish!"

"Go away."

"I need to tell you something."

"Then say it."

"Let me in."

"No way, *Jose.*"

"You don't want the neighbors to hear this."

He didn't think the veiled threat would get through to her, but he started when she flung the door open. "Go — "

He grabbed her by the shoulders and muscled his way in, kicking the door shut.

She yanked away from him. "This better be — "

"You need to get tested."

"What?"

"For HIV."

She sucked in a sharp breath and stared at him, wide-eyed. Her body started to shake, but he didn't dare touch her — she looked like she'd fly apart at any moment.

"I'm sorry. I know this is hard to hear. But ..." He had to take a deep breath before he went on. "About a year after we separated, Linda found out she had HIV. Matthew and I were tested, but we were clean. Linda had already broken up with Kazuo by the time she found out, so it's possible she didn't get it from him, but if you slept with him, you need to be tested."

Trish raised shaking hands to her mouth. Her eyes didn't move away from him, and he could see every corner of her fear. "Trish, did you ... did you ever have sex with him?"

Her denial erupted in a searing glare. "What kind of a question is that?" Meaning, *yes, of course I did.*

"Did you ever have *unprotected* sex with him?"

She tried to swallow, couldn't breathe for several long seconds. "Yes. Twice."

TWENTY-NINE

She had to ask him the question that could change the rest of her life.

Are you clean? When was the last time you were tested?

Kazuo had reassured her he was clean after the two times they'd had unprotected sex, but now, after hearing how he'd broken up Spenser's marriage, and about Linda's HIV, she wasn't so sure.

She pulled her legs up and tried to curl her body into her car seat. Spenser had hurt himself in telling her. She'd been able to see it in his eyes, in his voice. Maybe he'd also been earnest when he said that he liked her company and that it wasn't about Kazuo anymore. A part of her was intrigued, but she also didn't want to be intrigued. He was fun to banter with, but trusting him?

She needed to drive to Kazuo's place. No, she should take one of her cousins with her for protection. For support. For strength.

Because he'd just charm her again. He'd say whatever he wanted and she'd believe him. She still couldn't quite trust herself, despite the way she'd been able to spurn him the last few times she'd seen him.

But no. No matter how she felt — or didn't feel — about Spenser, she couldn't bring in someone else to witness her talk with Kazuo. She couldn't expose Spenser's failed marriage to anyone, not even her cousins. She couldn't even risk a hushed conversation that could be overheard. This was Spenser's secret. She didn't have the right to allow anyone else to know.

She had to do this alone.

But not alone. She hadn't been following rule number three very closely—she kept forgetting to pray—but not now.

"God, if ever I needed you, it's now." She rested her head against the steering wheel. "I almost don't want to know the answer. Please help me when I go to Kazuo's apartment. Keep my head clear. Help me not be tempted. Zap me with something, Lord, because I'm going in."

She missed the view from his loft apartment. As she waited for Kazuo to answer her knock, she stared up at the tall windows above the door, remembering the way the sunlight filtered into the room, warming the honey-colored walls. Remembering the days she could almost see San Francisco from the bay windows in his living room, when the smog had been blown away after a rain.

Strange, his apartment had seemed darker as their relationship started to sour. Or maybe she had looked out the windows less because he hadn't wanted her to be anywhere but inside, with him, inspiring his paintings.

He opened the door a crack, then swung it wide open—as wide as his smile. "Trish."

She entered cautiously, as if the room were booby-trapped with handcuffs or cages to trap her there so she could never leave. Then she noticed the show on the HDTV. "Is that one of those K-dramas?"

"Er ... no." Kazuo darted in front of her and turned it off. Then he faced her, opening his arms wide and his smile wider. "You've come back. Now I can finish my masterpiece, your painting."

"You still haven't finished it?" He'd been halfway done when they broke up months ago. "I thought you were going to show it at your uncle's new art gallery in Japan. That opens in only a couple months."

"I told you, you are my muse. I can't finish it without you." He tried to embrace her, but his hands felt slimier than a squid. Her gaze skewered him as she backed away.

Who cared about his art show? She was stalling. She needed to just confront him with what she really wanted to know. "I didn't come about your painting. I need you to tell me the truth. Do you have HIV?"

Well, that cooled his ardor pretty quick. Kazuo became very still. "No."

"When was the last time you were tested?"

He thought a moment. "Several years ago."

"You told me you were clean." She spat it at him through clenched teeth.

"What brought this up?"

"Spenser told me about Linda."

His eyebrows rose, then fell. Then he had the audacity to smile, the scum. "That was years ago. She means nothing to me, babe. Just you."

"I don't care how you feel about her."

"I know you don't." His voice had *patronizing* sprinkled all over it.

She shoved her fist in her back pocket so she wouldn't take a swing at him. "I care about the fact she has HIV, not that she was one of your lovers."

"Oh." He reached for her, but she jerked away. "Don't worry. About six months after we broke off, I found out. I had myself tested, I was clean. She got it from her boyfriend after me, whoever he was."

The relief crashed on her like a tsunami wave. Trish dropped into a chair, her head in her hands. She forced air through her lungs. Clean. He might be clean. She might be clean. She still needed to be tested, but the threat no longer oppressed her like a guillotine blade hovering over her neck.

She sat there for so long, she didn't notice his hand on her shoulder until her heart rate had settled down. She reached up to brush him off, and he grasped her hand instead.

But her body didn't respond to him as it had before, and her mind seemed almost disconnected. It was as if her brain had been tucked away safe behind a glass wall, to be able to see the lines of dissipation around his eyes, to not be influenced by warm hands or warm smiles. That had to be from God, this strange place of safety. She pulled away from Kazuo without a single drop of regret.

She stood. "Good-bye, Kazuo."

"I can't finish my masterpiece without you."

She walked to the door. "Use another painting for your uncle's art gallery. You've got tons."

"Ah, yes. I'll see you tomorrow."

Her hand froze on the doorknob. "Tomorrow?"

"At the unveiling."

"Unveiling?" Now she sounded like a parrot.

"Your grandmother said you'd be there."

"I don't know what you're talking about."

"At your grandmother's bank. She's unveiling the painting she bought from me."

Trish's heart pounded as she read the name on her cell phone's call waiting. She flipped it open. "Grandma?"

"Hello, dear."

No rancor, no anger in her voice, not even the tang of vinegar. What alien had abducted her grandmother and replaced her with this calm, pleasant woman? "H-hi, Grandma."

"Are you coming to the unveiling today at the bank?" Honey-sweet tones, as if she had talked to Trish yesterday rather than that last, rather short, highly upsetting phone call at work almost two weeks ago.

Translation: *You are off Grandma's Ignore List if you attend the unveiling today, and all will be well in the Sakai family.*

Trish leaped at the olive branch — even though it wasn't really an olive branch because it didn't mean Grandma actually forgave her, it just meant Grandma was talking to her again, conditional upon her attending the event. "Yes, what time?"

Since Kazuo was the star of the show, and it was sure to be large enough, she could avoid him for much of it. Plus she felt stronger after yesterday. She'd pray extra long in her SUV before going in. God would come through for her again, right?

"It's at one o'clock, but arrive a little early. And I hope you wear that pretty silk suit I bought you last Christmas."

Translation: *Wear the Christian Dior or be disowned.*

"Certainly." Trish had been a bit skinnier last Christmas, but she would cram her thunder thighs into that thing if it killed her.

The first people she saw at the unveiling ceremony surprised her. "Mom! Is it okay for you to be here?" She gave one parent a hug. At the other one she stopped, stood there awkwardly. Couldn't make herself move to embrace him. Dad turned away to mingle with the rest of the crowd at the unveiling, pretending not to notice or care.

Mom, on the other hand, pressed her lips together and dug her nails into Trish's upper arm. "That's not very respectful, young lady."

She honestly did feel bad that relations were so strange between them, but, well, Mom wasn't the one who'd caught him *in flagrante.* "How're you feeling? You look better."

"You're not changing the subject — Hello, Mr. Nakamura, so nice to see you." Mom nodded at a passing white-haired man in an indecently expensive suit before turning back to her. "Your father and I are working things out."

Working things out? For Japanese couples, that meant going on as before, pretending the problem didn't exist.

What was Trish going to say? *No, I'd actually like you to divorce the bozo and go against all the Christian principles I'm trying to model for you as a witness for Christ.* She also knew her dad. If they ever did actually talk about it, he'd charm Mom again like he always did, no matter what snit Mom had gotten herself worked up over.

However, Mom seemed different these days, less agitated. She even spoke with more calm than her normal NASCAR speed. "You're looking good, Mom."

"Life seems much slower lately, somehow. I've been so lazy, I've been watching these interesting Korean soap operas on TV . . ."

Trish caught sight of Kazuo—looking dashing in a black suit with his unruly hair pulled back in a neat ponytail—talking with an older gentleman, probably in Japanese judging from the deferential stoop of his shoulders and neck, the occasional short bow. Great! While he was occupied, Trish could talk with Grandma without fear of Grandma pulling him into their little *tete-a-tete*.

"Thank you all for coming." Grandma's voice aired above the crowd from the amplifiers set up discreetly on either side of the bank's large foyer, which had been cleared of islands and chairs. Too late to talk to her. Grandma stood behind a small podium slightly to the side of the bank's far wall, which had been partially covered with a white cloth.

"We at Sakai Bank have always supported our community. I am very pleased to have discovered this brilliant artist here in San Jose, and to have added to the bank's impressive collection of fine art pieces with this newest painting.

"Mr. Kazuo Kawakami has lived in our community for many years, but his family hails from Tokyo, Japan. In fact, his parents have flown in to the States to join us for this momentous occasion." She gestured to a Japanese couple standing to the side of the podium, who beamed and gave stately bows.

"And now, let me present . . . *Kubi ga nai Chikin*!" Grandma swept her hand upward in a dramatic flourish as the sheet covering the wall dropped.

Trish knew that painting. One of her least favorites of his, actually, possibly because of the bloody chicken head staring straight at the viewer with a look that mingled confusion and outrage at the same time. The same painting he had refused to mark down in price even when she told him it was too ugly for anyone to want.

Apparently not too ugly for Sakai Bank. She joined in the applause.

People rushed toward Kazuo to talk to him. Perfect. Trish left her mother chatting with one of her aunties and shoved her way through the crowd to the podium.

Grandma bestowed a pleased yet cool smile as she caught sight of Trish approaching, which was pretty much what she'd been expecting. At least she didn't turn her nose up and refuse to acknowledge her existence on planet earth. "Trish, come meet Mr. and Mrs. Kawakami."

Before she could get a word in, she found herself thrust before the elegantly clad couple bowing graciously to her. *"Hajimemashite doozo yoroshiku."* She managed a credible bow, although the waistband of the silk skirt threatened to slice her torso in half. She straightened with a soft grunt of pain.

Grandma spoke to them in Japanese. "This is the granddaughter who speaks Japanese with such a lovely accent."

Say what? Years ago, when Trish had been taking her Japanese classes, this was the same woman who had coolly informed her that her accent sounded like a country pig farmer with marbles in his mouth. Trish hadn't spoken Japanese in front of Grandma in years.

Mrs. Kawakami smiled and spoke in her native tongue. "All your cousins speak Japanese?"

"No, I'm the only one who speaks fluently." Trish spoke very slowly to make sure her accent and inflections were dead perfect.

"How wonderful that you keep up with your heritage." Mr. Kawakami fingered his Italian suit.

"You must be very proud of your son." Trish glanced quickly at the hideous painting and tried not to wince.

His parents looked rather pained, themselves. "We are very happy for him. When he settles down, he will be a good manager for our bank in Japan."

Whoa. She'd known Kazuo's parents were wealthy — after all, they supported all his financial needs rather effortlessly — but now she understood Grandma's insistence that Kazuo was such a *nice boy.* His parents had such a *nice bank.*

"Trish and Kazuo are very good friends." Grandma's smile was as slick as snake oil.

That's why Grandma had wanted Trish here today. That was the condition of Trish's return to matriarchal favor. Grandma had thought that Kazuo's parents' money would sway her. Maybe a few months ago, it would have. Now, it would be selling her soul.

A part of her ached like a festering wound at the thought that Grandma wanted her together with Kazuo because of what his parents could do for the bank, not because of what he could do for Trish. To Grandma, Trish's life and feelings were peripheral. Someone Trish had always wanted to please hadn't given a thought to pleasing her.

It wasn't Kazuo's parents' fault. They were collateral damage in this war of the Sakai women.

If her cousin Venus were in this position, she would baldly inform the Kawakamis that she'd broken up with Kazuo. Lex would announce that their son was a possessive demon with a temper and the last man she'd be interested in. Jenn would go silent and passive aggressive.

Trish turned on the charm. "Have you met others of my family? This is my Uncle Nakamura. He owns a resort in Beppu and goes back quite often." She eased shy Uncle Nakamura into the conversation and then turned to Grandma. "I need to talk to you."

Grandma hedged. "I have important guests I need to see —"

Trish steeled herself and wouldn't take the easy way out. "It won't take long."

"This is a very important event for Grandma." She must be suspecting what Trish wanted to talk about if she was speaking in third person again.

Her stomach acid went volcanic. What was she doing? This would kill her mother. The alternative was being guilted and nagged into a marriage with Kazuo — and she knew Grandma was already thinking along those lines, she could tell — which would probably topple Trish over the edge to homicide of said potential husband. Or maybe she was watching too much *CSI*.

For the first time in a long time, she really didn't care what Grandma thought. "I'm not going to marry him."

Wide eyes beneath Shiseido-blue lids. "Who said anything about marriage? Trish, you're being silly."

She gritted her teeth. "I mean, I'm not getting back together with Kazuo."

"Never say never, dear."

"He's abusive and possessive." Emotional abuse counted, right? She steeled her glare. "And I know you'd never want me with someone who treats me like chattel." *Ha! Try and wiggle out of that one, Grandma.*

She turned falsely innocent eyes on Trish. "He said he's changed. Don't you believe him?"

Aargh, Grandma was better at this than she was. "No, I don't. In fact, I haven't seen evidence he's changed at all."

"Doesn't everyone deserve a second chance? Isn't that what your *religion* teaches you?"

Oooh, low blow. Maybe Lex was right about the mysterious reasons behind Grandma's big fight with her long-time best friend—oops, *ex*-best friend, Mrs. Matsumoto, who happened to be an outspoken Christian. Maybe Mrs. Matsumoto had said something that hit too close to Grandma's heart.

"Jesus said to give people grace, not to put yourself back in dangerous situations." Not that he'd actually hit her or anything, but dumping her car keys down the toilet had to count for something.

"I think you're mistaken about the ... about his temper. It must be a misunderstanding. Look how nice his parents are."

"They're very nice, but I'm not marrying *them*."

"Who said anything about—"

Oops. "I mean, I'm not dating them. Him. I'm not dating him again." Arguing with Grandma always turned her into such an idiot.

"You're such a disappointment to Grandma. You were always one of Grandma's favorite grandchildren."

The petulance in her tone destroyed Trish's last remnants of guilt about disobeying her. "I'm actually protecting the family." She smiled, all sugar and spice.

Grandma's eyes narrowed. "What do you mean?"

"I'm guarding the family's gene pool. No neurotic artist genes in my children."

Grandma's mouth pinched tighter than if she'd eaten an *ume* sour plum.

Trish stood up straighter. "Good-bye, Grandma." She turned and walked away.

THIRTY

Trish only jogged when she felt fat, which was about once a week, which fell on a Monday this time. The stress was also prying open a hole in the base of her skull with a pair of flat-nosed pliers. Hopefully, some physical exercise would ease her neck pain.

She checked the time on her computer. Two o'clock. She had a two-hour incubation time, and she would need to stay late tonight to finish the assay. She'd be a good girl and go running now.

She changed into shorts and the extra pair of running shoes she kept at work but rarely used. She stood stretching outside the building when Spenser walked out, also in shorts and running shoes.

"Join you?" Tentativeness in his eyes belied his casual words and stance that seemed to assert nothing was wrong.

She didn't want company. She had too many things to hash over, including her own unusual defiance of Grandma yesterday.

Yet at the same time, she wanted to spend more time with him despite what happened on Saturday. But wasn't that looking, or at least encouraging him? Wouldn't she be breaking rule number one?

Well, she wouldn't actually be *looking* at him, he'd be next to her. Besides, who was she kidding? This was Spenser. When talking about how he thought of her, hadn't he used the *friend* word on Saturday? Not the *interested* word or the *like* word.

Another problem was the embarrassing fact that her cousins' kids on tricycles could beat her in a race. "I'm pretty slow."

"I'll try to keep up." He winked.

Well, it wasn't her fault if he didn't believe her. He'd end up walking while she huffed and puffed next to him.

They started off on a campus footpath used by the more consistent runners. She set the pace, following the concrete ribbon that wove through the green campus to a street, which twisted through the rolling foothills into a wealthy residential area.

She'd been following God's path for her, hadn't she? Why was all this trouble happening to her? Well, okay, right now she wasn't doing so hot on rule number three, persevere and rely on God.

Rely on God to do what? Protect her from Grandma's wrath now that Trish had told her no for once? Plus, Grandma had suddenly gone completely psycho on her and her three cousins because of their Christian faith. Fear of what Grandma would do next hung around in her stomach like bad *sashimi*.

Spenser had slowed down to match her speed, but with his longer stride, he was almost walking. "Hey, Trish." He breathed normally.

"Wha-aht?" she panted.

"I'm sorry."

"Fo-wha-aht?"

"About not saying anything about Kazuo."

"Izz-o-kay." She could understand. Kind of.

Trees *shushed* above them in the breeze, and the occasional car passed them and swept the early spring wildflowers into a waving dance. The winter rains had colored the foothills emerald green and mud brown, and dark jade juniper bushes dotted the hillsides.

Spenser cleared his throat. "So did you ...?"

"Whah?"

"Get tested." His mouth formed a grim line.

"Yes ... Results ... next ... week ... Also ... asked ... him."

"What'd he say?"

She couldn't talk, so she wheezed and gave an A-OK sign.

His face relaxed like he'd gotten a botox injection, although his mouth was still taut. "I'm glad. Let me know when you get the results back—I want to know you'll be okay."

A glowing warmth blossomed in her chest. No, that warmth must be her heart about to fail from this exertion. She should run more often than once a week.

"What are you doing tonight?" He suppressed a yawn, the more-physically-fit stinker.

She mimicked *Wax on, wax off.* "Wha-halls."

He gave an amused smirk at her gasping. "Scrubbing walls?"

She nodded.

"How about you take a break and go out to dinner with me?"

The air rushed from her lungs in a hacking cough.

"You okay?"

She stopped, folded over, and sucked in a few larger breaths. "What?" *Pant, pant.* "Date?" *Wheeze.* "Me?" *Cough, hack.* "Why?"

"Come on." He broke into a jog. "Don't stop."

So much for romance. She dragged herself up to speed while her legs protested and her side ached. "So?"

"So what?"

Her short break had allowed her to get some of her breath back. "Not ... about ... Kazuo?"

He looked her directly in the eye when he answered. "No, I promise this has nothing to do with him." He wasn't lying.

She reluctantly broke eye contact and turned her attention back to the road so she wouldn't trip over a rock and sprawl body parts all over the concrete. "Why ... a date ... now?"

He ticked off on his fingers. "I'm Christian, which is a good thing because you've been *looking.*"

"Shut up."

"We're friends."

"On ... good days."

"We have fun together."

"We do?"

"So, why not?"

Why not, indeed? Especially with him ignoring her interjections because he knew she was annoyed and about to collapse in exhaustion.

What about Grandma? Would she have a fit if Trish dated someone else? She really wanted to go out with Spenser. They'd had lunch together dozens of times, they had fun, and Trish was usually trying hard not to *look*.

"Sure." It zapped out of her mouth so fast, he blinked before he caught it.

He flashed that fabulous dimple. "Great. I'll ask my mom to sit for Matthew."

Oops. Maybe she should have prayed before answering him. *Uh ... sorry, God.* No bolt of lightning struck her down dead. Wasn't that a good sign?

He was her coworker — didn't that make it seem less like an "official" date? And maybe nothing would come of it — she'd feel nothing but platonic affection for him.

Yeah, right.

Trish strolled into Sushi Masa restaurant. She resisted the urge to smooth her pants over her ample behind, and stopped her hand from reaching up to make sure the jeweled clip still held her hair in place.

No one sat in the waiting area — she knew she should have waited longer to drive here. Spenser had suggested the place since it was only a few minutes away from her home. She'd thought a "few minutes" meant five. It had taken her about 90 seconds.

She took a seat, smoothing her khakis so she wouldn't stand up with creases, and crossed her legs with a show of indifference.

Why was she so nervous? It was just Spenser.

On a real date.

She couldn't even try to convince herself he wasn't attractive, not when they were on a real date. Would this make things awkward with them at work? Maybe she should call him on her cell and cancel. He'd understand.

The door opened and Spenser strode through. It was way weird to see him in date clothes. His Ralph Lauren short-sleeved knit shirt accentuated his broad shoulders but didn't caricature them. His gaze alighted on her, and he gave a wide, white smile softened by his dimples, which didn't come out often enough when he was with her.

She rose to her feet and dreamily returned his wide grin. Spenser paused and stared down at her for a moment, looking a little dazed. Strange, he did that randomly when they talked. She couldn't figure out why.

He blinked as if waking from a daydream. He turned to nod at the hostess, who had approached with two menus in hand.

"Tell me you like sushi." He sat gracefully into his chair.

"I'm Japanese. Of course I like sushi."

"Good. Let's order a platter."

They ordered, and Spenser started fiddling with the paper wrapping of his wooden chopsticks. Trish rested her cheek in her hand.

Tick, tock. Tick, tock.

"So, Spenser—"

Up went his hand, palm out. "You're going to start babbling, because you hate dead space. Don't. We're friends, we're past that stage. Ask me something. Anything."

"Tell me about Kazuo and Linda."

Oh, Trish. You should staple your mouth shut.

He looked like he'd swallowed a goldfish. Live. "You really go for the gut."

"Sorry, sorry."

"No, I did ask for it. I don't know how they met, I know she was modeling for his latest painting."

"Did you see it?"

"What?"

"The painting."

"And when would I have been at his studio?"

"Oh. Well, you'd be pleased."

"Why?"

"She's Asian, right? Besides mine—his current one—he only has one other Asian woman painting, and he cut her head off."

Spenser had a look on his face that indicated he really didn't know how to respond to that.

"Kazuo has a headless motif."

"Ah. Anyway, I found out when she told me she was leaving me and Matthew."

"*What?* What a tramp. I can't believe—oops, sorry, I shouldn't have called her a tramp."

"No, you shouldn't have." His heavy lidded eyes gave her a dry look.

"How old was Matthew?"

"Five months."

"She left her *baby*? I would never do that. Boy, do you pick 'em—uh ..." Oh, man. Shoe-leather diet. She was on a roll tonight.

"You're on a roll tonight, honey."

How did he do that? "I'm sorry, I keep forgetting this is a date and not lunchtime at work."

They stared at each other for a moment. The next thing she knew, she was laughing like her lungs were going to explode. He wasn't laughing quite so hard, but his dimple peeked out.

Trish saw a glimpse over his shoulder of a long ponytail of straight hair falling almost to the ground, swung in an arc over a bony shoulder. "Oh no."

She hadn't realized she said it aloud until Spenser's brows came together. "What is it?"

"My cousin Mimi. My eternal enemy, Dracula's daughter, Mephisto's mother, vamp of villainy ..." She couldn't come up with more flavorful descriptions before the she-devil herself sashayed up to their table.

Mimi's signature ankle-length ponytail measured a few inches shy of five feet, since Mimi herself had stopped growing at four feet, eight and three-quarter inches, to her frustration and rage and Trish's secret delight. Everything else in Mimi's life had gone according to her wishes—luscious pearl-pink lips and onyx eyes set in a face of pale ivory, a delicate bone structure giving the impression of frailty and triggering male-protectiveness, yet flaunting two bouncing C-cups and a tight little buttocks. It amazed Trish that Mimi's height wouldn't follow expectations, also.

"Hiya, Trish." Mimi rested her hand on the top of Spenser's chair, probably sinking her claws into his back.

"What do you want?" Somehow, Lex got along swimmingly with their cousin, but Trish still didn't see the girl's less repulsive side.

Mimi feigned ignorance of the prime object of her attack in a brilliant tactical maneuver. "We missed you at the *Obon* dance committee meeting."

Ah, a chance for a flush hit. "My mother went." Her saccharine tones implied the *Obon* committee was for the older generation.

"So did mine. You didn't want to help her?"

Ooooo, it had been a sacrificed pawn. "I haven't been to an *Obon* in years." Ever since Mimi "accidentally" shoved Trish out of the traditional Japanese line dance right into a mud puddle, ruining her great-grandmother's heirloom silk kimono and Trish's self-esteem.

Mimi's gaze oh-so-casually settled on Spenser's polite expression with a speculative gleam. Trish gritted her teeth. "Spenser, this is my cousin, Mimi Sakai."

Mimi gave a mysterious, seductive smile reminiscent of Lucy Liu.

Trish watched him study her down-tilted face—flawless, gorgeous, and dainty—everything Trish was not. But something he saw made his eyes chill to beads of black ice, and his wide smile curled short of a sneer. He confounded her by his indifferent, "Hi," before he turned back to rest both elbows on the table, shutting Mimi out.

Mimi's jaw plummeted to the floor. Trish saw all the way down her throat to her tonsils, while her mystical eyes bugged out into gecko orbs. Trish wished for a camera so the *Cherry Blossom Times* would run a front page spread: "MIMI DISSED!" Trish gripped her seat with both hands to prevent herself from jumping into the Snoopy dance right there in the restaurant. She rewarded herself with a cheerful "Bye, Mimi."

Her cousin swirled in a cascade of dark hair and flounced away.

Spenser's face shone with mirth and shared triumph. She wanted to reach over and kiss those adorable dimples.

Nononono. Stop thinking about kissing.

She actually had brain activity for an entire 0.2 seconds before blurting out, "Not to be mean, but I would think she was your type. She's like the stick—I mean, the Hong Kong intern at work."

He cocked an eyebrow at her.

"You said it yourself, I'm on a roll. Who am I kidding? We're friends. I can't expect to censor my mouth here when I wouldn't if we were both in the lab."

He sighed. "Good point."

"So? Mimi?"

"Girls like that expect every guy they smile at to fall at their feet."

"Mimi *is* gorgeous. It's always been like that for her."

Some of her wistfulness must have colored her tone, because his eyes gentled. "What's it been like for *you*?"

The question startled her. "What do you mean?"

"Oh, the bad blood between you two isn't obvious at all."

Trish remembered flashes of her childhood: at family parties, the girls a few feet away laughing about her, making her feel isolated in the middle of the crowd. Mimi making a habit—case in point—of stealing her boyfriends. "She always made me feel like I didn't measure up."

"Maybe *she* didn't."

"Did ya *look* at her?"

"She looks like Barbie's sister Skipper."

Trish sighed and her eyes drifted to Mimi's distant figure on the other side of the restaurant. "I'd kill to look like Skipper."

"Snap out of it." He glared at her. "You're being an idiot."

She gave a cheeky grin. "Now who's on a roll?"

"Trish, don't you know ..." He held her gaze. He wasn't being charming or flattering. Somehow, slowly, his serious expression made her feel as if she glowed. As if she was hotter than radioactive P^{32}. As if she was the most gorgeous woman in the entire restaurant.

As she studied Spenser's face, it seemed that in his eyes, she was.

She was ready. Body humming, mouth primed.

Dinner had been consumed with minimal public pigging-out on her part. Conversation had been witty and entertaining. Glances had been inviting but not too coy. If he hadn't gotten her message, he was dumber than a rock.

Kiss me, baby!

His kisses must be like Godiva truffles. She'd become conditioned — the whiff of his cologne made her salivate. She was ready to be smooched and see stars.

As she stood by her SUV, he enveloped her in a bear-hug that swallowed her in a rich sea of cologne, Lever 2000, and Spenser-musk. She contentedly drowned. "Thanks for a great evening," she spoke into his jacket pocket.

"Not bad for two friends, huh?"

Mmm, he had a solid torso. She wasn't close enough to feel his heartbeat, but she was fairly certain it beat faster than baseline, if this long embrace was any indication. Better and better. He loosened his hold and stared down at her for a long moment. She couldn't quite see his face because of the parking lot light shining behind him, but she felt the tickle of his breath on her forehead.

Her heart flipped cartwheels. Her senses came alive — she felt every light touch of the evening breeze, heard the faint roar of car engines, the skitter of some animal in the ornamental brush beside the restaurant.

He moved his head, leaning close.

Oh, yeah. She tilted her head up, but not too quickly, or else he'd think she was being too easy to get. Her lips parted.

He pressed a gentle kiss to her *cheek.*

What? Her heart smacked face-first into the pavement. Her muscles went into rigor.

Why didn't you kiss me, you freak?! Her cheek! A brotherly kiss.

But he didn't move away. His jaw pressed to hers. His breathing sounded harsh in her ear. Her body hummed where his hand, still embracing her, scorched her back.

Then another part of her realized, *Man, a guy with self-control! You scored, babe.*

Had she wrongfully assumed his playboy reputation? Or maybe he was being extra careful because she both worked with him and went to his church. Or maybe he had discovered during the course of dinner that she was too ugly and her mouth was too caustic for him to consider even thinking of her as other than his coworker and sometime friend, and he'd now go ask out that stick-skinny Hong Kong intern girl and they'd get married and have beautiful, skinny children together.

Then his voice rumbled in her ear. "Let's take it slow."

No! No! No! "Sure."

He drew back. She did *not* imagine that his hand lingered on her back longer than was technically necessary. And yes, she could barely see her hand in the dark parking lot, but she definitely heard his faster breathing. That took the edge off her disappointment.

She drove away with a smile on her face. She grinned at the empty intersection while she waited on the stoplight. She grinned at the drunken pedestrian who crossed Camden Avenue at a randomly chosen spot. She grinned at the suicidal rice-rocket as it zoomed past her, winking at her with a flash of red taillights.

She couldn't wait for work tomorrow morning. She wondered how long he'd want to take things *slow*.

THIRTY-ONE

He didn't know how much longer he could take things slow. Spenser activated his mother's car alarm and hustled into the church with Matthew between him and his mom.

She tucked her hand in Matthew's but spoke to Spenser. "Are you going out to lunch with your friend?"

"Don't know yet." He hoped so, just the two of them. "You're fine getting a ride with Mrs. Choi?"

"Of course." But she wasn't about to be distracted. "Did you have a good time with your friend on Friday night?"

"Yeah." They'd gone out to coffee after she'd finished worship team practice. "Thanks for watching him. Matthew said you both slept on the couch."

She smoothed down the collar of her favorite lavender suit. "VeggieTales. He fell asleep first, for a change."

They happened to see Trish in the foyer as they entered the church. She lit up the room with that smile. It seemed a bit brighter than normal, which made him lengthen his stride. "Hi."

"Hi. Oomph! Hey there, Matthew." She bent to peer down at the five-year-old attached to her leg.

"Tish! Tishtishtishtishtish!" Spittle rained on her khaki slacks.

"Machoomachoomachoomachoomachoo!" She tickled his ribs until he giggled and let go of her leg, to hang on like a monkey to her arms. While swinging him, she turned to Spenser's mom. "Hello, Mrs. Wong. How are you doing?"

"I'm fine. I keep wanting to tell you how inspiring it is to have you up there on the worship team."

Trish's smile turned nuclear. Spenser could feel the warmth. "Thanks so much, Mrs. Wong."

"Well, I better take Matthew to Sunday school. I'll see you." She disentangled her grandson from Trish's arms and led him down the hallway to the Sunday school room.

Alone at last.

Trish's eyes softened when she looked up at him. "Hi — oh, Olivia!" She reached around him to grab Olivia by the sleeve.

"Hey." She gave the two of them a speculative smile.

His gut clenched in an automatic reaction. But rather than wanting to ease away from Trish, his feet shuffled closer to her protectively.

Relax, Spenser. She was a big girl. Gossip wasn't bullets. Besides, Olivia wouldn't say anything, even if she did suspect they were more than friends.

"Olivia, I've been meaning to ask you, would you be willing to write a reference for my MDiv application?"

Olivia's teeth gleamed against her dusky skin. "Oh sure. Get me the form and tell me when you need it. Who else have you asked?"

"Griselle, and also Christina who works with me at Katsu Towers. My fourth one is on my supervisor's desk at work right now."

That's right, on Friday they'd talked about her wanting to get her MDiv. He tried not to feel left out that she hadn't asked him, but then again, if things worked out . . .

He shifted from foot to foot as they chatted. Weren't they going to lead worship together? Did they have to discuss all this now?

"See ya." Olivia hitched her gig bag higher on her shoulder and headed toward the sanctuary.

Finally.

Her smile said she had seen his impatience. "Sorry."

"No, you're not."

She laughed. "It's fun."

"To annoy me?" He flicked a lock of hair off her cheek.

"And it's easy." She stuck her tongue out at him. She also eased a little closer.

He liked that. "I have something for you."

Her eyes sparkled like she'd been handed a fat red envelope on New Year's. "What?"

He reached into his pocket and removed the earring. "I found this in my car seat after I drove away Friday night." He'd dropped her off at her SUV, still parked in the church lot, after they'd spent hours in Tran's Nuclear Coffee shop.

She held out her hand, but a cluster of people from the Singles Group suddenly walked into the foyer. Before he could give her the earring, her hand whipped behind her back and he straightened, trying to tip away from her so they wouldn't look like they were standing as close as they were. This thing between them was new and they were taking it slow, so they'd agreed to try and avoid the gossip that would fly around.

"Hey Trish, Spenser. Trish, great worship set last week."

"Thanks." She gave a lightning-short return wave.

Move along, people.

"Spenser, are you still training people to work the sound board?"

"Sure." He was glad the post-college grad was interested, but she could have picked a better time to talk to him. "I have another training session Wednesday night at six."

"Cool. Thanks." She flashed a wide smile.

He wasn't looking at her, but he could tell that Trish stiffened.

"Come on, I can see them inside already." Another girl pulled the brunette away, and the group of singles moved on.

He didn't realize his shoulders had been so tight until they suddenly relaxed. Trish's expression wasn't as warm as before, but she wasn't condemning, either.

He shielded the space between them with a rolled shoulder and passed her the earring more smoothly than James Bond himself would have. She loosed a short giggle.

But once she glanced at it, her animated face flatlined. Her spine snapped stiff as a spear, and she held the earring up in her fingers.

The ninja stars shooting from her eyes *thwacked!* him right in the forehead. "What's wrong?"

"This isn't mine." She flicked it from her fingers and walked away.

Clara's smile beamed in her wrinkled face as she announced, "We're having a girl!"

The other women in the Katsu Towers rec room *oohed* and *aahed.* Trish skewered her with a suspicious eye. "I thought your son was single?"

Clara flapped a hand. "This is my other son."

"The responsible one," Deborah added in a not-quiet-at-all aside.

Sumiyo shushed her, although not vehemently. "Clara's hearing is fine, you know. Don't start another squabble."

Trish turned to Deborah with renewed respect. "You fought with Clara?"

"She accused me of turning up my new hearing aid to overhear what she was whispering to someone else." Her voice was still pitched a bit loud since her nephew had sprung for the cheapest, and consequently, weakest hearing aid available. Trish was glad Deborah had finally agreed to get one, after she'd gotten her glasses. "How else was I supposed to figure out if her gossip was juicy enough to tell everybody else?" Deborah cackled.

"You were more fun when you were blind and deaf." Clara shook a finger at her, but she had a playful tone. She tapped Trish's wrist. "So, how did your date go? You told us last week you were going to see him again on Friday."

The ladies dithered and giggled. She wasn't getting out of this. Friday had been great, but because of Sunday, she had barely spoken to him the past couple days. She wasn't quite ready to talk it out. "Um … it was nice."

Deborah's gaze narrowed. "*Nice* isn't a word for a date — that's the word for when you're trying to compliment the cook and the casserole tastes like garbage."

"Deborah!"

"Be nice to the poor girl."

"She can't help it if the boy isn't marriage material."

Except he could be. Maybe.

No, she'd violated rule number one and had been looking. This was what she deserved. At least God was being nice to her and her tests had come back negative. Maybe at some point she'd be obedient enough and please Him enough that He'd send her a nice boy to marry her.

Deborah shrugged. "Well, can't bat a thousand every time."

Casseroles. Batting. "How great, you're reading the newspaper again."

Deborah self-consciously adjusted her glasses, but then her gaze sharpened. "Nope, missy, can't change the subject."

Trish sighed and told them about the earring incident.

The ladies clucked their sympathy. "Oh, that awful man." "Well, you're too good for him."

"You're being an idiot," Deborah barked.

Trish straightened in her seat. "No, I'm not."

"There is no such thing as a saint. Women just think some men are. Of course he's dated other women."

"I agree with Deborah." Clara nodded.

"*Et tu, Brute?*" Trish crossed her arms.

"What?"

"Are you speaking Korean or something?"

"No, Clara knows a little Korean."

Deborah leaned forward in her seat, her eyes wide behind her bifocals as she stared at Trish. "Are you pregnant?"

"*What?!*" Trish glanced behind her. "Who are you talking to?"

"You, you clueless girl. Your breasts are bigger."

At the word, the other women looked away, pink-cheeked.

"No, they're not." Trish dropped her arms from in front of her. "You're confused because of your glasses."

"I had glasses last week, too. I'm not confused."

Clara stared at her chest with her head cocked to the side. "I think Deborah's right."

Trish's head felt both fiery and lighter than air. "They're not bigger."

"Have you had nausea?"

"No." Well, only the typical stress-induced kind, and considering the past few weeks of her life, she wasn't surprised.

"Sometimes you don't get it. Is your bra tight?"

"I'm retaining water." Or gaining weight, but she chose to be optimistic.

"Are your breasts sensitive?" Trish had a feeling Deborah enjoyed saying the word just to make the other women uncomfortable.

"They're always sensitive right before my period."

"When was your last period?"

She closed her eyes. She barely remembered to pay her bills, much less her last menstrual cycle. She remembered the period right before New Year's. Right before ...

Oh. My. Goodness.

"Catch her, she's going to faint!"

"Sumiyo, move your walker, she'll fall forward into it."

"Somebody get some water."

When she opened her eyes, the room spun around the only focal point she had, Deborah's concerned hazel eyes. "Trish? Breathe. There you go. Another one. No, don't close your eyes again. Take another breath. Not too fast, you don't want to hyperventilate. There you go."

She gripped the arms of the old-fashioned metal library chair, feeling the molded edges bite into her fingers. She didn't think she could stand, but she had to. She had to get to a store.

She might be two months pregnant.

THIRTY-TWO

Oh, God. Oh, God.

She fumbled with the instructions. Maybe she hadn't read that right. Two lines meant ...

Oh, God. Oh, God.

She heard the insidious whisper and didn't immediately shut her mind to it. She could get rid of it ...

No. She wasn't so far fallen that she'd do that.

She cradled her forehead in her hands and curved her back against the cold porcelain of the toilet tank. A shiver shot through her, but her stomach didn't unclench when it passed.

She was single, and carrying Kazuo's baby.

What a mess. She'd been doing so well but now everything was crashing and exploding and demolishing around her without a sound.

Oh, God. Oh, God.

Why had God allowed this to happen? That last time she'd been with Kazuo, a couple days before New Year's, they'd used a condom. But look what happened! Why was God punishing her like this? Lately, she'd been trying so hard to please Him.

Why are you doing this to me?

Her nose closed and her head pounded with her heartbeat. She squeezed her eyes shut. The tears falling down her face scalded her skin.

This isn't happening. This can't be happening.

Two lines said it was.

Her cousins would faint dead away. Well, Jenn might look at her with sorrowful eyes. When she couldn't hide it anymore, her ruined reputation would destroy her mother, maybe bring on another heart attack. How could she possibly condemn her father's moral condition when she herself was in *this* condition?

Grandma ... she didn't even want to think about Grandma.

Could she hide it? At work, she'd seen a call for temporary transfers to the Pleasanton site for cell work on a short-term project. She could move. Have the baby. Give it up. Come back.

Everything would be the same as it was before.

She sobbed harder.

"Trish?"

Griselle.

"Trish? The door was open." The voice carried from the living room.

"Just a minute." She shot to her feet, tumbling the stick to the floor. She twisted the sink handles and splashed water in her face.

"I knocked a few times. Are you okay?" Griselle's footsteps sounded closer. She was probably in the kitchen. "I came to give you the reference for your MDiv."

Trish scrubbed her face with the towel, then peered bleary-eyed at the cloudy mirror. She didn't look too bad. Allergies. She had allergies.

She nipped into the open shower so she could open the bathroom door, clunking it against the toilet a little hard in her haste. She stepped out and entered the kitchen, where she casually hung herself against the doorframe. "How're you doing?"

Griselled eyes popped out of their sockets. "What happened to you? Are you okay?"

Trish sniffled. "Allerg—"

"Do you need to go to the doctor?"

"No, I—"

Griselle's brow wrinkled. Her gaze seemed to go lower. "Are you sure you're okay?"

"I'm fine." Trish crossed her arms.

Griselle fidgeted where she stood. It seemed to Trish she was trying not to stare at Trish's chest. "Are you … uh …"

"No, I'm not pregnant!" Trish's voice resonated off the newly scrubbed kitchen cabinets.

Griselle's eyes became freaky big, like the Japanese *anime* characters. "That wasn't what I was going to say."

Trish burst into tears. "I am pregnant!"

Arms came around her, and a shoulder appeared right in front of her forehead to rest on. Trish wailed into Griselle's blouse, smearing her tears and sniffles into the cotton.

"I was pregnant once."

It was so soft, Trish thought at first she imagined it. "What?" She lifted her head.

Griselle looked like she'd aged years in only a few minutes. Dark circles under her eyes, sunken cheeks. "I had an abortion." It was like a whisper from the grave.

"Oh, Griselle."

She gripped Trish's shoulders tighter than a vice, although her fierce gaze would have been enough to pin her to the floor. "You're not going to abort the baby, are you?"

"No! No."

Griselle backed down, obviously relieved. Her hands dropped from Trish's arms. "How far along are you?"

"Two months."

"Are you going to keep it? Give it up for adoption?"

Trish blinked and slid her eyes away. "I can't possibly keep it—"

"It's not quite the same as an abortion, but once you give it up for adoption, it's gone. No 'undo' button."

"I know." But she was single. In Silicon Valley, one of the world's most expensive housing markets. "I can't afford—"

"I'm just saying to be absolutely sure. You never want to look back and regret not keeping it."

Regret. Her whole life lately had been nothing but regrets. Griselle's haunted eyes radiated love for her, but she wouldn't be the one carrying it, facing the whispers, telling her family. Or making sacrifices in order to keep it, if she did decide that.

Another tear dripped from her eye. She swiped it away.

She wanted things back the way they had been before.

"Pleasanton?" Diana stared at her like she had a third eye. "Why do you want to transfer to Pleasanton?"

"It'll only be temporary."

"I know it's temporary, but it's completely routine work. Anyone could do it."

"I need a change of place. Time away."

Diana's gaze hardened. "Did you and Spenser break up or something?"

Trish choked and coughed. "We were never going out." Not really. They'd never actually had a conversation defining their relationship as a couple.

Diana blinked. "Oh. Well, you two get along so well, I thought ... did you fight with him?"

"No."

"Did you fight with Kevin?"

"No." He avoided her like there was a temporary restraining order out and he had to stay fifty feet away from her at all times.

Diana sighed and took off her glasses, rubbing her eyes. "Trish, I can't let you go. You're in the middle of a high-profile study, and I'm filing the IND for the projects we ran last quarter. I need you here."

"Maybe in a few months?"

"Maybe. We won't know until we get the results from this next experiment."

Well, it wasn't a no. Trish plodded back to her office.

Spenser saw her face as soon as she entered the doorway. "What happened? Are you okay?"

She almost turned right around and walked back out. Had she really thought coming late to work would help her avoid Spenser all day? He might have been in the lab when she arrived, but she should have known he wouldn't stay there until five, when he had to pick up Matthew from daycare.

"I'm fine." Her legs had turned into electrophoresis gel, and she dropped into her chair.

"You're not. What's wrong?" He leaned against the cubicle partition.

He was too close, both physically and emotionally. It was so unfair. She hadn't even gotten used to the news herself, but she had to decide what she was going to tell Spenser, what she was going to do about their sort-of dating.

She buried her head in her hands. "This is rotten timing."

"What is?"

"Nothing."

He didn't respond, but he didn't move away from her desk. "Look, I know you're still mad at me about the earring, but—"

"I'm not mad anymore." It all seemed so petty now.

"Oh." He looked down, rubbing the back of his neck. "Uh ... Do you ... need a moment?"

She was going to cry again. Maybe the pregnancy hormones were finally kicking in. "Thanks." She sniffled.

He would hate her because it was Kazuo's baby. She should sever all potential right now because she was guaranteed to lose him eventually. No normal male got involved with a pregnant woman, and most definitely not a pregnant woman carrying the baby of the man who'd seduced his wife and broken up his marriage.

But she couldn't do it. Couldn't make her mouth open to tell him the truth. Because a part of her—a very small, naïve part—hoped he might actually want to stick with her through it all, especially if she decided to give it up. He was a nice guy. He might do it.

And pigs would fly. Alongside Grandma.

It didn't matter. Eventually, she needed to tell him.

If only it was possible she didn't have to be there when she did.

Trish drove home, and despite the albatross hanging around her shoulders, the house triggered a wave of satisfaction.

She had arranged for painters to come next week to scrape the peeling strips of exterior paint and swab on a warm cream color. She had swept the garage, tightened a few screws, and used lubricant on the garage door so that it could close all the way. Eventually she would buy an automatic garage door opener—and be reimbursed by Mrs. Choi—but for now she kept the door locked.

Inside looked even brighter. The scrubbed walls revealed a modest beige color that a previous owner had painted a few years after the avocado-orange wallpaper era. She had reserved some heavy equipment for next week to sand down the hardwood floors exposed by the carpet removal. Then she would apply sealer, rent a steel wool polisher, and apply finish to her restored floors.

She had killed the mold on the bathroom ceiling and stopped the puddle under the toilet by tightening the spigot. At last, she could use the toilet without fear. She had hired a handyman to come in next week to check the joists for rotting from the water damage.

The kitchen still sported avocado-orange wallpaper, but also new grout between the tiles. She had replaced the yellow curtains with white cotton eyelet ones from a bargain store. In addition to cleaning the refrigerator, she'd scrubbed the grease from the ceiling and the cabinets, taking off some of the paint underneath. She'd strip the paint off and repaint later. The ceiling still had a beige stain, but at least it didn't look like it would drip on her when she cooked.

After she finished the floors, she could move her furniture into the house. It would look and feel like a home. And she had done it all herself. Herself! She, who had always been hopelessly helpless.

As she rummaged in the fridge for an apple, her cell phone chirped. "Hello?"

"It's Mrs. Choi. I'm afraid I have some bad news." The apologetic quaver in her voice made her stand up and take notice.

"What's wrong?" She squelched the burbling of unease in her stomach. It must be the pregnancy. Or maybe Mrs. Choi didn't agree with the amount the painters charged.

"My nephew George called me. He's decided against going on overseas missions."

Oh, no. Please God, no. That's all I need.

"I'm sorry, Trish. He's returning on Monday morning, and he said he wants his house back."

THIRTY-THREE

Lex was late, as usual. Trish slouched against the kitchen counter and tried to ignore Jenn's concerned looks, cast her way every few minutes. Venus leaned against the sink, her face tense, mentally preparing herself for whatever bad news had prompted Trish to call an emergency meeting for all four cousins that very night.

Jenn tried to smile. "You're doing a great job on the renovations."

She didn't answer, not meaning to be rude, but because she was going to hurl her entire dinner—salad, no dressing—onto the linoleum floor. Nerves, not hormones. She swallowed, and the wave of nausea passed. "Thanks."

"Where the heck is Lex?" Venus grabbed her Gucci bag from the counter and fished out her cell phone. "I should have picked her up myself."

The front door creaked open—Trish made a mental note to WD–40 the hinges. Oh, wait. She wouldn't be here in three days. George could oil his own stupid hinges.

"Sorry I'm late." Lex's voice rolled down the carpetless hallway as she hustled toward the kitchen. "Wow. Oh my gosh, Trish, you did a good job—"

"I'm pregnant." It exploded out of her mouth.

Lex froze in the doorway to the kitchen. Her purse dropped to the floor with a *thunk*, along with her jaw. Jenn gasped. Venus had gone perfectly still.

Her entire body felt like it had been overnight in a minus-seventy degree cryo-freezer. Cold, rock-hard.

"Oh, Trish." Jenn reached a hand to her.

"Don't touch me." Her lips barely moved. She'd shatter into a billion shards of ice if anyone touched her, the warmth of a human hand. She stared dry-eyed at the floor until Lex moved to stand in front of her.

"It's okay to cry, Trish."

"You always tease me about crying so easily." A tear burned a track down her cheek. " 'Crocodile tears.' "

Suddenly it was Venus who moved to her and grabbed her. Her head fell onto Venus's tall shoulder even as Jenn and Lex enfolded them both with more arms around her.

Her throat closed. She couldn't breathe. She gasped hard and air rushed into her lungs, filling and cracking her chest, straining her ribs. She shuddered as she cried, silently and open-mouthed.

Her cousins. Her friends. Her spiritual sisters. Her home.

Being in the center of a group hug was way too hot. She finally pulled away amid more sniffles, not all from her. Jenn—always pre-pared—dug tissues from her purse while Lex went to the bathroom and came back with a roll of toilet paper. She and Trish honked loudly while Venus and Jenn discreetly wiped their noses.

"What are you going to do?" Venus tossed her tissue into the trash bag.

"I don't know." Oh man, what was she going to do? She almost started bawling again.

"It's Kazuo's?"

"Yeah."

Jenn tossed her own tissue. "Are you going to tell him about the baby?"

"I'll have to, but not just yet."

"Are you going to marry him?" Jenn twirled the ends of her hair.

Trish bit the inside of her lip. "I don't know." He didn't know yet. Hadn't asked her to marry him. He didn't like children—she didn't even know if he would marry her.

But then she wouldn't be alone.

No, she and her baby would just be in the same house as a neurotic artist. Oh, joy.

But Kazuo had wealthy parents — they'd take care of her, even if he didn't. Wouldn't that be better than being on her own? Sure, her cousins would help, but she couldn't even live with any of them — Jenn was caring for her mother, Venus's condo was the size of a closet, and Lex was rooming with Mimi — the tramp — for free in exchange for help taking care of the house.

But marry Kazuo? She couldn't believe she was considering it. Yet what options did she have? Hardly any.

"How far along?" Lex studied her abdomen, which was rather embarrassing since she'd always had a small pooch there.

"Two months."

"Oh." Venus straightened in surprise.

Trish's nose closed again, and tears filled her eyes, but this time, she saw everything through a red haze. "Did you think I'd slept with him again? How could you? I've been trying so hard to *prove* to you that I was really trying to change."

"Trish —"

She didn't have patience for Jenn's placating tone. "No, you're my cousins. You're supposed to love me and believe in me, not wait around to see how I mess up again."

Venus looked away, and Lex scuffed the floor with her sneaker.

"Is that all I am to you? A screw-up?" Okay, now she had started screeching. Not a good sign. She needed to calm down, except she had a raging pot of *jook* rice porridge in her gut about to boil over.

"I'm sorry." Venus faced her with steady, humble eyes. She wasn't one to try to hide anything. "You're right, I wasn't believing in you. And I'm sorry."

"Me too." Lex wouldn't look at her, but her words carried clearly.

Trish gave a loud snuffle. It was kind of hard to be dignified with her nose running.

"You have been trying hard." Jenn touched her shoulder.

"What kills me is that I've been doing my best to follow my three rules and become a better person. I changed my image, my lifestyle, and what happened?" She wiped her face with her soggy tissue. "It's almost as if I hadn't even tried to regain my chastity in the first place."

"Your three rules weren't bad—"

"They obviously didn't prevent this from happening. I don't feel like being wholly devoted to God anymore, either."

Lex stabbed a finger at her. "But think about it. Why were you doing all that serving? Did you have a heart for the people you were helping, or were you just trying to look better in God's eyes?"

"Was it primarily to get references for your MDiv?" Venus didn't accuse her, but her tone said she wanted Trish to be honest.

"Maybe. At first." She liked the Sunday school kids, but she didn't really know what she could do to help them grow in Christ. She just liked playing with them. She didn't have anything to add to the support group at the Pregnancy Crisis Center—well, she did now—because those women had been through so much worse than what she'd had to endure with Kazuo. She did enjoy the time at Katsu Towers, but part of that was watching the K-dramas with the ladies. And even though people said they liked having her on the worship team, they didn't know she was so bad that they turned her mic off.

Was she useful at all for God? Did He make this happen because she wasn't pulling her weight or working hard enough?

Or maybe that whole thing about "the old has gone, the new has come" only applied to girls who stopped sinning as soon as they accepted Christ, rather than backslidden chicks like her who couldn't stop struggling with the same things over and over again. Why hadn't He helped her overcome her problems?

For that matter, why was it so wrong that she liked boys? It's not as if she'd ever been unfaithful to a boyfriend. Maybe God didn't like who she was, period. A red haze fell down over her vision. "You know why this is happening to me? Because God only sees the good girls. He doesn't give a flying flip about people like me—"

Venus's hand flew so fast she didn't even have time to blink before it slapped her across the face. Trish was so cold she barely felt the sting, but the blow knocked a gaping hole in her heart. Jenn and Lex both gasped.

"Don't you be blaming God." Venus's almond-shaped eyes had shrunk to dark sesame seeds. "He doesn't promise an easy life. We still have to face whatever the consequences of our actions are."

Venus's slap had jolted the hysteria bubbling inside her, but it hadn't dulled her anger. "Yeah, well I thought if we repented, He helped us out." Trish stabbed at her abdomen. "This isn't helping."

Her cousins were silent. A part of her wanted them to say something enlightening, to make her feel better or realize something profound about God and her situation, but another part of her wanted to feel angry and abandoned. Anger was easier to understand than why God had allowed this to happen.

"I honestly repented. I honestly wanted to turn my life around. But I can't even serve at church without messing up." Helping in the kitchen, the Sunday school Pet Day disaster, bonking into the microphone.

Lex flung her hands out. "God doesn't expect you to be perfect."

"Well, I still feel filthy. I feel like a whore, especially now. It makes me wonder if He really has forgiven me." She waved to stop Jenn's immediate protest. "I don't want to argue about it. I know in my head I'm forgiven when I confess, but I don't *feel* it."

Jenn's mouth worked back and forth a few moments before she asked a question Trish had been dreading. "Are you going to give the baby up?"

She closed her eyes. Griselle's words still haunted her. Would she regret giving it up?

"You could keep it, you know." Lex crossed one leg over the other. "Financially, I mean. You've got a good job, and we all know people who could provide daycare for you."

"We can help out, too. My work schedule is very flexible." Trish appreciated Venus's offer, although to be honest, she had a hard time picturing Venus holding a baby.

Jenn nodded. "I'm taking care of Mom, but I can help, too. And Mom loves babies."

"Thanks." She didn't know, practically speaking, how much they'd be able to help her, but their willingness to gather around her and shoulder some of her burden lifted some of the heaviness that had been weighing her down the past day.

There was so much she had to think about, so much to do. And so many other things to lay aside—would she need to give up her work on the worship team? At Katsu Towers? And she wouldn't need references for her MDiv anymore—she couldn't take classes right away, not with the baby.

She sighed as her eyes strayed to the paper strewn on the kitchen counter. She'd been trying so hard to impress others, including God. What use had she been?

"Well, but your dating life would be down the toilet." Lex started to laugh, then suddenly choked as she gasped. "Did you tell Spenser yet?"

"Spenser?" Jenn's brows furrowed. "Your coworker?"

Trish glared at Lex. "We're not even serious yet, loudmouth." And probably never would be.

"Sorry." Lex ducked her raspberry-red face.

Venus's sympathetic look seemed to mirror the ache in Trish's heart. "Do you like him?"

"I don't know." Yes, she did. More than she wanted to.

"Will he ..." Jenn licked her lips. "Would he stand by you after, you know ... finding out?"

She couldn't answer.

Venus had the courage to ask the hardest question. "Will it devastate you if he walks away?"

She swallowed—or rather, tried to. A gigantic pinecone had lodged in her throat and lacerated her esophagus, making it painful to breathe. "He'd never stay." The words fell in the quiet kitchen, lying there like dirty snow.

"He might—"

"No, he won't. I don't blame him. Kazuo had an affair with his wife, broke up their marriage."

Jenn's hand flew to her mouth. Lex stared at her in disbelief.

Venus sighed. "You have to tell him, then."

Her heartbeat went from zero to sixty in 0.4 seconds. "What do you mean?"

"Think about it. Spenser's involved with you, even if it's not serious yet. Kazuo stole his wife. You need to tell him before he finds out himself."

Jenn and Lex spoke at the same time.

"He'll think you were trying to hide the baby from him."

"He'll think you were trying to deceive him."

"At the very least, you have to let him know so he can break it off without too much emotional involvement from either of you." Venus scrutinized her face. "You'd want that, right?"

"I want him to stay." Trish buried her face in her hands. "I don't want to be alone."

"That's not a good reason for him to stay."

"I know. I'm being selfish." She felt the tickle against her fingers and grabbed the fresh tissue from Jenn. She blew her nose. "It would have been nice to find out if he were The One or not. Now I'll never know."

"You might—"

Venus cut Jenn off. "Don't give her false hope. It'll be nice if he surprises her, but don't make her believe it would happen."

Lex stuck her hands on her hips. "You are so cynical."

"I'm realistic. People with their heads in the clouds trip and fall."

"Hmph." Lex crossed her arms.

"When are you going to tell him?" Venus shifted her weight to one hip. Trish almost expected her to start tapping her toe.

"I have to set a date?"

"If you don't, you'll never do it."

Trish sighed, but Venus was right. "Sunday after church."

"I'll drive you," Lex said. "That way you won't have to drive home afterward."

Trish felt like they were planning military strategy. "Fine. Thanks." She cleared her throat. "There's something else. I kind of need housing ..."

She was going to throw up all over his nice Italian leather shoes before she even got a word out.

"Hey, Trish—whoa. You don't look so good. You're pale." Spenser guided her to a seat in the sanctuary.

"No ..." She didn't want to tell him here, with stragglers still making their way out, with people chatting in the foyer through the sanctuary doors. At least the worship team had finished clearing their equipment away, except for the few cords in Spenser's hand.

"Sit down." He pushed her into a seat.

She pressed her palms to her temples. "I need to tell you something—"

"Hey guys. Going out to lunch?" One of the singles came up to them, then caught sight of Trish's face. "Are you sick?" He took a large step backward. "You're not contagious, are you?"

She growled at him.

"Uh ... yeah. See ya later." He headed up the aisle toward the doors. His voice carried back to them as he spoke to someone else. "Man, she's crabby."

This was just great.

"Spenser, I need to tell you something."

He sat in a seat in the row ahead of her, twisted around so his arm draped over the back of the chair, but he didn't look at her. "Diana told me you wanted to transfer to Pleasanton."

"I did, but she won't let me." Maybe that was a good thing, making her stay and face this. It would be shameful and deceptive to run away. But it would protect her reputation—whatever good she'd accomplished for it, in this church and with her family.

"I don't want you to move because of me."

"Oh, no. Nothing like that." Fabulous. Now she'd hurt his feelings before she'd even talked to him. "It's something else. And I might not move."

She cleared her throat. She didn't want to tell him. She had to tell him. The silence in the sanctuary roared in her ears. She couldn't do this.

She could. She had to.

"Spenser, I'm two months pregnant."

At first she thought she'd said it too softly for him to hear. He sat there, blinking, not looking at her. His face didn't change.

Then his jaw flexed.

His skin turned white. Whiter than white. Translucent enough to almost see the skeletal bones underneath. His eyes had sunk back into his head and his mouth disappeared into a thin line.

He said a single word. "Kazuo."

"Yes," she whispered.

He stood and walked away.

THIRTY-FOUR

She didn't know how long she sat there, staring at the empty stage, still lit by the front lights. She must not have been there that long, because Olivia found her.

"Are you okay?"

Dry-eyed, she shrugged. She didn't have any more tears. She'd been emptied. She was like a burned-out building, a charred shell.

Olivia's touch on her hand made her jump. "Trish, you're like ice."

Funny, she felt like she was on fire.

Olivia sat down, ironically in the seat Spenser had vacated. "Did you guys have a fight?"

She took a deep breath. "No, he just ... did what I expected him to." She hadn't expected it to hurt so much. She'd been skewered straight through the sternum, leaving jagged edges that burned and throbbed. Yet the rest of her body felt nothing. Nothing.

"Did you want to talk about it?"

"I'm pregnant from my ex-boyfriend." She didn't care anymore. She felt both numb and reckless at the same time. "Spenser just walked away."

"I'm sure he has a reason." No mention of Trish's utter lack of moral fortitude.

"It doesn't matter if he does. It's over. Not that we had anything. Only a couple dates. It shouldn't feel this bad." She rubbed her chest. She had almost expected to feel a gaping hole.

"Let me pray for you —"

"I don't want to pray. I can't pray."

Olivia turned away to look at the empty stage. She swiveled back. "Tell me about it."

She shook her head and shrugged again. What was there to say?

"Trish, I'm not going to give you platitudes. I want to help."

"With what? There's too much and too little."

"Honey, He's God. It's not too much for Him."

"He did this to me." Dad's affair, Mom's collapse, now this. "He's punishing me for all my bad choices when I should have known better."

Olivia's eyes darkened. "He doesn't punish people anymore. But bad choices have consequences."

"But I was trying so hard to *be someone He'd forgive*." The words hit her square in the chest like a blow.

"He did forgive. He forgave as soon as you said you were sorry. You're still His child. But that doesn't mean you don't have to take responsibility for the things you've done."

Responsibility. "I was trying to be a responsible person." But it didn't erase what she'd already done when she should have known better. Her three rules weren't the Dry Erase alcohol solution that could wipe it all away.

"Let me say this again: He's God. He has His reasons. Who are any of us to question them?"

Trish stopped and felt the weight of those words, the weight of the truth of it all. She felt especially small in the empty sanctuary. "I feel so alone." Her voice cracked.

"Even—and especially—when you don't see Him, He sees you."

"Yeah, but what does He see in me?" *Whore.*

"He sees Christ's blood."

She shook her head, and her hands started to shake, too. "That doesn't mean anything to me anymore."

"Trish, blood is more precious than gold."

Precious. "I don't feel precious." She sobbed into her hands.

Olivia moved to sit beside her. She surrounded her with light cinnamon scent and arms wrapped tight around her shoulders. "You are more precious than you know."

The tears rained down her face. "I don't have anything."

"You are even more precious to Him when there aren't any walls between the two of you."

The darkness behind her closed eyelids was too black, too deep. She wanted this mercy, like a light, like a ribbon of silver, like a hand on her head.

"You are His. You don't have to follow certain rules or be a perfect Christian to be His. You have to trust and believe how much He loves you. That's all that matters."

She cried harder. Even her heart was crying. Her soul cried out like a physical hand reaching out to Him. And she thought ... she thought she felt Him take it.

She sat there, and sobbed, and hung on.

Trish sat on her concrete front step, staring at the newly-cleared front lawn in the fading sunlight. The neighbor's teenage son had done a great job pulling up the weeds on Friday. Twenty bucks for his labor had made him ecstatic. Trish considered that cheap compared to the quotes from commercial landscapers.

Of course, she'd enjoyed it for all of one weekend.

Luckily, most of her stuff was still stored in her parents' garage. The rest had been packed into her SUV, ready to drive to Venus's place tomorrow. Trish would get a spot on the loveseat. Woo-hoo.

She needed someplace else for long-term. How could she find anything she could afford with a baby?

There she went again, thinking like she should keep it. She shouldn't. She couldn't give it a nuclear family, a stellar life. She could barely take care of herself.

She looked out over the front lawn and remembered her rejoicing that she could finally see the sidewalk from her front door. Well, maybe she wasn't that helpless.

Oh. She sat up straighter. What she should do was pray about it. (Imagine that!) The reconciliation and peace she felt in the sanctuary still covered her, embracing her like a soft chenille blanket. *Lord, I don't think Kazuo would want this baby. Do you want me to keep it?*

She didn't expect a voice in her ear, but she suddenly saw a picture of the child in her arms, her mother's smile beaming at her, maybe Grandpa's dimples peeking out.

If you want me to, I will.

No writing on the wall or in the sky, but she also knew somehow—deeper than emotions, from somewhere down inside her—that He'd let her know definitively. Eventually.

She shifted when the crack in the step started digging into the seat of her pants. She breathed deep of the cooling twilight air and dropped her head into her bent knees. She should go inside soon.

Then she heard the car engine. Deep and growling, massive power held in check. Prowling down her street. Slowing near her house.

She looked up. A black Mazda RX–7 in perfect condition pulled into her cracked driveway. The door swung open and Spenser stepped out.

As he approached, Trish rose to her feet, lifted her chest up, set her jaw. But then he stopped and removed his sunglasses.

His eyes had aged a hundred years. He was a man with no soul left in him, a wraith left all alone.

It shocked her, then angered her. Fury trembled in her chest, quivered in her hands. No. She wasn't going to forgive him just because he came with that hangdog look. She wasn't.

"I'm sorry, Trish."

She burst into tears.

She hadn't thought she had any tears left in her. She felt his hand guide her back down onto the step. He sat next to her and shoved a white linen handkerchief into her hands.

Handkerchief? Who carried real handkerchiefs these days? She buried her face in it and let it muffle her sobs.

After a while, she quieted and blew her nose. Hard. Oh. A handkerchief was much better for blowing her nose than a tissue. She mopped her face and peeked at him.

Spenser returned her look with those horrible dead eyes, sitting with his knees pulled up. He didn't say anything, and neither did she.

Her breathing calmed from gasping back to normal, but her whole face felt swollen. She probably had splotches all over it. She felt lumpy and upset, and why in the world was he here? He'd been pretty clear about his feelings.

A tiny little corner of her heart had hoped he was a better man.

She thrust the crumpled handkerchief at him. Spenser looked askance at it and muttered a strangled, "Keep it."

A watery giggle burst from her.

A smile flitted across his face, then disappeared. He looked away, at the empty street. He wet his lips. "I'm sorry."

She stared at the ground between her feet. She couldn't get herself to toss off a flippant, *It's okay*, because she didn't feel okay. She wiped her nose to stall for time. He solved her dilemma by continuing.

"I've hated him for a long time."

"Kazuo."

"When Linda first left me, I thought maybe Matthew wasn't mine."

The world shattered around her in booms and sparks and falling shards. She started hyperventilating. He shoved her head between her knees but quickly assured her, "He is mine."

Eventually her world righted itself and she raised her head. She had a billion questions and no tactful way to ask any of them.

His eyes slid sideways at her. "Just ask them."

"Are you reading my mind?" This was way bizarre.

"It's all over your face."

Oh, the face with red eyes, red nose, red cheeks? Lovely. "How do you know?"

"Matthew and I have the same birthmark on our arms." He pulled up his sleeve to the shoulder to reveal an apple-shaped black spot. "But I hated him for making me doubt it."

She couldn't say anything.

His jaw clenched. "I loved Linda. It's been years, and I still can't forgive him."

She didn't want to hear this. Would he ever forgive her for carrying Kazuo's child, after what he'd feared about Matthew?

Kazuo wouldn't have cared even if Matthew had been his. He hated children. They required attention and time away from his art. He wouldn't even babysit his cousin's baby the one time they'd called to ask. He wouldn't care about the one growing inside her.

"I still shouldn't have walked away from you."

She couldn't answer that. A few more tears spilled out of her eyes and she caught them with the handkerchief.

"I'm sorry. I'm so sorry." His voice had a catch to it. "I shouldn't have walked away and left you alone."

Like Linda had done to him. The thought made her chest unclench. She still didn't feel okay, but she could say the words she needed to say. "I forgive you."

He swallowed, and his mouth pressed into a thin line. He looked away, but his hand fumbled for hers and caught it in a painful grip. She felt the trembling that ran through him.

She squeezed back. She understood what he didn't tell her. He released her hand.

They sat in silence until the sun dipped low on the distant foothills. She drank in the crisp night air, listened to the distant rush of a car driving past the street.

Finally, she became aware of the chill that settled over the dimness. She shivered. "I wanted so much to change into a different person."

"You have changed." Spenser sat so still. His face was an outline in the darkness. "Nothing we do makes change happen in us. Only God can do that."

His hand, palm warm and fingers cold, covered hers again and wrapped around it. He squeezed and loosened.

"Are we okay?" she asked.

"Yeah, we're okay." He swallowed. "It'll take some ... getting used to."

"I know. Things are different." She didn't want them to be different, but it wasn't like she was three years old and could throw a tantrum until God gave in. At least Spenser was still her friend. It made her glad. "I can't handle anything complicated right now, anyway."

He let go of her hand, stood, and stretched. He reached down and pulled her to her feet. "C'mon."

"Where?"

"To get something a pregnant woman can eat."

She dusted off her jeans. "I'd never even have suspected if the old ladies at Katsu Towers hadn't ..."

Old ladies. Gossipy old ladies. Gossipy old *Japanese* ladies. The realization punched her in the throat.

By now, Grandma knew.

She prayed with all her might that Grandma hadn't told them already.

She didn't think so. Something that major, wouldn't her parents call her immediately? At the very least to demand an explanation why they were the last to know? Among other types of ranting and raving.

Her stomach growled as she parked in her parents' darkened driveway next to Dad's car. She could have been out to dinner with Spenser by now, but the panicked paranoia of Grandma calling them made her refuse.

He'd seemed to understand when she explained the situation. "Chinese families are the same."

She fumbled in the dark for the latch to open the side gate, steeling herself for its usual haunted-house screaming. But it swung open on silent hinges. She thrust her hand out. Someone had oiled it. Weird.

To get to the back door, she had to pass the wide picture window in the dining room. Tonight, Mom hadn't drawn the curtains yet and light streamed in a rectangle on the grass, turning it silver.

Trish did a double-take at the sight in the window. Both her parents at the dining room table, sitting *next to* each other, heads bent *close together*, working on a jigsaw puzzle.

A puzzle! They hadn't worked on a puzzle in forever, and certainly never just themselves — it had been one of the few things they did as a family.

She didn't feel left out, exactly. She hadn't been close to her parents — specifically, Dad — since New Year's. She should be happy they were actually enjoying something together for a change. For the past several years, it had seemed as if they only lived together and didn't have anything in common anymore.

Dad said something. Mom laughed and swatted his arm. He smiled, reached out, and touched her waist, leaning in for a peck on the lips.

Aaack!!

Dad never indulged in PDA with Mom. He never even indulged in *private* displays of affection with Mom. She felt like a voyeur standing outside the dining room window, watching her parents act like ... lovers.

Ewww.

Who had kidnapped her parents and replaced them with these strangers who looked exactly like them and acted twenty years younger?

Mom's head popped up from staring at the puzzle. "Did you hear that?"

"What?" Dad looked up, too.

Mom's eyes went wide, and she leaned in closer. "I think someone's outside."

Dad shot to his feet. "Stay here. I'll get the gun."

"Mom! Dad! It's me!" Trish raced the few steps to the back door and pounded. That would have been a good headline — shot by her own father for peeping.

Dad opened the door. "We didn't know you were coming."

"I should have called. I'm sorry." She joined her mom at the dining room table, Dad trailing behind her. "A puzzle?" She tried keeping her voice nonchalant.

"We started it last week." Mom's smile fluttered in and out. Why would she be embarrassed? Had she been trying to keep the puzzle a secret for some reason? Mom pointed at a seat for Trish. She didn't move at her usual bird-like speed, but she seemed to have more energy than the last time she saw her.

Dad sat down next to her. "You haven't come around much lately."

She avoided her initial impulse to give her father an *Are you kidding me?* stare and instead kept an admirably neutral face. "I thought Mom needed some quiet to recover."

Mom made dismissive noises in her throat. "You're our only daughter. I'd always want to see you."

"It's probably a good thing, Marian." Dad wouldn't look at her. "She needed some time to herself."

Trish turned her face away. She hated that he knew her so well.

He cleared his throat. "We've been going to counseling, Trish."

"Arvin —"

"No Marian, she needs to know."

Trish could only look from one to the other. She knew she needed to close her mouth, but it had frozen in place. Japanese men did not go to counseling. Japanese men were strong and stoic and never admitted to mistakes or wrongdoing. Well, in general. "The counselor suggested the puzzle?" And the oiled hinges maybe indicated other little things her dad had done around the house?

"Don't tell anyone." Mom wrung her hands. "Especially Grandma. We don't want the family to know. It's no one's business but ours."

Trish nodded even as her mind whirled. Grandma wouldn't want it known anyway, that one of her sons had to have therapy. That was weakness, a blemish on the family. She still couldn't believe her father had agreed to it. And had volunteered the information to her, who knew the ugly truth and hadn't exactly been the loving daughter the past couple months.

Maybe she'd been wrong about him. She wanted to be wrong about him. She'd been wrong about so many things lately. Tonight, after everything that happened today, she could see things differently. If God had been able to forgive her, touch her, promise to help her — she didn't really have a choice about doing the same for her own father.

She didn't want to keep shutting Dad out. It wasn't natural because their relationship had always been close. Maybe she'd worshipped him, in a way, which was why God allowed her to see something that would bring him tumbling down.

After all, could she really throw stones with the secret growing in her?

She took a long breath that shook. "Mom, Dad. I'm two months pregnant with Kazuo's baby."

She heard the ticking of the wall clock. The faint whistle of the wind outside.

Well, if they didn't have anything to say . . . "It happened before I officially broke up with him." She needed them to know that.

"You're Christian, you're not going to abort — ?"

"No, Mom."

"Are you going to keep it?" Mom twisted her wedding rings, which were so loose that they clinked.

"I don't know. I might."

"Are you sure about that, pumpkin?" Dad's soft, concerned voice made her nose stop up and her eyes swell.

She sniffed. "I don't want to regret giving it up."

He reached out and clasped her hand too tightly. She squeezed back, needing to feel the pain, which was his love for her.

"Are you going to marry him?" Mom sounded hopeful.

"I don't think he'd even ask."

Mom's gaze dropped to the unfinished puzzle. But then her face warmed with a joyful smile. "A grandchild."

"They'll talk about me at Temple. I'm sorry." Great Christian witness, too. *God, is that what you wanted?* "I don't know if I can do this." She bit the inside of her cheek.

"We'll help you, honey." Dad released her hand. She missed the warmth. "You shouldn't be doing those renovations on the house. You might hurt the baby."

"About that ... The guy wanted his house back."

"When?"

"Um ... tomorrow."

Mom gasped. "Trish."

"Don't worry, I'm moving in with Venus."

"You should move in here."

"Dad, it's too far to commute to work."

"Telecommute."

"I can't really do that with biology studies. I have to actually dose and harvest the cells and run assays."

"Venus's apartment is too small." Mom's chin jutted out. "You should move in with us. We can help you better than Venus can."

A three-hour commute every day. "I don't know, Mom."

She reached across the table and covered her hand. "I want you here, sweetie."

Suddenly she wanted to be here, too, to rely on her mom and dad again. Not as much as she did before, but she wanted to be close again after two months of strained phone calls.

"I'll think about it."

THIRTY-FIVE

She couldn't believe she was thinking about it.

On Wednesday night, Trish stumbled through the door to her parents' house after a nearly two-hour commute that had practically sucked the life out of her. Mom had invited her for dinner, and she'd thought she'd at least try the drive after work to see what it was like.

A descent into hell.

But as she entered the house, she was enveloped by the aroma of frying chicken. She was wiped out, and that smelled heavenly. Maybe the commute would be worth coming home to Mom's cooking every day.

Mom's head peeked out from the kitchen doorway. "Chicken *katsu* for dinner. Almost ready. How was work?"

Trish collapsed into a seat at the dinner table. "Okay." Spenser had been a smart-mouthed pain in the neck. She probably should be glad they were still friends considering their almost-relationship and the upheaval that cut it way short. But she didn't really want to tell her mom about that. "My boss, Diana, requested a last-minute graph, but it took me over an hour to finish because my stupid graph program had fritzed on my computer and I had to call the IT guys to come rescue me."

"Aw. Here, sit and eat." Mom dropped in front of her a plate of steaming white rice smothered with breadcrumb-coated fried chicken and sweet-salty *tonkatsu* sauce.

With one look at the overfilled plate, Trish threw her arms around her mother's waist. "Oh, Mom, you're the best mother in the world," she sobbed.

Her mother started at the sudden physical affection. She hesitated, then awkwardly patted Trish's shoulder. "Eat up." She extricated herself and bustled away to poke her head out the back door. "Dad! Dinner's ready." She filled a glass with juice and set it before Trish. "Why couldn't you join us for dinner last night instead? One of the aunties brought over shrimp *tempura*."

Aw, she'd missed deep-fried shrimp? Shucks. Not that she could eat shrimp right now, thanks to baby. "I volunteer at the Pregnancy Crisis Center on Tuesday nights."

Mom's eyes got as big as *musubi* rice balls. "You do?"

"Relax, Mom. This was before I found out. Ironic, huh?"

Mom bustled back to the kitchen. She thought she heard her mutter, "You can say that again."

"I, uh ... told them last night." Griselle had squeezed her hand so hard, she thought she'd cracked a few bones.

"That's probably good." Mom slid two more plates of food onto the table as Dad walked in the back door.

After a staid dinner, punctuated by Dad's complaints about the broken lawn mower, the doorbell rang. Trish opened the door to Mrs. Choi.

"Hello, Trish dear. Oh, you must be Mr. and Mrs. Sakai. Hello, I'm Mrs. Choi, from Trish's church."

"Hi, Mrs. Choi. Did you come all this way to deliver my mail? You only had to forward it—"

"Oh no, dear, I didn't bring the mail. I brought something for you." She held out a bank draft with a triumphant smile.

Trish caught a glimpse of the amount. Astronomical. "What's that for?" She straightened her back and kept her arms at her sides. She didn't dare touch it. Once she touched it, she'd never get Mrs. Choi to take it back, and she had a feeling she knew why she'd brought it.

"I got George to reimburse me for the amount we paid for your repair costs, but this is additional for your labor."

"Labor? But Mrs. Choi, I stayed there rent-free."

"You did so much work, and then you had three days' notice to leave." Mrs. Choi's face wrinkled like a shar-pei dog. "I'm so embarrassed by all the trouble this entire thing has caused you. Please, take it."

"No, Mrs. Choi, I couldn't." Not with Trish's *mother* standing right next to her. If she did something so rude as to accept this, she'd never hear the end of it: *Oh, what kind of a daughter did I raise? Have you no respect for your elders? How could you accept that check? So discourteous. Oh, this generation is so bad-mannered.*

"Trish, I insist."

"No, Mrs. Choi. I appreciate the gesture, but I couldn't. You take it. You did so much for me."

"No, I got you involved in that house in the first place. You deserve this." Mrs. Choi attempted to grab Trish's hand and shove the check in it, but she snatched her limb away.

"No, Mrs. Choi. I'm serious, you should take it." The older woman tried to shove the check in Trish's front jeans pocket, but she scooted backward and hid behind her father. "You provided a place for me to stay rent-free."

Disappointment etched into her face, Mrs. Choi lowered her hand. However, Trish's mother beamed her supreme pleasure that her daughter had evaded the check. "Mrs. Choi, won't you stay for a while? We're eating dessert. I have hot green tea. Would you like some?"

"Oh, no, I couldn't —"

"Oh, but I insist —"

"No, I couldn't impose —"

"Oh, it's no imposition."

"Oh. Thank you, I'd love some."

Trish followed her mom into the kitchen, but felt a tug at her back pocket.

"No, Mrs. Choi, you keep it." She removed the crumpled draft and held it out to her, but the woman clasped her hands in front of her ample stomach, turned her head sideways, and stared at the wall.

Trish marched to Mrs. Choi's handbag, which had been left by the door, and dropped it in.

She wasn't too worried about losing that money—and boy, did she need it—because she knew the drill. Mrs. Choi, thinking she was so devious, would slip it into Trish's jacket pocket for her to find later.

Trish found it in her father's jacket pocket, because three jackets hung on the coat rack near the front door. She sighed as she fingered the thick paper and traced all those lovely zeros. She'd have loved to see George's face when Mrs. Choi submitted the "bill."

Thank You, Lord. And please forgive me for earlier when I was hoping the contractor I'd arranged to come this week would find his joists rotted through.

She had pulled on her jacket to drive back to Venus's apartment when her cell phone rang. Uh, oh. "Hi Grandma."

"I heard something rather surprising about your state of health today."

Oh, no. "I'm actually feeling rather good—"

"Are you still at your parents' house?"

"I'm about to leave—"

"No, you stay right there. I'm ten minutes away."

Oh, no. No, no, no, no, no.

But she hauled off her jacket. She wasn't about to disobey a direct matriarchal order. She sank into the sofa, biting her cheek.

"Trish?"

"Grandma's coming, Dad."

What would she say? Grandma wasn't going to be happy with Trish, but then again, they hadn't exactly parted on the best of terms at Kazuo's art unveiling at the bank. Would *anyone* sympathize with her that she didn't want to get back together with Kazuo? Well, maybe the point was moot. Kazuo wouldn't want her now.

So why was Grandma coming?

Round and round and round. Mom and Dad chatted in the kitchen, cleaning the dishes, while Trish sat on the couch, jiggling her leg, staring at the clock.

Grandma must have been speeding because she got there in eight minutes.

Trish opened the door before she'd even rung the doorbell. "Hi, Grandm—"

Kazuo loomed in the doorway.

"Aack!" She jumped, feeling like a *kendo* stick had beamed her right in the forehead. She heard her parents come out of the kitchen behind her.

Kazuo took a giant step forward over the threshold, grabbed her, and planted a big kiss right on her gaping mouth.

Yuck, yuck, yuck! His mouth was slimy and hard and disgusting. She slapped at his chest and squirmed in his grip until he let go. She gave him a good shove for extra measure. "What are you doing here?"

"I brought him." Grandma stepped into the house, nose in the air, choosing to ignore the PDA that had happened not three feet from her.

"You brought Kazuo? Have you become *his* grandmother, too?"

"Trish." Mom's voice had that warning in it that usually preceded sending her to her room for a timeout.

Grandma smiled, an evil upturning of scarlet lips that would have made Medusa proud. "I might."

No. Way.

Kazuo dropped to one knee. "Trish—"

She backpedaled even as she heard her mother's sigh of joy. "No. Absolutely not."

He clasped his hands to his chest and looked up, falling into the throes of artistic vision. Except he looked a little silly since he was still on one knee. "This is the very thing to complete my masterpiece. Marriage with you, my muse. We will forever and truly be one, heart and soul. It will be magnificent. My uncle's gallery will be known for debuting the most brilliant artist of this century."

Okay, no delusions of grandeur there. "What about the word *no* did you not understand?"

His eyes blazed dark with passion as he rose to his feet and moved toward her. "We will be alone again, you and I, in our world of artistic freedom and decadent creativity—"

"That is not appealing and you are making *no* sense. As usual." She planted her heels, rammed a sword down her spine, and stood her ground. He towered over her, his face inches away, but her basilisk glare prevented him from trying to take more liberties.

Grandma's voice suddenly came from right at her elbow. "Trish."

She started and turned away from her staring match with the Clueless Wonder. "Grandma, we already talked about this."

"Kazuo's parents love you and they will always take care of you." Translation: *When Kazuo divorces you, they'll ensure you get a nice alimony package and child support for the baby.*

"But I'm not marrying them. I'd be marrying him." She'd rather eat *uni sushi* and gag to death.

"This is an ideal alliance with the bank."

She knew it would eventually come around to that. "Why me? I have plenty of cousins willing to put up with him."

"Do you really want to cause embarrassment for your family like this?" Grandma gestured toward her parents, who stood frozen a few feet away. "People will shun your mother. She will lose all her friends." Marian Sakai, mother of an unwed mother. Trish swallowed. There were lots of unwed mothers.

But very few with grandmothers who owned the largest private bank in Japantown.

Trish bit her lip and glanced at Mom. She was blinking rapidly and clinging rather hard to Dad's arm.

No, Trish wasn't going to be guilted into this. This was her entire life. This was doing what God wanted her to do, not what Grandma and her family wanted her to do. "If they won't be Mom's friends because I choose not to marry this scumbag, then they aren't true friends, are they?"

Grandma's eyes started to glitter in a very unpleasant way. "They'll boycott Grandma's bank and bankrupt the family."

"Now you're being melodramatic." As soon as the words flew out of her mouth, Trish's heart stopped beating for a second or two, then resumed.

She'd smart-mouthed Grandma. She sounded like Lex or Venus. Her, Trish. She never talked back to Grandma, especially when her grandparent had become so agitated that she was speaking of herself in the third person.

Grandma had turned an interesting red-orange color, rather like those Chinese octopus appetizers at wedding banquets.

"I'm having this baby and I'm not marrying him."

Kazuo's brow furrowed as if he were just catching on. "Baby?"

The world stopped. She stared at him. He stared back, completely ignorant.

She rounded on Grandma in amazement. "You mean you didn't tell him?"

"Ah . . ." Grandma's mouth worked open and closed. Trish couldn't believe it. Grandma was speechless.

And Trish had her trump card. She turned on him for the attack. "Yes, Kazuo, I'm carrying your *baby*."

He visibly flinched at the word.

"Do you really want a *baby* around your studio? Playing with your paints? Ruining your artwork? Chewing on your brushes? Your apartment isn't exactly *baby*-proof. And there's no way I'm letting you get out of changing the *baby's* dirty diapers—do you know how much they *smell?*—and burping the *baby* so she upchucks all over your shirts, and did you know that *babies* always start screaming and wailing right when you want to watch TV, like, oh, Korean soap operas?"

He'd turned pale as she pressed him with mutilated brushes, dirty diapers, and slobbery burping, but when she threatened his K-drama watching, he balked. "No K-dramas? I cannot miss my K-dramas."

"Trish, stop scaring him. I'm sure his apartment is fine and he'd make a wonderful father." But even Grandma didn't sound so sure.

Kazuo was even less sure. In fact, he'd turned the color of Elmer's glue and was inching backward toward the door. She'd been right — no way would he want a baby.

Now she only had Grandma to deal with. Trish crossed her arms. "Grandma, this is my decision to make."

"Not if it influences the rest of your family."

"Well, my family supports me." Trish gestured to her parents. They gave her bewildered looks. Her chest tightened.

She gestured at them again, widening her eyes at them. They finally nodded in response, and she loosed a breath.

Grandma's eyes narrowed, but she couldn't really fire her own son, especially when he was so popular with the bank's wealthier clients. "If you do not marry Kazuo, Grandma will *not* support you." She hmphed and crossed her arms.

Trish stared her down. "I'll have this baby on my own, with or without you. I don't need your permission to do anything in my life, Grandma."

She deepened her fierce frown.

"What'll you say when your friends ask you how Trish's baby is, and you can't answer them?"

Grandma visibly faltered.

"I'm sure it'll look so good when people notice my own grandmother, a pillar in the Japanese community, won't visit her great-grandchild."

Grandma shifted into hasty retreat. "No, no. You misunderstood. As if Grandma would abandon you." She whirled toward the door so fast, Trish blinked, and Grandma was already turning the knob.

Trish's chest swelled. So this was how Mel Gibson — er, William Wallace felt when the English were vanquished. Victor. Conqueror. Master and commander —

Grandma wasn't finished. She looked back at Trish, her lips pulled into a highly miffed line. "At the very least, you could be a *good grand-*

daughter for a change and find some nice boy who'll marry you, baby or not." It sounded more peevish than threatening. Grandma exited with a flourish.

Kazuo was right on her heels. "Good-bye."

The door closed with a solid *thunk*. Trish stared at it for a moment. The silence seemed out of place for a moment.

She took a deep breath and clutched her hands around her midsection, waiting for her heart rate to climb back down. She'd really done it. All by herself.

She'd defeated a dragon.

At least they weren't carrying rotten tomatoes.

As Ed finished the last song before he could dismiss the congregation, Trish's heart thudded like someone taking a mallet to her breastbone. She almost rubbed her palms against her slacks, until she remembered these were new and she didn't want sweat stains on them.

She'd been pretty cavalier with Grandma about people shunning her mother, but visions of people snubbing her on the street had kept her awake last night. She didn't like it when people didn't like her. She knew in her head that not everyone would be her friend, but she didn't want people who previously thought she was a nice Christian girl to suddenly treat her like a leper.

She didn't need to do this. She could do this later. Or she could go privately to the pastor and tell him first, and maybe he could make the announcement to the congregation. It wouldn't be as bad, coming from him, right? Or maybe he'd tell her to leave the church and the congregation would never need to know why.

Except that for the past few days during her Bible-reading and prayer time, she'd felt like she needed to do this. In front of everybody, not hiding behind the pastor. Funny, it seemed like she heard God a lot clearer these days.

"Let's pray." Ed bowed his head.

She sighed. "I don't want to do this."

Her words resonated clearly through the speakers and out over the hushed congregation.

What? She thought her microphone was off. When had Spenser turned it on? Why hadn't he told her before she made a complete idiot of herself in front of the church again?

Her gaze spat sparks as she found Spenser way at the back in the balcony with the sound board. He gave a *What do you expect me to do now?* gesture.

Ed cleared his throat and started the prayer.

Her legs jiggled as she stood there, waiting for the prayer to end. Could she really do this? Did God really want her to do this? Well, if He wanted her to do this, maybe He'd make it turn out okay and the congregation wouldn't turn their collective backs on the Fallen Woman.

"Amen."

Oh man, oh man, oh man. Maybe Ed would forget she'd asked to say something after the prayer ...

"Before we're dismissed, we have an announcement from one of our newest worship team members, Trish."

Rats.

She reached for Olivia's mic before remembering hers was hot. How could she have forgotten to easily? She must really be losing it.

"Um ... hi. I'm Trish Sakai."

Now what? The pretty speech she'd memorized had dribbled out of her ear.

"Uh ... okay. Before I came to this church, I was really bad." *Oh, that was eloquent.* "Really, really bad." *You're making it worse.* "I did things I'm not proud of." *Okay, maybe now you're getting somewhere.*

"Then I repented." *Good word.* "And I joined this church, and I really like it here. A lot." *You're back to idiot-speak.*

"Now ..." She took a few heavy breaths. *Courage.* "I'm forgiven, but I still have to face the consequences of what I did. I'm pregnant, about two months."

All she heard was a baby squeal faintly from the nursery. Ironic.

"The baby's father isn't a Christian, and he doesn't want to have kids." *At least not until he stops watching K-dramas.* "So I'm going to keep the baby and raise it alone. I wanted to let you know before I started to show so you wouldn't wonder about it." *Or gossip, or snub me, or anything depressing like that.*

There was a rustle from the side of the sanctuary. Oh, no. People were going to leave their seats and walk out in protest that she was a member of the church and on the worship team and ...

No, it was the pastor coming back on stage. That was even worse. He'd denounce her in front of the entire congregation and tell them to never speak to her because they wouldn't want the stain of her sin to rub off on any of their pure singles or teens.

"You're very brave to tell us, Trish."

Yeah, but ... ?

"I'm very proud of you."

Really?

"I want to pray for you now. Let's pray."

"Dear heavenly Father, thank you that Trish is now part of our family."

Oh man, she was going to start bawling up here in front of everybody.

"Thank you for the precious life growing inside her. We pray for good health for both of them. She has a difficult season ahead of her, raising a child alone. Give us wisdom to know how we can each help her and support her."

Trish didn't hear the rest because her heart kept repeating "help her and support her." She wasn't being kicked out. Some people might feel she should be, but if the pastor supported her, she wouldn't hear about it, and really, that was fine with her. She was such a coward.

"Amen."

Olivia embraced her before the pastor had even finished speaking. "You did good, girl."

She nodded into her shoulder.

The pastor dismissed the congregation, and as they were breaking down equipment, Griselle came running up the steps to the stage. She barreled into Trish and nearly cut off her air supply with her hug. "You're so brave."

"Urk."

She noticed a few women following Griselle up the stage. "Um, Trish?"

She extricated herself from Griselle and approached them warily. "Hi."

The shorter of the two girls burst into tears.

Oh, no. This was not looking good. "Uh ... Are you okay?"

"You're so fearless," she sobbed.

"Huh?"

"You worship with such abandon." The other girl gestured to the rest of the worship team. "The worship sets have been so great. And now you're going to have a baby on your own, and you announced it in front of the entire congregation."

Put like that, it made Trish wonder what she'd been smoking to even contemplate doing what she'd just done. Whew. Good thing it was over with.

"You're such an inspiration."

"Whoa, whoa, whoa." Trish held up her hands. "This isn't a virgin birth, you know."

"We know." She giggled.

"And I'm not condoning sex before marriage." She pinned the two girls with a fierce gaze.

Their faces fell. "Oh. Really?"

Dingbats.

THIRTY-SIX

One month later

Spenser bullied her into running with him on Monday.

Trish dug her heels in as he pulled her toward the door. "I'm pregnant."

"You ran last week."

Rats, he remembered. "It's a hundred degrees outside. Wait until it cools down."

"It's only eighty, I checked. Perfect for running."

"It's lunchtime. It'll be crowded with everyone else jogging."

"So? You can't breathe enough to talk to anyone anyway."

"Grrrr ..." But in pausing to growl, she loosened her hold on the doorframe and Spenser yanked her outside.

He even let her set the pace. She dragged herself along in the humidity, stifling after the recent rain and like sloshing through hot soup. The direct sunlight stung her skin, but the temperature didn't seem much cooler even under the dappled shade. They headed down the concrete path, with sprinkler-fed green grass on the side closest to the research buildings and the early spring wildflowers on the side next to the street.

Trish panted like a dog, so Spenser did most of the talking. "How're things at your new place?"

"Okay."

"Got everything unpacked?"

Trish nodded. "Thanks ... helping ... move."

"No prob. I'm glad you found something."

So was she. Strange how she had suddenly found the perfect apartment at the perfect price. She knew now God wasn't her personal genie, but she had thanked Him and jumped on the place nonetheless.

"Did your parents get back from their vacation yet?"

"No." Trish had almost had a heart attack herself. The fact they'd decided to go on a cruise had been enough to shock her — although it had also made a calming warmth settle in her chest to see them vacation together for the first time in years, to see them so happy in each other's company. Then they'd called her last week to say they were extending their time in the Bahamas another two weeks.

"Kevin has a new girlfriend."

"Wha-ha?"

"I saw them together at lunch. The tiniest Asian girl I've ever seen."

How nice for him to rub in that she herself was getting larger. "Happy ... for him."

"Really?" He actually seemed concerned.

"Why ... not?"

"You've seemed kind of down the past month. Not happy."

He would be too, with his body gaining weight like a fiend, his hormones all out of whack, and his dating life down the toilet.

Oh, and Grandma was still not talking to her, although the sting of that had started to ease. Lex and Venus kept reminding her that being on Grandma's Ignore List was a good thing. "Oh?"

"I know what'll cheer you up."

"Sushi?" Man, she missed it.

"No, no raw fish. Even I know that's bad for pregnant women." Spenser cleared his throat. "How about dinner with me?"

Trish ground to a halt, but her lungs heaved so much she couldn't speak at first. She pierced him with a glare like a dagger. "You big ... dork!"

He looked like he'd suddenly landed on the Planet of the Apes. "What's wrong?"

"All ... month ... nothing!" Not even a hint of interest. She'd finally gotten used to the idea that he'd never be interested. She didn't want to get her hopes up again.

His eyes softened, and she had that feeling again that his gaze wrapped around her like a blanket. "I know. I was waiting."

"For what?" As soon as she got her breath back, she was going to sock him one.

"I had to know how I felt about you."

She stared at the grass. Her breath roared in her ears. Did this really mean what she thought it meant? "And?"

"I needed to know I liked you apart from the mess with Kazuo. I needed to know I'd be okay with the baby. I needed to know if this was serious, because I didn't want you to be just another girlfriend."

"You didn't answer my question."

She hadn't realized how close he stood until he clasped her upper arms, his thumbs working in gentle circles against her skin. Her breathing quickened. The musk of his cologne smelled stronger now in the sunlight. She saw the awareness in his eyes. The desire tensed the air between them and caused a delicious fluttering in her stomach.

This was Spenser. Hunky, annoying, growling, glowering, glaring, teasing Spenser. Touching her and making her insides feel molten and trembly.

His eyes burned with something she'd never seen in them before. "I've prayed about it, and I'm ready to start dating seriously."

His face bent lower, and she closed her eyes as his breath caressed her cheek, feathering her ear. "I'd like to date you seriously, Trish."

She felt his lips, warm and smooth, against her mouth. He pulled on her lower lip, floated a kiss at the corner, and then pressed his kiss full upon her, firm and purposeful. She kept her eyes closed, feeling his mouth follow along her jaw, before planting a soft kiss below her ear.

"Are you free tonight?" His whisper tickled her earlobe.

Her heart pounded as if she'd sprinted a mile. His hands pressed on her arms, his fingers circled in a mesmerizing motion against her skin. His mouth wooed her with soft kisses on her neck. She was intensely aware of his body as he leaned close to her, his accelerated breathing, the pulsing of his heartbeat.

This was Spenser, her friend. Who had mopped up her tears with his handkerchiefs, who knew about her past (very bad) love life, her erratic moods, her annoying quirks. Oh, and her unborn child. Who stood seducing her as if she were the most beautiful woman in the world.

And all she could do was croak, *"Gaaa ..."*

He lifted his head and blinked at her. "Um ... I guess I'll take that as a yes."

ACKNOWLEDGMENTS

Thanks to:

Wendy Lawton, my awesome agent, for your terrific advice and encouraging words.

Sue Brower, Karwyn Bursma, Karen Campbell, and the rest of the team at Zondervan for doing so much for this series.

Rachelle Gardner, my fabulous macro editor. Becky Shingle-decker, my stupendous developmental editor.

Aunty Gail and Mom for their info on the K-dramas.

My terrific critique team who got this puppy done in only a few days: Robin Caroll, Sharon Hinck, Pamela James, Ronie Kendig, Dineen Miller, Trisha Ontiveros, Heather Tipton, Cheryl Wyatt.

Kenta Akaogi (with help from Rena) for translating Kazuo's painting title. David Kawaye for translating Marnie and her mother, even though he probably doesn't remember doing it for me years ago.

Captain Caffeine, for the kick in the pants when I needed it, for washing dishes for me, and for not watching *24* until I had the time to watch it with you.

GLOSSARY OF ASIAN WORDS (CAMY STYLE)

Baka— (bah-kah) (Japanese) (1) Stupid. (2) The nickname of your siblings/cousins/anyone particularly annoying whom you can't run away from.

Char siu— (cha-sue) (Chinese) marinated and grilled pork. This is some of the yummiest stuff on the planet. It's also this alarming radioactive red-pink color.

Chicken hekka— (heck-uh) a country-style Japanese dish that my grandma makes often when there are several family members gathered for dinner. It's technically a stir-fry, but there's so much stuff in it that it's almost like a soupy stew.

Chicken katsu— (caught-sue) (Japanese) chicken breaded and deep fried, cut into fingers and served over rice with salty sweet tonkatsu sauce. See *tonkatsu*.

Hanaokolele— (ha-nah-oh-koh-lay-lay) Hawaiian for Nani-nani-boo-boo. Many modern Hawaiian terms have seeped into California Japanese American colloquialisms, and vice versa.

Inarizushi— (ee-nah-ree-zoo-shee) Also called cone sushi, this type of sushi is flavored rice packed into fried tofu pouches. The pouches are light brown color and look a bit like footballs when they're stuffed. This is a really good appetizer.

Kagami mochi— (kah-gah-mee moh-chee) decoration (Japanese) This is a New Year's decoration that people set out in various places in their homes just before New Year's Day. It consists of two pieces of round mochi (they look like white hockey pucks) with a tangerine balanced on top. This is placed on a paper sheet (*shihobeni*) supposed to ward off fires. There are other things that some Japanese add to their kagami mochi, but these elements are the basic ones that I'm used to.

Katana—(kah-tah-nah) Japanese sword. I actually learned a little bit about sword strokes when I took martial arts, except I used a wooden sword, called a *bokken* (*beau-ken*). A real katana is way heavy and super dangerous. It's meant to kill with a single stroke.

Kendo stick—(ken-dough) Kendo is Japanese fencing, but instead of a solid sword, opponents typically use a *shinai* (shee-nigh), which is a set of four long thin pieces of wood bound off at the bottom with leather. The shinai is not really a sword, nor is it technically a "stick," but for lack of a good English word, I think that's closest to what it is.

Konbu–(cone-boo) edible kelp. It's the dark colored seaweed shreds or sheets in miso soup that you get at Japanese restaurants. It's quite healthy for you. Since I've grown up with it, I think it tastes normal, but many people who eat it for the first time say it has a distinctive flavor. I usually tell them, "Then give me yours." (Japanese)

Kubi ga nai Chikin–(coup bee guh-nigh chicken) literally, Headless Chicken. (Japanese)

Kuromame–(coup-row-mah-may) This is a cold red (azuki) bean and chestnut salad (sometimes it's made with soybeans, but we always had it with red beans). It's slightly sweet. Mom always says it's good luck to eat it on New Year's Day, but I've never been a fan of chestnuts. (Japanese)

Musubi–(moo-sue-bee) rice balls. Possibly some of the yummiest things to eat in a Japanese-style brown bag lunch. Traditionally, it's just plain rice balls with *nori* seaweed wrapped around it, but the ladies at my church make it with a little salmon inside, or sometimes salty fish. Oh my gosh, their musubi is to die for. Hawaiian style is with a slab of fried Spam, which I think tastes great, but then again, I've grown up with it. (Japanese)

Noh – (no) Japanese musical drama. Noh masks are often collector's items. The most familiar noh mask is the plain white mask, but there are also red demon masks that would fit in with Freddie Kruger's wardrobe.

Obon – (oh-bone) Buddhist festival of the dead. Our local Buddhist temple (*hongwanji*) would throw their Obon Dance every year. It's a fun festival, typically running from afternoon until evening. Obon dances are easy, repetitive steps and hand motions that people do while circling a short tower (called a *yagura*) with the musicians in a box on top. (Not all Obons have a yagura, but the dances in my home town always had a yagura.) The *food* is the best part of the Obon. Man, those Japanese people can cook. When I went to Obon dances on Hawaii's North Shore, people would buy floating paper lanterns with candles inside. They'd light them and set them adrift on the beach, where the tide took them out in a twinkling line. The lanterns are supposed to guide the spirits of people's ancestors. (Japanese)

Sashimi – (saw-shee-mee) raw sliced fish. It's not as yucky as it sounds. When the fish is fresh, it's refreshing and tasty. I guess since I've grown up with it, it's nothing unusual to me. We always have sashimi as appetizers at family gatherings. (Japanese)

Shihobeni – (shee-hoe-ben-knee) see *kagami mochi* (Japanese)

Taiko – (tie-koh) Japanese drums. Taiko drum ensemble performances are way cool to watch. It's a little bit of showmanship, not just the drumming. I enjoy the rhythms and cadences — it feels very *Japanese*, to me.

Tonkatsu – (tone-cut-sue) breaded, deep-fried pork cutlet, cut into fingers and served over rice with tonkatsu sauce drizzled over it. Tonkatsu sauce is thick, dark colored, salty and sweet. I've heard it described as Japanese Worcestershire sauce, but it doesn't taste much like regular Worcestershire sauce. I personally like katsu without the sauce, but I have relatives who pile it on. (Japanese)

Ume – (oo-may) Japanese pickled plum. The ume I had growing up was small, bright pink, and hecka sour. My mom likes dropping one in the green tea she drinks after dinner. Sometimes Grandma would make musubi rice balls with an ume in the middle of it, but I personally thought it ruined the rice ball. However, most of my relatives love ume. There's even ume-flavored candy (significantly sweeter than actual ume) and ume tea.

Wasabi – (wah-sah-bee) Japanese horseradish. It's a lot like those yellow Chinese mustards at Chinese restaurants, but without the pungent flavor. Wasabi has a very clean taste — it's mostly just extremely hot. It's meant to give a spicy kick to sashimi and sushi. You're only supposed to use a small amount (like the size of a grain of rice) because it's so hot, but my dad piles on so much when he eats sushi that he needs a big ole honkin' marble-size glob.

ABOUT THE AUTHOR

Camy Tang is a loud Asian chick who writes loud Asian chick-lit. She grew up in Hawaii but now lives in San Jose, California, with her engineer husband and rambunctious poi-dog. In a previous life, she was a biologist researcher, but these days she is surgically attached to her computer, writing full-time. In her spare time, she is a staff worker for her church youth group, and she leads one of the worship teams for Sunday service.

On her blog, she gives away Christian novels every Monday and Thursday, and she ponders frivolous things, like dumb dogs (namely hers), coffee-geek husbands (no resemblance to her own . . .), the writing journey, Asiana, and anything else that comes to mind. Visit her website at www.camytang.com.

Sushi for One?

Camy Tang

"*Sushi for One?* is an entertaining romp into the world of multi-culturalism. I loved learning the idiosyncrasies of Lex's crazy family—which were completely universal. Enjoy!"
  —Kristen Billerbeck, author of *What a Girl Wants*

"In Lex Sakai, Camy Tang gives us a funny, plucky, volleyball-playing heroine with way too many balls in the air. I defy anyone to start reading and not root for Lex all the way to the story's romantic, super-satisfying end."
  —Trish Perry, author of *The Guy I'm Not Dating*

Lex Sakai's family is big, nosy, and marriage-minded. When her cousin Mariko gets married, Lex will become the oldest single female cousin in the clan.

Lex has used her Bible study class on Ephesians to compile a huge list of traits for the perfect man. But the one man she keeps running into doesn't seem to have a single quality on her list. It's only when the always-in-control Lex starts to let God take over that all the pieces of this hilarious romance finally fall into place.

Softcover: 0-310-27398-6

Pick up a copy today at your favorite bookstore!

SUSHI
SERIES

Camy Tang

author of *Sushi for One?*

SINGLE
SASHIMI

Read the first chapter of
Single Sashimi, the third book in
Camy Tang's Sushi Series!

ONE

Venus Chau opened the door to her aunt's house and almost fainted.

"What died?" She exhaled sharply, trying to get the foul air out of her body before it caused cancer or something.

Her cousin Jennifer entered the foyer with the look of an *oni* goblin about to eat someone. "She's stinking up my kitchen."

"Who?" Venus hesitated on the threshold, breathing clean night air before she had to close the door.

"My mother, who else?"

The ire in Jenn's voice made Venus busy herself with kicking off her heels amongst the other shoes in the entryway. Hoo-boy, she'd never seen quiet Jenn this irate before. Then again, since Aunty Yuki had given her daughter rule over their kitchen when she'd started cooking in high school, Jenn rarely had to make way for another cook.

"What is she cooking? Beef intestines?"

Jenn flung her arms out. "Who knows? Something Trish is supposed to eat."

"But we don't have to eat it, right? Right?"

"I'd never become pregnant if I had to eat stuff like that." Jenn whirled and stomped toward the kitchen.

Venus turned right into the living room where her very pregnant cousin Trish lounged on the sofa next to her boyfriend, Spenser. "Hey, guys." Her gazed paused on their twined hands. It continued to amaze her that Spenser would date a woman pregnant with another man's child. Maybe Venus shouldn't be so cynical about the men she met. Here was at least one good guy.

"Venus!" The childish voice rang down the short hallway. She stepped back into the foyer to see Spenser's son, Matthew, trotting down the carpet with hands reached out to her. He grabbed her at the knees, wrinkling her silk pants, but she didn't mind. His shining face looking up at her — *way* up, since she was the tallest of the cousins — made her feel like she was the only reason he lived and breathed. "Psycho Bunny?" he pleaded.

She pretended to think about it. His hands shook her pants legs as if it would make her decide faster.

"Okay."

He darted into the living room and plopped in front of the television, grabbing at the game controllers. The kid had it down pat — in less than a minute, the music for the *Psycho Bunny* video game plinked into the room.

Venus sank to the floor next to him.

"Jenn is totally freaking out." Trish's eyes had popped to the size of *siu mai* dumplings.

"What brought all this on?" Venus picked up the other controller.

"Well, Aunty Yuki had a doctor's appointment today — "

"Is she doing okay?" Venus chose the Bunny Foo-Foo character for the game that was starting.

"Clean bill of health. Cancer's gone, as far as they can tell."

"So that's why she's taken over Jenn's domain?"

Trish rubbed her back and winced. "She took one look at me and decided I needed something to help the baby along."

Jenn huffed into the living room. "She's going to make me ruin the roast chicken!"

Venus ignored her screeching tone. "Sit down. You're not going to make her go any faster by hovering." She and Matthew both jumped over the snake pit and landed in the hollow tree.

Jenn flung herself into an overstuffed chair and dumped her feet on the battered oak coffee table.

Venus turned to glance at the shoes piled by the door. No Nikes. Lex wasn't here yet. "Where's Lex?"

"Late. What's new?" Jenn snapped.

"I thought Aiden was helping her get better about that."

"He's not a miracle worker." Spenser said as he massaged Trish's back.

"I have to leave early." Venus stretched her silk stocking-clad feet, wriggling her toes. Her new stilettos looked great, but man they hurt her arches.

"Then you might not eat at all." Jenn crossed her arms over her chest.

Venus speared her with a glance like a stainless steel kabob skewer. "Chill, okay Cujo?"

Jenn pouted and scrunched down further in the chair.

Venus ignored her and turned back to the game. Her inattention let Matthew pick up the treasure chest. "I have to work on a project."

"For work?"

"No, for me." Only Spiderweb, the achievement of her lifetime, a new tool that would propel her to the heights of video game development stardom. Which was why she'd kept it separate from her regular job-related things—she didn't even use her company computer when she worked on it, only her personal laptop.

A new smell wafted into the room, rivaling the other in its stomach-roiling ability. Venus waved her hand in front of her face. "Pffaugh! What is she cooking?"

Trish's face had turned the color of green tea. "You're lucky *you* don't have to eat it. Whatever it is, it ain't gonna stay down for long."

"Just say you still have morning sickness."

"In my ninth month?"

Venus shrugged.

The door slammed open. "Hey, guys— *blech.*"

Venus twisted around to see her cousin Lex doubled over, clenching her washboard stomach and looking like she'd hurled up all the shoes littering the foyer floor.

Lex's boyfriend Aiden grabbed her waist to straighten her clenched posture. "Lex, it's not that bad."

"A locker room smells better." Lex used her toes to pull off her cross-trainers without bothering to untie them. "The *men's* locker room."

"It's not me," Jenn declared. "It's Mom, ruining all my best pots."

"What is she doing? Killing small animals on the stovetop?"

"Something for the baby." Trish tried to smile, but it looked more like a wince.

"As long as we don't have to eat it." Lex dropped her slouchy purse on the floor and walked into the living room.

Aunty Yuki appeared behind her in the kitchen doorway, bearing a steaming bowl. "Here, Trish. Drink this." The brilliant smile on her wide face eclipsed her tiny stature.

Venus smelled something pungent, like when she walked into a Chinese medicine shop with her dad. A bolus of air erupted from her mouth, and she coughed. "What is that?" She dropped the game controller.

"Pig's brain soup."

Trish's smile hardened to plastic. Lex grabbed her mouth. Spenser sighed. Aiden looked at them all like they were funny-farm rejects.

Venus closed her eyes, tightened her mouth, and concentrated on not gagging. Good thing her stomach was empty. She clutched her midsection.

Aunty Yuki's mouth pursed. "What's wrong? My mother-in-law made me eat pig's brain soup when I was a couple weeks from delivering Jennifer."

"*That's* what you ruined my pots with?" Jennifer steamed hotter than the bowls of soup.

Her mom caught the *yakuza*-about-to-hack-your-finger-off expression on Jenn's face. Aunty Yuki paused, then backtracked to the kitchen. Thankfully, with the soup bowl.

"Papa?" Matthew's voice sounded faint.

Venus turned.

"I don't feel good." He clutched his poochy tummy.

"Oh, no." Spenser grabbed his son and headed out of the living room.

Then the world exploded.

Just as they passed into the foyer, Matthew threw up onto the tiles.

Lex took one look and turned pasty.

A burning smell and a few cries sounded from the kitchen.

Trish sat up straighter than a Buddha and clenched her rounded abdomen. "Oh!"

Spenser held his crying son as he urped up the rest of his afternoon snack. Lex clapped a hand to her mouth to prevent herself from following Matthew's example. Jenn started for the kitchen, but Matthew's mess blocking the foyer stopped her. Trish groaned and curled in on herself, clutching her tummy.

Venus shot to her feet. She wasn't acting Game Lead at her company for nothing.

"You." She pointed to Jenn. "Get to the kitchen and send your mom in here for Trish." Jenn leaped over Matthew's puddle and darted away. "And bring paper towels for the mess!"

"You," she flung at Spenser. "Take Matthew to the bathroom."

He gestured to the brand new hallway carpet.

Aunty Yuki would have a fit. But it couldn't be helped. "If he makes a mess on the carpet, we'll just clean it up later."

He didn't hesitate. He hustled down the hallway with Matthew in his arms.

Venus kicked the miniscule living room garbage basket closer to Lex. "Hang your head over that." Not that it would hold more than spittle, but it was better than letting Lex upchuck all over the plush cream carpet. Why did Lex, tomboy and jock, have to go weak every time something gross happened?

"You." Venus stabbed a manicured finger at Aiden. "Get your car, we're taking Trish to the hospital."

He didn't jump at her command. "After one contraction?"

Trish moaned, and Venus had a vision of the baby flying out of her in the next minute. She pointed to the door again. "Just go!"

Aiden shrugged and slipped out the front door, muttering to himself.

"You." She stood in front of Trish, who'd started Lamaze breathing through her pursed lips. "Uh ..."

Trish peered up at her.

"Um ... stop having contractions."

Trish rolled her eyes but didn't speak through her pursed lips.

Venus ignored her and went to kneel over Matthew's rather watery puddle, which had spread with amoeba fingers down the lines of grout. Lex's purse lay nearby, so she rooted in it for a tissue or something to start blotting up the mess.

Footsteps approaching. Before she could raise her head or shout a warning, Aunty Yuki hurried into the foyer. "What's wron—!"

It was like a Three Stooges episode. Aunty Yuki barreled into Venus's bent figure.

"Ooomph!" The older woman's feet—shod in cotton house slippers, luckily, and not shoes—jammed into Venus's ribs. She couldn't see much except a pair of slippers leaving the floor at the same time, and then a body landing on the living room carpet on the other side of her. *Ouch.*

"Are you okay?" Venus twisted to kneel in front of her, but she seemed slow to rise.

"Venus, here're the paper towels—"

Jenn's voice in the foyer made Venus whirl on the balls of her feet and fling her hands up. "Watch out!"

Jenn stopped just in time. Her toes were only inches away from Matthew's mess, her body leaning forward. Her arms whirled, still clutching the towels like a cheerleader and her pom-poms.

"Jenn." Spenser's voice came down the hallway toward the foyer. "Where are the—"

"Stop!" Venus and Jenn shouted at the same time.

Spenser froze, his foot hovering above a finger of the puddle that had stretched toward the hallway. "Ah. Okay. Thanks." He lowered his foot onto the clean tile to the side.

Aiden opened the front door. "The car's out—" The sight of them all left him speechless.

Trish had started to hyperventilate, her breath seething through her teeth. "Will somebody do something?!"

Aunty Yuki moaned from her crumpled position on the floor.

Smoke started pouring from the kitchen, along with the awful smell of burned ... *something*.

Venus snatched the paper towels from Jenn. "Kitchen!" Jenn fled before Venus even finished speaking. "What do you need?" Venus barked at Spenser.

"Extra towels."

"Guest bedroom closet, top shelf."

He headed back down the hall. Venus turned to Aiden and swept a hand toward Aunty Yuki on the living room floor. "Take care of her, will you?"

"What about me?" Trish moaned through a clenched jaw.

"Stop having contractions!" Venus swiped up the mess on the tile before something worse happened, like someone stepping in it and sliding across the floor. That would just be the crowning touch to her evening. Even when she wasn't at work, she was still working.

"Are you okay, Aunty?" She stood with the sodden paper towels. Aiden had helped her to a seat next to Lex, who was ashen-faced and still leaning over the tiny trash can. Aside from a reddish spot on Aunty Yuki's elbow, she seemed fine.

Jenn entered the living room, her hair wild and a distinct burned smell sizzling from her clothes. "My imported French saucepan is completely blackened!" But she had enough sense not to glare at her parent as she probably wanted to. Aunty Yuki suddenly found the wall hangings fascinating.

Venus started to turn toward the kitchen to throw away the paper towels she still held. "Well, we have to take Trish to the hospital—"

"Actually ..." Trish's breathing had slowed. "I think it's just a false alarm."

Venus turned to look at her. "False alarm? Pregnant women have those?"

"It happened a couple days ago too."

"What?" Venus almost slammed her fist into her hip, but remembered the dirty paper towels just in time. Good thing, too, because she had on a Chanel suit.

Trish gave a long, slow sigh. "Yup, they're gone. That was fast." She smiled cheerfully.

Venus wanted to scream. This was out of her realm. At work, she was used to grabbing a crisis at the throat and wrestling it to submission. Trish was heading somewhere without her, and the thought both frightened and unnerved her. She shrugged it off. "Well ... Aunty—"

"I'm fine, Venus." Aunty Yuki inspected her elbow. "Jennifer, get those Japanese Salonpas patches—"

"Mom, they stink." Jenn's stress over her beautiful kitchen made her more belligerent than Venus had ever seen her before. Not that the camphor patches could smell any worse than the burned Chinese-old-wives'-pregnancy-food permeating the house.

At the sound of the word Salonpas, Lex pinched her lips together but didn't say anything.

Aunty Yuki gave Jenn a limpid look. "The Salonpas gets rid of the pain."

"I'll get it." Aiden headed down the hallway to get the analgesic adhesive patches.

"In the hall closet." Jenn's words slurred a bit through her tight jaw.

Distraction time. Venus tried to smile. "Aunty, if you're okay, then let's eat."

Jenn's eyes flared neon red. "Can't."

"Huh?"

"*Somebody* turned off the oven." Jenn frowned at her mother, who tactfully looked away. "Dinner won't be for another hour." She stalked back to the kitchen.

Even with the nasty smell, Venus's stomach protested its empty state. "It's already eight o'clock."

"Suck it up!" Jenn yelled from the kitchen.

It was going to be a long night.

Aiden returned with the Salonpas patches, which Aunty Yuki took an abnormally long time applying. Venus finished cleaning up the mess with some cleaner from the hall closet and more paper towels. By that time, Lex had a drop of pink in her cheeks and was leaning back against the sofa.

Venus dropped into the brown corduroy recliner. Jenn returned to the living room and sat in the farthest corner from her mother, refusing to look at her.

"Um . . ." Trish rubbed her stomach. "I guess since everyone's here, we might as well do it now."

Venus glanced at her. A tightness in her chest made her drop her feet from the coffee table and sit up.

Trish suddenly seemed older, calmer. And happier. Venus somehow felt distant from her, even though she only sat a few feet away. She again had that vision of Trish walking down a road she couldn't follow.

Trish reached into her purse and pulled out something small. That glittered.

She beamed and held it out to the room at large. "Spenser and I are engaged!"

We want to hear from you. Please send your comments about this book to us in care of zreview@zondervan.com. Thank you.